NATALIA'S PEACE

ADRIAN DE HOOG

Adytum Publishing, Ottawa

Natalia's Peace

ISBN 978-0-9869666-0-6

Published by Adytum Publishing
www.adytumpublishing.com
Ottawa, Canada

Copyright © Adrian de Hoog 2011

Library of Canada Cataloguing in Publication Data

De Hoog, Adrian. 1946 –

Designer: Sian Elin Thomas

Editor: Hannah Mae Cartmel

Author Services by Pedernales Publishing, LLC.
www.pedernalespublishing.com

Praise for Adrian de Hoog's Novels

"The main attraction of de Hoog's novels is the people who inhabit them. His visual portraits are economic, but his psychological profiles are detailed and filled with subtle brush strokes. Recommended for those looking for something more than boom and bang in their spy fiction. These are "literary" spy novels that make you think."

MARK HOOKER, SPYWISE.NET, OCTOBER 2008

"Greed, revenge and political retribution are the driving forces in *The Berlin Assignment*. Characters are skilfully drawn and the story unfolds like a career diary with a climax as unexpected as it is satisfying. The tale is rich in gossip and loaded with scandalous traps. All in all, an auspicious debut."

DON GRAVES, THE HAMILTON SPECTATOR, MARCH 2007

"This well-crafted spy thriller combines an exciting, well evoked time – Berlin just after the destruction of the wall – with some engaging characters."

JOAN SULLIVAN, THE TELEGRAM, SEPTEMBER 2006

"*The Berlin Assignment* is easily the most gripping novel I've read this year."

JEAN GRAHAM, BOOKCASE, THE NORTHEAST AVALON TIMES

"*Borderless Deceit*, clearly, is a book with brains."

MIKE GILLESPIE, THE ITTOWA CITIZEN, MAY 2008

"Borderless Deceit is fast-paced, with lots of page-turning intrigue. There are enough twists and turns to the plot to keep you reading."

GAR PARDY, BOUT DE PAPIER, FEBRUARY 2008

For Regina
In Memoriam

Also by Adrian de Hoog:

The Berlin Assignment
Borderless Deceit

Acknowledgements

I would like to thank the following for helping to make this book better:

Bhalwant Bhaneja, winner of the Canadian Peace Award and co-chair of the Canadian Peace Department Initiative, who over many lunches helped me to identify and scope out many of the substantive ideas in the novel.

Glenn D. Paige, author of *Nonkilling Global Political Science*, Professor Emeritus of at the University of Hawaii and Chair of the Governing Council of the Center for Global Nonkilling, for reading an early version of the manuscript and giving me important feedback.

Erika Bruce and **George Haynal** for reading an advanced version of the manuscript and, as de facto editors, for making many perceptive suggestions which led to numerous character and descriptive improvements.

Keira Dickinson and **Julian de Hoog**, whose enthusiastic reading and close questioning identified countless errors, ranging from plain syntax to inappropriate hyperbole.

Hannah Mae Cartmel, who fulfills an author's dream to have a steadily supportive, yet detached and sharp-eyed copy editor.

Sian Elin Thomas, for her great artistry in designing the novel's lovely and arresting cover and for typesetting the book in a way that will please any reader.

Chapter 1

In the evening, out over the North Sea, the fog arose as if from nothing. Then came a silent movement towards land. The menacing way it spilled forward in the darkness, an evil will could have been at work inside.

Holland's dunes are equal to the tides and render solid defence during the most wicked storms, but in seconds this fog overran them. The roads behind the dunes were next, then the towns and villages nearby. Lights were on and yet were out. Objects a few steps away became effectively invisible.

In this sudden blackness all around, in the turbo prop about to land, the pilot was momentarily bewildered.

Suppose the fog had not swept in during the plane's last seconds of descent, or that the landing had been minutes earlier. Suppose the pilot had not been battling with fatigue. Would, months later, have there been the funeral in Delft?

~

The rite in Delft's central cathedral was fine and flowery, as splendid as any funeral can be. Yet the band of mourners looking on was small. A trio played a sombre Schubert movement, the doleful notes moistening many an eye. Natalia, unexpectedly a widow, held a handkerchief and dabbed. She raised her gaze from the casket to the cathedral ceiling. What was she seeing up there in all that space? Her deceased husband's restless spirit? The meaning he conveyed with his lazy, understanding smile? Or was she contemplating something else, something equally immaterial, such as her dream of a peace dove ascending? She had nourished that dream for months, although it had ended, seemingly coincidentally, in the same week that her husband died.

Among the mourners, Robbie, three pews behind Natalia, alternately stared at the casket and at Natalia's back. Of all the people there she had the clearest view of many strangely linked events. From the plane crash that started it all to the accident that had claimed Carlos's life, and all that happened in between, Robbie saw quite plainly that something like a scythe had been swinging. Unleashed by the February fog, it had been mowing things down with a hidden and terrible rhythm, things like dreams and hopes and expectations. And now, here in the cathedral, with the Dutch pastor gutturally pronouncing that ashes were returning to ashes and dust was becoming dust again, the many cut-down illusions – this one and that one and then still more, some belonging to Natalia and others to Robbie – were all being entombed. Robbie sensed them disappearing, slipping away forever into the cracks between the cathedral's ancient stones.

Master Planner, how did your good intentions for us get so fouled up?

According to the eventual enquiry into the crash, one problem with the turbo prop's flight, even before the fog consumed it, was that the pilot had been in the air too long. He initiated the final descent just after 21:00, by which time he had been on duty fifteen hours. Yes, he admitted to the investigators, he had been tired, quite tired, but not asleep. He had seen the runway clearly. It lay before him brightly defined by two long lines of lights. The claim was corroborated by his voice on the flight recorder. In fact, throughout the approach, the pilot's communications with the tower were factual, accurate and crisp. During the approach, the tower informed him of the possibility of fog, adding it was not expected until later. The runway to be used was RWY 34. The crosswind, coming in at an angle of between 35 and 50 degrees, might be a touch gusty, but nothing extraordinary.

So why wasn't the landing routine like many hundreds of others? Because, seconds before touchdown, the fog destroyed the lights. It was as if the earth with one huge bite had gulped the whole of Holland down. "What the hell ...?" said the pilot, not believing his eyes. He stared out through the cockpit window, looking left and right. At this distraction, and because he was tired, his brain didn't immediately catch on. By the time he consulted the instruments the plane, in its stall, had advanced well over the runway. Was he reading correctly? Was he really only meters above the asphalt, yet couldn't see a thing? "Where the fuck am I?" he muttered.

It was picked up by the tower. A helpful airport-jargon reply in a friendly Dutch accent informed him that though they couldn't see him, they could confirm he was on the runway.

"Like hell I am," the pilot growled.

"But you are."

"Well then, I'll put her down."

Too bad he hadn't seen that the crosswind had blown him slightly to the right. The plane hit the rough next to the runway and bounced hard, the landing gear crumbling. There was a rearing up, a brief airy fluttering before violently coming down again, this time on its side. No one saw the machine twist then, somersault and break up. The final moments had to be reconstructed.

The approach speed of SX-PAX had been 103 knots, which was correct – according to specification for a King Air B200. That was the velocity with which the plane touched down. The first markings on the ground continued for 22 meters, causing a probable velocity reduction of some 40 per cent. The gap between the first markings and the much deeper gouging further along was 57 meters, suggesting the plane had been in the air again for 1.85 seconds. When it hit a second time it was on the right wing, which immediately broke from the fuselage. The plane's nose then hit, the whole cabin flipping over, whereupon SX-PAX, upside down, twisted and broken, slid to a halt. The fog absorbed all sound. Miraculously, no fire broke out.

As mishaps go, this one was not considered major. Dutch radio news the following morning curtly announced an accident at Valkenburg, a small airport some miles north of The Hague, almost in throwing distance from the North Sea coast. The plane was privately owned, registered in Greece. Two people were on board. The pilot was American, the passenger Canadian. Both were in hospital in poor shape.

It was scarcely a story, so no wonder that at the Canadian embassy no one picked it up.

~

But the news did arrive.

It came during the ambassador's Thursday morning embassy management committee meeting. Natalia was in grand form, flattering and cajoling her program heads, faking a grumble about the increasing volume of official visitors, then turning intimate. In a voice that was almost a purr, she shared some snippets of cocktail circuit gossip and fragments of secrets she had picked up on the phone from the big guns in headquarters. Whenever their ambassador went at them this way her sturdy program overseers generally wilted.

"So now, Gus," she said brightly as she initiated the *tour de table*, "I was informed that the social workers from Montreal loved their program in Amsterdam. Took them to the red light district, did you? Tell us about it. I want to know."

Gus considered himself a serious political analyst (his normal speaking pattern was precise, slow and monotone), but the ambassador's innuendo – that he knew his way around Amsterdam – put a glimmer in his eyes. "Gave that part of town a pass, Natalia," he said robustly. "They came to see how clean needles get handed out."

"Of course!" Natalia cried. "Cleanliness is glorifying. Ah, I see your purpose, you devil. You believe Dutch glory is transplantable. Imagine it, Dutch order in Montreal. Can that be possible?"

"It may not be impossible," replied the careful political commentator, proceeding to describe the visit in excruciating detail.

The ambassador broke in and switched from Gus to the embassy cultural attaché. "Marcel, about your marvellous plan to bring Inuit art to Groningen next month, is everything on track for a riveting winter show? I'm keeping my fingers crossed the canals will be frozen."

In this way, reports on embassy events sprouted from each seat in the room. Everyone wanted Natalia to know about their busy files, and she got excited about each one. Just as it was Robbie's turn to provide a briefing on the week's list of Canadians in Dutch jails, the door opened. Marge, the ambassador's assistant, a heavyset woman with self-assured eyes, came in and went directly to Robbie. She whispered something. Robbie rose, lifting her eyebrows in silent apology. "A policeman on the phone," she informed the meeting.

"Off you go then," said Natalia. "Politeness costs nothing and we should be polite to the police. Give me that list of our teenagers in jail. I'll present it for you." Robbie signalled to Marge to transfer the call to her office and departed, gently sealing the conference room door as she left.

Another consular crisis.

Thank You, Great Fixer!

The escape couldn't have been timed better. The crowd in that committee! Five drab males stumbling over each other in their haste to impress the ambassador. But fortunately Natalia was nice. Her one problem was fervour. A kind of love for substantive issues sometimes took her over the top. One more silent note went up.

Dear Humongous, it's all fine but, please, can you bring the enthusiasm down a notch?

The call forwarded by Marge was blinking on Robbie's phone when she arrived at her desk. "Consular Section. Robbie Warren speaking."

"Ah, Ms Warren. Yes. I am Inspector van Zanten, Leyden Police Department."

Another student at the university, Robbie thought. Drugs.

"I have before me a passport belonging to one of your countrymen. He is here in a hospital. His condition is not so good."

Maybe not drugs. Possibly alcohol. A drunken student duel with real swords, like in the good old days.

"There was an accident yesterday in the evening. There was a fog." The inspector factually described what he knew of the crash.

"Anyone dead?"

"Not yet, Ms Warren. On that plane were two men. As far as we can know until now, your countryman was the passenger. His name is Alistair Edward Paradis. The birth date on the passport is October 1, 1947. We are until now saying to the media only that there was a crash. But we are not releasing names. Can you inform the family in Canada?"

Robbie jotted down the passport number, date and place of issue and asked if more documents had been found.

"We have the wallet and the briefcase and also a small suitcase. You are welcome to come and look."

The committee meeting had finished and the ambassador, back in her office, asked Marge to inform Robbie to come see her. "Robbie's gone out," Marge replied curtly. "To Leyden to see the police. She left this note." Natalia took the note, read it, then repeated it out loud to Marge. "I see," Marge observed tartly. "A plane crash. Big planes are bad; little ones are worse. Death traps. I'd never get on one."

Natalia nodded. She enjoyed her assistant's simple clarity. Teasing her lightly, she mused, "There's also the view that the moment life starts the appointment with death is already fixed."

"Ambassador!" Marge exclaimed. "That's…that's fatalism."

"Or realism." Natalia smiled. "Would you mind putting a note on Robbie's door saying I want to see her the minute she's back? And I'm having lunch with my husband in an hour, right? Could you make a booking for us somewhere and let Carlos know? Some place that's intimate. You know the saying: there's more to a marriage than four bare legs in a bed."

"Ambassador!"

Late in the afternoon, when Robbie was back from Leyden, she didn't immediately do as the note asked. She took off her coat and spent ten minutes entering information into a database. After

6

an email had been sent off to headquarters about the new file, she made her way up one floor. Marge was long gone and the ambassador's door stood open. Robbie knocked.

Natalia, standing at her desk, was on the phone. With a great swing of her arm she waved Robbie in and pointed at an easy chair. The person on the other end of the phone was doing all the talking, which allowed Natalia to put on a show. She grinned at Robbie, made dancing movements with her head as if to say *ho-hum, ho-ho*, then winked. Robbie grinned back, asking herself what it was that made this ambassador so attractive.

Natalia was on the short side and not exactly thin. On the other hand, her waist came a good way in, nicely defining the hips. Overall, physically, she was about average. So maybe it was the hair. Natalia had special hair, dark grey and speckled, vibrant and buoyant. It swirled at every movement of her head. There's art in hair that tells the world that, although no longer young, your vitality hasn't left. Natalia's Slavic features helped too. A strong nose, high cheekbones, small tidy lips and eyes radiating mischief and humour. And then there was her jewellery. Lots of it. Natalia loved precious stones and each day coloured gems adorned her: red rubies, white sapphires, black opals, blue tanzanite. The rocks in her long whirling earrings scattered light as if they possessed internal energy.

Yet Robbie had also observed – not in the management committee meetings, but at the Friday after work staff socials – that Natalia holding a drink would sometimes retreat to a corner for a private moment. Freak minutes those, when Natalia ceased performing. Her eyes turned heavy, becoming lidded and losing focus. An unspoken burden, a great weariness of some sort, seemed to come over her. Robbie recognised the glaze. She was sure it came from having too much knowledge, of life and of the world. She'd seen the same look on her aunts' faces, though they had their reasons for it. No vibrant coiffures for them, no overflowing jewel chests. All her aunts possessed was a clinging to survival – lives played out inside a filmy, barren interface between a no longer fertile ocean stretching out before and a destitute land of rocks behind.

Robbie concluded that, yes, outwardly the ambassador had much you could admire. But what really made Natalia attractive was something else. It was the special *way* she had with people. She knew how to reach out. And once she had, you next sensed she would bring you in – by sharing with you something of herself.

Supremo, my suspicion is, she is a special favourite of yours.

~

At last Natalia squeezed a few parting words into the phone conversation. "Interesting idea, Heiko. A non-killing world. Who wouldn't want that? I agree, it's good long-term goal. Yes, yes, don't worry. Mum's the word."

She hung up and said to Robbie, "Heiko de Bruyn. Heard of him?" Robbie shook her head. In three years of consular work she'd come to know, she believed, every one of Holland's police inspectors, but she doubted the ambassador had been on the phone with one of them. "De Bruyn is the foreign policy advisor in the prime minister's office. He asked me to come around earlier today. *To get acquainted.* I dropped everything for that. Marge has been trying to get an appointment with him for months, but the great man was always too busy. No time for mere courtesy calls. Today, oddly, it was the other way around. He asked *me* to come in. I was like a beggar delighted with a few sudden crumbs. At last I meet the man. He is very bald, though very charming. He asks me questions. Question after question. About my career, where I've been, what I've done. I wondered, is he this interested in everyone? Then before I have a chance to show I can be personable too, he stands up, shakes my hand and says, *Very nice to meet you, Ambassador. I hope to see you again.* Sure, I thought. When? Then, just now, he calls. Out of the blue. Not his secretary. He personally did the dialling. He wants to know if I can come in again next week. I say that should be possible. Next he launches into a sort of sermon. The topic? A non-killing world. And the punch line? That our contact must be kept secret. Shhh, Robbie, don't breathe a word to anyone. But does it make sense? I don't think so. On the other hand it could be fun."

Natalia had come around to sit across from Robbie. "Well now, your afternoon in Leyden, Robbie, did the police cooperate?"

"They were sweet."

"With you, naturally. You're such an opposite to the sour things they have to deal with. Of course they love you. But the plane crash, how did it happen? Foul play?"

"Human error they think. The fog last night. No visibility. The plane missed the runway. We went through the Canadian's belongings. Nothing points at foul play there either. All ordinary stuff. I went to the hospital afterwards. The poor man is in a shocking mess. Lots of broken bones, some vertebrae included. He's over sixty and overweight, so a surgical risk. The doctors were still deciding whether to operate."

"His name?"

"Paradis. Alistair Paradis."

"What was in his things?"

"Clothes. Toiletries. Documents. I mean, texts of speeches by all kinds of people. Also what looked like position papers on world peace."

Natalia frowned. "World peace?"

"World peace."

Natalia began to shake her head, as if questioning something. "I'll say this, peace is sprouting up all over. Your Mr Paradis has a briefcase full of documents on peace. Heiko de Bruyn is thinking of organizing a high-level conference, a summit, on it. And Carlos doesn't know what to do with all the invitations he gets nowadays to give lectures on peaceful solutions to ethnic conflicts. All of them ploughing the same field. Why is that, one wonders. Is something in the air? Is a desire ripening to do something, not to stand still?" Natalia got up and went to a painting hanging over a cabinet. It was in an aboriginal style, of a West Coast Indian village with totem poles. Other pictures like it hung in her office, abstract renditions of animals and spirits in blissful natural settings. "Feel the harmony in it, Robbie?" Natalia asked. "Why is that mood so rare?" She trailed off, then regrouped, "Tell me, what identified Paradis?"

Robbie explained it was the passport, issued in Vancouver.

"Vancouver? I went to school there. Was he born in Vancouver?" Robbie said Paradis's birthplace was Saint Boniface.

"Saint Boniface? Well, why not. We all had to be born somewhere. I came into the world in an emptiness south of Edmonton."

Natalia, peering again into the painting's forest depth, seemed to be watching her own birth taking place. She began to describe it. On *her* passport, place of birth was listed as Red Deer, but strictly speaking that wasn't true. She took her first breath in a farmhouse near an Albertan village called Mirror. A doctor from Red Deer dropped by the next day and the form he filled out was pre-stamped with *Red Deer Regional Hospital*. Scratching it out, replacing it with *Farm House with Leaking Roof 3.3 miles east of Mirror* would have been bothersome. So Red Deer it was. Soon after, Natalia's papa and her accommodating mother took their baby and left the family farm, moving to Vancouver to find a job that would pay. Natalia shrugged. "I think the real reason was he wanted to get away from the local Ukrainian community. Anyway, that's how I grew up on the West Coast." She leaned down to open the cabinet, extracted bottles, cans and glasses, and continued her questioning.

Did Paradis have a business card? Robbie replied that, yes, a small quantity of business cards had been found. What was his address? No address was shown, nor a phone number or email account. "Before we go on," Natalia interrupted, "can I offer you a martini? I have to improvise them here, but they generally turn out not that bad." Robbie said she was fine without. "You sure? Not even a diluted one? The working day is over, you know. This is social time. I can also mix up something with tonic. Or a virgin tonic? No ice though. Sorry."

Robbie yielded to a virgin tonic. Natalia energetically opened a can and poured. "Do you like my paintings?" she asked. Robbie said the colours were lovely, very strong, but she didn't understand the meaning of all the figures. "I love Indian paintings," Natalia said, without explaining. She handed Robbie a fizzing glass, began constructing a martini for herself and enquired further into the business card. Robbie repeated there was nothing on it except Paradis's name plus an acronym.

"An acronym?"

"Sure."

"Which was?"

"P-E-A-C-E."

"P-E-A-C-E? Intriguing. Peace keeps stalking us, this time as an acronym. I love acronyms. They can be so amusing. What could this one stand for? Don't tell me. Let me think. I'll take a stab." Natalia looked into her martini. "To you Robbie, to your good work, and to avoiding fogs, especially the ones we can't dispel." She extended her glass towards Robbie before taking a delicate sip. "So, P.E.A.C.E. *P* could be *Program*. Or *Partnership*. *E* could be a verb such as *Enact* or *Establish*. *A* could be *Agreement*, or *Arrangement*, possibly *Action*. Ah, I've got a candidate. *Partnership to Establish an Action Committee on the Environment*. No. Not right. Doesn't mesh with the peace documents he had with him. Wait. *P* could stand for *Peaceful*. Just a sec. Another one is emerging. *Peaceful* uh *Elimination of* uh *Activities Contributing* to uh, uh *Enmity*. Or, *Program to Eliminate Agreements Causing Enmity. Enmity* as in hate. Oh, this is fun."

"Enmity? On a calling card?"

"There are thousands of non-government groups with weird names. But you're right. Well, what is PEACE? Was I close?"

"I don't know. I haven't found out. The closest thing I could find on the Internet was *Palestine-Europe Academic Cooperation on Education*. I think your two were better than that."

"Palestine and a briefcase full of documents on peace. That's like oil and water. No way it could be that. This *is* getting good. Mr Paradis works for, represents, belongs to, or may be in the process of giving up his life for something to do with peace, yet whatever it is, it seems not to exist. A mystery. A good acronym is one thing, but one that stands for nothing deserves a toast." Natalia held her glass forward again. "To nothingness in life, Robbie. And let's not lose sight of the fact that the deeper you dig for meaning, the less likely you are to find any." She sipped again. "I'm glad Carlos didn't just hear me say that. He prefers to see life as randomness rather than a nothingness. I guess today proves him right. See what randomness has done for us. If it weren't for the fog and that crashed plane we wouldn't be having this enjoyable chat. I think we should do this more often. Don't you?"

~

11

They did. In the weeks and months that followed, Robbie came to appreciate that socializing after hours with the ambassador could be compared to a joyride on a carousel. Natalia, her martini dangerously swaying, told engrossing stories. The events she described were ordinary enough – it was her rendition of them which made them fabulous. Her tomboy childhood (ringing laughter), the fight against acne in high school (done in bass vibrato), gangly boyfriends in university and her first lover (whoops and war cries), menial work right after that (a monotonous wailing, as out of a bagpipe), her guitar-playing first husband called Nav, or Navvy, short for Donovan (a shaking head and a full minute of silence for him). The best stories were about breaking the solemn hush in the inner sanctums of the Foreign Service. "As if, each time I was in some meeting, I was smashing precious crystal, Robbie. I couldn't help it. I didn't understand the culture. I learned the hard way to tone myself down."

Robbie loved the carousel's whirling. Natalia's second martini usually brought on breathless descriptions of the day's ambassadorial conclaves. Ripe insight and dangerous confidences passed from the older to the younger woman. Robbie's expression sometimes posed a question: *Natalia, why are you telling me all this?* To which Natalia once replied, "Unshared secrets, Robbie, are a burden for me. Having a bosom pal scales that down." And so Robbie, reclining far back in the armchair, was carried along. Around and around past crowds painted by Natalia – people with eyes set deep in inky sockets, whose foreheads were furrowed and cheeks were sunken, who had crooked noses and mean, sallow lips. Caricatures, all of them. "Our colleagues, Robbie," Natalia would solemnly conclude, though a slight quiver in her voice betrayed the irony. Robbie tried to keep up with Natalia's way of seeing the world.

She eventually claimed that Natalia's portrayals were easily generalized. The lacking, decrepit figures of diplomacy could be found elsewhere too. During any day on any ordinary street you could see them struggling to make their way.

"You mean, they exist where you come from?" Natalia asked.

"In Ramea? For sure. In spades."

"In that case we'll have to get around to talking about Ramea," Natalia threatened. "Where is Ramea anyway?"

"It's a small island off Newfoundland's south shore."

"I see. I like islands, so finding out about a little island off a big island is doubly special. Is the Newfoundland spirit double the size there? Are Ramea's myths twice as big?"

Nothing in Robbie's background was spared. Her origins became fodder for the ambassador's happy-go-lucky revisioning over an after-work drink. Robbie and Natalia talked much about themselves, about their dreams and expectations, and about men. Natalia revealed that she loved Carlos because he was low maintenance and the funniest intellectual she'd ever known. "Mind you, physically, he's kind of a throwback. If you see him naked you have to think you're looking at an ape-like missing link. Nothing but thick black fur, front and back. Funny thing is, for me, that has been appealing from the beginning – the subtlest of minds in a body covered by the skin of Australopithecus himself." No more needed to be said. Robbie had already seen that Carlos was burly and affable, an instant hit with everyone.

The two women drew closer as the forces set free by the plane crash rippled along, and in the end it fell to Robbie to untangle them. When Natalia suddenly became a widow, Robbie took it as her duty to console, but what was she to do with the knowledge she had gained? What should she do about the evidence that Carlos's death was not an accident?

Chapter 2

Carlos grew up in Granada, in an old part of the city, in the shadow of the Alhambra. As far as he was concerned, the palace complex up on the hill was timeless. All that ever seemed to change was its colour, in accordance with the weather and the seasons. As a child he ignored that other world suspended over him, but by the time he was eleven or twelve it began to beckon. The way in wasn't a secret. Some rustling through undergrowth at the bottom of the gardens, a rabbit run along a stone wall to a gate, a quick climb to the top and a jump back down. Inside, he got to know every walk, courtyard, garden and arcade, and all the palaces and holy places. By what marvellous workings of whose mind, he wondered, had this feeling of peace been created? He started reading books on the Alhambra's history. Which brought him to religion and the development of beliefs.

As Carlos read up on the origins of the Alhambra's aura of spirituality, he naturally discovered that the culture that built it thought nothing much of killing off members of other cultures that happened to have a different religion. There seemed to be a paradox in that. Or, if not a paradox, at least a conundrum. He set about unravelling it and halfway through his teenage years he succeeded, to his own satisfaction at least.

He went back to first causes. What, he asked himself, determines human existence, and as part of that how do beliefs arise? He developed a theory. At its center he placed the notion that certain great forces direct life. His tag for them was 'determinants'.

One day, sitting on a shady bench in a quiet space defined by dozens of slender columns lightly holding up arches over a fine mosaic floor, Carlos reasoned that each individual's determinants are unique. There are primary ones, that is, the genetic blueprint that springs into existence at the moment of conception. Secondary ones immediately follow, such as the mother's health while she carries the foetus and, after birth, the character traits of the parents, as well as the prevailing culture to which the parents belong and how they are positioned in it.

As he deliberated further Carlos recognized, though not from personal experience, that conception is spatially and temporally a minuscule event. The sperm that completes the job of tunnelling into an egg is one of many available and the one that manages it does so randomly. Therefore, since the primary determinant, the set of genes that form the individual, is unpredictable, the precise interplay between that individual and the secondary determinants can't be foretold either. It follows that the way in which the existence of every newly born individual unfolds is generally unpredictable.

On another day, sitting by a softly gurgling fountain, Carlos began to explore a related notion: that during the early years of a human's existence he or she is a complete captive of that unique set of personal determinants. You have the parents you have, they impose on you who they are, and they try to get you to believe what they do. But once an individual is a little older, he is free to think this through. An individual can try to understand what his determinants add up to. He can develop insight into why he is who he is. And once that has happened, once an individual has a more objective perspective of what his determinants have fashioned, a new possibility arises. An individual can make changes. An individual can alter his imparted behaviours and beliefs.

In line with this approach, Carlos decided that henceforth he would direct his own beliefs and behaviour. He began to work at blunting certain personality traits that he considered to be less than stellar, such as being demanding on his mother in the same way that his father was. And he began to emphasize behaviour he considered beneficial, such as reading – his objective here was to double the number of books he went through in a week. He also began to question his beliefs. The effect was immediate. His awareness and understanding exploded. As his horizons expanded, he felt he was developing a distance from everything around him. Sensing that he was sublimely assuming control over who he was and could become, he acquired a solid streak of idealism. And that made him decide that from that day forward he would only act to maximize the common good of all humankind.

Carlos now generalized his thinking, moving from the individual to the group. He began with the one around him, his neighborhood. Contemplating its intense Catholicism, he concluded that nearly everyone had that faith because they happened to have been born into it. Looking at their religious belief through the lens of his theory of randomness and determinants, he immediately understood that, for example, had he been born into the culture a few hundred kilometers to the south on the other side of the Mediterranean, his brain would have had altogether different religious notions poured into it. The conclusion? Religious belief is easy and relative, if not plain quirky. How strange, he thought, that groups turn to killing each other because of something as whimsical as that.

The randomness of culture and religion fascinated Carlos as much as his own accidental spot on the planet. He saw that the people in his neighborhood were convinced they had been divinely chosen to be Catholic. They were proud of their convictions. Actually, you could say they loved their convictions. Yes, they were in love with their determinants. Self-love. Self-adulation. It was plain to see – his neighborhood had a big religious ego. How sad that it didn't contemplate the foundation for it, that it was unable to free itself from that conceit.

When Carlos tried to talk about such things at home or school, or with the priest, he was rebuked and told to follow the neighborhood's way of thinking. But he didn't back off and there was some confrontation. He was accused of siding with the devil, which was hard on his mother. She cried about him quite a lot. His response was to stay calm, quietly convinced that it would be unfair if his neighborhood's love of its determinants became his prison.

Generalizing still more, Carlos concluded that if this problem was arising in his neighborhood, it must exist elsewhere too. And so it was that in the tranquil spaces of the Alhambra, Carlos developed his own, very personal understanding of why Muslims kill Christians and vice-versa, and why Catholics killed Protestants and vice-versa, and why, more broadly, *homo sapiens* tends to run around killing other members of its own species. He doubted that the urge to kill flowed from the primary determinant. Killing was surely the by-product of secondary determinants. And the question he now posed was this: if an individual through mental effort can move beyond his or her secondary determinants, can overcome imposed beliefs and leave the desire to kill for them behind, are groups capable of that too? Can societies reject their conceits? Can they survive without the illusion of supremacy? Furthermore, when societies enter into conflict and acquire the urge to kill, might it be possible to end such contest by getting them to understand that their beliefs, though comforting, are not absolute?

This cleared the way. Carlos, his idealism loftier than ever, decided to maximize his contribution to humanity by becoming a student of cultures. And so it was that he turned to ethnography.

~

After running off from Granada, he lived in huts in Africa, caves in India and yurts in Mongolia, absorbing languages, probing customs and, generally, learning how to live like the indigenous people. When he was twenty, he searched out holy lakes above the Himalayan tree line; during his thirties, he spent time in steamy Cambodian jungles visiting shrines first built for Vishnu; he celebrated his fortieth birthday, most esoterically, in Temple Square in Salt Lake City pondering the Mormon Tabernacle and the irrationalities it stood for. His understanding of culture and religion became sought after. A professorship came his way from the Collège de France in Paris. As his approach and understanding of ethnography became steadily more authoritative, he began working with international commissions and committees. UN agencies picked him out and offered lucrative consulting contracts. With an expanding travel schedule, time for teaching dwindled. His message did not waver – build peace by acquiring a deep understanding of cultures. This brought him to the Malta conference where he met Natalia.

The topic was globalization and peace, the paper he delivered at a workshop setting out new perspectives on tribalism's contributions to genocides. Natalia attended the workshop because she was organizing a foreign ministry project to promote democratic institution building in societies traumatized by war. After the workshop, at a reception, Natalia approached Carlos to question him on several of his ideas. The acoustics in the reception hall were terrible, the noise rising off the scale, and not wanting to shout their interests at each other, they broke away from the crowd onto a terrace overlooking Malta's harbour.

Their conversation took a much-tried path – from the problems of the world to how they came to be in Malta. "Interesting," Carlos said after Natalia had laid out her career with a few broad strokes. "Yours is pretty good too," she admitted when he'd done the same. Carlos became more personal. Was there a husband? No longer, said Natalia. When a student she'd become convinced she wasn't meant to live in one only place and so she joined the Foreign Service. The man she had married, a West Coast songwriter and guitar player, was at first content to move around, but after a decade changed his mind. His own career, he was sure, was still waiting for him in the back alley pubs of Vancouver. "At the time my posting was in South Africa. He left, and we divorced soon after. It was amicable enough. He qualified for alimony. He thought that was a good deal. I'm still supporting him."

Carlos chuckled. "I never married. The idea of alimony – me qualifying for it – scared me silly. Anyway, such women as were interested in me wanted to settle down, whereas I always had a roaming spirit." He shrugged and changed the topic, complimenting Natalia on her contribution to the conference. The experiences she set out, the preparation of a basis for democratic processes amongst African tribes, were fascinating and advanced the conference's objectives. Natalia in return admitted that she had admired his composure during an intellectual shootout with a caustic British academic who objected to Carlos's observation that genocide doesn't come from ordinary people, but from their belief structures when manipulated by a political class, such as tribal chiefs of shamans.

Their chatting drifted this way and that and back to the disjointedness of their lives and to the chance events that brought them to Malta. Carlos smirked as if he knew something. He explained the theory of his youth: primary and secondary determinants. Natalia said "But isn't that just the old nature versus nurture chestnut? Are you saying that, for you, the role of nature, your primary determinant, is stronger?"

"I am saying," an amused Carlos replied, stroking his clipped beard, "that according to my theory the act of nature, and everything ever after, is random. How else can we account for this completely unpredictable but thoroughly delightful conversation?"

Natalia began to laugh. "Randomness? You know, I had a wonderful, wise grandmother. I'll tell you what she said about life being random. She said, chance will bring the things for which we do not dare to hope."

"That is very good. An optimistic outlook. And I agree with her. We should not be afraid of moving forward randomly. Your grandmother and I are on the same wavelength. Is it too late to meet her?" Natalia nodded. Carlos said he was sorry, and added, "Let me tell you about my grandmother. She also is no longer with us. In her thinking hope also stood at the center, but she treated it differently. Yours was prepared to live with what chance would bring her; mine prayed a lot. She believed in the divine and what came to her was his design. Mostly, she told me, she prayed for me. I loved her so much that I never told her it was my opinion that prayer is a waste of precious intellectual time."

Over the next months, Carlos and Natalia coordinated their travel schedules, spending weekends together in various cities and in other out-of-the-way places. A year later, he insisted she come to Granada so that he could show her the Alhambra. They visited it three days in a row, he recounting stories about each hall, alcove, court and atrium. On the third day, in a private ceremony – no presiding official, no witnesses – standing in the Court of the Lions, Natalia and Carlos declared to each other that henceforth they would consider themselves married. Carlos had drawn up in Spanish, on parchment, a marital contract. They signed it, then jointly held a stamp wet with red ink, into which each had squeezed a few drops of blood from a fingertip. They pressed the stamp onto the parchment, thereby rendering their contract inviolable. The stamp that Carlos had ordered to be carved for the occasion was imposing. The outline of a god, or demon, stood at the center. It was according to a sketch Carlos once made, which itself was based on descriptions he had from a tribe that lives, still undisturbed, in the rainforests of the Amazonian highlands. An exchange of marriage vows sealed by a non-existent god that looked ever-so-much like a devil? For Natalia, this fateful event truly was one for which she had not dared to hope.

Afterwards, she called her friends, adding that her second husband wouldn't have the problem of the first. "It makes no difference to Carlos where we live," she explained. "His career is to attack ignorance, which means he can work everywhere." The marriage, illegal in a narrow sense, was a great success. Natalia and Carlos were not made to be joined at the hip. They lived together sociably, but worked in separate worlds. When Natalia was named ambassador and Carlos learned they would move to Holland, he was more excited than she. "Did you know," he said, "that the Dutch and the Spaniards once waged an eighty year war? Eighty years of conflict because of minor differences over how their same god should be worshipped. As an ex-Spaniard, I'm eager to find out what the Dutch thought then and what they think now about that." Carlos made it sound as if the discovery of a mysterious new tribe was awaiting him, as if for him Holland would be as enthralling as the upper reaches of the Amazon.

~

An ex-Spaniard striving to become intimate with the Dutch.

One place Carlos started out was the embassy social club. On Friday afternoons (if he wasn't away travelling) he would step out of the ambassadorial residence, blow kisses at the deer, numerous part-owners of the great park surrounding the house, jump on his new bike – it was of the local upright variety – and, irrespective of the weather, pedal eight kilometers to the embassy. A rich journey, which allowed him to focus on its sounds. As Carlos leisurely cycled along, he mostly heard the deep sucking tone of reliable tires grabbing the bike path – no-slip rubber meeting a frictionless surface. What did that tell you about the local culture? That it was stolid and staid enough to match its slippery underpinnings? Sometimes a friendly ringing crept up on him from behind, a courtesy from another rider swooshing by. The speed! Such little apparent effort! Slipping away from Carlos, soon out of sight, was something obviously abnormal, a mythic figure.

Carlos's bike also had a bell. He liked to sound it along the rhododendron-lined driveway on the residence grounds. Sometimes he rang it for the deer, other times for himself. One loud ring meant that he was leaving, two that he was back. He rang it during his journey too, sometimes randomly when he idled through an open stretch, but mainly at intersections. Intersections were an excuse to send long strings of happy notes out into the grey Dutch weather. For Carlos they ascended cymbal-like up into … well, into Holland's pantheon, whatever that might be, whatever might be in it. By the time he joined the crowd at the embassy social he would be so giddy that some of the staff thought the ambassador's consort was high.

That notion deepened when he talked. The locals left their offices punctually at the end of the work week, assembling on the ground floor near a kitchen area with a sink and a fridge, and Carlos eagerly entered the small talk. He might describe something Dutch he had observed that week, such as herring being eaten raw. He mimicked holding the fish by the tail over his mouth, then chomping his way up. How delightful it was, he said, that the Dutch ate this way in public. Several of the girls claimed they had never done it, but all the same they laughed along. Carlos probed other customs, such as scrubbing your house's piece of a sidewalk with a strong disinfectant once a week. Did such thorough cleansing really make a difference? Was it the cause of Dutch tallness and longevity? Or, why must Dutch drapes and curtains hanging by the front windows be so lavish when no one ever closes them? He wanted to know about other things, too, such as rituals used to celebrate religious events. After that, he would turn to topics such as the nation's self-image. Carlos didn't have to scratch at beliefs too long before the locals tripped over their own tongues trying to clarify and describe their culture to him.

Other times he went at the Canadians. Gus, for example, often stood around looking solemn, stroking a glass and saying nothing. Soon enough, Carlos discovered his hobby was wine. Gus planned to practice viticulture in his retirement; he already owned land on Prince Edward Island. Carlos stroked his beard and studied him. Why put money into something that risky? And wouldn't running a vineyard be hard work? Apart from that, who would buy the wine? Gus's reticence disappeared with one monumental downward gulp of a nearly full wine glass. The reason was his dad, a steel worker in Hamilton who drank too much beer and whiskey all his life. When he was too old to go to the plant, all that remained was booze, TV and a couch. He was soon dead. Only then did Gus come to grips with something he had always suppressed: that he always wanted to be his dad's total opposite. Therefore, retirement would be in a place without steel mills. Therefore, in in his future home there would be neither TV nor couch. Therefore, no beer or whiskey. Only wine. This made good sense to Carlos who clasped a hand on Gus's shoulder. "Pruning vines and drinking wine lie at the root of the world's deep civilizations. Your country needs you."

Another time Carlos fixed on Marcel. Marcel had grown up next to the Saguenay River, close to where it joins the St Lawrence. The scenery there, by any standard, is spectacular and Marcel could go on and on about it. *C'est beau. C'est vraiment très, très beau.* Carlos probed: what went into the Québécois identity there? What made it special? He asked about the river, the towns along it, how people earn their living and what they do in their spare time. Marcel's English was accented with a round, rustic Québécois tone.

He claimed that despite having traveled and gained much pleasure from working in many countries, Saguenay remained unbeatable.

"Say something in Québécois," Carlos urged. Marcel thought, then with a scowl turned to his dialect: *un sympa Espagnol est rare comme la marde de pape.* A likeable Spaniard is rare as pope shit? Carlos stroked his beard. The force of the compliment in the insult registered. He began to laugh. Marcel too. It escalated. Carlos took his head in his hands and shook it. Tears flowed down his cheeks and into his beard. He used his shirt sleeve to mop up the excess. Others looked their way while he smoothed his hair to regain composure. "Rare as pope shit," he repeated, touching Marcel's shoulder with a fist. "I like that, but I know a few things about pope shit too. Unlike most shit, pope shit never disappears. It doesn't turn into plant nutrition. Pope shit accumulates century upon century, which means its smell is always worsening and becoming more permanent, too."

In due time Georgette, the immigration councillor, became a Carlos discovery. His first impression of her was primness, but after a mere five questions she confessed to him that she knew how to abandon herself to passion. Her passion, she trilled, was duck hunting. Lines around Carlos's eyes tightened. Clasping understanding hands beneath his chin, he asked, "Do all women hunt where you're from?" Georgette's head bobbed. In her clan, oh yes, there were quite a few. Each year she took her annual leave in September, spending the weeks at the family cabin in the Qu'Appelle Valley. How utterly beguiling, Carlos answered. And where is the Qu'Appelle Valley? Well, in Saskatchewan dontcha know. Georgette now confided that she loved roughing it there with her sister, who was an even better shot. In hip waders they hid in the reeds of the marshes and when the ducks returned from feeding on the wheat fields in late afternoon, they popped them off one by one. And then? Well, ducks have to be plucked and cleaned before roasting. Surplus carcasses were stored in the deep freeze.

"Self-reliance," Carlos concluded. "Is that how you grew up? Were you more of a hunter and less of a gatherer?"

"For certain," Georgette replied. "We just always went at it, know what I mean? We never liked stuff getting too precious. This immigration work I do, it pays the bills, but it isn't the same as living off the earth." Carlos was forming a picture of Saskatchewan culture.

"There's a tribe in Africa that's good at catching migrating birds," he said.

"Betcha they don't match our dancing," Georgette answered.

Carlos was so captivated by the specimens at the Friday socials that he observed to Natalia: "So much randomness in one place, all of it just thrown together. I ought to pen a monograph on it. *Embassy Identity: The Synergetic Convergence of Divergent Tribal Emissaries*. A good idea? Would you read it?"

Her reply was regal. "They're my staff. They're good. I like them, Carlos. Drop the word *divergent* from the title and write it."

~

Carlos steadily worked his way through the group, but had not got around to Robbie. Months later, he still lacked her contribution to his unwritten monograph. She often slipped into the party quietly and stayed on the sidelines. He observed that she usually took a soft drink or a glass of juice to a corner where other singles, local women her age, clustered. Robbie was easily both the tallest and the plainest – like a striking weed shooting up out of a bed of carefully pinched petunias. Her hair was bundled into a simple ponytail, straight back from the forehead. It narrowed her head and sharpened her features, which looked gaunt, even undernourished, next to the made-up faces of the Dutch girls. "A waif," Carlos concluded. "A waif locked up inside herself. She doesn't know what belonging is."

He asked Natalia about Robbie, and she partially agreed with him. "She occasionally has that I'm-lost-in-the-world look," Natalia admitted, "but beneath the surface there is pure bedrock. When you talk with her you discover her core is absolutely solid."

Natalie and Carlos seldom compared impressions of embassy staff and never discussed embassy matters. But Natalia hadn't been able to hold Robbie's report on the plane crash back and, anyway, it was public knowledge. With her head still full of the details Robbie had provided, and being free that evening of formal functions – the residence staff were gratefully enjoying a night off – she had joined

Carlos in the kitchen. He was clanging pots around, deciding on a good one for heating up a soup. Natalia began searching out cutlery. With her voice rising above this din she described the crash and its aftermath. "So we have the business card," she half yelled like a foreman in an assembly plant, "but are we the wiser for it? What's the point of a business card with an acronym that says nothing? PEACE. It would be no surprise to learn that John Lennon had one with just his name and that word on it, but suppose my business card consisted of my name plus the acronym G.O.D. Wouldn't a lot of people say, 'Yes, yes, dear girl, and now please give us your hand so we can lead you to the chalky mansion up on the hill where delusions are managed'? You know what Robbie found on the internet, Carlos? Palestine-Europe Academic Cooperation on Education." Natalia snorted. "It's a total enigma."

Carlos stopped clanging. In one hand he held a large saucepan, in the other the lid. "Paradis?" he asked. "Alistair Paradis?"

Natalia ceased rumbling through the cutlery drawer. "You can't know that. The name hasn't been released."

"Alistair is close to death? Holy dumping pope. I was expecting to see him next week at a local think tank seminar. We have been traveling on the same circuit for years."

~

Natalia's program was taking her to Holland's eastern regions the next day. Since the return would be late, would Carlos help out? Some of what he knew about Paradis would round out the consular file. Could he call Robbie to transmit them?

Early on Friday, as the official vehicle pulled away with Natalia in the rear – she immediately sank away and turned to a stash of files Marge had prepared for reading – Carlos retreated into his study. He soon sank away too, into his work, and completely forgot the promise to contact Robbie. It came back to him only as he was climbing onto his bike for the ride to the late afternoon embassy social. "I'll have a one-on-one chat with her," he rationalized. "More fun than phoning anyway."

At the party, he waited. Robbie came in slightly delayed and when she did went directly to the bar. In an instant he was next to her, hearing her order a juice. "End of the work week?" he broke in pleasantly. A sideways glance questioned him. "Fridays are special," he continued.

"For sure." She went back to watching the busy bartender.

"How was the week? Not tougher than the others, I hope?"

"About the same."

Now they both studied the juice jug freshly hauled out of the fridge having its cap removed. "Natalia says you do consular."

Robbie nodded. "I do consular."

"Sounds special. Ancient Rome had consuls. The work has deep traditions."

"Ancient Rome? Golly. Well, they surely didn't do what I do. Thing is, often it's crisis work. Running around all the time. Sometimes you have to get it done with just a lick and a promise."

"A lick and a promise. That's colourful. Licking and promising. I'll try it next time perspiration threatens. Where did you pick that phrase up?"

"I don't know." Robbie had begun to sip her juice through a straw and placed the glass on the counter. "My aunts used it. Where I'm from it's just a normal expression."

"Folk expressions fascinate me. Know any more, you know, ones used where you're from?"

Robbie laughed. "Loads."

Carlos asked to hear a few. She hesitated, but with a motion of his hand, a signal to just let it roll, he urged her on.

Out popped another one. "Don't be breaking your leg on a stool that's not in the way."

Carlos was delighted. "Don't stop. Tell me more."

"Stunned as me arse. It's often used for repairmen of all kinds."

Carlos clapped. "Vivid. Illuminating. You know, sayings are windows into a culture." As Robbie sucked more juice through the straw, he added. "Newfoundland, right? You're from Newfoundland?"

Robbie raised her glass. "The Rock. Actually I'm from a little rock which sticks up out of the ocean next the big rock."

"A sub-island. That's neat. But what do I know about Newfoundland? I read that Spain scooped up all your fish, which is typical of Spain. Its culture is to believe that what others have belongs to them. You only have to think of the conquistadors. Any fish left?"

Back home, Robbie revealed, Spaniards were known as fish killers. They weren't the only fish killers, but they ranked high. So, yes, the fish were gone. She took her juice and began to move towards the cluster of single girls.

Carlos, stepping with her, asked, "Did you see Alistair Paradis today?" Robbie stopped in mid-stride and, seriously perplexed, looked Carlos in the eyes. He started smoothing his moustache with two spreading fingers. "Natalia mentioned the accident and, as fate has it, I know him," he explained. "Will he pull through?"

"I don't know. He was operated on today. I haven't seen him yet."

"He isn't young. Let's hope for the best."

"Where do you know him from?"

Carlos began tugging at his beard. "The peace circuit. We're always the same few hundred sharing the latest thinking on the world's festering sores. Mostly non-government types. Diplomats sometimes show up but you get the feeling that for them to be in the same room as us is purgatory. Alistair is our bridge – to the diplomats, the UN crowd, exiles wanting their country back, you name it. He chats everybody up with every charm available to man. And he has a budget. The whole crowd is invited to his cocktail parties. No holds barred. The finest ballrooms in the most lavish hotels. And you know what? At his parties everyone talks to everyone. No silly you-and-them stuff. You always find him at the center, embracing, kissing, laughing, and singing in baritone that there's just too much love in the universe for all the little guys to be running around needlessly killing each other. He was coming in for next week's seminar."

"Did Mr Paradis ever tell you anything about himself?"

"Not much. I can say that he's the only one on the circuit who gets around in his own plane."

"I know nothing about him either, not even if he has next of kin. There's only the acronym on his card. So far, no luck tracing it."

"Of course, PEACE. Natalia asked me about that too. Alistair is an Executive Secretary."

"An Executive Secretary? Of what?"

"People Everywhere Against Conflict and Evil."

Robbie looked blank, but slowly a smirk of recognition formed. "That's not too mouldy," she said, nodding. "People Everywhere Against Conflict and Evil – that must be some mountain-sized organization."

"Not mouldy? That's good. Natalia said it sounded more like motherhood. Well, Alistair claims PEACE speaks for millions, though I don't know how he counts them. But we shouldn't laugh, at least not at Alistair. He's got influence. Everywhere he goes he meets the leading politicians, opinion makers and others who pull strings. When will you know about his operation?"

"Monday. I'll be informing the ambassador as soon as I'm back from the hospital."

"She will want to know. Meanwhile, can I ask for a favour? I plan to read up on the complexities of sub-islander societies. If I find something that needs more explanation, can I ask you then?"

"Asking costs nothing," Robbie said, excusing herself and slipping off.

Carlos watched her go. A sub-islander who seemed self-exiled, who was born on a rock and was rock-solid. And a diplomat too. More exquisite randomness. Sumptuous input for the monograph.

Chapter 3

Natalia's office was lit up bright, bright as a big city, and the West Coast paintings on the walls, worlds of indigenous myths and spirits, served as vibrant conduits out of it. On her desk, a cup of tea, the wisps of aromatic steam slowly drifting up. All snug. All convivial. A conspiracy to drive the Monday morning doldrums off.

But Natalia, tense in her chair, wasn't registering this. Her mood was more in sync with the weather. Outside, a cold rain was falling through a dark grey mist. All gloom and melancholy there. Staring at the tea cup, her fingers drumming at the desk, she was trying to connect some dots. But no picture was emerging. No more today than yesterday, or for that matter since Saturday when a ringing phone had disturbed the residence's afternoon silence.

Natalia. She recognized the growl. *Irving Heywood here. Got a minute?*

If Natalia were asked to describe Heywood in one sentence or less she would have said – master of self-absorption. He was a typical power-loving headquarters man and though she never trusted him, nothing ever happened for her to dislike him either. Actually, she often found him amusing. His precise, short question about her availability, which had more the tone of an order, was one of the dots. And though it lent significance to some earlier dots, it also made connections between them still more tenuous. After he had said his piece and the line clicked dead, Natalia sat transfixed. All kinds of thoughts swirled around in her head, wayward thoughts, none landing and none adding up. A case of ambiguity, and dealing with ambiguity had never been her strong suit.

The first dots had blipped on Thursday, one after the embassy management committee meeting in the morning – the urgent request to meet the Dutch prime minister's foreign policy advisor – and another some hours later when de Bruyn phoned to follow up. A third dot came on Friday. She was out of town when, late in the afternoon, her cell phone buzzed. De Bruyn again, not really saying anything, only that he looked forward to seeing her early the next week. He rang off before she could say: *What will the topic be?* In the back seat of the car speeding from Maastricht back to The Hague, she began to wonder why de Bruyn, coming from nowhere, was suddenly pursuing her. Then the Saturday interruption from Heywood, the fourth dot, the final dot. It was connected to the other three, but did nothing to explain them.

And now, on this cheerless Monday, within the hour, she would be undertaking the trek to the prime minister's office again.

Heywood had put her right off. For a start, the moment she realized who it was she felt foreboding. There had to be a crisis of some kind. Why else would Ottawa be disturbing the weekend? Had a cruise ship full of Dutch pensioners gone missing in the cold waters surrounding the Queen Charlotte Islands? Was a Dutch bank in Toronto being nationalized first thing Monday morning? But no, nothing like that. No emergency required a diplomatic intervention. All Heywood did was give her some advice. Of the worst kind. Tips on how behave during her upcoming meeting with de Bruyn.

"No problem." Natalia tried not to sound too snappish. "Of course I'll listen to him. It's not as if I've never done that before. But if there's something you expect he will say to me, do we have a position on it? Do you want me to tell *him* something?"

"For the time being, Natalia," the stern voice from Ottawa commanded, "just be your sweet self. As I say, smile and hear de Bruyn out."

Heywood had a reputation for being ignorant about many things, and Natalia caught herself thinking that Dutch pronunciation could safely be added to the list. Through the medium of Heywood's rusting vocal cords de Bruyn came out as *Duhbrouyeen*. For an instant Natalia saw the Dutch foreign policy advisor in a fresh light, as a desert warrior wearing a head cloth, brandishing a rifle, possibly a Kalashnikov. But the image, though amusing, lasted no more than a second.

Natalia couldn't shake Heywood's order. *Act sweet, smile and listen.* It was a provocation that, as it replayed in her head, posed questions too. How did Heywood know she'd met with de Bruyn once before? And who told him she'd been called in by him again? Had some diplomatic subtlety, some sub-surface issue started spinning during that first chat, which triggered off not only two more phone calls from the great foreign policy advisor himself, but also the one from Heywood? Had she missed something? Again she went over what had happened on Thursday. In de Bruyn's office she had looked up from a low sofa, making a mental note that his manner was graceful. Could they continue on a first name basis, he had asked. "Call me Heiko. Please. I prefer it." No problem for Natalia. She liked familiarity too. He asked about her family name. "Plavniuk. Ukrainian. Correct?" When exactly, he wanted to know, had her ancestors moved to Canada? For over thirty minutes he'd prodded her this way, and she grew more talkative the whole time.

Not until after Heywood had hung up did she ask herself if maybe she'd poured out too much of herself. Why otherwise would he have instructed her to do no more than smile and listen? Had de Bruyn wanted to say something important to her on Thursday, but she had somehow prevented it? Was that the reason for his phone call late on Thursday when Robbie walked in? *He* did all the talking

31

then. A long ramble, a kind of homily, a bunch of scrambled up sentiments mostly on the pious side, of a sort you're more likely to hear in church. All about the importance of doing more to create a non-killing world. A non-killing world? Good idea, Heiko. Sure. Why not. Good sermon, by the way. Now that you're finished, why don't we go over to the church annex for a social hour and some tea?

How was all this connected to Heywood's order that next time she should say little? She wanted to explain to Heywood that the foreign policy advisor had led her on, that he had *asked* her to describe her forebears' pioneering lifestyle. That was why, in a voice tripping over itself, she had talked about her grandparents' tough journey from Ukraine nearly a century ago, their first wretched sod hut and their ramshackle farmhouse on a bleak patch of land on the vast, western fringes of the Canadian prairies. But she never got around to articulating this to Heywood because he had hung up.

So there was ambiguity. Plenty of it. More of it arriving every day. And ambiguity made her restless. It wasn't long before it darkened her mood. For the rest of Saturday it had gnawed at her. That night she suffered from insomnia, which meant that Sunday morning she felt still more rattled. In the afternoon it got to her. She marched into Carlos's study not caring that she was shattering his concentration. He threw her one look and thought for a second, then put down his pen, pushed a writing pad away and closed the books he was consulting. "Good idea," he said curtly. "Let's go."

Natalia got into a fur coat; he donned a worn, plaid woollen jacket. In her car, from within a high collar of soft Arctic hare, she said, "Sorry Carlos. I interfered with your work." She was driving in the direction of the coastal dunes.

Carlos shrugged. He hadn't taken a break since early morning and was beginning to feel stale anyway.

"What are you working on?" she asked. "It seems you've been deep into something for a while."

Natalia's style when she operated her private car, a sleek German saloon with a big engine, was expressive. She liked to push the machine to the limit. Carlos, not a driver himself, loved it. Usually he reclined his seat a bit, so as not to see anything, to concentrate on the feel of the car's rally-type manoeuvring. It was from such a position of near repose, with eyes closed, that he serenely answered her question. "I have been looking into the Sentinelese. A remarkable tribe. Heard of them? They inhabit a small island in the Bay of Bengal and remain unspoiled. If outsiders come near, by sea or air, they attack. Volleys of arrows and spears drive intruders off. Effectively, we know nothing about them. I'm mentioning them as a case study at the seminar next week."

"If they like to be left alone, why drag them into a seminar?" Natalia was swerving around a corner, close to the limits of control.

Carlos, hanging onto his seat belt, loved the forces generated. "Varoom," he purred as the car stabilized. Peaceably he continued. "The Sentinelese are a symbol. For centuries they have successfully resisted outside change. They deserve respect. A high wall should be put up around them."

"Around an island?" Natalia pushed the gas pedal to the floor, holding it until the tachometer neared the red zone, then backed off.

"A metaphorical wall, a barrier put up by us against our own best intentions. We must keep our customs away from them. Mass tourism, all the silly gawking, that should be kept even further away. No one should be allowed to disturb cultures that want to be left alone. The Sentinelese are not the only ones. We have the Pygmies in Africa, the Ayoreo and the Cacataibo in South America, the Penan in Malaysia. Proud people. We should value and respect them.

"Too many want to turn them into theme parks. Imagine Disneylanding them. There ought to be a law restricting Disneyland's imitations to the country from which it sprang." Carlos chuckled. "Or which imitates Disneyland. As I say, high walls around vulnerable cultures. But how?"

"Interesting seminar."

"There's more on the agenda than that."

The car tore down a straight stretch. The speed, plus Carlos's unruffled voice, soothed Natalia. She adored his calm and she liked that his talent had a high international demand. She reached over to squeeze his hand. "You do good work, Carlos. Good work praises the workman."

Carlos shrugged. "I don't know. I sow maybe, but who reaps?"

"What a desolate attitude. Not like you at all. More like me. By the way, I should have asked, did you talk to Robbie? Was she interested to find out about PEACE? So many coincidences. Your seminar this week, you knowing Paradis, him travelling here for it, his plane crashing, Robbie responsible for dealing with that. What did you think of her?"

"Robbie? Well, she is most interesting. I thought afterwards, she resembles a seal. I mean, she has an inquisitive head. Cute how it sticks up from below to study the world. Then she goes back down, spending most of her time out of sight. In her own domain she moves swiftly and gracefully, I'm sure."

Natalia laughed. "She must have seen enough seals when she grew up. There's also a spiritual side to her, don't you think? The way she looks at you, but past you, as if more important things are happening in another realm."

"As I say, the seal's perspective. She takes a peek at how humanity lives, sees awfulness, then retreats. She mostly lives elsewhere. On the other hand, she knows some earthy sayings. *Stunned as me arse.* Don't laugh Natalia. Really. She said that. Good, don't you think? Well, I liked it. What a treat it would be to do some ethnographic research on her little sub-island."

"*Stunned as me arse.* What made her say that?"

"I sort of dragged it out of her," a sheepish Carlos admitted.

The idle talk continued until they pulled into the parking area of a small pavilion, a teahouse, overlooking a North Sea beach. The dunes around were muffled, crushed into silence by the dark season. A dense pewter vapour hung over the sea. A choking mood. But inside the teahouse the many lively voices converged into a bright din. "A perfect place to come," Natalia said when she and Carlos were at a table. Tea and pastries were soon served.

"Something weird is going on," she finally revealed.

Carlos had to agree that Irving Heywood's message was on the cryptic side, but why would Natalia let that get to her? "Did Mr Heywood sock it to you in your weak spot?" he asked.

"My weak spot?"

"You know, where your bravado and self-doubt intersect."

Natalia's eyebrows rose. "Oh, there. Maybe. For sure he threw me. There's a loop of some kind – I seem to be in it, but really I'm not. Being out of the loop when you should be in is not good. Could it be linked to what he said last summer?" Carlos looked blank. "We had dinner at his cottage."

"That! An enjoyable evening. His wife was very charming."

"And Irving was doing his best to be modest. Remember what I said driving home? That the whole evening he struggled to hide his pride in his own successes, including orchestrating my being appointed ambassador."

"I don't know, Natalia. You may be taking this too far. That evening was to celebrate. He wanted to say bon voyage. You said you felt honoured. I'm not sure he was hiding pride. He was drinking a lot and blathered a bit, but all of it struck me as pretty innocent."

"That wasn't my take. Irving has always concealed his true agendas. That's what has kept him rising through the ranks and almost to the top. Head of the Service. He was in the running for it. A month after that dinner he was told he wouldn't get his ultimate promotion. He was pipped at the post."

"I rather liked him, I mean, the way he talked. All trumpets blaring. That was the sound he used when he placed you on a pedestal. He thinks the world of you. That much was obvious."

Natalia threw Carlos a doubting glance and began to nibble at her pastry. Carlos took his tart, spooned out the thick cream and dark berries, licked his lips, wiped the hairs around his mouth clean with the serviette and finally consumed the tart shell whole. He signalled a waiter and ordered wine.

"Think back, Carlos," Natalia said when the waiter had gone. "Irving spent a good part of the evening reminiscing about his career, all forty years of it. He dropped steady hints that he was expecting to be named the new Service Head and talked about how for months he'd worked for my best interests. He also made it more than clear he'd had to overrule some naysayers to my appointment."

"Naysayers? There are always many and they are never silent. One has to expect them."

"What he was really saying was that I owe him one, that I was indebted to him. In debt, in danger. It's that simple. The most consistent part of his reputation is being friendly, friendly, friendly until his own survival is on the line. Then, poof, the camaraderie is gone. Anyway, he didn't get the nod to become Service Head and apparently it nearly killed him. Why not retire? they said. Forty years is a good run. But he hung on. Couldn't let go. The standard scenario unfolded – a rebirth as a senior phantom with assorted powers and an unspecified role. I'm guessing the reason he was vague on the phone is that he's cashing in that IOU. Something bizarre is happening. It could get dangerous."

The wine arrived. Glasses clinked. "Cheers," Natalia mumbled.

"Dangerous?" Carlos continued.

"Careers are whimsical. They get snuffed out."

"Ah, that kind of danger. Well, if you're in danger, probably he is too. Maybe he wants to pass a danger along. When cultures grow more complex, systems emerge for that specific purpose. Priests exist to manage the intricacies, but when eventually they can't cope, when something goes wrong – you know, a plague or a bad harvest, or in your case, in your Service, some failure on the foreign policy front – the priests search out a culprit. Scapegoats are needed. It's never the priests who get strapped to the sacrificial altar. Almost always adversity gets delegated down."

"You're describing my anxiety. Where Irving sits now, he's not far from the prime minister's hitmen. Priests, witch doctors, shamans – that's them. Maybe they are on his case. Maybe you're right. He may be passing something on." Natalia mimicked Heywood's gravelly voice. "*You'll be seeing quite a bit of Duhbrouyeen, Natalia. That's my prediction.*"

"Did he say that? How interesting. In addition to his many other talents, Mr Heywood seems to have a capacity for soothsaying too."

~

Few things excited Marge as much as big changes to the ambassador's schedule – if the cause was a VIP – and early Monday, when Natalia entered the office, she was over the moon. "I've got de Bruyn's office on tenterhooks," she trilled. "They insist you must see him today. I hummed and hawed and bluffed and said that could be problematic. It was so delicious to play hard to get. It would turn your whole day topsy-turvy, though. Want me to go ahead?"

"Did they say why the rush?"

"No. But I know why. It's your magic. It touched de Bruyn and now he's hooked."

"More likely he is half mad."

"Well you could handle that too. Here's what I could do: switch Gus so that he's first after lunch; the courtesy call by the Mali ambassador would come after that; I'd also cancel your meeting at the Economics Ministry, and so on and so forth. The appointment at the Foreign Ministry would be at eleven by the way. De Bruyn's office explained there was an unexpected opening in his schedule."

"Unexpected? The unexpected keeps happening. It's becoming tiresome."

Marge picked up a vibe. "Everything alright?" she asked, studying the ambassador.

"A touch of brain flu, Marge. Stuffy thoughts, that's all. Let's go with what you suggest."

At her desk, Natalia propped her chin up on one hand. Something was being done to her, maybe even violating her. With fingers drumming, she tried once more to lift meaning from events. De Bruyn growing so chummy so quickly. It suggested he knew something. Plus, when she first walked in, he had cocked an eyebrow like someone scrutinizing. Later, his eyes had been sharp as a hawk's. Does that happen at routine courtesy calls? Not too often. If anything, last Thursday had been more like an interview.

An interview? Natalia stopped drumming. Was that it? Had de Bruyn been testing her? Had he called her in to have a look at her? Had she been, so to speak, on view? Like a model strutting on a catwalk? Was Heywood in on this?

From nowhere an awful image came to Natalia. She saw a phantom bureaucrat and a prime minister's right hand man negotiating zones of influence. She even heard a raucous Heywood chuckle. *That proposition, Duhbrouyeen, is one we can't refuse. Yup, we'll pony up. 'Course we will. I offer you our gal. She's just down the road from you anyway and has time on her hands. Call her in. Give her the eye. Get her to do a turn. If she tweaks your fancy, well, I'd say the business is on.*

Natalia grabbed a pencil and snapped it. *The snakes,* she thought.

~

Dirk, the embassy chauffeur, consulted his watch when she came down. 10:45 am. He was outside by the main entrance holding a large umbrella. The distance between the building and the car wasn't much, but it would be a shame if a raindrop defiled the ambassador's perfect hairdo. Just as Natalia moved through the foyer, Robbie walked up too. "Ambassador," she exclaimed. "Good morning. You look nice." She had taken in Natalia's tailored black suit and contrasting white pearl brooch, the dark blouse, the Hermès scarf wound round the neck, the day's earrings – brightly coloured opals set in silver – the black Burberry raincoat draped over one arm, and the extravagantly patterned purse dangling from the other.

"And you, Robbie," Natalia countered gravely, "look ready to slay hordes. Also going somewhere?"

Robbie said she was catching the train to Leyden. A few minutes with Alistair Paradis were possible before he went in for surgery.

They remained on the foyer side of the double security doors, Natalia placing a hand on the handle of the first one without pushing it open. "Carlos said Paradis was flying in to attend a seminar on culture and conflict."

Robbie nodded. "And he told me about PEACE. I still don't have much detail on what they do. If the doctors let me talk to Paradis I may find out more."

Natalia opened her coat and talked as she pulled it on. "We sure missed that PEACE acronym by a mile. I feel for the poor man. Carlos says he wants to build a better world. *Against conflict*

38

and evil. We should all sign up for that. Join the billions. Well, I do hope he pulls through."

They fell silent, both considering that Paradis might not make it. An old man dying alone in a foreign land. Natalia sighed and again took the door handle. "You're off to a hospital and I'm going to the Foreign Ministry. Remember that phone call Thursday? The non-killing world? Today may bring a new instalment. Not sure I'm ready for it, Robbie. I sense something isn't right. And it's no fun finding out that those who seem to be the best are actually the worst."

"How do you mean that? Non-killing is a meaningful topic. You'll be good at it."

Natalia grimly shoved the door open. "Come to my office when you're back, Robbie. I want the latest on Paradis. And then we'll compare notes, mine on non-killing with yours on not dying. We could adopt a motto too: a trouble shared is a trouble halved. Sound good?"

Outside, the ambassador slipped underneath Dirk's large umbrella. Robbie was invited to squeeze in, but declined and, on foot, brought up the rear of the small procession departing the embassy.

As the car pulled away, Natalia from the back seat waved at Robbie who energetically threw an outstretched hand back. For a second Natalia took her in, struck by the determination of the young woman's forward stride. Robbie stooped a little on account of her height, and her feet angled slightly outwards. Not exactly a candidate for the catwalk, though she made up for it with a plucky, psychic poise.

When the car was speeding through traffic, Natalia thought further. How had she been at Robbie's age? Nowhere near the same. She'd lacked the quietness. If anything she had been loud, even clamorous, though for a reason. To push back a phobia, the phobia of failing, which came courtesy of papa. It seemed he never ceased yelping that she had to be the best, or else. Complex adjustments were necessary. When she was older, when the phobia had settled, disrespect for papa joined it. Papa was long dead, yet in her head he remained as demanding as ever. Had Robbie's daddy done that too?

Natalia doubted it. Robbie achieved, but didn't seem burdened. She seemed free of the urge to compete.

~

The same attendant as last Thursday came up to the car, swung the door open and escorted her into the building where de Bruyn had his office. Up some stairs covered by a thick carpet, along a tomb-like corridor and into de Bruyn's ante room. His assistant dotingly came over to help her slip out of her coat. "So grey and cold today, don't you think?" the woman said. "We call it *guur*. That's *cold and bleak* in English, isn't it? Please sit here. Will you have coffee?"

A good idea, Natalia thought, to sit for a few minutes and be idle. Why not use the occasion for something worthwhile? Such as learning to pronounce *guur*. Do it repeatedly, since its component sounds, the full back-throated *g* and the *uu* as in French *menue*, at first seem totally unutterable. Say it again and again. An acceptable version could come eventually. She did it silently. *Guur, guur, guur.* Cold and bleak, cold and bleak, etcetera, etcetera. The inner chant described her state perfectly.

Alas, de Bruyn appeared too quick. Her tonality of *guur* did not seem flawless yet.

"There you are," he remarked pleasantly. The voice was deeper, more resonant than she remembered. "Very nice to see you again. Was the weekend satisfying?"

"Thank you, Heiko. An excellent weekend. And yours?"

"I felt imprisoned by the weather. Please, do come in. Let us get started."

With a sweeping gesture he directed her to the guest settee in his office. His own tall chair, ornately carved from oak and resembling a throne, stood angled towards it. When she had settled he sank back too, crossed his legs, grabbed the armrests and transformed into a potentate. Grimly quiet, he waited, perhaps for the coffee. Natalia steeled herself to say nothing. No small talk. No hint of clamor. Adopt a Robbie pose – a presence of warmth, but beyond that determined stillness. De Bruyn pressed his lips together. After a slight upward pull of the corners of his mouth he spoke. "I told my wife about your forebears. She was fascinated.

What you revealed of frontier life – the focus on survival – there's wisdom to be found in that. She thought it should be shared. She thought you ought to write it down."

"You keep talking about my background."

"Because it interests me. Are you not interested in mine? It has its own peculiar features. My ancestors belonged to the nobility. That was centuries ago, in the north, in Friesland. Admittedly, the nobles were only on my mother's side. Over several generations, the family's fortunes deteriorated. By about a hundred years ago, my forebears were mere merchants. Since then some have even had to turn to functionary work. I'm one. By now the family is quite anonymous and possesses absolute predictability. A century of family history has been laid down as thick seams of dullness. In contrast, yours is a story of rising. The irony is that our directions are opposite, yet have brought us to an identical level. For me this is very interesting to know. Beyond that, I believe that acquiring an understanding of our respective backgrounds is vital."

"Vital? Vital for what?"

"For the influence it may have on how we conceptualize things."

Natalia shifted on the little sofa. Her career had spanned more than two dozen years, long enough to have had to deal with her fair share of both deep thinkers and serious borderline cases. She had learned that at first blush the two extremes can look uncannily similar. Where on the continuum between them did de Bruyn have his perch? She decided to smoke him out. Taking a cue from Carlos's theory of randomness, she turned de Bruyn's obsession with ancestral influence on its head. "Aren't ancestors just a lottery? Why would one think they have importance?"

"A lottery? Indeed. Yes, they are. Naturally. And yet they shape us. Mine, frankly, have made me feel confined. I feel I live a very small life. In all its minute details it is a mere repetition of how my forebears lived. Of course, the smallness of my country isn't helpful.

"But your roots are the opposite. You radiate an open future. Your country's geography must stimulate feelings of expansiveness. I think, in between my understanding of minutiae and your capacity to make grand sweeps, we may create interesting synergies. That will be beneficial for our work."

Natalia darkly remembered Heywood's admonition, yet could not prevent two words from slipping out. "What work?"

"You don't know?" One of de Bruyn's eyebrows rose.

A soft knock on the door created a pause. A gleaming pot of coffee and a plate of ginger cookies arranged on a tray were brought in by de Bruyn's cheerful assistant. Precisely, fastidiously, she arranged everything on a low table. Natalia watched de Bruyn, who patiently studied the ritual. His stiff posture remained throughout – an unassailable self-assurance coupled with fiercely observing eyes. Was the pose, she wondered, reminiscent of his private life? Did his wife serve coffee in an identically careful manner at precisely predetermined times? Was such ceremony essential because it brought structure to their lives?

Could de Bruyn truly be convinced his ancestors were confining him? If anything, he seemed to soar over the affairs of state with a sure sense of direction and a ruthlessness to strike. De Bruyn might think he was no longer up there in the ranks of noble forebears, but, Natalia concluded, he hadn't fallen far.

They sipped coffee and nibbled on cookies before de Bruyn quietly picked up where his question had left off. "I was told you would be informed that my prime minister was in communication with your prime minister. Someone was to contact you."

Natalia's mind shifted, focusing on what she had suspected. Her outward reply was a dismissive shrug. "Someone did."

"Then you know our task."

Natalia gazed cordially at de Bruyn, took another sip of coffee, put the cup down and spread her hands. "I must confess, the call … it was rushed. It lacked precision."

"I understand. Long message chains. They often distort. I am fortunate to speak with my prime minister directly since he is not far away." A thumb gesture indicated a general direction behind him. No more than a wall or two seemed to separate them.

"Why were you so sparse with details when we met on Thursday?" Natalia asked.

"At the time some things were not yet clear."

"Heiko," Natalia crisply intervened, "to make sure we're on the same wavelength, describe to me your understanding of the sequence of all this. Something began which you knew about fully, but I did not. Not yet. And now we have this task. Please also tell me if you think the task is feasible."

"Our task? Feasible? Oh yes. I believe so. On Thursday I became convinced that you were an inspired choice to take it further."

"Well, I think you are too."

"Thank you. At first I expected that my counterpart in your prime minister's office would fly in once a month for half a year or so to do the work. Then I was told you would be equally, possibly still more effective. Since the finest policy minds in Ottawa will be supporting you and you will speak for your prime minister as I do for mine, I became convinced we had arrived at operational concision. After meeting you, I was sure we would make a potent team. But we have much to do. Time is not on our side."

"It surely is not. Time shrinks hour by hour. About the sequence of events, though, give me your perspective. I'm interested to know if it is similar to mine. Begin with when our two prime ministers talked."

"Yes, in New York, at the UN, during the luncheon the week before last when they were table companions."

When Natalia first sat in de Bruyn's office, she talked and he smiled, listened and said little. Now it was her eager nodding doing all the spurring. And de Bruyn responded. He had a raconteur side, which was taking over. Natalia concentrated on every word.

My prime minister congratulated yours ... on the Canadian initiative ... timely and important ... a well-executed piece of work ... my prime minister agreed that the global community cannot, must not, sit on the sidelines when civilian populations get slaughtered ... when that happens as a by-product of war it is loathsome ... when a military does it by design it is an atrocity ... but when a state systematically kills its own citizens it is a great and ultimate crime ... my prime minister said to yours that Canada had shown the way out of a human morass ... your breakthrough concept that the world community has a responsibility to step in to prevent genocide ... my prime minister said Canada's work was on a par with that of the great Dutchman, Hugo Grotius, nearly 400 years ago ... Grotius argued for more order in the

43

world ... in his famous books he advanced the notion of a global rule of law in times of peace as well as war ...

Natalia felt a tug of pride. The new international doctrine, the "responsibility to protect," R2P. She knew it well. R2P was a milestone, a major shifting of the goal posts of world order. Too few knew of it, but it had boosted her sense of national dignity. All the same, she wondered, how would it link up with what de Bruyn said earlier? What further concepts were there for them to put together? What was their task?

When my prime minister returned to The Hague, he reflected on your country's initiative ... the responsibility to protect now exists as an advanced idea ... but how to implement it, how to give it a more forceful standing in international law? ...

My prime minister thought: The Hague has a long tradition as a center for world peace ... two important peace conferences took place here a century ago ... the International Court of Justice is here ... so is the International Criminal Court ... former heads of state accused of crimes against humanity are now routinely put on trial ... clearly, new traditions are strengthening as we speak ...

Despite this, the concept of world peace remains underdeveloped ... humanity still goes about exterminating specific populations ... in some countries genocide is still a tool of public policy ... as a species, politically, humans are not yet non-killers ...

My prime minister concluded there should be another push, another large step forward ... as with Hugo Grotius, as with the conferences one hundred years ago ... Canada's concept of the "responsibility to protect" should become a global imperative ... for building peace, for creating a non-killing culture ... a new world order should not be beyond our reach.

My prime minister then contacted yours ... last week ... by telephone ... to propose that our two countries initiate this work ... he said your prime minister agreed ... my prime minister summoned me one hour later and directed me to assume the task of looking after details ... someone would be named by Ottawa to work with me ...

For Natalia, a haze as thick as the one that had been blanketing the city for days began lifting, causing her to see a reality that was much more foreboding than she had feared. It chilled her to the bone. She heard the finale to his speech only distantly. De Bruyn had telephoned the prime minister's office in Ottawa the next day, wanting to talk to his counterpart, but had run into disorder. No one there had the slightest idea what the two prime ministers could have discussed. Someone would call back. It didn't happen. Next day de Bruyn was back at it, this time having more luck. He was put through to someone, a certain Desmond Mckilroy, who listened to de Bruyn's polite request for operational clarity so as to implement the prime ministerial agreement. Mckilroy peremptorily replied he was too busy. When de Bruyn pressed him he snapped, "Try our ambassador there," then hung up. An odd response. Upon reflection, however, de Bruyn perceived it as having had a certain ring – of invitation. In a quaint but candid frontier style he had been invited to check out whether good interpersonal chemistry would come into play between himself and the ambassador. The Ottawa concern had to be that he and the ambassador would hit it off. That led to the Thursday afternoon tête-à-tête with Natalia. During a renewed exchange with Ottawa on Friday, Mckilroy's office suggested that he should really focus on the Foreign Affairs Department. De Bruyn asked if there might be a name. There was. Mr Irving Heywood. He was direct recipient of detailed instructions given by Mr Mckilroy. This time it proved challenging to locate Mr Heywood. He did not pick up his phone. Nor did anyone else. Again and again the voicemail clicked on. Late on Friday, The Hague time, the elusive Mr Heywood announced himself. He scarcely said a word, but confirmed to de Bruyn that, on this initiative, Ambassador Plavniuk would speak for Canada. And yes, naturally – why ask? – he would convey this to her. De Bruyn waited an hour, more than enough time he believed for the instruction to be passed on, before calling the ambassador to say he was delighted he would be seeing her again soon.

"And here we are," de Bruyn confirmed with genuine delight. "We have organizational precision. An important initiative awaits our attention. Much engrossing foreign policy territory will have to be explored. More coffee?"

Natalia's nod and smile signalled that she approved of his account of how events had unfolded, but her inner chill was worsening. She knew of Desmond Mckilroy. He had swaggered into the heart of the prime minister's office out of the merciless barrens of the advertising world. His task? To implement numerous weird political whims and wishes using a time line of zero. Which is to say that everyone around him got clubbed or cracked open, after which meek obeisance oozed forth – like the innards of crushed limpets. The instant nickname for Mckilroy in the bureaucracy was *The Sledge*, as in *Hammer*.

For Natalia, all the dots had now connected up, save for how Des the Sledge and Heywood the Phantom had cooked up some deal. She took a deep breath and damned the instruction to do nothing except smile and listen. The line she uttered was frigid. "I began to suspect last Thursday afternoon was an occasion to look me over, an inspection of a kind."

De Bruyn was unfazed. With a bass resonance he replied, "I was sure you would suspect that. I am sorry for it, but the suggestion came from your side. In some ways their caution was understandable. A fresh approach to global peace requires magnanimity and creativity. There had to be some certainty that you and I could jointly fashion this new crucible."

"Whereby overnight I became a prime minister's personal representative."

"Well, it truly is an honour. In my experience, Natalia, such situations always arise unpredictably. Now let us look forward. We will have to set a brisk pace. A blueprint for new peace commitments, the evolution towards a non-killing world, prescriptions for the global community to function according to high moral principles – there is much for us to wade through."

Natalia had heard enough. Whole chapters had been written about a story in which she would be a major player, though throughout she had been kept entirely in the dark. Furthermore, she was to be the personal envoy of a prime minister who had no creative interest in foreign policy and who, in accordance with his reputation, had spoken to her solely through the dark, back channels populated only by venomous spiders of the Heywood-Mckilroy type. An urgent need to get away seized her.

She began to rise. "A daunting task, no doubt," She said calmly.

De Bruyn's outstretched palm forced her back down. "Wait. Yes, it may seem daunting. It will not happen overnight. We both have heavy schedules. Close coordination will be necessary to identify the many hours needed. Even today I could only see you because of an unexpected cancellation."

"It was the same for me. Luckily, some minutes could be freed up."

"I'm sure. It may amuse you to know that the person I was scheduled to see was also a Canadian. A peace advocate. He suffered an accident and couldn't keep the appointment. As a result, the hour available today for peace went from him to you. Isn't that a coincidence, a sort of little irony? We still have fifteen minutes. Shall we start? We could begin by making a closer comparison of our prime ministers' initial views."

"Was the accident a plane crash?" Natalia asked, moving forward to the edge of the settee.

"It was. A private plane. The police found his appointment diary and discovered my name. They called early this morning."

"And his name? The peace advocate's, I mean. Was it Paradis?"

"I believe so. Do you know him?"

Natalia sighed and rose. "He is important. I must leave on that account. The accident brings some communication challenges to the embassy. They need direction. I have already overstayed."

De Bruyn came forward and took her hand, squeezing rather than shaking it. "In that case we will leave our future to our assistants. And we must stress to them to be discreet. Should our purpose leak out, it would cause serious misunderstandings."

Leaving the executive suite, Natalia waved off an offer by de Bruyn's assistant to be helped into her coat, instead draping the garment over an arm instead in one swift move. Nor did she wait for the door to be opened, cranking the handle herself to hasten departure. In the corridor, eager to escort the ambassador out, the woman caught up. "*Goeie genade*," she said, voicing a well-meant opinion. Immediately she translated it. "*Goeie genade* is *good heavens*, isn't it? What I mean is, you have a very large hurry."

The ambassador was wearing high heels, yet the assistant in her functional shoes was straining to keep up. When the ambassador nodded concurrence, the assistant continued her pleasantries. "It is nice that you know that expression. You have good Dutch already. Are you learning more?" At the building exit they exchanged their *tot ziens*, whereupon Natalia slipped into her coat and clattered ahead.

Dirk was timing the opening of the car's rear door, but instead of getting in, the ambassador remained on her feet and issued him brisk instructions. He passed her the umbrella, touched his cap, slammed the rear door shut, circled the car, got into the driver's seat and motored off. Natalia departed on foot in the opposite direction.

The rain had run its course, replaced by a piercing, icy damp. She ignored the water it brought to her eyes. Her feet in the dainty shoes were chilling fast and Natalia disregarded that too. Her turmoil was deepening. She was on autopilot now, scarcely aware of her route. Much had gone on behind the scenes, and now one emotion prodded others. All of them competed: anger at being blind-sided; foreboding that she was in a maze with no way out; contempt for having been shuffled about and treated like a pawn. Emerging from the toxic mix and towering above was the feeling of self-doubt.

On unsteady clickety-clack shoes, wobbling through cobble-stoned alleys, Natalia struggled to order her thoughts.

You have led delegations at global gatherings. You have survived the quicksands of international negotiations. You understand the problems of humanity pretty well, in both their simplicity and complexity. If asked, you could say constructive things about building more peace in the world. You have always kept up with the best. But none of that counts. Not now. A new game has started and your credentials for it are weak. In fact, for this game, you've got no credentials at all. Unlike Heiko who, with one thumb jerk to the wall behind him, proudly demonstrates his are unbeatable.

How so?

Heiko's prime minister is a man who seems to think about humanity and is prepared to push issues that advance its progress.

Your prime minister isn't Heiko's. Your prime minister doesn't wish to know that he could act to build a better world. He claims there are no votes in it. Face it, Natalia. Your national tradition, the will to force the international pace, has been shredded into nothing but a heap of tatters.

The upshot?

Heiko is empowered to shine whereas you've been sent into the world to hide that your country has become a vacuum. Representing the prime minister? What a precept for an absolute disaster.

As Natalia made her way through the city's medieval heart, she began to sense the despair a warrior might have when his armory is empty yet he is expected to do battle. In a near trance she passed the central pond from which, on one side, Holland's ancient governing buildings rise. The damp air was coagulating now, draining energy from the light, seemingly exhausting life. In the wintry wretchedness it was becoming difficult to tell whether the shapes on a small island in the pond were shivering water birds, or a collection of dark rocks. When a new gust of frigid air brought more water to her eyes, she halted, hauled out a handkerchief and cleared her nose. Before her she now saw a broad promenade lined on both sides with leafless trees. The way they stood in the half light, like skeletons fixed and in formation, it turned the avenue into one of ghosts. Was this a metaphor for her?

It pushed her thinking a little. If those *were* her ghosts taking form before her eyes, and if ghosts can have an overlord, her papa would be ruling here. That tree would stand for mediocrity and the tall one further on for insignificance. Failure was there too, of course. And let's not overlook ineptitude. And so on and so forth. Second-rate performances, inconsequential deeds – this was the avenue of her worst inner fears. Given the abysmal imbalance she faced with Heiko, how could these ghosts not be rattling her?

Dear Papa, you had your problems, I know, but why did you ordain that I must carry them too?

The stark trees were too awful and Natalia scampered off into a narrow passage. Her feet had become unbearably painful and she half-stumbled into a coffee bar. She spotted an empty corner bench where she frantically shook the shoes off, pulled her legs up and started massaging warmth into her feet. When a double rum and a cappuccino had been ordered, the way was cleared for revival. The first question that posed itself was how the waiter might be viewing her. As a crumpled up bundle of misery, she supposed.

And what would Carlos say, if he were to see her in this state. It forced a wry smile from her lips. He would be teasing her. *Robustness conjoined with fragility*. To which she would be delivering a riposte. *My negative secondary determinants, Carlos, are a bit bothersome today. Sorry, I haven't risen above them.* He would laugh at that and offer her a high five. Carlos understood her to the core and she loved him for it.

She might not yet have mastered her hang-ups, as Carlos with his endearing look of irony always claimed he had. But she had delved into them. She had spent time analyzing her papa's destructive influence, his rule of terror which began the moment his daughter showed promise. Two decades it took her to understand it. Most of the reasons were based on a conviction that life had conspired against him, that he was a victim.

Robustness conjoined with fragility.

The source of her fragility was papa's years of hectoring. But how did her other side arise? Where did the robustness come from? Was it courtesy of her first husband, Donovan? It had been in full view with him. Which posed a related question – why was Donovan there at all? Why had she latched onto him? Well, because Donovan's existence pissed papa off. Donovan pissed papa off so royally that Natalia decided to marry him. With Donovan she had no fear. With Donovan it was easy to be strong. Donovan was like a cute puppy licking her. No, robustness didn't arise through Donovan. It preceded him. Natalia had put her finger on that long ago. Robustness was a gift from papa's mother.

The rum, when it arrived, disappeared in one determined swoop and the cappuccino warmed as it went down. Physical warmth led to spiritual warmth. And to thoughts of Baba. Holding herself tight, leaning forward over the coffee, Natalia felt that Baba, suddenly near, was nudging her.

~

Imagine spending summers with a twinkly-eyed grandmother who lives alone, surrounded by nothing but the prairie. Her patience has no limits. Every complex emotion a young girl may feel can be talked through.

You're thinking something, Nataliascha. What is it?

Baba is bulky and her expression nurtures. Baba likes to hum and loves laughter. When Nataliascha voices her observation that Baba's thick socks are slightly dirty, Baba becomes merrier still. Outside the house Baba wears heavy shoes over those thick socks. The shoes stick out from under a long dark skirt covered by an apron.

Behind the house is a big garden, cared for by Baba's leathery hands, out of which emerges pail after pail of vegetables. Inside at the kitchen table, grandmother and granddaughter peel, pare, scrape and slice. And they laugh, they laugh so hard sometimes that their heads sink down and disappear into the mounds of beets or beans.

They also talk. Nataliascha states she is worried that if she's not first in school again her papa will stop being proud. On the other hand, when she *is* first, her friends stop liking her. Furthermore, suppose, once she's grown up, she does not gain fame? What will papa do then?

Baba places a hand on her granddaughter's head. *We dream, Nataliascha, about the thousand paths we cannot take. Accept that's how it is. All you can do is take one and follow it with dignity.*

But Baba, papa doesn't want just any path. He says I have to be the best.

Your papa grew up feeling he was living in a prison. No matter what he did or where he went, that didn't change. He may think that you were born to free him. But you weren't. Only he can unlock the door to the cell he believes he is in.

I worry though. I fear I can't become what he wants me to be.

No need for that. Why feel fear if there is no danger?

~

In the café, warmth cruising through her feet, sensing the presence of Baba, Natalia's resilience flowed back. She had urgent things to do, for which she had to summon up her dignity. On the cell phone she placed a call to Marge, to say the afternoon was cancelled. Dirk was next. He was to come to take her to the residence. She planned from there, mid-afternoon, to contact Irving Heywood. An ultimatum to him had been forming in her head. Finally, she accessed Robbie's voicemail and left a message. Robbie was to join her right away in the pedigreed house in Wassenaar. The pretext was Robbie's report on Paradis, but what Natalia really yearned for was a kind ear.

Chapter 4

The phone broke into Irving Heywood's reverie, but he ignored it for a while, silently counting the rings, not picking it up until just before voicemail came on. He took his time bringing the handset to his ear. "Heywood here," he grumbled, conveying he was being inconvenienced. The reply instantly transformed him. Sweetly he continued, "Natalia. Hello. I've been expecting to hear from you. Did you see Duhbrouyeen?" He was already envisioning a round of warm telephone companionship with her.

The answer was hardly warming. In fact, it was ice-cold, like chilled water, bucket upon bucket, being poured down on him.

Which made him think.

What had happened to the affable minutes of telephone play he had always enjoyed with his protégés? Where, nowadays, were the harmless little jokes that used to get the phone line lubricated? Frolicky starts to serious conversations were among his finest career memories. Telephone long-haul, transporting the heavy stuff, always progressed more fluidly if the first minutes were pleasingly uplifting. Long-distance camaraderie, that advancing of professional partnerships – it used to impart so much meaning.

Too bad that today's five thousand kilometer link to Natalia wasn't unfolding according to the ancient script. The arriving blasts were distinctly unfriendly. Distasteful really. He held the handset at arm's length and, from an angle, contemplated the thing. How could that insignificant piece of equipment be violating him? "Wait, Natalia," he tried to interject. He repeated himself with force. "Natalia. Whoa. Hold it. Just wait a sec, won't you." She wouldn't. All that led to was her volume ratcheting up a few more notches.

Heywood began to reflect on the other Natalia he had known, the bouncy, cheerful, clear thinker, the ultimate professional, extracting the best from every situation, the one person who, if you had a choice, you would want to be in the same meeting with. Could this really be her, this near choleric? He had never known her to complain before. Nor had she ever expressed herself in run-on sentences that didn't pause. When would the real Natalia reappear? Certain that she would, he decided to wait, though with the hand piece held afar. And in this pose, he fell into philosophizing. Sensitivity to the moods of others, he believed, had always stood him in good stead. Rants, he'd learned, should run their course. So vent, Natalia, and as you do I will apply my mind to other things.

What other important topics were at hand for him to mull over? Not too many actually. Not nowadays. Nor could he entirely stop himself from silently reacting to what she was saying. Unspoken rebuttals flashed through him. *You're right, Natalia. Of course, you are*, he wanted to squeeze in, though couldn't. *But look at it from my perspective. I was in a tough position, darn it. I wasn't being treated as I have treated you. If someone has a right to snarl, it's me. … But Natalia, all I was doing was protecting you from the dark angels … But I received no details, so could pass none on. But … But … But …* Explanations such as these, he was sure, would turn the tide if only he could get her to listen. He couldn't, which prompted punchier thinking. *Now pray, do tell me, Natalia, objectively speaking, what in the end was so horrible? Was it really that painful for you to sit with a civilized Dutchman, to listen and observe good public policy manners at work? … And, furthermore, what is the use of concluding that our own political class requires centuries more of development to get to his level? …. And, have you considered that more than your own pride and career are on the line?*

The imagery of a career on the line, more specifically of a career getting strung up in broad daylight to experience the slow, painful death of desiccation, caused a shiver to go up Heywood's spine. Natalia's accusations were pounding him, yes, but Lord Almighty, echoes of other telephone conversations did too.

~

How do you spot the moment when a career's downward spiral sets in? What signals tell you that others think you've peaked, that you're past your prime? How attuned should you be to admiring voices becoming disingenuous, too regular and loud and crossing over into simple syrupiness?

Heywood's antennae were sensitive, no doubt. The only problem was that over the decades he'd used them only to navigate bureaucracy's raging battles. His feelers had no practice detecting that he was wanted out. And so, when *his* moment came, when he began spiralling down, it hit him hard, doubly hard, because he was sure the opposite was happening.

For a month, the top job in the Service had stood vacant and Heywood, believing he been *de facto* number two for years, was sure he'd get the call. *Congratulations, Mr Heywood, you are being entrusted with a larger challenge.* For days he'd waited for the phone to ring, but steadfastly it remained silent. Occasionally he picked it up just to be sure the dial tone was still there. All around him the annual high-level new appointment activity in the Service was swinging into gear. A replacement was named for his own position, confirming he would be moving on. To where? No one said. The tension grew. Next, a significant shuffle filled a whole batch of other senior positions, many as ambassadors, ruling out a lateral stagnation – another sign in favour. Silence descended on the Service. Who would the new top dog be? Who would win the sweepstake? Heywood was cocky. "By now I've outlived pretty well everyone," he reasoned. "Plus I've got more experience in the neurons of my middle finger than others have in their entire central nervous system." Informal feedback from the Service peons on his chances was good too. He picked that up from the adoring sideways glances they sent his way in the elevator. To get ready Heywood began formulating the decrees he would issue during his first ten days as Deputy Minister.

When the blow landed, it crushed him utterly. A short article, buried in the gossip section of the local paper, reported on a rumour that Harry Berezowski would get the nod. The article speculated that Berezowski was already in town, recalled from a high-profile diplomatic assignment in Asia. Heywood stumbled across the piece while drinking his mid-morning coffee. Berezowski? He gagged. His eyes and nostrils opened wide. His heart started pounding. His brain, his mind, his soul fell into the grip of a spasm. His breathing stopped. He sat as immobile as a wax figure.

Once breathing restarted and some brain function returned, he tried to think. Who held a grudge against him all these years? Berezowski? Had Harry surreptitiously outflanked him? No. Not possible. Harry was a protégé too. He'd helped Harry get that plum job overseas. On the flip side, true, not that much was really wrong with Harry. He wasn't timid and had shown he could manage tough issues. "But all the same," Heywood reasoned, "he isn't me. He hasn't shown yet that he possesses guile. His subtlety needs more development too." Heywood read the article again, skimming the humdrum biographical stuff, fixing on a quote from a certain Mr Anonymous: *Berezowski is the right leader for us at this difficult time. He is a refreshing thinker. No one's mind is more inventive and vigorous.*

Heywood's brain cramped up all over again. Harry's mind more vigorous than his? A grotesque untruth. Who was this ignorant Mr Anonymous, anyway? How could anyone overlook his intellectual mettle? Everyone knew that for decades he had been a fountain of innovative policy. No one was leaving as large and deep a legacy as his.

Then it hit. Youth. That was it. The only thing that had slipped away from him over the years was youth. He was being bypassed on account of the flow of time. One day you're a commander with a sweeping vision; the next you're treated as if you're no more than a shadow that can't shoot, box or wrestle. Heywood stared at his future, now an abyss, and groaned. He saw that, henceforth, the most exciting event each day would be a shuffling back and forth between the couch and an easy chair.

His assistant tip-toed in later that day, saying she was really sorry, but she had been told to tell him to clear out his office. "By whom?" he asked curtly. She cowered, mentioning a clerk's name. Heywood contacted the clerk.

"Where am I supposed to go?" he asked.

The clerk said, "No job, no space. If you don't like the policy, call Berezowski."

That's when the first of the echoing conversations took place.

"Why, Irving! Hello. Good of you to call. Ah, thank you. Yes, I was surprised by the appointment. Of course, yes, I was honoured. But humbled too. Yes indeed, I am looking forward to the challenge. You're right, it has no equal. So true, so many gifted people to work with. Indeed, yes, I will be relying on them to get things done.

"Your future? Well, Irving, let's be frank. You've been contributing for how many years? Three dozen I believe. Forty-three? Oh my. That many? One hell of a run, Irving. One hell of a run. Most of us are out of breath in half that time. But you were never afraid of the extra mile. You ran hard and you deserve rest. You also deserve an award. I'll be putting your name forward for a distinguished service medal."

At that point Heywood had a thought: *Go to hell, Harry. If I have to spend my days on the sofa at home I will cause Hannah's premature death. And if she dies, I won't be far behind. What you're really doing is telling me to kill myself.* Fortified by an urge for something better than that he said to his new boss, "Actually, Harry, I'm feeling pretty chipper. Lung capacity is holding up. Still got a few circuits in me."

"I'm sure you do, Irving. I'm sure. Let me think about it. There may be other possibilities. First thing I'm doing is taking a vacation. You should too. We'll compare notes when I'm back."

Three weeks later, another conversation happened that never stopped echoing.

"Hello Irving. Thank you, yes, it was a lovely holiday. Ruth and I went to the Galapagos. Get there soon before that world is finished too. Well, let's focus on you. Thought about your future? Forty-three years, Irving. What's the highest accolade we can think of? Can't promise a knighthood, but there are some other orders that aren't really all that bad. What? You don't want a prize? You want to keep your old job? Well then, here's a better idea. Occasions may arise when I might need some good old-fashioned help. Work with me directly, Irving. When I get busy, too busy, I'll spin you this or that issue. You run them as I would, you know, as my alter ego. Take a couple of days to think it over.

"No? No need for that? Why can't you stay in your old job? Sorry, it's gone. Other possibilities? I'll be frank. There are only two. One, you slip into your long-deserved rest. The other is to be my alter-ego. Well, good, the alter ego route it is. Your new title? Oh … I suppose … something along the lines of Senior Advisor. No? You think people would see you as a stud put out to pasture? That could be true, I guess. Yes, yes, I know you've still got oomph. Not Senior Advisor then. How about Ambassador at Large? Ah, you think you would be made fun of on account of your figure. You want my title with something in front? Associate? You want to be Associate Deputy Minister? Sorry, Irving. I've got someone else in mind for that. No, you can't be Assistant Deputy Minister either. What about, Special Assistant to …? Sounds like the stud farm again? Alright. Yes, alright. Yes, yes, have that. Co-operant to the DM. If that's what you like, that's what you'll be. Yes, no problem, you'll have an office nearby."

An office? The clerk, a former Heywood sycophant, assigned him a square cell without a window and barely enough space for a filing cabinet, a desk and a chair. And what happened in this sparse compartment? Not much. Not at first. Irving Heywood, aged sixty-seven, after more than four decades of bureaucratic contest, a man convinced he had not yet peaked, sat sidelined and silenced. He felt as if he had been finished off. Except he was alive and able to reflect on being dead. Some time was spent reading journals and looking at the internet. Mostly, though, he waited. He waited for the phone to ring. Every day he imagined Harry would be calling to seek input. *Irv, sorta feeling out of my depth just now. Can't really see what's going on. Need your help. Ought to do more travelling, you know, get away for a while. While I'm gone can you sort some problems out?*

Eventually the phone did ring. It was Harry's assistant. "Mr Heywood, Mr Berezowski has a scheduling conflict. He promised to meet with the Red Deer Junior UN Club, but now there's also a Chinese political delegation coming to explain their record on human rights. He doesn't want to let the kids from Red Deer down. Can you listen to what the Chinese have to say?"

"I'll look at my schedule," Heywood said gruffly. "I hope it's not until the week after next. What were the dates? OK. I've got some things going, but I'll get them rescheduled. I guess you'll send me Harry's briefing book the day before? I'm pretty sure I can get the Chinese to treat their intelligentsia more humanely."

During office hours Heywood went to a printer in the local mall for a new calling card. He considered his title. *Co-operant to the Deputy Minister.* Too long. Tough to explain to the Chinese. Shorten it, he thought. Take out letters that don't matter. It you remove *operant to the*, what's left? *Co-Deputy Minister.* Even the Chinese should be able to get their heads around that.

Co-DM. The impact was magical. The delegates bowed respectfully and listened attentively. Heywood quoted Confucius, putting them at ease. Word of the visit's success spread, so Heywood began pinch-hitting for Harry more often. He wasn't exactly appearing before Parliamentary Committees, or delivering speeches to the UN General Assembly, but he did listen to greenies wanting a ban on hydroelectric dam building in the Amazon basin, advocates for a global minimum wage, and health groups seeking a Security Council resolution declaring non-fluoridated drinking water to be a fundamental human right. The big issues brought forth thick briefing books and his filing cabinet filled up nicely. He was also copied on emails again. And invitations to attend strategy meetings reappeared. Heywood was back in, his credibility was rising. Harry sometimes asked him to stay back after a meeting to share ideas on next steps and who were the new, young high flyers. In the hallways other senior people stopped ignoring him. Joking started up again. *Irv, are you looking for a hair of the dog that bit you?* To which he growled a warm reply. *The beast is in my sights and pretty soon I'm gonna chomp its ears off.* Judging from the glow on Heywood's cheeks, years were being added to his life.

Harry did start travelling, finally. He was in Africa when his assistant informed Heywood of a call from the prime minister's office. "It's in the middle of the night in Burkina Faso and Mr Berezowski needs his sleep," she said to Heywood. "Can you call the PMO back for him? They said it was urgent."

"One of them dark angels, eh," Heywood said laconically. "No probs. I've dealt with that type all my long life. This one's name is?"

"Desmond Mckilroy."

"Des the Sledge, huh. This should be fun." Heywood dialled Mckilroy's number and was put through. "Mr Mckilroy, my name is Irving Heywood. You were calling Harry Berezowski. He's in Africa this week. I'm the Co-DM responsible for things."

This was when the third echoing conversation began.

"Time is short, Mr Heywood. Listen closely. Yesterday, I was contacted on the phone by someone with a name that's difficult to pronounce – Duhbrouyeen, something like that. Said he was in the Dutch prime minister's office in The Hague. Said his man and my man had talked peace. In New York. Then his man followed up with mine to get going on a big new initiative. I'm not aware those conversations happened. If they did I assume the talk was casual and the contents a form of drivel. Otherwise I would know. This fellow Duhbrouyeen – Is he legit? Nobody knows – then asked if I would be his interlocutor for the next steps. That irritated me since I don't do interlocution. I do execution. I informed him we deal with foreign governments through our embassies and suggested he check out the Canadian ambassador. He said he'd do that.

"Same guy called again just now. More nonsense. Said he checked the ambassador out, considered her imposing and believed he could work with her. Asked if this weekend she would receive instructions to get the discussion started. That irritated me all over again. Which is why I'm making him your problem, Mr Heywood.

"My instruction is this: call this Duhbrouyeen and tell him to stop phoning me. If our Madame Ambassador in The Hague can help in this regard, use that route, I don't care. Bottom line – I want that Dutchman off my back. Peace is not our priority. Nor is taking part in the international gabfests. We don't care about that. We only care if my boss is the sole guy orchestrating the music. If we don't run the show we're not interested. Is that clear?"

No problem, Heywood had replied right away. He would have liked to have added something about his decades of experience ensuring that international hip-hop outings go well, but Des the Sledge was gone.

~

Heywood could sense Natalia was running out of steam, and silently reviewed all that Mckilroy had not instructed. No instruction not to talk to the Dutch. No instruction not to look more closely into this or that peace concept. No instruction not to pinch some good Dutch ideas. The picture, overall, was ambiguous, and ambiguity can be artfully exploited if it is given structure.

"What I am saying, Irving," Natalia was summing up, "is that if the two prime ministers agreed to pursue a new peace initiative and I'm the one to lead it for our side, I want that put down in black on white. I also want a direct line to the policy group. I will not meet with de Bruyn again unless I've got solid proposals to put forward. Maybe it's best I take this up with Harry. When is he expected back?"

Heywood was strategizing fast. Natalia had done well. She got Duhbrouyeen to sing like a canary without offering him so much as a feather mite in return. Also, The Hague had a reputation. On the peace front, historically, the place had been productive. All along he had intuited that a decent peace package could emerge there, which was the basis for his decision to send Natalia in to find out. Suppose the Dutch had something interesting on the go. Suppose they could be led on to show their cards. And suppose they were sitting on a royal flush? They could be outflanked. Their cards would drop into his lap and the royal flush could be presented to Mckilroy as *Ours!* Imagine the opportunity in that. Imagine a decent international conference – *Our Show!* – being conducted by the PM. Wouldn't he, Heywood, be asked to brief the PM? And what would the PM say? *Mr Heywood, this pleases me.* Just imagining it made Heywood's ears turn pink.

There was also a tactical consideration. No new peace process stood a chance in hip-hop heaven if headquarters' thinkers took control. The term he coined for them long ago was *complexifiers*. If you looked at it objectively, they sort of worked like ancient alchemists. They transmuted clear crystals of common sense into mucky foreign policy tenets which they called gold, but in reality was foolish stuff. Ditto for the lawyers and the UN crowd. All such wonks would have to be kept in the dark. An appealing picture formed in Heywood's mind. Natalia would do the policy running and she would check her ideas out with him. Natalia had always been creative and resourceful. No one cut through policy dross faster than her. If she could heave a couple of solid peace ideas onto the Dutch and next get a good read on their stuff in return, he would present the policy package to Mckilroy as a hellishly irresistible political opportunity. Why wouldn't votes for more peace in the world accrue from one end of the country to the other?

There was only that that last challenge: managing Natalia. After she'd threatened to talk directly to Harry, Heywood's response was indifference. "Wouldn't bother if I were you, Natalia. Harry and I are like conjoined twins. We act as one. The only thing distinguishing us is that Harry is younger, so does the travelling. I manage the shop."

"Does Harry know the two PMs agreed to cooperate on a peace agenda?"

"Not yet. That didn't come out of the woodwork here until Friday. You know how it is. The PM's people have been pretty busy. Details about the foreign lunches – drab stuff that. It gets stuck in a mill that doesn't grind fast. Only last week, though, Harry and I spent an afternoon brainstorming new policy. What, we asked ourselves, is the next big step to take after that great ride we had when we pushed the UN Doctrine of the Right to Protect? So on Friday I was on the phone with Des to sound him out on some of our ideas. Des voiced no aversion. He used that occasion to brief me on two conversations he'd had with Duhbrouyeen. Funny, isn't it, that the Dutch and us are thinking along the same lines? So, chatting with Des was how all that Duhbrouyeen stuff came out.

"By the way, apologies from him. Des knows we should have gotten to you sooner. Anyhow, this is the picture we are looking at, Natalia. Two progressive countries are thinking similar things, an indication, we think, that there's something in the air. It could be very fertile. Des's bottom line was to jump on it. Which is why I called you. Alright, I was short on detail, but our strategy was to smoke the Dutch out, you know, obtain convincing evidence that they are committed without saying much ourselves. You did that masterfully, Natalia. Kudos. I'm confident from what you say this thing will be a go. I'll be talking to Harry in Africa tonight. I'll bring him up to speed then."

Heywood sensed a hesitation on the other end of the line.

"And policy support," Natalia asked, "how will that work?"

Heywood answered breezily, "You know the rule of thumb for the skill of planning policy – do it or lose it. It's been a while since our brainy guys worked on something with profile. Fact is, you've gotta go back years to look at their last decent project. We're worried about them. It seems nowadays that they often stand around leaning on their shovels. No proper digging going on. They've gotten out of shape. What's our solution? Harry and I thought back. Turns out the only transformational stuff pushed forward this past half decade was yours, Natalia. What you did on human rights and democracy building was pretty potent. Don't laugh. It's a historical fact by now. Fledgling democracies got beyond crib death on account of you. So for this new global peace thing – you know, the PM finally seeing there's such a thing as history and why not try to get a spot in it – since creative thinking is needed, we thought of you. You need no support in that department. We don't want to table the timeworn stuff that seeps out of our policy cubby holes. The Dutch would laugh at it. That's why I said to Des that you and I, Natalia, can run this thing. He asked if that was a bottom line and I confirmed it was."

In the residence in The Hague there was a pause. Heywood patiently waited. Natalia came back on. "Let me see if I fully understand. I know de Bruyn speaks for his PM. Am I doing that for ours? Is that abundantly clear?"

"It is."

"The marching orders from Mckilroy are that I do it?"

"They are," Heywood intoned.

"But I talk only to you."

"There's very few in on it, Natalia. Same on the Dutch side. Of course, through me you talk to others, such as Des, and through Des to the PM. You know what Des asked me? God love the guy. He asked me, *Can I expect Madame Ambassador in The Hague to become one of our dream team players?* Something close to that."

"It sounds too neat, Irving. You're asking me to go out on a limb. How do I know the day won't come when they'll suddenly saw it off?"

"That's where I come in, Natalia. I'm the insurance policy." Heywood heard a sigh. "Let's step back a sec, OK? Let's view the big picture, as the two PMs did in New York. They were thinking of the world's kiddies. They want the kiddies to grow up with decent opportunities to live fulfilling lives. That means building a better world. Which is why you and I joined the foreign service, Natalia. We joined to work on that big picture. It sounds corny I know, but it is the truth. That's how I see it. And what happened? During our careers we intimately came to know the characteristics of a world in conflict. We never saw much of kiddies growing up to live lives more fulfilling than their elders. Did we get to understand the characteristics of a world at peace? A couple maybe. There should be less poverty and more health. We worked on those two or three good things, but there's a long way to go. That's the chance we have now, Natalia, a chance to do something good, something really big for the lives of unborn generations. That has been the leitmotif for my career, hokey though it sounds." Heywood detected one more sigh, but it was different, perhaps of acquiescence. "So what's wrong with some good old-fashioned idealism?"

"I'm glad you're still thinking utopia, Irving. Sorry to keep pouring cold water, but you're not convincing me. Desmond Mckilroy is Des the Sledge, right? Is he motivated to think about doing something for children? Does the PM entertain thoughts about humanity's big challenges? Sorry, I don't see it."

"They're busy people, Natalia. Just like the ones before them. They rely on us to do the right thing. To do that, we fall back on our values. Our values tell us this thing with the Dutch is right. That's why we'll do it and why we'll do it well." When the phone line brought renewed silence, Heywood played his final card. "While we're on the topic of values, Natalia," he said softly, "let's talk about their origin, you know, growing up. I did that in the forests of New Brunswick. Even today, that makes me feel proud as a peacock. All the volumes written on philosophy can't express what that has caused me to think and do." He waited.

"No one can take your upbringing from you."

Heywood detected a note of empathy. "A lovely sentiment, Natalia. Thank you. And you? What can no one take from you?"

The ice dam seemed to be breaking, for Natalia replied that she grew up in Vancouver, but really she came from the Great Plains. As a child that's where she acquired her values – during summers spent with a grandmother. When she revealed that happened near a little place called Mirror, Heywood murmured, "Mirror? Really? Mirror?" He practiced it, repeating the name. Mirror Alberta. Mirror Canada. Mirror Planet Earth. "That's just so good," he cooed. "Tell me, Natalia, did Mirror reflect humanity's complexities? Is that how you came to understand just about everything? Is that why you blossomed?"

She laughed. "Blossomed? There's a problem with blossoms."

"There is?" Heywood laughed too.

"Blossoms are not fruits."

"Sorry, I don't read you."

"The problem with this peace initiative is that deep down I don't think I'm up to it. I doubt I can produce the fruit. I'm a people type, Irving. I'm best in a group. I need to hear what others think. That sets me off. By myself I'm pretty barren. I've got an example. Three days, that's how long it took me to figure out that you and de Bruyn were negotiating me. I'm still kicking myself for not twigging."

"But that is not true. Not remotely. Drop that suspicion this instant, Natalia. It was the other way around. You and I were negotiating de Bruyn. We had to be sure that in his head, you know, he's got the goods. Now we know he does. If we had played it otherwise, we might still be in the dark. Anyhow, if you need a group around you, I'm there. Twenty-four seven, Natalia. Every hour of everyday I'm yours."

"Wouldn't work, Irving. I need someone present, literally next to me, someone who has time and with whom I can really let a conversation flow. I'd like someone unafraid and who, when it come to new ideas, is free."

"But that's so easy. Use your number two. I would authorize him getting briefed. Sorry, his name isn't coming …"

"Gus."

"Gus. Right. I know Gus. Rock solid. Swear him to secrecy. Make him a companion."

"Gus? Rock solid? Salt pillar is more like it. His problem is looking backwards. Every time he does he sees the horrors of the past and freezes."

"OK, not Gus then. Hmm, let's see. Who else?"

"I have someone in mind."

"Whatever you think, Natalia. Carlos? I forget now, did we ever put him through a security check? It can be done fast if needed."

"Not Carlos. He and I draw a line. He stays away from my work and I keep out of his. I'm thinking of someone younger, someone who thinks fresh."

"The spontaneity of youth, eh? I'm with you. That's important."

"I'm thinking of my consular officer. When something needs a dose of common sense she packs a punch."

Heywood couldn't object to Natalia having a confidante of choice, but he turned ecstatic when he heard the consular officer was a Newfoundlander. More solemn than a priest he stated that since he'd come out of the forest and Natalia was from the plains, for this new venture someone from the sea would be a natural fit.

~

When Heywood finally put the phone down, he breathed out loudly, took a minute and with a surge of energy sprang up as fast as his great frame allowed. Time to get another morning coffee from the cafeteria. Forget the hair of the dog that had bitten him. The beast had just been leashed. His career was on the up and up again. With Natalia's energy working for him the future had seldom looked brighter.

When the coffee had been hauled back up into his cubicle and he sat sipping it, his mind roamed over a few defensive moves he perhaps ought to make. Mainly, he thought of Harry. Harry had to be informed when he was back from Africa, but in a special way. Harry's standard response to everything was co-ordination, always ordering his forces from A to Z to sit together tightly, on each other's laps if necessary, to talk things through. Committees everywhere and all the time. This was fine if you wanted to know what others were up to, but not so good if you wanted a decent free range of control. Definitely there should be no peace committee. Nothing should threaten the great outcome that now seemed likely. Heywood allowed his mind to run on awhile. How he loved these moments of unbridled creativity, of the innovative impulse blasting forth, of operational routes towards efficient results being laid clear.

Actually, a solution came fast. Disappointingly so. A slightly longer divining spell would have been nice. Heywood planned to brief Harry once a week, sort of incidentally, on the margins of meetings. He would tell Harry about Natalia's involvement in a modest Dutch academic exercise. A couple of interesting thinkers were meeting every once in a while in an ornate room in the International Peace Palace. She was the group's sole foreign member, mostly an honorary one, on account of Canada bringing peace to Holland at the end of the last war. He foresaw the end product likely being a small pamphlet to give peace inspiration to young people.

Heywood was certain Harry would buy into this, that he would like Natalia contributing because, well, it would be a good example of the fine contributions ambassadors can make to the intellectual life of other countries.

"And that," Heywood thought with pleasure, "will get us through the next few months quite nicely."

Chapter 5

The whole way back from Leyden, Robbie was in a state of deep exhilaration. The train was crammed with noisy travellers and she sat squeezed in tight, but the half hour journey passed in an instant. During the tram ride from the central station, too, she continued to be oblivious to all, even to the trolley bell clanging at the intersections. The short walk to the embassy, despite a new outbreak of the day's cold drizzle, had the same quasi-hypnotic quality. Outwardly, there was rote movement, but inwardly, as she later described it to Natalia, there was rapture, an absence of time, a strong feeling of an absolute oneness, though with what she could not explain. Natalia answered, "Are you sure you spent the afternoon in a hospital room? Sounds more like you were in an ashram. It makes me wonder. Our PEACE man, is he a guru? Some of them, you know, they take on cover. They hide what they are."

Natalia's ashram observation was not too far off the mark.

Alistair Paradis, weak, uncomfortable and in pain, had made an impression on Robbie. She stayed with him as long as she could.

With faint, sometimes scarcely audible whispers he pulled her into a new world, drew her into a state which she hazily knew existed, yet had not discovered until now. At least, not in words. He unfolded it for her and confided its splendours. But why her? Why, before the orderly arrived to wheel the injured man out for high risk surgery, did he use his few minutes of wakefulness to bequeath great truths to her? Robbie was dizzy thinking what this could mean. Paradis may have gone off believing he might die within the hour and in that dire moment had he chosen her? Were his truths now hers? Was it her sudden duty to carry them forward?

Great Revealer, you ought to have prepared me better for all this.

~

In a sterile medical environment he lies with eyes closed, his majestic white-maned head deep in a pillow. Cables cling to a hand and tubes remain inserted in an arm. Blinking monitors high up on both sides of the bed indicate that although life is feeble, it is continuing.

"Mr Paradis," Robbie says gently, having tiptoed in and taken a chair next to the bed. "Can you hear me?" His eyelids tighten slightly. "I'm Robbie Warren from the embassy. I'm so sorry your airplane crashed."

The eyes stir into a narrow opening and the arm on the blanket with the drip hose attached inches towards her. His lips quiver before producing a faint, rolling sound. "Give me your hand." Robbie leans forward, places her fingers into an open palm, which immediately closes. She begins to rub the back of his hand lightly with her thumb. More words rise from the wan lips. "Thank you for coming."

Immortal Source of Life, you've got to help this man.

"Can I do something for you?" she asks kindly, moving closer, observing the silky strands of hair spread wildly out over the pillow. She believes she picks up a hint of relaxation on the face. Seconds go by. His lips, though moving, form no words, until finally she hears, "Robbie? You say you're Robbie?"

"Yes."

"You console me, Robbie. Your presence is a blessing."

"Oh, it's nothing. I wanted to see you. Are you well looked after?"

"Will you acquaint me with your story, Robbie? Not now, but when I'm better. I'm sure it's special."

Robbie feels his weak hand squeeze hers. "My story? It isn't special. Not really. When you're better you have to tell me yours."

"I sense we will find similarities. That gives me strength."

"Mr Paradis, I don't want to tire you, truly I don't, but I have a question. Is there someone I can contact for you, someone who should know what's happened?"

The gaps between his eyelids widen; eyes move sluggishly in her direction. "I see you now, Robbie. I see that inner joy sustains you. It does me too."

"Do you have family? A friend somewhere?"

"I do." Robbie leans very close. "I do have a friend, but no need to contact her."

"Why? I mean, why not? If she's a friend she'll want to know."

"She knows."

"How?"

"She is here. She is with us."

Robbie scans the small room and empty doorway. "I don't understand."

"My friend is not visible. But I know when she is near. She is the source of love. And of tolerance. I discern her now. Do you too?"

For an instant Robbie is confused. Hesitantly she replies, "I may. I suppose I may."

"You do, Robbie. I'm sure you do. Your eyes bespeak it."

"How did you find her? Or who brought her to you? And what do you call her?"

"No one brought her and I did not find her. She found me. I call her Truth. She opened my eyes and I began to see love and peace and tolerance. Everywhere I looked, I saw it. Then she helped me see once more. She helped me to perceive limits. My limits. All limits. Our limits cause the struggling we must all go through during our short human period."

"Our short human period?"

"Robbie, my child, our lives are like sneezes. So quickly over. That is obvious to all, yet too few know, despite this, that each of us has always been and will always be. We are continuous before and after the sneeze. We are eternal. I want to share Truth before my darkness comes. If I don't come through at least you will know it. So listen, Robbie, listen."

What is the universe? A weird place for sure. Robbie has always been certain of that, though she could never explain it. But Paradis can. His whispering carries Robbie off.

"We are certain of our senses, Robbie, yet they tell us nearly nothing. We think the universe is energy, which is somewhat true. Matter is energy. Light is energy. We detect many energies. But few realize that energy is partial and imperfect. Energy is not eternal. It came and one day will be gone again. Energy explains nothing. Something lies behind it. I have been helped to understand that only essentiality is forever."

Robbie is bewildered. Essentiality? A realm beyond materiality? She often feels that she can touch that realm and that it touches back, but no words have ever come to her which capture the sensation.

Paradis continues in a throaty, slow and raspy voice, "Essentiality gives rise to all, also to energy and so to the energy universe. There is more. Essentiality allows for the qualities that energy cannot have. Essentiality spawns the worthy intangibles – love, compassion, gratitude, tolerance, wisdom, trust."

Robbie is transfixed. For sure, she has always believed in good. But she never clearly realized that good is a force, something objective, an agency that comes from beyond nature.

"Good came, my child, when life did. Essentiality's life force reached down and imbued energy, some little parts of it, with the capacity to replicate. And you must know something very wonderful. The life force coming through into this universe was always coalescing. It coalesced and coalesced, becoming steadily denser. In humans it is densest of all, which explains our capacity for awareness and our spirits. Not only that, but our spirits are strong, so strong that they have the capacity to understand essentiality. We are able to know that we are in the energy universe and – more exhilarating still – that we are also part of the essentiality that gives rise to it. We have been endowed to know *that* there is good and *what* good is."

Robbie's eager eyes question Paradis. She feels new tremors of excitement. A life force from beyond transports good into us? She has always believed she was in touch with her spirit, always felt a force for good inside her, but she has wondered how it is that she has a spirit.

"The basis for our spirits may seem complex, yet is simple. Essentiality is dynamic. Within essentiality, spirits conflate. They form as clouds do on a summer day. Bursts of spirit cross into the energy universe to occupy material forms for a while. They are infused into our bodies as long as our bodies live. That allows human existence to be meaningful.

"In the energy universe, bodies one day cease to be alive, but spirits don't. They burst back into essentiality and once more diffuse and co-mingle within it even as new outbursts form. Momentously, cyclically, in different forms, something of the spirit that our bodies used to house is always reappearing somewhere. The spirits of those who came before are in us and our spirits will be in those who follow."

This is what Robbie always vaguely suspected, though could never define. The reason she ventured into this kind of thinking was her mother and father who were question marks for her, immaterial entities that seemed real but had become hidden in a haze. She sometimes tried to think of a framework that contained both their short earthly existences and her relationship with them. But what framework might exist that is here and now, yet also forever? The framework she sought shimmered, yet stayed elusive and distant, like a desert mirage.

Robbie's gaze on Paradis takes on more urgency. Is the framework she sought being defined? Can it be that her parents are not gone, are not permanently put away, are not interred in nothingness?

"My child, parents are never gone. In essentiality the spirits of the generations constantly rejoin. Parents are forever present."

Excitement turns to rapture. She is not, after all, alone?

"You have never been alone. No one is, or has been. We are all in everything."

Robbie wants more. What about that other part of living? What about struggling? Struggle in the world is pervasive. What explains that?

"Struggle in our lives arises because when the life force brings good, an opposite comes too. We believe, yet we doubt. We possess knowledge, but know we are ignorant. There is love and there is hate. We experience good; we confront evil. Intangibles exist only through their opposites. We struggle, Robbie, because through that, good can flourish."

Robbie has begun stroking his hand with both of hers. Is that why PEACE exists?

"Everywhere, Robbie, everywhere I go, I meet people who struggle to oppose conflict and evil. They are in touch with their spirits. They act to pin evil down, to deny it expression. I can tell you, Robbie, there are very many such people. Very, very many. Though they occupy a tiny corner of the energy universe, their aim is celestially magnificent: peace without interruption. To achieve it they imitate the life force. They wish to infuse peace into everything. What they do is irresistible."

~

Entering the embassy, Robbie thought back to the moment Paradis was suddenly exhausted. The whispering grew weaker; the words became more halting. She had other questions to ask. Why did no one know about essentiality? Was it a secret? If not, how was it that no one had ever used it to explain things to her? The conjunction of the now and the forever and the fate of her relationship with her parents had been wrapped up in a haze too long. She had also wanted to ask more about PEACE. But Paradis could talk no more – his eyes had closed. For a few more minutes they communicated through touch. When an orderly interrupted them, she asked what chance the patient stood. The orderly shook his head and frowned. Even so, as Paradis was rolled away, Robbie's new understanding began to resonate. It transcended into a state of joy and fulfilled her utterly.

Her office, naturally, shattered the mood. Robbie threw her coat across a chair, resisted the computer turn-on habit, ignored the flashing telephone and went directly to the ambassador's office. Factually, there wasn't much to report, but Natalia would understand that she had partaken in something grand. Anticipating the experience of sharing, she entered the ambassador's anteroom.

"She's not here." Marge's tone was unusually frigid. She did not lift her eyes from her monitor. "The ambassador went home. Maybe a migraine. Lying down. Who knows."

"She asked me to see her the minute I was back."

"Sure. She was scheduled to see a lot of people. It's been a crazy mess here rearranging."

Robbie returned to her office where she closed the door, hung her coat, sat down, tapped the desktop a few times, then jabbed the computer's power to on. The mood of rapture was gone, replaced by a base sense of corruption. The computer whirred and Robbie turned to the phone. Two messages. She pressed a button.

Ah … yes, Ms Warren. My name is Maarten Valk. I am with DINPOL. Can you give me a telephone call back please?

DINPOL? International police coordination? Robbie occasionally had contact with them. Valk said his number before repeating it slowly, a sign of some consideration. All the same, Robbie was not in the mood for him just now and a button press put him aside.

Another press. *Robbie. It's Natalia. I'm at home this afternoon. It's just past three. I'd like to see you. Today. No time is too late. My car will be at the embassy. Ask Dirk to drive you.*

~

The stone mansion on the vast estate carried an ancient title dating back to the thirteenth century: Groot Haesebroek. The mansion itself was newer, an Art Deco affair, a brick house of mixed exterior aesthetics put up in the 1930s. The odd effects of war and peace made it Canadian.

When Dirk dropped Robbie off in the fast fading light of the February day, the mansion looked almost like a bunker, dark and dangerously sulking. But in a drawing room the light was strong, exposing a melee of patterns and colours. Bright flower arrangements stood on side tables; expressive oriental carpets adorned the floor; swirling abstract paintings hung on the walls. A scene for festivity and celebration.

Once drinks were poured, Robbie began her long report to Natalia, no prompting needed. She scarcely stopped to sip her juice. Natalia, in an easy chair, feet up, was lounge-suit comfortable and in a whiskey glass nursed a significant martini. As Robbie talked about essentiality and the life force, the energy universe imbued within it, and co-existence with parents unknown and long dead, the older woman smiled sympathetically. Robbie didn't miss one of Paradis's concepts. Her face had acquired the sheen of conviction working within her.

"It's clear to me, Natalia. All along I sort of fancied my mother and father were not far away. And now I know they're here, this minute, in me. I know now that my whole life I longed to know that I'm not an orphan. What I don't understand is, why it was Alistair Paradis who gave me this insight. Why did no one else tell me about essentiality. He said Truth found him. But why only him? What's your take on it?"

Natalia was always careful not to trivialize the experiences of others, and was especially so with Robbie's epiphany. She was slow to answer and did it gently. Paradis, she was sure, was a fascinating man, a guru of some kind. Or part guru and part mystic and prophet. As such types are supposed to do, he had communicated insight into how the physical and spiritual realms are linked. Natalia speculated he could have drawn on ancient ideas. Perhaps a little of Zoroaster, a sprinkling from Buddha, a pinch or two from Plato. But who could claim he wasn't right? Too many dogmas acquiring standing over the past centuries had ended up becoming excessively defined and therefore narrower and then still narrower, snuffing out tolerance for other faiths. It was always nice, Natalia said, to hear about a faith that was simply expressed and based on equality and inclusiveness. Therefore the concept of the spirit being a coalescence, to be followed by re-diffusion and then more coalescence, was perfectly fine. Unity possessing plurality and plurality reverting back into a unity. Why not? Why not believe in a metaphysics that is generous?

"I sure felt I was on his wavelength." Robbie admitted. "That feeling of oneness – it made me shiver. It was a beautiful sensation."

"And PEACE. Did he say anything about it?"

"Only that it consists of hundreds of millions, maybe a billion people ready to struggle against conflict and evil. They all want their little corner of the energy universe to be characterized by a pan-human harmony. He called PEACE an irresistible force."

"Did he say whether it had an action program?"

Robbie shook her head. "We seemed to be coming to that, but suddenly his strength was gone and he disappeared on me."

"I ask because since this morning my future has changed too. PEACE may become useful for me. I want to tell you why, Robbie. You're the only one I can talk to about this, but you must keep what I say secret. Swear?"

Robbie sat still, considering this, then replied, "I swear." Impishly she added, "the life force in me is my witness."

Now, in the drawing room, the day's happenings on Natalia's side were graphically relived. She became caught up relating them; her flair for drama was set loose, as if the day had given rise to a new legend and this was the first occasion for its telling. Nothing was left out, neither facts nor feelings. Not even the cross-link with Robbie's hospital visit – that the time slot of Natalia's appointment with de Bruyn had originally belonged to Paradis, who couldn't keep it and, in its place, had one with a surgeon instead. In Natalia's brand new legend, Act One, she presented the morning as a confrontation with a challenge so impossible to meet that, right away, it led to deep despair. Lunchtime was spent drinking a coffee and something else, and was rather like time spent in a psychological wilderness with a bouncing back and forth between competing emotional forces. Next, bubbling up from below, came the impulse to prevail. This was followed by a resolve to confront heinous manipulations of recent days, plus the determination to call Ottawa's double-dealing by its name. Ultimatums were formulated. They crossed an ocean and were hung around the neck of an arch dissembler who was instantly weak-kneed. *I held nothing back, Robbie. Nothing.* When the ultimatums were met, the morning's challenge became more acceptable. And that brought on Act Two with the current scene, this one, here in the residence, opening with the heroine planning to gird herself.

Halfway through Act One of her epic, Natalia stopped and left to prepare a new, still more considerable, martini. Robbie joined her in the kitchen and helped assemble a plate of crackers, fresh cauliflower pieces and raw carrots. Back in the drawing room, more celebratory than before, they laughed freely when Natalia painted the scene of how the overseas trickster had grovelled.

"I didn't entirely take his word for everything. As soon as I hung up I got hold of Ranford to check out that New York lunch."

"Ranford?"

"Ranford Tolman, our ambassador to the United Nations. If anyone knew about the PM's lunch, what was agreed to etcetera, it would be him."

"And?"

"He confirmed the lunch took place. The two prime ministers were table companions. Ranford was waiting outside when it finished and asked the prime minister if something needed follow-up. The prime minister said his Dutch counterpart talked a lot about peace. Our PM claimed he tried to slow him down. At one point he said, *If global peace were a puck, I agree it would be nice to see it at the back of the net.* Ranford was inclined not to give the remark too much credibility since the PM seemed uncharacteristically jolly just then. More likely the PM was trying to say he wished he had something of substance to add to a conversation like that. I've know Ranford for years. He is a sharp, honest and discreet man and I levelled with him. To a degree. When he heard that I was contacted by Ottawa to pursue some discreet follow-up work on peace with the Dutch, he said, 'Good for you, Natalia. That won't be wasted time. In which direction will it go? New ways to fund poverty elimination? Rapprochement amongst the religions?' I replied it wasn't clear yet, that people continued to play it close to their vest, that the two sides were still feeling each other out. 'Well, The Hague is a good place for it. Thank God you're there to do it. If

I can help, Natalia, you know, information, ideas, the role of devil's advocate, I'm here. What passes between us will stay between us, but I think that's not something I need to say.' He then asked about Carlos and I did the same about his wife and that was it."

"Your moment of conversion."

"It helped." Natalia sighed. "Yes, I'm in. A big new peace initiative. I have no choice but to do it. And you're the one I will turn to. Ready for it?"

Robbie shifted. She put down what was left of a carrot. "You want me to stick my face into your big challenge?" A shaking head answered her own question. "I'm doubtful, Natalia. That's not me. Better you stick to Mr Tolman. I don't think like you."

"That is the very point. That's what I want – you not thinking like me."

"You don't understand. I see what you do as a bog. Policies on this, policies on that – to me that's like bogs. Bogs aren't difficult for you. You begin to dance and all of a sudden you've crossed, you're on the other side. In comparison I'm thick as a brick. When I try to keep up on policy, soon as I'm a half step in I sink from sight. Sorry, but that's reality."

"You think I dance to where I'm going? It's been a while since someone has used that imagery for me. I guess it may look as if that's what I do, but it's really my way of hiding a deeper problem. Long ago when I used to visit my grandmother she would listen to me rambling. I would describe to her my dreams for my own fairytale future. One time she said: *Sounds as if you plan to dance to it. Take care, Natalia. You might think you're dancing, but all you may be doing is kicking up some dust.* She knew me. That soberness helped. That's what I need from you, Robbie. You have similar candidness." Natalia turned conspiratorial. "OK, so this is how I see it working: if I'm dreaming up peace things that are follies or if, you know, I'm just creating a dust storm, something along those lines, then you wince. You wince hard. If you want, you may also say something honest, as my grandmother did. It won't be your role to get to the other side of the bog."

"Suppose I do that, suppose I bring you down to earth, suppose that rubs your nerves, suppose it rubs them raw."

"Not possible. I'm not like that. I can take it. I've thought about it and decided. We are venturing all, Robbie, and we will see where it takes us."

Natalia's second martini was pretty well gone and Robbie thought she was detecting a slight slur. "That's fine then," she replied. "I suppose that's fine. Anyway, I promise I won't be in a hobble about it. I'll look sour at you from now on, if that's how you want it."

Chapter 6

"Of all my born days," Robbie was thinking, "never before was there one like this."

She was back in her apartment spooning yoghurt from a bowl. She was also reliving the day's unexpected, fanciful moments. The remainder of the week, in comparison, was likely to be pretty tame. Paradis's whisperings came back, and goose bumps came on all over again. The time at the residence had been uncommonly good too. Only when Natalia's tongue began to sound a little thick and she fell into making outrageous judgements of famous men she had known did Robbie decide it was time to leave. An unsteady Natalia accompanied her to the door where she exuberantly called out, "The hill, Robbie, is steep but our hearts are stout." Robbie stopped, turned and cried back, "You sleep tight now, Natalia, you hear."

Setting the empty yoghurt bowl aside, Robbie smiled to herself.

Sitting still, traversing the day once more, Robbie felt a surge of affection – for Natalia and the way she had taken her in, and for Paradis who had opened her eyes. One day, two people, both opposites to her, both opposites to each other, yet bestowing much rich new meaning to life. How good was that? Was this part of essentiality already working its magic?

Robbie contemplated this, and slowly she became certain – now that she possessed that word and therefore the concept – that essentiality was truly seeping in. A lovely tingling had started in her toes and fingers, was moving up her legs and along her arms and was spreading all through her. It took a while, but eventually she knew essentiality had merged with her. She shuddered, thinking she was as one with infinity and eternity. Such bliss to feel united with the parents she never knew. Transfixed and motionless, she sat glowing for an hour.

~

The glow lingered when the new day began.

Source of All That Is Miraculous, why are you doing this for me?

She stirred only because there were practicalities to confront. A shower, breakfast, dressing, a fast walk to the tramline through a bewitching hoarfrost. In her office Robbie dialled padlocks and opened filing cabinets.

Before she turned to the computer she contacted the hospital and learned that the news was guardedly good. The operation on Paradis had been long, but broken bones had been successfully reset, and life support systems were keeping his condition stable.

Robbie, relieved, phoned Marge to ask her to pass the news on to the ambassador. Her attention shifted to voice mail. Only one message, the one saved yesterday afternoon. She jotted down the number.

Before dialling she reflected. Another police officer. A new one. From DINPOL. Why DINPOL? Robbie seldom dealt with the international police liaison group in Zoetermeer. She tried to think what the issue could be. A drug smuggling case maybe. Had a Dutch destroyer forced, say, a Newfoundland trawler into the harbour at Scheveningen? The harbour wasn't far from where she lived. Regularly, she walked around it to hear the sound of gulls and take in the smell of the sea. She imagined the trawler's crew as a bunch of well-meaning refugees from the defunct Grand

Banks fishery. You never knew, several might be her first or second cousins, that is, once proud fishermen with nothing useful left to do. She visualized them sailing east, away from Newfoundland's rugged cliffs, jubilant in spirit, eager to cross the Atlantic, delighted to be delivering their new bounty – bales of quality Canadian pot – to the ardent markets of Holland.

At DINPOL her call went through directly. She heard the same pleasant voice as on her answering machine. *Goedemorgen. U spreekt met Maarten Valk.* Robbie identified herself. He switched to English and forthrightly asked if she could come to see him.

"For what reason?"

"It has to do with the airplane crash at Valkenburg."

Robbie explained she was already in contact with the police, mentioning the name of the officer in Leyden. Valk graciously responded he was aware of that, but the flight having been international caused the scope of the investigation to have widened.

"Can't we discuss it now?"

"It is not very wise to review certain points through the telephone."

Robbie let this sink in. She glanced at her planner. DINPOL was in Zoetermeer, a kind of suburb of The Hague. It wasn't far. She agreed to a time that afternoon and hung up.

So, no unemployed sods from The Rock had been taken into custody in Scheveningen. No cousins, near or distant, needed to be visited in jail. That was too bad. Instead it was about the crash again. Poor Alistair Paradis was hanging on by his fingernails, but she herself had gained from it. How could she repay him? Nothing much came to mind except doing everything she could to help him get through.

~

By train, Zoetermeer is a mere dozen minutes from The Hague's central station, so no problem getting there. And normally Robbie enjoyed the train. She liked its regularity and the independence which resulted from lines that stretched everywhere.

Today's short trip was through a pervasive greyness, however. A dense cover of unbroken cloud filtered the last vestiges of joy out of the light. Holland felt sedated, with nothing taking on colour. As the train pushed on she had little to look at – an occasional football field in hibernation, now and then a small antique chateau looking forlorn on a tiny space between regular square blocks of flats. All clean, all neat, all planned. In this light Holland was stripped of its frivolity. Robbie also knew that the conurbation's gloom would soon break up. Spring was mere weeks away and millions of flowers would bloom.

In Zoetermeer the sky was raven-dark and sent down a steady driving rain. The DINPOL building stands in a modern, planned neighborhood. Under the overhang she tapped her brolly before collapsing it. The building door opened. "Ms Warren?"

"Yes."

"I am Maarten Valk. I was expecting a diplomatic car."

"I took the train and walked."

"You did that? That is good. I do it too. Please, will you enter? Our weather is very bad. I am sorry."

Robbie seldom formed mental pictures of policemen on the phone and was not often surprised when she met one face to face, but this one broke the mould. No uniform. Instead, a grey turtleneck. No precision to the hair. It was blond and somewhat messy. No lifeless law-enforcement eyes either. His were tinged with something opposite, a hint of mischief perhaps. He was more or less her age and thin, though taller.

"Thank you for coming," Valk said, leading the way into the complex. "You know this building?" Robbie said she had been in it once with a Canadian group for a cheerful discussion about tackling cross-border crime. Valk laughed and asked what she thought of Holland. Robbie answered she had lived here for so long she was beginning to feel local. "I would like some day to feel local in Canada," he replied. "Holland is very squeezed. If you know how to follow rules then it is not so bad, but we have very many rules and sometimes you don't want to spend every day paying attention to them." He laughed again. "Sometimes you don't want to have to wash your front windows every week. If you compare, in Canada, are there fewer restrictions?"

"Fewer restrictions, but fewer conveniences too. No trains."

"No trains? That is a pity."

Half way up the building near a corridor's end, Valk unlocked a door and preceded Robbie through. Neatness jumped at her. A spotless desktop; orderly well-labelled file boxes; a computer screen without dust. "It's like my work place," she observed, "but with some differences."

"You have plants? Are you a plant person?"

"I think I live with less order and fewer rules."

Valk grinned. "I have to say that after talking to you this morning I cleaned up a little."

"It's been washed and polished, for sure. Is there a rule which makes you do it once a week?"

"Once a year only, or when I expect a visitor. Will you sit down? And can we be informal, I mean, speak off the record about the crash and your countryman?"

"Alistair Paradis?"

"Yes."

"Formal or informal, does it matter? The poor man was operated on yesterday. The surgery was high risk. He's hanging on by a thread."

"Yes, I know. You spent time with him yesterday and, informally, I wish to ask if you know something about him, his position in Canada for example."

"The police in Leyden allowed me to go through his briefcase. His business card says PEACE."

"Yes, I know. But do you have information on him from Canada?"

"No. We don't know if he has a residence there, or even next of kin. Not yet, anyway. What is DINPOL's interest?"

"We are not yet sure, I mean, if we have an interest, or should have an interest. The insurance company wants many details. An investigation has begun. I will not work on that." Valk shrugged. "It was very foggy that night. The pilot missed the runway. Such accidents occur. Insurance can pay up as far as I'm concerned. But it has come to our attention – I must ask that you keep this between us – that the plane landed earlier that day in a strange place. I mean, a strange place if you work for peace. We don't know yet if he met people there."

"Which place?" Robbie asked. Her tone was taking on an edge.

"The airplane," Valk continued neutrally, "took off from Akrotiri early in the morning. It took a course west and slightly south …"

"Akrotiri?" Robbie interrupted.

"An airport on Cyprus."

"Greek or Turkish?"

"British. Military. Also used by the Americans. The flight was to Libya and it landed there at another military airport. Surt. Near a town named Gardabya. It was on the ground for nearly two hours. After Surt it went to Madrid – spending a short time there only to refuel – then to Valkenburg. A very long day. I mean, for the pilot."

"And this means?"

"Nothing maybe. Well, we do not know."

"But you suspect." It came out like an accusation. A simple situation – a fog, a tired pilot – was threatening to turn complex and Robbie didn't like it.

Valk, steadily neutral and pleasant, seemed not to notice. "It strikes us as interesting that the plane would land at a military base in Libya, which is not on the shortest route to Valkenburg from Akrotiri. The plane's registration was SX-PAX. The prefix SX is for Greece. We do not know yet why it was registered there. PAX is, well, sort of the same as what is on his calling card. That is cute, but overdoing it maybe just a little bit.

"It may also be noteworthy that so little information is available. I mention this so that you understand why I ask about Mr Paradis. You know nothing more? Do you know if PEACE means something?"

"It stands for People Everywhere Against Conflict and Evil. My ambassador's husband informed us of that. He knows Mr Paradis from peace seminars they both attend. They are busy with them all over the world. Mr Paradis was coming to one here this week. He also had an appointment with someone in your prime minister's office. That proves his credentials are excellent."

"Thank you. Very much. That information is very helpful. Is PEACE what you would call an NGO?"

"That is our understanding."

"What impression did Mr Paradis give you?"

"I don't know what you mean."

"I mean, what type of person is he? A businessman? Or did he appear to be more like a politician?"

"He struck me as a spiritualist. And he is very wise. Like a teacher, a guru, or even a prophet."

"A spiritualist? A prophet? Such people can be very interesting. Did he explain PEACE to you?"

"It is to fight ..." Robbie halted, sensing that a forensic examination of the precious time she spent with Paradis was starting. The experience had been magnificent, it did not deserve to be pulled apart into a thousand petty, police pieces.

"PEACE is to fight?" Valk prompted. "Fight what?"

"Sorry, Mr Valk. Mr Paradis was in pain. He was struggling to remain conscious. I felt sorry for him. I did not press him. He did not say."

"My information is that you were with him for nearly an hour."

"I sat with him. I wanted him to know he wasn't alone, that I wanted him to pull through."

Valk nodded. "A very good thing to do. Please excuse me for asking many questions. In this place that's how we make progress. Is it possible to ask you not to write a report on our conversation?"

Robbie frowned. "A weird request."

"It is because we know so little. We don't really know anything beyond just the plane crashing. We don't want to stir the pot if the pot is going to stay empty. A plane departing from the Akrotiri airfield is not abnormal by itself. It is only that a peace man visiting Libya is, well, not very normal if you know anything about that country. If we think that no answer can come, we will move on. In our work, Miss Warren, we fish. That is all."

"And if there are no fish to catch?"

Valk smiled disarmingly. "For us that is good. As I say, we go to a new pond. Will you tell me about your work? Is there a good word to describe it?"

Robbie hesitated, unsure where Valk was going. Was the reason for her visit finished? Was he starting final social pleasantries? She felt she had not really driven home the point that suspecting Paradis was a waste of police time, that angling into Paradis's travels would only uncover compassion for humanity.

Valk prodded. "If what I do is fish, what do you do? Diplomats cultivate, do they not? Does that mean you also harvest?" He was grinning again, like a school boy enjoying a word game.

It relaxed Robbie. "Not harvest," she said. "Rescue. We rescue. We throw people lifelines."

This delighted him. "Good. That is good. Very good. I use a fishing line, you throw out a lifeline and we both pull our lines in. It's nice to think there is a parallel."

"May I predict something?"

"Yes. Please. I like predictions very much."

"I predict that in fishing for Mr Paradis your line will end up with nothing on the hook."

Valk thought about this. His face darkened. "I do hope that's how it will be, Ms Warren. There are enough other fish to catch. We don't need more. And I do hope that with your lifeline your luck will be better."

Chapter 7

Carlos, upright on his bike – dignified and unhurried, the very picture of a solid burgher – was pedalling along the pristine lanes of Wassenaar. The winter had shifted early, and spring's power to renew was evident everywhere. The sheet of lead that had been serving as a sky was gone. Light and lightness were triumphant. "A post-gloom world," a spirited Carlos thought.

In his upbeat mood he saw that flowers were as numerous as in paradise. And, all around, the rhododendrons' swelling buds were about to transubstantiate into celestial glory itself. As for Wassenaar's lawns, young though already flawless, each one seemed to symbolize an immaculate conception of a kind. What had caused all this regenerating perfection? Carlos in his happy mindset grinned and threw a quick glance up.

Good morning, Sun.
Good morning, Carlos.
I believe in you, Sun.
I love you, Carlos. I bless you with my splendour. I reward you

with my warmth.

Carlos's grin became permanent. On days like this, you felt a need to worship. Three times in quick succession he rang the handlebar bell, a clarion call rising up, a signal of his own intentions for renewal.

The destination was a clinic about an hour off by bike. The rhythmic pumping of his legs allowed some downtime for the mind, an occasion to touch randomly on many pleasant thoughts. Some good news had arrived courtesy of Robbie. Alistair Paradis's surgery had been successful; he was rehabilitating well. Internal organs were healing; reset bones were knitting. A week before, after six weeks in hospital, he'd been wheeled out, eased into an ambulance and delivered to a luxurious health complex set in the middle of a spacious meadow. Robbie had supervised the move from start to finish. Carlos could imagine how she fussed over every detail to ease the old man's burden. According to Robbie, Alistair had been chatty, which was how Carlos knew him. At the clinic, as the stretcher rolled him into a roomy private suite, the man of peace had declared that his contact with the world, to promote its well being, would be re-established soon. "And tell Carlos," he made a point of pressing Robbie, "that I would love him to visit. I know he travels a great deal. I won't expect him tomorrow. But some time when it's convenient for him, if he comes, it would warm my heart."

There was no stopping Alistair when he got onto the topic of Carlos. He described to Robbie the many conferences they had attended together. "And, Robbie, I have to say this, his company was unfailingly elevating. As is yours. You're like an angel to me. Thank you for taking charge and arranging things. Thank you. Thank you."

At the Friday embassy happy hour, Robbie detached herself from the locals and went up to Carlos to let him know what Alistair had said. She handed him a map with the route to the clinic traced out in red. "It's a ritzy place," she said, then adding in a filial hush, "but all the same I'm worried he'll get bored. He says he's got stuff to read, but I think it's just stale documents on global peace. It would be good for his state of mind to have some diversion."

So now, today, pedalling through unimaginably glorious weather, having dropped his desk work, Carlos planned to accomplish two things. The first was altruistic – entertaining Alistair. To show an interest in his well being was simple decency. The peace man could be garrulous, but he was amusing too. In any case, Carlos was convinced, their social time would not last long, given Alistair's need for rest.

The day's second event, if there was time and everything worked out, would be personal and private. Carlos planned to find a unique spot for acting out a fantasy. For months, an urge had been growing. He wanted to feel Dutchness. He wished to sense Dutchness flowing through him. A bag slung over the rear carrier of his bike bulged with some accoutrements for that. First a visit to Alistair, then a search for a dyke and a polder.

~

The map Robbie gave him was well-intentioned – the shortest route from the residence to the rehab clinic situated near some pretty lakes a few dozen kilometers northeast of Leyden. But the wind was still and the day was his alone, and because all paths in every direction were equal and even, Carlos decided on a zig-zag route. The thought delighted him. Let this hither and thither journey be a metaphor for life. Canals, drawbridges, villages modern and ancient, townhouses next to fields with contented cows grazing whichever way he turned, all was finely manicured. A delightful expression of culture. He took in the precision. Was there a match anywhere for this kind of all-permeating order? The Swiss perhaps. The Singaporeans maybe. What bliss to be immersed in it. A good reason for losing the way. And gleefully he did, practicing an orderly disorder. Or, disorder within order! This zig-zagging – it described his life.

After a few hours he had traversed a good subset of Holland and found that he had been unable to get lost, since suddenly he was pedalling through two tall gateposts. In the distance, beyond countless crocuses fusing into an unbroken varicoloured sheet and majestic daffodils standing dense and at the ready to turn golden, he saw robed figures reclining on lounge chairs in the sun. They were arranged in a parallel and rectilinear fashion – more order! – and immobile as statues, seemingly fixated on something beyond the meadow where trees stood thick. What was out there? Were they waiting for a phantom to appear? Would a stirring in the treetops be a druid's signal that a miracle was near, that their maladies were actually ending?

An attendant guided Carlos to a shaded patio where Paradis dozed in a wheelchair underneath boughs of blooming forsythia. His large head was slouched forward; a double chin rested against a barrel chest. Carlos touched his shoulder. "Alistair," he said softly.

Paradis shook. His head lifted. "Carlos!" He pinched his own cheek. "Am I dreaming?"

"Not an apparition, Alistair. It's really me. I've come to see how your limbs are mending. Well, well, you ancient bear, so you decided to tempt mortality to its limits."

Paradis waved a hand as if that subject wasn't worth a second comment. "We don't often contemplate how the world will be if we are no longer in it, Carlos. A close call, yes, and it humbled me. It made me think. I have realized, had I expired, the loss would scarcely have been noticed."

"Nonsense. You're a vital cog in the world of peace. You speak for millions."

"And you are a poor flatterer, Carlos. I am easily replaceable. Unlike you."

"You have it backwards, Alistair. Most of us come up with theories and think they matter. You bring something rarer. Inspiration. A vision. I was glad to hear that you're through the worst. I have been receiving reports from your newest admirer."

"Robbie? Is she not a pure delight? If I had a daughter, Carlos, if only ... Well, wheel me to that table. We can sit there. And if I push this little button someone will come running, which means I can offer coffee."

They settled at the table with the sunlight angling at them from the back. Paradis asked, "That seminar in February I was coming to attend, was there a result?" He was keen on this news, but also for all the other events on the peace front because his deep voice raced on. "How much have I missed? What have you been up to? Have you been busy providing humanity with still more proof that it's the only species in existence eager to bring about its own extinction? And what has become of that zoology spinster from Portugal? Isabelle, I think. Remember at the Tehran conference last December how we enjoyed her slide show of a group of African great apes demonstrating pacifist behaviour? We saw not one picture of aggression, but we were forced to observe by her how many of the primates used their plentiful free time for routine fornication. If I recall right, she concluded there were lessons for mankind, and for pacifism, in that. She appeared to be making an offer, but I don't recall anyone taking it."

What was it about Paradis, Carlos thought. At international events, participants mobbed him during the breaks. In widening circles, spellbound, they listened to his anecdotes, his reassurances and his prognostications that sounded more like prophecies. With Paradis, they set aside professional rivalries. Occasionally he would halt, survey them with darting eyes set in black hollows and, having taken the group's pulse, would go on with controlled cadences, deep tones ceaselessly rolling on and a rich vocabulary deployed with wit and confidence, as would any other born orator. With Paradis comfortably at the center, each occasion was like attending a mesmerising performance.

As now.

Sipping coffee, Carlos was drawn in by stories of the famous peace laureates whom Paradis personally knew. Suddenly Carlos was jarred because in the context of several truly great international peace advocates Paradis used his name. "Stop right there, Alistair," Carlos said quickly. "Please. You call me a poor flatterer, but you're worse."

"But no. I remember the workshop in Phnom Penh, Carlos. Oh, I do. Every minute of it. The analysis you gave of Cambodia's conflicts, the dark years of genocide, the cultural self-immolation so seemingly inexplicable – you explained them so clearly. The hush in the room was palpable, as if a light not known before had been switched on. Everyone felt the moment, the understanding of why the genocide happened and why it continued for so many desperate years. Had we only known those deeper causes earlier. I saw how humanity refuses to understand itself, how, unless it matures, it will always continue to kill its own members. The narcissism inherent in so many societies – no one is better than you in laying bare the challenges *that* poses.

"Your next coup. Two months later in Djakarta. What a wonderful paper you presented. How is it that some cultures are non-violent? I adored your insight into the Semai. Perhaps I'll have a chance one day to visit the Malay Peninsula to see them for myself, to do what you did, to be part of the community. Your description of how they manage conflict, the whole group exploring the causes of discord and how embarrassment, not punishment, is used as a disincentive for unacceptable acts – it was more gripping than watching an action thriller, though the lessons were pivotal. I began to think, why can't that way of proceeding be followed by more cultural groups? You went on to elucidate other cultures that function as peacefully as the Semai ..." Paradis paused, trying to come up with their names.

"I mentioned the Nubians that day," said Carlos, "and the Malapandaram in India. Also the islanders on Tristan da Cunha in the South Atlantic. Plus the Anabaptists and the Ifaluk." He rattled more names off. "There are some two dozen low-conflict cultures. If they have a common characteristic it is a psycho-cultural atmosphere of warmth and affection rather than of competition and wealth acquisition."

"Indeed, yes. If you have new papers on such issues, please send them along. Reading about that kind of upbeat work speeds my healing. You always point at the potential for spreading the commonalities underlying peaceful cultures. I live for such optimism."

Carlos often noticed that although Paradis liked to bring substance into conversations, it was never really his. He was always quoting others. His own rhetoric was sky high, up in the clouds, and, Carlos supposed, if you speak for millions that's where it has to be. That was probably the reason for Paradis never ceasing to acquire knowledge from others, though praising them for it. This meant that when he enticed you to share what you knew it was tough to stay mum. You began to tell him more and more until you couldn't stop. Carlos was not immune to this ego-tugging. He enjoyed the limelight and liked being the *primus inter* a hundred *pares*. Not only that, but the peace circuit was not badly funded, a gravy train of sorts, with his performance fees commensurate. So here, amongst the pretty boughs heavy with the small yellow flowers, he was feeling successful and began doing most of the talking.

His own diction, once it warmed up, could be as fluent as that of Paradis. Carlos described the ways in which cultures practice harmony, how avoidance of physical violence becomes a basic necessity, a daily staple as it were, like eating and drinking. He spoke of the role of self-restraint, of the absence of the compulsion to be in the right, of the willingness to allow others to mediate, of the ability to see humour and of the capacity to laugh. "But," he added in a scholarly tone, "by and large, peaceful cultures are tightly knit and not especially complex. Other cultures usually have a tough time commingling with them."

"Is that where your cultural compass comes into play, Carlos? That marvellous analytical tool. It has never ceased to amaze me."

"My compass? I had forgotten it. That was long ago."

"It was pure genius. I memorized it, you know. For me it remains a handy guide to determine which cultures are likely to misunderstand each other and bare their fangs."

Carlos thought back. He'd arrived at the compass by focusing on very strong features of different societies. One day on hotel stationery he portrayed this schematically. As with a compass he drew two axes: north and south, east and west. With a little effort you could place cultures somewhere on the four resulting squares. He was keynote speaker that day at a symposium of UN officials working to rebuild post-conflict regions. He described the compass to them as an amusement, but the response was enthusiastic. It became part of the meeting's record and word of it spread. Not long afterwards, at a seminar of ethnographers like himself, he was asked to explain the compass in more detail, but he declined. For such experts he considered it superficial. Paradis was present and cornered him afterwards.

A patient Carlos had explained to him the axes of the compass. The north-south axis represented extreme cultural characteristics – strongly pragmatic cultures being north and rigidly ideological ones south. The east-west axis, on the other hand, depicted cultural behaviour, the east representing submissiveness to authority and the west an orientation towards the opposite, that is, critical thinking and analysis. Every culture fitted somewhere on one of the four squares.

In the talk to the UN group Carlos had observed that the Anglo-Saxon world is generally northwest. It is broadly pragmatic and has a focus on learning from experience, especially from failed experience. Southwest cultures are those that prefer to begin with principles that are held to be universal, from which conclusions are logically drawn. Southwest cultures often have strong state-planning, China being one example, but France and Germany are somewhere in there too. Northeast cultures are ones which address existential challenges on a case-by-case basis, yet practice strong conformity. By and large, they are self-contained traditional societies. And southeast cultures start with universal principles and apply authority to force conformity in society with no individuality allowed. Strong southeast cultures are often nationalistic or missionary in their orientation. Many practice xenophobia. A good example, Carlos had stated, would be the Taliban.

Paradis had murmured words of awe and had prodded Carlos for more. Apart from characterizing cultures, did the compass have a deeper power? But yes, a giddy Carlos had replied. Going out on a limb, he claimed that the compass also had predictive power. The greatest potential for conflict arises when the most opposite cultures, say the extreme northwest and southeast groups, come into contact. Some irritant, a flashpoint of some kind, will cause instant misunderstanding; right away, the two sides dig in and turn belligerent. Dialogue becomes nearly impossible. Take the Americans, always pragmatically pursuing their wealth-acquisition using all others as tools. Put them opposite to extreme conformity-imposing groups such as the Taliban. They'd sooner kill each other than figure out why the other thinks the way it does. Similarly the USA and the ayatollahs in Iran.

The same thing between southwest and northeast cultures. The communists running China can't stand Tibetans. But there's hope too, Carlos had added. Cultures develop. Under the right conditions, forces at work within cultures, education being prominent, tend to push societies from the eastern part of the compass to the west, from submission to authority towards critical thinking, and from the south to the north, from rigid ideology towards pragmatism. On the other hand, forces come into play that oppose the cultural drift towards the northwest quadrant. One is that, in all cultures, individuals are born who are driven to possess power. Once they have some power they won't stop, can't stop, until they gain absolute control. When tyrants and dictators take over, societies are usually forced back into a southeast direction. Hitler, Saddam Hussein, Mugabe, there are plenty of examples. If nothing can contain them, for example, the media or other strong institutions, such men are fated to sow death.

"For me, the explanation you gave that day came like a beacon of light," Paradis said, still revelling.

"It was a convenience, Alistair," Carlos said, downplaying the compass, "but it's fun to deploy from time to time, if only to see the broad generalizations it will generate."

Paradis sighed. "If it brings fun I will want to deploy it often. I haven't had much fun these past eight weeks. But I should not be morose. One must never lose sight of the prospect of fun and soon enough I'll start to partake in the circuit again. And thank goodness you are well. I assume your wife is too."

"Natalia? Oh yes. Always the whirlwind, Alistair. I hope you'll see her in full flight sometime. Not a day goes by without her undertaking something new. Whatever it is, she gives it structure, a future, a good polish and turns it until it's positioned to look its best. She's like a talented impresario. Compared to her, you and me, we're just scoffers and duffers. She's interested in how you are, by the way. She has asked about you several times. And about PEACE. Peace appears to be on her mind these days. She often enquires into the results of the workshops and seminars."

"Wonderful. A diplomatic interest in peace will do no harm. Do you think something is afoot?"

"Difficult to tell. For years she worked on democracy building. Democracy and peace – there is a strong link. It's what brought us together."

"Married to a fine diplomat. You are much blessed. I suppose it is imaginable that diplomats are thinking peace again. Any rumours on that front on the circuit?"

"Nothing, Alistair. No buzz, no gossip, nowhere, not from any quarter. But if Natalia is engaged in something, our seminars would be like children playing in a sandbox relative to what she and her peers could get done."

"So true. I have often thought, if we could get closer to where the political decisions are shaped, our cause would leap forward. I try to see as many opinion makers as I can. They listen to me politely, but that is all." Paradis drew in a deep breath and shook his head. A silence set in. His eyelids drifted downwards. It seemed something startled him then, for suddenly they reopened wide and he looked about for several seconds like a wild man. His calm returned and mournfully he whispered, "apologies, Carlos. It is a bad host who drifts off into himself. I am sorry. I am tiring. Will you give me your hand before you go?" Carlos extended it. Paradis took it and bowed his head. "I have learned from you over the years, Carlos," he said, his voice shaking. "Your explanations and optimism that peace breeds peace sustain me. How grand it would be were your wife to join our struggle."

~

Visiting the sick, Carlos told himself when he was on his bike again, is a form of comfort delivery. He hoped that's how it had been for Alistair because that old white grizzly bear deserved it.

With a coddled conscience, Carlos changed the focus of the day. Having skirted Leyden to the north on his way to the clinic, he now set a course directly for the town. He didn't intend to go into Leyden. He merely wanted to approach it, to look at it from afar, to see it whole from a distance, to focus on its history, that is, on a great drama that unfolded there centuries before. His imagination would have to function as a time machine, taking him back, letting him experience all that happened.

Interestingly, a time transformation set in long before he was even close to Leyden. It started right away, on the bike path he was following in his methodical, stately manner. The path was like a twisting line pulling him from the present into the past – the way it took him past classical Dutch windmills and paralleled a narrow river guarded by great overarching, ageless willows. A short rise took him to the top of an ancient dyke. On both sides, Carlos observed, checker boards of pastures were defined by standing water in perfectly straight lines, another scene unchanged for centuries. After a half hour of drifting through this bucolic tranquility, he spied in the distance some spires rising out of the flatness. Were they Leyden's? Was that bulky greyish form the town? A quick perusal of Robbie's map proved it was. Four and a half centuries ago the view from here would have been as unhindered as it was now.

Carlos got off the bike to establish an accurate bearing. It was somewhat past noon and since his shadow would approximately be pointing north, south was behind him slightly to the left. That was the direction from which the inundation came. Next, he studied a drainage ditch at the bottom of the dyke's grassy slope. The ditch would be as old as the dyke, probably as old as Holland. How far did the ditch run? As-far as his eye could see, perhaps the whole way to Leyden. Yes, this was the ideal vantage point. For what? For watching a historical moment when two cultures collided. All that remained was to trigger the mechanism for transforming himself, for looking like a contemporary eyewitness of one of Holland's great transformational moments. All that was necessary now was to become Dutch. Carlos sent a quick, sly glance upwards as a prelude to opening the bags dangling over the rear wheel of his bike.

Hello again, Sun.

Warm greetings to you once more, Carlos.

I love what I'm doing.

Nothing is ever new for me. You go ahead. I allow all.

Under Egypt's sun Carlos wore a dirty galabya. In Bangladesh, he made his way bare-trunked with a lungi draped from his waist. The Arizona desert brought on moccasins and a loincloth. Leather shorts, a chequered shirt and a feathered hat had served him in the Alps.

Culture and costume. Ancient cultures and ancient costumes. Dressing up like them provides the feel of being an insider.

An old blanket emerged from the bags. He spread it on the grass. First his jersey, then his shoes and finally his pants came off.

In ghostly white underwear contrasting with thick black swaths of body hair, he bent forward over the bags to haul out more items, such as black linen pants, which he put on. They were loose, more billowy than pyjamas, though fitting tightly around the ankles. Next he donned a dark blue top coutured as a blouson. It had a frilly collar, which closed snug around the neck behind his beard, and black lace cuffs that covered his hairy wrists. There was a cap as well, flat and black. Frizzy locks were squished in, though right away most squirmed back out. Finally, the *pièce de resistance*: wooden shoes painted bright yellow and lavishly decorated in swirling strokes of red.

Carlos was recast. He'd turned into the spitting image – save for some excessive hair – of a sixteenth century Dutch farmer dressed up in his Sunday best. But Carlos wasn't done yet. Out came a white-clay pipe with a long stem, into which he stuffed tobacco. It lit easily and he drew on it vigorously a few times to get it glowing hot. Stretching out on the blanket, propping himself up on an elbow, ancient fashion covering his body, smoke filling his lungs – Carlos relaxed. For months he had dreamt of doing this. The tobacco brought on a high and as he closed his eyes he felt that all he had been was draining out and behind it Dutchness came rushing in. The transformation was fully in progress. Dutch contrariness, the impulse for freedom, the urge for order, their speaking bluntly – he comprehended it all. When this new round of otherness had entirely seized him, he opened his eyes. He was ready now. The drama could start. He would witness the crux of Holland's political creation.

~

It is 1574.

From the dyke top the dark outline of Leyden's encircling wall is easily made out. In the polder before the wall a military encampment has been struck. A Spanish army, which has been marauding through Holland, is laying siege to the town. Leyden's citizenry has been presented with a choice. Death by starvation or submission to King Philip II of Spain.

A conflict, but for what reason?

Philip inherited these low-lying northern lands in 1555 from his father, Charles V, Holy Roman Emperor, King of Castile and León, King of Aragon, Archduke of Austria, Duke of Burgundy and Ruler of the Seventeen Provinces of the Netherlands. Too much political real estate for one man? The emperor's son knows little about the people in this cold, damp extremity of his inherited realm. But he does know there is heresy and, being a fanatic Catholic, he is determined to exterminate it. The Inquisition is deployed. Holland's protestants are to be flushed out and burned.

Fifty years after the Reformation's start many non-Catholics are living in the free-thinking low countries. This population reacts. The nobility and town burghers get involved. Anti-Spanish opinion coalesces around Prince William of Orange who organizes resistance, which further incenses Spain's king. To quell the revolt he sends an army north, led by a pathologically brutal commander, the Duke of Alva.

By 1574, the religious revolt has been going on for six years. To crush it once and for all, Spain's army adopts the tactic of besieging towns. The burghers, starved out of their minds, eventually open the gates, whereupon the town's leaders and protestants are murdered off. Near to Leyden, Haarlem and other towns like it have in this way been forced back into the Spanish fold. Leyden is next. Its fate is crucial. If Leyden falls, the revolt will effectively have run its course. William of Orange tries to raise a mercenary force to lift the siege, but this is taking time, too much time. The Spanish commander, on the other hand, wants to get the bother over with and offers Leyden's leaders amnesty should they unlock the gates. Their reply is brief. They say his words sound sweet enough, but they know full well that his heart pumps gall. The gates stay closed, though inside the walls the situation is becoming desperate. The siege began in the spring, the fall is coming on, the plague has arrived and hunger is claiming lives. Prince William has but one option now. Breach the dykes; let the sea flood the land and the encampment; force the Spaniards to flee or drown. The dykes are cut. The wait is on for a decent North Sea storm. Finally one blows in. The water gets whipped on. Dutch barges carrying roughnecks set off. They punt their way over pastures to the town.

The Spaniards, up to at least their waists in water, flail and go under, or scatter. Leyden is freed and the Dutch revolt goes on.

The siege of Leyden is a turning point, not only for Dutch independence – history more broadly lurches into another direction.

~

Drawing smoke from the pipe, Carlos gazed at the unchanged pastures and steadfast spires. This cultural-religious conflict had a balance sheet and he began to draw it up. Suppose Philip of Spain had not thought one-dimensionally in matters of faith. Suppose other beliefs hadn't been designated as heresies. Suppose the King had allowed religious consciences to be free. And suppose he had permitted the distant Dutch to keep on running their affairs pretty well in their own way. Would they have revolted? If not, would Philip have lost his northern realm so thoroughly?

Suppose, Carlos reflected further, Philip had hung on to Holland. Economically, wouldn't Spain have done better? The Dutch had a talent for business. That talent could have flourished within a framework linking them to Spain. Meaning that fourteen years after the Leyden debacle, in 1588 when Spain clashed with England, Philip could also have counted on his Dutch possessions to provide support when he launched the Armada. Would the English fleet have been able then to defeat the Armada the way they did by keeping it bottled up in the Channel? Because with Dutch war ships sailing from Amsterdam through the Zuiderzee into the North Sea, threatening Drake's rear, the English wouldn't have had their pivotal and exclusive strategic windward advantage. England could well have been defeated. As victor, what would Philip have done with Queen Elizabeth? Would England's post-1588 commercial empire have come into existence? Or, without strong English competition, would Spain's imperial reach not have spread still wider than it did?

At Leyden, King Philip of Spain probably lost all this.

Historical second-guessing was an entertaining pastime for Carlos. It might even provide lessons. He taps the pipe against the sole of the wooden shoe to empty the bowl. What lesson can be gleaned from that bleak Spanish king? That monomaniacal thinkers who crave control over the consciences of others invariably fail – because the conscience of a reasoning mind is indomitable.

~

In a minor way Carlos saw himself in all this. Philip's tyranny reflected something larger. Ignorance. For centuries that ignorance continued. It busied Spanish priests who kept their religious pots boiling. When Carlos was a youth the family priest was still that way. No real harm was done to him. Carlos easily survived the attempt to terminate his conscience. On the dyke, a look of *ex post facto* satisfaction spread across his face.

The thoughts you have if you dress up! Carlos's, though pleasurable, were also slightly tiring. Stretching full out on the blanket, the sun continuing to bestow its blessing, Carlos dozed off. In a state of partial dreaming he saw William the Silent and King Philip II square off. Tolerance pitted against bigotry. Reason confronting prejudice. Generosity wrestling with mean-spiritedness. In this fantasy Carlos progressively began to see his own hairy head positioned between Prince William's shoulders. He dreamed that, centaur-like, he was prancing off to vanquish all the King Philip types in history.

Awakening, back in the present, Carlos savoured the dream. Suddenly an idea hit. He consulted his watch and saw there was time. Quickly he slipped out of the farmer's costume, back into his humdrum ethnographer's garb. The bike bags were repacked and he was off. Next stop? Delft's great cathedral. Why? Because that's where the Dutch Prince lies buried.

Carlos knew the cathedral well. When he and Natalia arrived last summer, almost their first act of tourism was to view it. She walked up and down its vast interior with mostly an architectural interest. He in contrast stood quietly for some time next to William the Silent's mausoleum. Having read Dutch history prior to arriving, and having developed his own perspective of the sixteenth century Dutch-Spanish conflict, he was fascinated by the epithet behind Prince William's name: *The Silent*. Feeling close to the man, to his style and stand against tyranny, Carlos had gone back several times. "Why shouldn't I go on a pilgrimage now and then?" he would say to Natalia. "Where the Prince is, is where I wish to be." Hastily he added, "I mean, not down there in the crypt. I mean, in terms of conduct. Imagine using silence to advocate tolerance."

Having witnessed Prince William the Silent of Orange's act of drawing on the sea to send the Spanish running, Carlos raced to Leyden for ten solemn minutes of silent proximity.

Chapter 8

"You should have told me!" Natalia exclaimed over a pre-dinner drink. "If I'd known you planned to dress up that way, I'd have joined you." She and Carlos were on the patio, and the late day sunlight touched the treetops, giving each fresh spring leaf up there a private halo. Spare rays trickled through to down below and bathed them too.

Carlos bit his lip. He had described his outing in detail – the gear he lugged along and why he wore it – but he had not expected Natalia to react with this sharp disappointment.

"I've seen postcards of traditional Dutch costumes," she continued. "Imagine me looking like a farmer's wife – tight bodice, ballooning black skirt, pointy white cap, big gold hairpins sticking out. I sort of have the figure for it. And all that on a dyke. Too good for words. Why did you leave me out?"

"I changed on the dyke, Natalia. It was in public. I stood in my underwear. People passing by on their bikes whistled at me."

"You think that would have stopped me? I'd have smoked from your pipe too. And guzzled Dutch gin from a jug if you'd thought to bring some. Well, here's to your hour of Dutchness. May it make you a better person." She raised her glass and changed her tone. "So the Dutch slashed their dykes to save themselves from tyranny. Do you really think that if they hadn't, if Philip had starved Leyden into submission and Holland had remained a Spanish province, the end play would have been the Armada sending the English packing?"

"Oh sure," was Carlos's glib reply. "A few dozen war ships sailing out of Amsterdam, going around North Holland into the North Sea, getting at Drake from behind, him squeezed in between Dutch warships and the Armada – an English defeat would have been as good as certain. England was pretty well defenseless apart from their navy. Without it, the Spanish army would have marched into London for sure. *That* would have changed the world. Spanish might have become North America's mother tongue. Think of it. English hanging on as a quaint local language, sort of like Danish."

"Next time I see Heiko de Bruyn I'll mention that theory. I think he would like it. The siege of Leyden as a turning point for the modern world. He says the Dutch revolt made his ancestors wealthy. The wealth didn't last, but at least he knows that three, four centuries ago his family was prominent. Which is more than I can claim. I have no idea how my family lived before 1850. I think they scratched an existence out of the Ukrainian steppes."

"You know my views on ancestry, Natalia. I can understand ancestral worship by ancient cults, building Stonehenge for example. Ancestors were a spiritual force reaching through the generations. But overall, ancestry can be a burden. Minimizing baggage from the past brings more levity to life, that's my philosophy."

"I know, but it's a tough attitude. Most people draw strength from knowing their roots. Speaking of life and levity and the like, how was our peace man? Is Paradis back on his feet?"

"Almost. He's vertical enough now to get into a wheelchair. I predict, in a month or two, he'll be pumping hands at the peace meetings again."

"Let's invite him over for a drink sometime, when he's up to it. I'd be interested in his ideas."

~

Ideas. Ideas for peace. Or, peace as a big idea.

On the patio, in the pleasant spring air, Natalia enjoyed bantering with her husband – a golden hour, of which she had too few. But elsewhere, further back in her mind, ideas were besieging her. They arrived from everywhere – from within herself, from Carlos right now, from Heiko last Saturday at their meeting, from Robbie when she saw her, from Ranford Tolman, ambassador to the United Nations in New York, when she talked to him. Sometimes, Natalia thought, her brain was like a roaring mill that crushed and processed ore so that minute amounts of value could be extracted. It had been this way for weeks. So yes, amidst all the other stimuli, she really was interested in Paradis's ideas, especially since his calling card said PEACE.

As her husband listed details of Spanish atrocities in ancient Dutch polders, she would have liked to question him more closely about the underlying causes for all that. An issue she had begun wrestling with was mediation, that is, how to file the edges off cultural conflicts. Carlos, committed student that he was of the forces of religion, identity and tradition, was never short of ideas for turning origins of wars into arguments for peace. But she couldn't probe him too directly. It could cause him to turn the tables. Suppose he began asking why the subject interested her so constantly these days. "If news of our pursuit leaks out," de Bruyn reminded her routinely, "if it gets into the media, we would have to issue a denial. That would end it. Very few know what we're planning. Let's be vigilant so that doesn't change." So openness was denied, including with her husband. It wasn't natural for Natalia not to share her excitement, to be forced into silence, to pursue the ambassadorial humdrum with an outward show of nonchalance. She itched to tell her husband that she had been asked to take the structures supporting global peace a huge leap forward. If only she could say, *and by the way, Carlos, since you're the world's expert on the ethnic underpinnings of conflict, I'd like you to contribute to this work.* Imagine the depth of insight and variety of opinions – the richness of the ore – that would come her way then. But no, she could only get to his ideas casually, by steering their marital banter.

"That war went on for eighty years?" Natalia enquired in between sips. "Was it avoidable?"

"Naturally," Carlos replied laconically. "Philip had no notion of building bridges between cultures, no sense of levering political progress out of demonstrating respect for others. He had an absolute conviction there was no way but his. Rebellion became inevitable and rebellion usually shrinks a realm. He was just another of all the many inept tyrant kings, and he paid for it. Mind you, most rulers have that blind spot, a certainty that they are always right. But then, that's why they are rulers."

"What do think would prevent it?" Natalia asked lightly. "I mean, rulers becoming tyrants."

Carlos shrugged. "The remedies? They are known, but difficult to apply. Less power for individuals and elites. Strong competing institutions. Religion pushed back into the only place where it may do some good, the individual's inner life. And there should be privileges and prizes everywhere for the cultural heralds of this world."

Natalia leaned back, slowly lifting her arms into a lazy stretch. "Cultural heralds? That's got a nice ring. Do you mean the people who get other people to talk and listen, rather than to point muskets?"

"I mean the people who know how to open eyes and bring down barriers. Your glass is empty, Natalia. Let me get you a refill." Carlos rose.

"When you're back tell me more about those remedies," she called after him. "You make it sound as if there's an apothecary somewhere that's got drawers full of them."

Carlos stopped and laughed. "I can tell you in one second what their common key working ingredient is. Faster political evolution. Humanity's big problem is that the rate of progress is set by states that love inertia. Sovereignty means we all have to go at the pace of the slowest. Fortunately some good people are pushing to speed things up." With a hand flip he seemed to wave the topic away, as if it had received the attention it deserved and he had nothing more to say. Natalia watched him head towards the kitchen.

~

Continuing to lean back, she looked up into the sky, which was translucent, like a huge crystal in perfect cobalt blue. She closed her eyes to focus on what Carlos said. Revving up political evolution. Thanks for the suggestion, Carlos. That sure would be good, but how? How do you force politicians out of torpor?

So typical of Carlos to advance his ideas so casually, to make them sound like afterthoughts, as if he'd left them behind, or dismissed them, his mind having moved on to more fertile territory long ago. This was another good example. No sooner had she zeroed in on the vast, fascinating topic of culture and conflict – with much outward indifference – than he declared it could be summed up in a few words. Reducing the power of individuals and elites, push back religion. If only it was that simple. Then he threw in, fairly enigmatically, that some good people were working on this. Who were they? And how were they going to be pushing it? It interested Natalia because de Bruyn had said something quite similar. So here were two men, different in almost every way, both arguing that global politics needs to take on new forms. Natalia wished she could explain to Carlos why she wanted him to expand on this.

De Bruyn had come to the notion of political evolution early on, not long after the two of them had settled into meeting in his office once a week on Saturday mornings, regular as clockwork. Weekend work brought an advantage, he claimed. "No one around. No one to become nosy."

All week Natalia would have been crushing and refining intellectual ore, and by the time she settled on the small sofa opposite de Bruyn's oak throne she tried to have a few nuggets ready. Social niceties were dispensed with, allowing them to plunge right in. Their topics? Ending conflict, preventing violence, protecting civilians, stopping the killing, building durable peace. As they worked their way through options, Natalia often felt excitement coming on, as if something rare and beautiful, something elevated, was calling out to her. De Bruyn, in contrast, appeared about as emotional as a stone. Well, she thought, that's your fate if the sober blood of aristocratic forebears fills your veins. Despite de Bruyn's detachment, however, he had ways of lifting discussions. Occasionally Natalia experienced doubt. She asked him once if he did too. "How do we get governments to agree to all this?" she wondered. De Bruyn refused to think that way. "We are building a temple," he said flatly, like someone talking about a fence that needed painting. "It's a temple to sanity. I am one of those who take the view that the world is becoming saner, that the main problem today is that it's going too slow." His voice was emotionless, yet signalled idealism. He elaborated on this "temple to sanity" metaphor. He was convinced that in recent decades humanity was showing signs of rising.

"Rising?"

"Out of its starting conditions."

"As in Adam and Eve?" Natalia asked lightly, laughing.

De Bruyn's eyebrows knotted. "Yes, its starting conditions." He said it severely, as if her glibness aggravated him. "What was our original state?" he asked. Natalia made no attempt to answer and he delivered a little speech about tribal behaviour at the beginning of time, the focus on survival, the competition, the suspicion and distrust, the thievery between clans, which led to quarrelling, skirmishing and killing. Tribes formed nations, nations grew into empires. Throughout, combat became more formalized and soldiering more professional. As carnage escalated, war brought ever more glory and battle became steadily more honourable. Finally, humanity had its ultimate war experience – one detonation and, in seconds, hundreds of thousands of people were dead. Even for the most warlike this proved too terrifying. "A few sane people declared *no more*," de Bruyn continued. "I believe the large, formal wars are behind us. We have learned they bring no advantage. But we do have the local wars and the dispersed informal wars. What are their causes? For me there are two. One category is containable. I'm talking about causes such as greed, poverty and those specific individuals amongst us who crave absolute power. The second category is more difficult to address. It consists of things that form the core of ordinary people. I'm referring to kinship, beliefs, the collective memory, which are fundamental, constructive aspects of the human condition. They provide us with our identities and satisfy our social needs. Regrettably they all have flip sides that are irrational and terribly destructive."

A slight tremor of ardour crept into de Bruyn's voice. "Our job, Natalia, is to figure out how such cultural conflicts can be contained. I believe the world is ready for it. There are signs enough. We are moving from distrust to cooperation. We are becoming more respectful of differences. Standards of living by and large are improving. And we have the doctrine your country steered into existence – the overarching, collective duty and right to provide security to civilians when their own governments refuse. Is it not interesting that now, after five thousand years of recorded history, we finally have the insight that individuals must be called to account if they commit crimes against humanity. My conclusion? As a species we are showing signs of rising out of our starting conditions. Equally obvious is that the pace should be speeding up."

Waiting for Carlos to return with refills, Natalia dwelt on de Bruyn's stamp-sized summary of the history of humanity. His conclusion and Carlos's flippant summary were neatly identical. How many others thought that same way, she wondered. How many millions share the view that a global *nous* exists, that it is becoming more aware, that it understands the time has come for humanity's killing habits to end? Which brought her back to Paradis. His PEACE organization. Could there be ways to bring its huge membership – the ordinary people everywhere who abhor conflict and evil – into the secret peace initiative? Natalia really did want to see him and harvest his ideas.

When Carlos was back and handed her a fresh martini, he joked, "your remedy. It comes with a warning, though. The apothecary who dispensed it is unlicensed."

~

Weeks went by and Natalia's peace pursuit eased into a higher gear. But the embassy dross continued, too. Keeping the programs humming, seeking a little wriggle room inside the straightjacket of the never-ending diplomatic invitations, lifting grains of common sense out of bizarre headquarters instructions, valiantly lubricating the ten thousand interconnected gears known as the administrative rules, which had been designed to grind life to a standstill. No one detected that the ambassador's charisma was now just a mask that had a higher purpose seething behind it. This fissured way of functioning wasn't easy for Natalia. She wasn't used to maintaining silence if a topic or an issue was inflaming her. So thank God Robbie was around. Monastic Robbie, taciturn Robbie, Robbie as confidante, Robbie as listener. Robbie brought relief. With Robbie, Natalia could rip the mask off.

This happened once or twice a week, in an atmosphere of stealth. It had to be that way. Suppose Gus, or another of the program heads, picked up a pattern and started questioning why the consular section was getting so much of the ambassador's attention. And suppose Gus, with his forehead furrowed, then whispered through the phone to one of the headquarters' minders that the ambassador's behaviour had abruptly turned odd. Someone somewhere would start digging. Questions would get asked, perhaps about Robbie's files. What was she up to that gave them this undue political importance? Nothing would be found, but then what? Would off-colour insinuations get sprinkled into stray conversations? Could titillating rumours about the older and the younger woman get floated just to see where they might drift to? It was obvious. Collusion with Robbie had to be kept secret. A secret within a secret. They met in Natalia's office only if the embassy's top floor had emptied for the day. If Gus or someone else worked late, they went to a safe place, a teahouse a few blocks away. The scruffy-cozy atmosphere there catered to an indecorous milieu, which explained why it was Robbie's favourite. Natalia also saw the advantage: no embassy program head, Gus especially, would ever be caught dead in a place like that. But during evenings when Natalia had no social obligations, and if Carlos was away, Robbie would drop in at the residence. Relaxing on sofas, sipping drinks and munching celery sticks, they would talk about peace as if comparing glossy photos in fashion catalogues. That is, they wandered off topic a lot. Spending time this way with Robbie was relaxing for Natalia. With Robbie she didn't have to weigh each word; rough thoughts could be voiced. The hours with Robbie felt whole. Of these places – office, residence or teahouse – which was most productive? Where did the best big, bold, free thinking happen? Where were they least off topic? Natalia wasn't sure. Her office brought rigour, whereas the residence drawing room induced something opposite to that. As for the teahouse, though they were never there for long, the herbal beverages seemed to render their minds unusually fertile.

"So now, Robbie, we're outside the box. Can you feel it?" Natalia had positioned them this way the first time they sat amidst the slovens, haggard mothers ignoring their infants and young pimple-faced intellectuals who talked non-stop. "We begin by emptying ourselves of preconceived notions. Imagine we are observing the dawn of the world. Let's say it is the day of Creation. We know now that in the model which came along that week, when humanity appeared on the planet, greed, envy, jealousy, bullying and the lust for power were immediately in existence." Natalia was shamelessly borrowing de Bruyn's starting conditions. "Slightly later, frustrated ambitions, threats to security, double standards and denied freedoms came along. Unless you can think of more reasons why people fight, let's say these are the essential causes of conflicts."

Robbie lifted her tea mug and closed her eyes, savouring the aroma. "Why *do* people fight?" she said introspectively. She looked at the scene around her and thought a little longer. "Misunderstanding is a cause too. Misunderstandings do terrible things. As does an absence of understanding. And then there is victimization."

"Victimization?" Natalia sat up. Thoughts of papa flashed through her head.

"I've got an example." Robbie began to explain her home, Ramea, once a decent place for people wanting to work and earn a living. Existence in the village had idyllic cycles. The men went out to fish; the women did the shore things. There were tragedies, to be sure. Fishermen didn't always make it back. "My daddy was one. His boat went down in a storm. I was a baby, so I never knew him." There was tragedy, yes, but good times too, plus reasons to hope the next catch would be especially good. Then suddenly the fish were gone. Centuries of abundance were followed by nothing.

"Everybody nowadays knows why, sort of, but nobody really understands it. Many people in many places could have prevented it, though they all claim someone else was responsible. The scientists didn't do it. Nor did the politicians. The Spaniards deny it was them. Ditto the Portuguese. And absolutely not the Eurocrats in Brussels. Nobody." Robbie described how, although it was preventable, the ancient rhythm of the sea had been extinguished, and the fishing communities along with it. "The fishermen were victims. They felt that others had played with their livelihoods, which they then lost and they were powerless to stop it. It created an urge for retribution."

Natalia had been looking into Robbie's eyes, seeing the slight scowl of bitterness. But Robbie shrugged it off, satisfied perhaps that she'd finished her rant about power hierarchies far away screwing up life's vital strands. "I see you are a firebrand in hiding," Natalia said. "I should be shaking up a double martini to show my deep commiseration. I know about victimization. I've seen it too. Victims do ugly things. OK, one more reason why people fight and kill. Victimization is added to the list. Does that complete the picture from the Ramean perspective?"

"We could talk about democracy denied, you know, people not being heard."

"I had that, I think. Denial of freedom."

"Sorry. Yes."

"Good. Let's go back to standing outside the box. Let's now say that humanity's been around for a while and it's been doing its squabbling and killing for all the reasons we've identified. Suddenly, humanity speaking as one comes to you, Robbie, and says it has come to its senses. It begs *you* to instruct it how to stop the killing. It will do whatever you say. What would you say?" Natalia sipped tea and waited.

Robbie's hands remained wrapped around her mug. "Sounds like a trick question."

Natalia chuckled, but not loudly, more a private kind of chuckle, its sound not rising above the café din. All the same, Robbie laughed along. "You're dodging," Natalia accused her. "You know, not long ago I had a question like that put to me and my reaction was the same. I dodged too. But that simple question – *What would you do?* – grows on you. If you were empowered to stop the killing, what steps would you take? You don't have to answer right now. Next time if you want."

When Natalia faced this question, she had transported herself to many places and situations. What is the answer to Africa's tribal killing? Why doesn't Balkan ethnic and religious hatred end? What can be done about government policies that create hatred and nurture terrorism? What solutions can counter absolutist beliefs such as the ones held by America's evangelists, Iran's mullahs and other robotic religionists?

Robbie scarcely moved, apart from lifting the mug of tea to her lips, as she worked out an answer. "If humanity tasked me," she finally said, "I would start by dealing with testosterone."

Natalia was taken aback. "Testosterone? OK … Good. You mean we go around the world and cut off testicles. Well, why not, I guess."

"I mean it figuratively."

"I'll say this, that *is* an outside-the-box idea. What do you have in mind?"

"When I went to school, then university, looking around, I saw a lot of young male chest beating – great ape behaviour. It wasn't too different from tomcats tearing each other to pieces and moose pounding their horns at each other."

"I get the point. I get it. Let's think of the solution. Let's postulate that humanity is in agreement with you – that we're trapped like all the other animals, competing and fighting on account of the urge to pass on our genes. Let's also say that humanity, being capable of reasoning, decides to get a grip on that aggression. It wants you to deal with testosterone and gives you green lights the whole way. Now what?"

"It's not that tough," Robbie replied sweetly. "Figuratively speaking, we only have to find an anti-testosterone and deploy that. We start small. We start with governments. We know there's lots of testosterone in government. Would squirting some anti-testosterone into them be that difficult?"

"You're losing me, Robbie."

"I thought about this in a university history seminar. The seminar was about armies, battles and dead soldiers piled up in mass graves. I thought, governments seem to have an urgent inner drive to fight. The next question is, where in government is the aggression institutionalized? Where in government does the level of testosterone reach a peak?"

"Prime ministers' offices," Natalia remarked glumly.

"I was thinking of the war departments. If you think of anti-testosterone in the context of war departments, it leads you to consider creating anti-war departments. What's a good name for an anti-war department?"

Natalia gazed at Robbie, her eyelids dropping until they were half-shut. A slow smile formed. "That's good, Robbie. Peace departments." Natalia's tea mug rose in a salute. "This is a eureka moment."

~

The ore processor in Natalia's mind was roaring when she hurried from the teahouse to a diplomatic dinner. It turned out to be cold and sluggish, a glacial type of evening. Her table companion was a retired Amsterdam judge and the only thing on *his* mind was a monograph he was writing on the emerging jurisprudence for certain ethnic minorities who, on religious grounds, claimed the right not to pay interest on their mortgages. In other circumstances she would have egged him on, but she had become too engaged by the question of how peace departments could function. The venerable judge eventually concluded the ambassador was boring and showed her his back. Silently consuming the dessert, Natalia was framing points to put to de Bruyn. *If governments decide to attend a peace summit, Heiko, they have to show they're serious. They will want to institutionalize the new peace focus. Developing a strong counter-balance to fighting-ready defence departments would be a minimum step, don't you think?*

The next day, too, Natalia's mind churned along. Just before leaving the embassy for Rotterdam to attend a harbour development celebration, she left Robbie a voice message. *Good morning, Robbie. Your take on testosterone yesterday was good. Must have been the tea that did it. Keep drinking! I'm busy today, but I don't want your anti-war department idea to get cold. I've got nothing on tonight. Carlos is in Africa for three days. Can you come to the residence? Say about eight? Lots to discuss. Call me on the cell phone to confirm.*

In Rotterdam, Natalia listened to long speeches on yet another Dutch reclamation project, the construction this time of a marvellous industrial peninsula, planned to reach far into the North Sea. A stiff breeze blowing in from across the frigid waters played with the microphone, making most of what was said incomprehensible. A seafood lunch followed. It was inside a tent struck on a spot where, not long ago, ocean waves had rolled towards land.

Back in the car, Dirk announced that Miss Warren had called. "She said to say *OK*." Natalia nodded. Still before her was an afternoon of meetings, Bulgaria's national day reception and a tequila reception at the Mexican ambassador's place for a delegation touring Europe to promote that drink.

When she was finally home, the obstacle-course day over, Natalia took stock. At lunch, two glasses of very good white wine and one chilled aquavit. During the afternoon meetings, several cups of coffee and too many cookies. Then two glasses of Bulgarian red, followed by three shots of classy tequilas. It was enough to make her pine for a decent martini just to forget. The chef had left her something in the oven and Robbie would arrive in twenty minutes. She allocated the remaining time: change into her ancient, favourite wine-red house coat, mix up a martini, then wolf down some dinner. Or better still, have dinner first, then the martini.

The doorbell rang when Natalia was halfway through her food. She set the plate aside, tightened the house coat belt and strode to the door in slippers. Robbie stood there, tall and smirking like a loyal co-conspirator. "Hi Natalia."

"You bring with you the essence of the light spring air. I'm glad you could make it. Excuse me for looking frumpy."

In the kitchen, cracking ice cubes for drinks, Natalia remarked that all day long wherever she went she had seen testosterone. "Men. Only men. Mostly nice ones, mind you. Except for two Mexicans. The things they said! Total captives of their hormones." She poured a thimbleful of vermouth and a liberal dose of vodka into a thermos, added ice and shook it. Robbie poured herself a glass of tonic water. When they were settled in the drawing room

Natalia said, "My day was full of men. Was yours?" She poured from the thermos into a large whisky glass.

"Only one. A detective. We had tea."

"In his workplace?"

"In a café."

"A young detective?"

"About my age."

"Business?"

"At first. He had news of the investigation into Alistair's plane crash. The report is done. It concludes what we've known all along: the plane missed the runway on account of poor visibility and a wind gust during landing. Case closed. After that we talked more generally."

"You enjoyed it?"

"He has good manners."

Natalia pulled her feet up under her, lifted the glass and sipped before snuggling into the sofa pillows. "This is nice. If you weren't here I would be – I don't know – I'd be reading a briefing book. So you spotted good male manners, Robbie. Where did you learn to do that? Ramea?"

Robbie laughed. "Another trick question."

"Don't dodge again. I want to know about male manners on Ramea. Or were there none? Is that why you left?"

"I left because there was nothing there for me except stressed-out aunts. I was accepted into university, took out student loans, and applied for jobs in far away places. Miraculously, offers came back. Someone out there wanted me! I had difficulty believing it. I thought, though, that consular work would be neat because it was about helping people." Robbie grimaced, as if to say, *That's me. That's all there is.*

Natalia had suspected all along that Robbie, like her, was a refugee of sorts, and hadn't come close to describing the full experience. She muttered, "I think you're holding back. I think you have more tales to tell." Briefly, she lifted the glass to her lips. As it drifted back down she made an admission. "What you did is sort of what happened to me too. I also decided to leave others behind. But unlike you, I made a mistake. I got married before I left."

"You said that. To Nav, right? Or was it Navvy?"

"I called him Navvy. He called me Natty. Sometimes he added Nifty. Nifty Natty. In that case, I said, I'm adding Narco to you. That made him Narco Navvy." Recalling this amused Natalia. "He wasn't a hard core narco," she said fondly. "He just liked to puff a few joints. When I told him I was going to become a diplomat, he was high. It took him five minutes to process the information and he said that just totally blew his mind. I was having problems with my papa in those days. My hanging out with Nav bugged him a lot. When I decided to go away it added to the stink. My papa wanted me to go into real estate. He said I had a good personality for it. He wished to see me rise through the ranks, maybe end up as president of the Vancouver Real Estate Agents Association. That world was magical for him. So much easy money. By then I was rejecting everything he had in mind for me, and I announced I was also planning to marry Nav. It just about killed him. A day or two later I proposed to Nav. When we tied the knot, I did it with bitter determination. A funny-sad relationship began, but it lasted a surprisingly long time."

Natalia described Nav having a preference for very thin books, a serious interest in folk music, and empathy for the underprivileged. He also had numerous friends, all light, all volatile. Conversations for them consisted of one-word sentences interspersed with grunts. Nav had an aversion too, to regular work and steady hours. But hey, Nifty Natty was good at that. Bread on the table courtesy of your chick. After Vancouver, when Natalia was in the diplomatic service, they moved around. The places were groovy and the bread got better. With Nifty Natty's loot, Narco Navvy flew back to Vancouver a couple of times a year to see his pals. He told them freaky sagas about pigs in blue suits running the world. Natty didn't mind any of this. Keeping Nav going was sort of like donating to charity. It also brought advantages. Going home at the end of the day to a man who had spent one hour composing a new folk song and eight more going out of his mind with lust wasn't all that bad a prospect. The Nifty-Narco show lasted for over a decade, until Nav's frustration spilled over and trumped his comfort. Strumming the guitar year in year out was nice enough, until it dawned on him it would be nicer still if others heard it. He had a brainwave. Since he went where Natty was sent during their first dozen years, the next twelve should be his.

Natalia made a face – *My lunacies in life.* She took two quick sips and rolled on. "Nav wanted us to go back to Vancouver, where his musical career would blossom. I asked what that meant. Playing the guitar and singing in bars, he answered. Will that earn us a living? I wanted to know. He confirmed it would, though for the first while it would require patience. Anyway, why worry about it since I would find work in a bank, or something along those lines. We were on our third posting at the time. South Africa. We had already put in years in Moscow and Islamabad, but I liked South Africa. I didn't want to pull out, go back to the West Coast and count twenty-dollar bills all day long.

"The following weeks were rough. Harangues. Tantrums. Things like that. It was clear I had to cut my losses. I comforted him, promised him a nice financial package and we parted. It wasn't easy for me. The relationship did have a perverse juiciness. He was my man, but also my child. I didn't like the idea of that failing. I still pay alimony. It gives me a good feeling, sort of like making an investment in a child's continuing education. Then Carlos came along. He allowed me to understand that the fit I needed with a man was the opposite of what Donovan brought. I wanted to explain Donovan to Carlos, but it didn't interest him much. He shrugged and told me he didn't think that I was meant to be a tomato ripening slowly on the vine. I had to think about that for a while."

Natalia leaned forwards, took the thermos and refilled her glass. Once more, she hugged a sofa pillow. "So good talking with you, Robbie. I want you to promise, if you meet up with that young detective again, you have to inform me. What is his name?"

Robbie studied her tonic water. "Maarten Valk. I doubt I'll see him again."

"Why not? If he invited you for tea, why not invite him back? Men don't invite charming women to have tea in restaurants just to pass on bureaucratic reports. The mail can do that just as well." With Robbie continuing to look down, she added, "Well, if nothing else, let's at least toast him. To Maarten." Robbie didn't budge. "Well, if not to Maarten, then to Maarten as an idea. I'm in an ideas phase these days." She raised her glass.

Robbie's detachment broke. "OK. As an idea. Rejecting an idea isn't difficult. Cheers."

"Oh," Natalia cooed. "It sounds like this is a toast to a man rebuffed." Their glasses clinked. "I have to say, Robbie, sometimes you worry me. You are hyper sober, which is fine. Just don't be that way all the time." Robbie didn't bite. "Well, who am I to talk?" Natalia sniffed. "I'm sort of hyper sober's hyper opposite, but let's not get into that. We wanted to talk peace and we should." She became serious. "I'm meeting Heiko again on Saturday and I need to have something clever ready. Alright if we spend five minutes on peace departments?" Robbie nodded.

Natalia, with exaggeration, as though she had just arrived to chair a meeting, assumed a formal posture on the sofa. "I have thought about peace departments, I have. I have thought about them ... and began to wonder ... would anyone respect them? What, concretely, would peace departments do?" Natalia's voice was louder now. She recognized it, halted, and brought it down. Very calmly, she said, "We can't just get rid of war departments. Belligerent regimes and terrorists won't go away. War departments ensure order." She tried to sit stiffly, but her torso tottered slightly all the same.

"I can see that," Robbie answered. "But if billions are spent on soldiering, why not some on anti-soldiering?"

Natalia closed her eyes. "Elaborate please. What are the functions of peace departments?"

Robbie, hyper sober dear soul that she was, obliged and Natalia, sitting very still, as if asleep, was lulled. She saw a picture being painted, a scene that really was quite beautiful. On the canvas in her mind, highly trained legions, not wearing uniforms or helmets, nor carrying rifles, were spreading out over human landscapes threatened by war. Their objective? To build societies up, not tear them down. She saw skilled mediators giving hope to people threatened by conflict and, as differences between cultures were bridged, new prospects arising for mutual respect. The actions were potent, disciplined and professional – commando troops that reach into the mind.

Robbie had long ago ceased speaking, but Natalia – her eyes remaining closed, not wishing to lose the moment – sat stiff. Finally she was jarred out by Robbie announcing that it was time she left. "I guess you must," Natalia muttered. Robbie got up and Natalia did the same, holding the side of the sofa until she had balance. In her slippers, she slid more than walked alongside Robbie to the door. Slurring a little, she said,

"F-f-resh thinking, Robbie. We're not finisshed. How you gettin' home?"

"The bus. There's a stop up the road." Robbie kissed Natalia on the cheek and was gone.

When Natalia turned in the hallway, dead weights seemed to hang from her. Dumbly she studied her course. A final martini? She shook her head emphatically. So it was to bed. With both hands on the banister – a heavy self-lifting – she ascended. In the bathroom she got around by grasping at the towel racks. In the bedroom she found a way to get the house coat off. When she fell backwards onto the mattress her head was swimming. Swimming through what? Through Robbie's landscapes? Gathering a last quantum of awareness, she thought, *Natty is canny, but Robbie is brilliant.*

Chapter 9

What if she stumbles, Robbie thought, stepping away from the front door, *or feels dizzy going up the stairs and falls.* An ingrained habit, dormant for years, brought her to a halt.

There was a time when Robbie was accustomed to playing the role of ministering angel – to cousins, their friends and other wayward types. The attention they needed was always the same: a steadying arm, patience at the pit stops, an ear open to heartfelt confessions and, of course, some back-patting when violent retching occurred. The black sheep were guided home with sympathy, stripped of coats, boots and other layers, and ordered to sleep it off – on a soiled mattress, a sagging sofa, worn-out floor mats, or nothing special at all.

Not that Natalia fell into this category. You couldn't compare her to the rudderless, blaspheming descendants of Ramea's noble fishermen. Nor to the crowd she hung out with in university – the bleary-eyed and pasty-faced sons of the shifty merchant class in St John's. Not a bit. But all the same, shouldn't she go back in to make sure? *Hi Natalia. Me again. Think I left my house key in the vestibule. Managing OK?* Robbie debated. A minute passed. When a second story window sprang to life she broke into a grin. Staring up, she briefly entertained an inner image. A lonely soul in a dinghy was returning from an outing on the sea. The water had turned restless. Waves were heaving. There had to be some hard pulling on the oars to get past the headlands. A short while later, in snug harbourage, the calm that followed was utterly complete.

That Natalia! She sure lost count of her drinks. Why did she overdo it like that? What caused her to throw back those great big martinis? To escape the ambassadorial hassles for a few hours? Or for pure enjoyment on a rare night without duties? Robbie had never fully understood the drinking habit. Her cousins poured buckets of booze into themselves. They claimed it was to forget. To forget what? They said, to forget their small island existence. Robbie agreed that conditions on the island weren't ideal, but all the same, with a shove-of-self you could set your sights higher. This wasn't applicable to Natalia, though. As far as Robbie could make out, there was nothing seriously major that Natalia needed to forget or achieve. So what could her reason be? *I could ask*, Robbie thought. She's given me a green light to be merciless. I could go into her office tomorrow and make it seem I've got a concern. *Natalia, you were three sheets to the wind last night. Whatever for? Were you pretending to be drinking holy water?* What would Natalia say to that? You had to anticipate a reply that would freeze you in your tracks. Robbie tried to think how Natalia would leave you dumbfounded. *Why practice moderation if you were born to love excess.* Something along those lines.

That Natalia.

In the darkness, on the lane twisting through the residence's grounds, rhododendrons towering on both sides created a gorge that seemed deep and squeezing. At intervals there were night-lights, which gave a sense of widening. Compression, expansion, compression. A rhythm. Which acted as a cue. Robbie's concern for Natalia gave way to amusement, which flipped into generosity before tipping into merriment.

Take the ambassador's affair with her martinis. She wasn't out to keep it secret. As an example, at the Friday office happy hours, should the ambassador be in town and join in, the staff winked at the disappearing drinks. The first glass was often slow, sipped with introspection, but the second freed her, as if the issues of the week weighing down on her were vaporizing. During the third martini, if she had time for it, an expansive, fun-filled discourse would begin with anyone nearby. There was a pattern to this, a modest pattern, but still a pattern that did nothing to erode the staff's respect. Because surrounding this little pattern was a bigger one, for which the staff thanked their lucky stars. All week long the ambassador provided them with purpose. If something went off the rails, as happens in an embassy, she refused to let them stew in it. Some palliative phrase would pop out. *Why let worry stain life's beauty.* Natalianisms. That's what they were called. Each one the ambassador delivered was shared, remembered and reused. So who cared if occasionally she had one martini too many?

Making her way along the lane, Robbie smiled inwardly at Natalia's eagerness to lift all and sundry out of tedium. Look at this evening. Another one spent as full-blown theater: touches of melodrama, much satire, personal flaws presented as farce. The piece about Nifty Natty and Narco Navvy. How good was that?

Other fragments drifted back. Natalia's self-description as a hyper-opposite to hyper sobriety. Its meaning wasn't entirely clear. Was it plain deadly honesty about her relationship with alcohol? Or was the use of *sobriety* meant differently, more along the lines of *solemnity*? A self-pigeonholing, in other words, as being anti solemn.

Robbie now came around to what Natalia had said about her, and it made her grimace. Was she truly hyper sober? Was that how others saw her? As sober, somber, colourless? Robbie didn't like to think so. True, she wasn't ostentatious. She lacked Natalia's flair for jewels and clothes, and generally had simpler tastes. On the other hand, if Natalia lived theatrically, she did too. Therefore, no, Robbie convinced herself, leaving the residence grounds and aiming for the bus stop, she was not somber, nor colourless. It wasn't theater all the time. Not every day. Nor were her dramas terribly intense, or overwhelmingly chromatic. But in her own way, she did appear in sideshows that were not uninteresting. Just today there had been one – tea with the detective from DINPOL. Granted, a tea date is not that exotic, although Natalia did her best to make it seem so, yet in its own way it had been theatrical. Tea with Maarten Valk had a prologue of a sort, and a finale, plus a few acts and scenes in between. As female lead, Robbie had even experienced butterflies.

She plonked herself down on the bench in the bus shelter and, leaning forward, rested her head in her hands. In this pose, waiting for the bus, she watched the curtain rise on *her* afternoon of drama.

~

ACT 1, SCENE 1

Robbie's phone rings.

"Ah, Miss Warren, hello. Maarten Valk here. Me again … Thank you, yes, I have been well … Yes, the report on the crash. The investigation is over. It was the fog … Yes, I know that Mr Paradis has left the hospital. The rehabilitation clinic will do a good job on him … Why am I calling? Well, the day after tomorrow I will be in The Hague for a meeting. It will be finished in the middle of the afternoon. Would you like to join me for a cup of tea or coffee? … Yes, I will wait a moment … Ah, it will be possible? That will be very nice. Shall we say half-past four? … Good. Very nice. Would it be convenient to meet by the statue of William of Orange in front of the entrance to the Royal Palace?"

ACT 1, SCENE 2

Replacing the phone, a puzzled Robbie stares at it with confusion. *What was that about?*

The question doesn't go away. It remains in her thoughts like a seed that germinates.

Throughout that day and the next, the question becomes: *What will it be like?* The answer is unknown, but the thought does cause a glow. Tea with Maarten Valk could be agreeable. Her memory holds certain details, such as his height and disordered blond hair, the rising forehead and a significant nose.

Robbie tracks the final hours, counts the last few minutes and is off. Her route is along familiar streets, across a bridge, past the teahouse where she sometimes goes with Natalia, then along the walls of the stables behind which the royal horses are kept. The last corner comes, and Robbie takes the plunge … or it takes her.

ACT 2, SCENE 1

Maarten is standing next to the pedestal of the large statue, in front of the royal palace. It is of a prancing stallion carrying a triumphant Prince William of Orange. As Robbie comes up, he grins. "Miss Warren. Goeie dag!"

"Goeie dag, Meneer Valk," Robbie replies in her best accent. It comes off pretty well and she grins too.

"Mooi gezegt." Nicely said, he counters. "You walked?"

"It's not far. Twenty minutes."

"And no rain today. I thought, if the weather is good, this is a nice place to meet. Do you like the palace?"

"Well, yes. And it's in a lovely part of town. Many cosy alleys."

"Shall we go this way? I believe there may be a place by the canal." On the way he asks if they can use first names.

"We may as well."

Maarten nods, satisfied that the name hurdle has been crossed. "*Robbie*," he says, "Nice. Robbie sounds nice." He pronounces it several more times, rolling the R with a slightly too masterful trill.

Maarten also contains an R, but it's half hidden and although Robbie can get the double '*a*' out fine, as in *aah*, she can't quite get the tip of her tongue to vibrate at the right time, so it comes out sounding muffled.

"We must accept," Maarten says, shrugging, "that we may spoil each other's first name."

ACT 2, SCENE 2

They enter a café and settle at a table by a window. It is framed by extravagant lace drapes, with the scene beyond – the flux of cyclists, the canal and red brick buildings opposite – acting as a

126

lively backdrop. The beginning of the dialogue is cautious. Maarten asks about Robbie's day. Robbie enquires whether his afternoon meeting took place. The polite questions serve as a warm up.

Has Robbie been enjoying the spring weather?

Yes, naturally. That is, when possible. Last Saturday she planned to walk the boulevard in Scheveningen because she enjoys the sea breeze and likes to watch happy dogs run around in circles on the beach. But it rained. Maybe this coming weekend will be dry.

"You like to walk on the boulevard? How nice. I grew up in Scheveningen." Maarten is pleased that they have this fishing village in common.

"You were raised in Scheveningen? I live there. Well, just outside. I like it – the pier, the harbour, the lighthouse, the other connections to the sea. I go often."

"My mother still lives there. So you like the sea?"

"I grew up on a small island, just a piece of rock sticking up out of the ocean. The sea is all there is. You read its moods. One moment it's asleep, then in no time it's so violent that you wonder how anything on it can survive. I've only seen calm seas in Scheveningen. Fairly calm, I mean. I haven't gone to the beach when the weather was bad."

"The North Sea can be barbaric. My father would have told you stories about that. He worked in the harbour office. He kept files of stories about fishermen who had to be saved. Sometimes help didn't arrive in time. He was a Scheveninger all his life. As his father was. Long ago, when you could still catch fish, my grandfather was captain of a fishing boat. His boat went down in a storm. No trace was ever found."

"How old was your father when that happened?"

"Seven or eight."

"A family tragedy."

"It was."

"My father was a fisherman and his trawler sank in a storm too."

"I ... I am sorry to hear that."

The confluence of family sorrows causes Maarten's face to cloud over and he seems to disappear into his thoughts. When a tray with tea, coffee and a plate of cookies is brought to their table, he stares at it, as if such petty orderliness is suddenly incomprehensible. Quietly he says, "I am truly very sorry. How old were you?"

"Two."

"Only two." He passes the tea to Robbie and takes the coffee for himself. "You know, my father was not at peace with losing his father. Whenever something made him recollect his eyes filled with tears."

"I don't remember my father. A year later my mother fell ill and she died too. I don't really remember her either. I have a vague mental picture of a room with a large iron stove and a figure in an apron standing in front of it, stirring a pot. She must have been my mother. After she was gone, my aunts took me in. I have three aunts. One is a sister of my father and two are of my mother. They lived close by and every few months I moved from one to the next. They rotated me to share the burden."

ACT 2, SCENE 3

"You grew up with difficulties," Maarten says gravely.

"I remember my aunts were often downcast, but I had plenty of cousins and the days were a riot. Anyway, death was not unusual. It was always in the neighborhood somewhere. Death made us sad twice – once when it happened, and later at the funeral. After the funeral we did chores and after that we played."

"I think that when my grandfather was claimed by the sea my father lost his hero and also his joy. He never overcame the emptiness. I don't recall him ever being happy. My mother was a sunny woman and she and I both laughed easily. But he did not join in. We often felt like we didn't really exist, for him. He was unreachable. As I was growing up, my father was mostly an unknown. I never understood why my mother married him."

"That's not how it was for me. I wanted to believe my mother and father were watching me, or with me, enjoying everything I did. They became an unknown for me only when I was older, when I began to think it would be good if they were still alive. There were many unknowns at that time. Having one less would have been nice. I had my aunts, naturally, and they were kind, but it seemed, if I had my own parents, it would have been better."

Maarten rubs his forehead. "Unknowns," he remarks.

"To tell the truth, some people can't cope with them. I learned that unknowns drove my aunts into a form of captivity. They dreaded the future."

"What is unknown terrifies many people."

"The good thing about my aunts' fear was that it allowed me to realize that if I wasn't careful I could become that way too. I began thinking that maybe I didn't have many answers, but that didn't mean that there weren't any. And if that's true, if answers exist somewhere, why spend the days fearing?"

"You know," replies Maarten, brightening, "I'm also convinced there are answers." He lifts a finger as if he wants to make a special point. "The problem, in my opinion, is the realm in which we experience things. It is very restricting. It is not possible to find true certainty in it. Real answers lie beyond it."

ACT 2, SCENE 4

Robbie is nodding vigorously and sends up a silent message. *Great Source of Truth, is he in communication with you too?*

She grasps that Maarten may be a man of a type she has not met before. He seems to do what she does sometimes – examine an experience, generalize or maybe abstract it, and then determine if what is there yields higher meaning. One minute he is appreciating a story of three aunts, limited by life on a small island, who are anxious about the future. In the next, he concludes that facing unknowns can be terrifying. But there's more. For good measure he goes one step higher. He spins out the view that a grand sphere of certitude must surround the graceless little one in which human experience pointlessly swirls about. Should she share with him the concept of essentiality, given the similarities between Alistair's philosophy and what Maarten has just said? Robbie decides against it. She has had a few encounters in which metaphysics became problematical. Metaphysics can be counted on to deaden easy-going chitchats, and why not keep this pleasant one nimbly moving along?

ACT 2, SCENE 5

Robbie asks Maarten about something that had come up earlier. "Your father. Tell me more about him. He administered the Scheveningen harbour?"

"He was in the administration, yes."

"I've seen postcards of Scheveningen the way it was fifty years ago. The harbour looked so full – trawlers moored so dense you could practically hop, skip and jump your way across from wharf to wharf. It isn't like that now. Did your father ever talk about what happened? Do you know?"

"Do I know?" Maarten breathes in deeply and adjusts his posture from leaning forward to stretching back. He is an expert on the whole sorry story. At the slightest hint of interest, his father would pull out scrapbooks and albums packed with photos of countless ships in port, finely decked out with flags on every mast and strings of them hanging from the riggings. Company pennants, long orange streamers, provincial flags, national flags – everything that will flap in a breeze was there. The mood was always festive. Other photos showed mountains of empty fish barrels stored on the quays waiting to be filled with herring. The North Sea fishery was rich back then. The holds of the trawlers returning from the fishing grounds were so full that the sea swell washed over the decks. And not just herring. There was cod, sole, haddock – all the species, and in abundance. The bounty lasted until the late 1960s, when the catch disappeared to almost nothing. Years of quotas produced faint signs of fish stocks reviving, but that didn't last. Fishing moratoria were decreed. Fishermen became unemployed. The odd load of fish that still came in had been bought in Iceland at dockside. "Compared to how the harbour was, it looks alien today," Maarten says.

Robbie has felt the harbour's queer, impotent mood – a barrenness layered over by gaudy strip mall developments. "As a harbour administrator, how did your father see that?"

"My father saw the harbour as if it was his father. Both hit their peak at the same time. Some years after his father drowned, my father was taken in as an apprentice in the harbour office.

He never left. I think it was his way of honouring his father. The fishery began to disappear progressively, meaning that for decades he was responsible for administering that break-down. That is, of the harbour's heroic qualities. Year upon year of decline. I believe that for him each new unproductive year was like one more year of irreverence to the memory of his father. I believe that made his own existence steadily more tragic." A wry smile fleetingly crosses Maarten's face.

Or is it a smile of anguish? Robbie isn't sure. She asks about the partners-in-crime of the demise of the North Sea fishery. Did they consist of plundering vessels from foreign lands, unregulated new technologies, governments applying hindsight instead of foresight, scientific panels of every description tripping over each other, plus endless international conferences incapable of acting? Is that in the scrapbooks chronicling the destroyed livelihoods of Scheveningen's fishermen?

All of that, says Maarten.

"You had a head start. What went wrong in Scheveningen in the seventies happened to Ramea in the nineties."

Maarten nods. He knows. The disaster on the Grand Banks is famous. "In my opinion, what is interesting in such episodes is the absence of learning. Destruction occurs, reasons are identified, yet in other locations the pattern repeats itself. A few fisheries still operate in the world. Will they exist in a decade? No one wants their disintegration, but nothing can stop it. Is this not strange?

"You seem amused. Did I say something funny?"

ACT 2, SCENE 6

"Sorry," Robbie says, taking another cookie, "I was just thinking, here you are, a detective chasing after international criminals, and you talk like my ambassador." She bites a piece off. "She likes to think about solutions to big problems. Do you have one for fish?"

"Maybe we have talked enough about fish."

"One last question. Suppose you had all the necessary power to bring a solution to the fish problem, what would you do?"

"That's easy. I would create a true authority, one that could pass and enforce laws, I mean globally." Maarten spreads his hands and shrugs.

Robbie continues nibbling on the cookie and says teasingly, "Sounds like a policeman's approach. Law broken, culprit chucked in jail."

"Mostly it works."

"Why are you a detective anyway?"

Maarten explains that as a child he liked to solve puzzles. "And why are you a diplomat?"

"To run away," says Robbie, "without it seeming so."

ACT 3, SCENE 1

Their cups have emptied and the evening crowd has begun filing in. As they get up to leave Robbie's curiosity gets the upper hand. "What is it like to live in Zoetermeer?" she asks. "What do people there do apart from polishing windows and scrubbing sidewalks?"

"Zoetermeer? I don't live there. I only work there. I take a train in the morning and go home that way in the evening. I live in Delft. I inherited my grand mother's house. It's more than four hundred years old, in the middle of the town on a canal. The date it was built is on a tile above the front door.

"Maybe I can show you Delft sometime?"

ACT 3, SCENE 2

A tramline connects Delft with Scheveningen. They will both take it, though in opposite directions. Strolling to the closest tram stop, Robbie casually inquires, "Is the Paradis investigation over? You haven't said anything about him."

He laughs. "If I did, wouldn't I have to call you Miss Warren again?"

She replies with equal merriness. "Can you only talk about him in your office, Inspector Valk?"

"No. It is alright here. It has been slow getting some information about him, and it may not be of interest to you anyway."

"What did you find out?"

"That he is strange."

"Strange?"

"Yes. Quite strange. For a start, he has no address. If he does live somewhere, that is unknown. We determined that a very long time ago, in your country and in the United States, he worked as an actor in a small travelling troupe that put on Shakespearean plays. It folded and it seems that for awhile he traveled from one small town to another, acting out one-man dramatic shows. When this did not work out, he joined a circus as a clown. Eventually he developed a special personality. Wazzock. Don't laugh. Wazzock. Wazzock the Clown. Wazzock must have had a good following because the act continued for a decade. Overnight, then, Mr Paradis dropped out of sight. No details on him for several years. When he reappeared, it was to attend an Episcopalian seminary in New England. That didn't last. I think he realized its doctrines weren't right for him because soon after he dropped out he resurfaced in Quebec. There he spent some time in a religious house preparing himself for the Catholic priesthood. But that ended early too. Can you think of something that would explain this?"

"I ... I can't," Robbie stammers. "I have no idea."

"I can't either, not with certainty, but one can speculate. What psychology could explain that kind of behaviour? He seems to like to entertain. There appears to be a love of disguise. If you think about it, clowns and priests have certain common aims. Both set out to affect people's feelings. Both learn how to manipulate their moods."

Maarten's story hits Robbie like a blow from a hammer. Paradis is an old man for whom she has developed tender feelings. In return, she has acquired concepts from him, which she considers very meaningful. Her meditating has become more rewarding with his philosophy enriching her. She takes a breath. "I ... I would be careful with speculations like that. You seem to think he isn't genuine. But it could be the opposite. Maybe when he was a clown he was searching for a purpose. Then he thought he could find it as a holy man. Maybe that didn't work out either and finally he turned to a cause that's higher still."

"Do you think that's what PEACE is for him? A higher cause?"

"Is promoting peace not the best thing anyone can do?"

Maarten shrugs. "I'll add one more wrinkle. Mr Paradis did indeed become the public face of PEACE, but unfortunately it also has a funny smell. Like Mr Paradis, PEACE has no location to which mail can be delivered. PEACE exists only in one place – on his calling card. I admit, it has links to numerous peace organizations. One of them pays his bills. It is called Peace Musings. Peace Musings takes in subscriptions and small donations from people all over the world. It has an account with an Austrian bank.

"Of interest is that Peace Musings does not do anything except handle funds. If you pay or donate, you receive a code that allows you access to a website, called Peace Concordance. There you do get something for your money, but not much. That site lists all the considerations, contemplations, sermons, homilies and quotes on peace that people have formulated over thousands of years. Next to some of the entries, you see a photograph of Mr Paradis, as if he is the source, or author. Once a day, one lovely thought about peace is sent out to everyone who subscribes. Peace Concordance claims to speak for, or represent, thousands of peace groups, mostly small ones, clubs and community groups and the like. The site is hosted on a server in Geneva, but maintained from Athens. It doesn't somehow seem genuine. So one asks, is Mr Paradis authentic?"

Robbie, tense now, blurts, "I don't understand why ... why you theorize like that. Why read something so complicated into who he is and what he does? You interpret everything negatively, but he could just as easily be legitimate. I haven't heard anything that proves Alistair is not a voice for people who want to live in a world without conflict. He searched for years. Finally he found his calling."

"Possibly, but possibly not. Is Mr Paradis a true convert to peace, or has he merely changed the circus in which he performs? Has he traded a clown's costume for the gown of a prophet? He could be a sham. A good one too. Think of it. Wazzock the Clown transformed into Sham the Prophet. But you are right. We don't know this. And that was the conclusion of the investigation: that we don't know."

~

At the bus stop in Wassenaar, Robbie didn't want to sit through the third and final scene of that last act. It consisted of her getting into a tram heading west and Maarten onto one going east. They parted in a strained, nearly frosty manner, which did not at all match the mood of the earlier scenes.

The night bus rolled up and Robbie climbed on. It coasted back to The Hague, where night revellers, unshackled by the fine weather, were shrieking and shouting. Quietly, she transferred onto the Scheveningen tram. It rocked and swayed her back to her current ex-fishing village. At home she summed up the day for herself – it had two decent pieces of theater, really, and in both she had played a leading role. The final scene of the afternoon show with Maarten was forgettable. A down-note for sure. But the evening event with Natalia ended on an upward beat with some lovely, histrionic qualities. What did the day add up to? It hadn't been bland, not hyper sober at all.

What now? Natalia wished to draw her ever deeper into the peace topic. Which was fine. And Alistair was in the picture too. Frankly, Robbie didn't care one whit that he had been a clown once upon a time. He was a role model now. He had a grandiose view of life. Could anyone live more positively than him? She resolved once more to get him back on his feet and back into the affairs of the world. As for Inspector Valk, she had to admit he had some things going for him. He was intelligent, sensible and capable of empathy. On the other hand, he was a policeman too and paid to be suspicious. But should she dislike him on that account? Was it right to feel antipathy towards him for the job he had? Suppose she hadn't asked that question about his investigation. Suppose she hadn't pushed him into his policeman's function. For sure there wouldn't have been that tiff. And in that case, how would the final scene of the last act have played out? Would the parting have been warm? Could there even have been a hint that a further act was still to come?

Mightiest Advisor, take your time, but when you're ready, let me know: Should I do what Natalia said? Has my turn come to invite him?

Chapter 10

Effusive, fluid accolades were a Paradis trademark and whenever Robbie called to ask him how he was he showered them on her.

My best-ever good Samaritan. Or, *you are too vibrant a young woman to spend time on an old cur like me.* Or, *why do I deserve the earthly good fortune of being nursed by a heavenly angel?*

Today, however, as Robbie's latest call came through, he wasn't in his suite to pronounce an elegant salutation. An automatic redirection took her to the clinic's admin office where the attendant – in full, throat-accentuated English and with all Rs rolling – prosaically described how the patient left early that morning. Unexpectedly, he had wheeled himself into the foyer and then sat there waiting, still, very still. *Spreekt U een beetje Nederlands, mevrouw?* she asked. I speak some Dutch, yes, Robbie replied. *Prachtig. Nu, hij was gewoon een standbeeld. How do you say that in English?* Motionless as a statue, Robbie guessed. Yes, that's how he sat! Exactly. As a statue. A quarter hour passed and a van drove up, two male nurses spilling out and marching towards him.

The three engaged in a brief exchange, some jokes it seems, bawdy perhaps, for there was robust, loud laughter. Mr Paradis removed a cane from a side harness on his wheelchair, which he then twirled and jabbed into the air before pointing the tip towards the van, a signal that they ought to get going. A ramp became operable from the van's side, which allowed him to be rolled up into the back, where the wheelchair was carefully secured with catches and belts. All highly professional. They departed down the lane, very slowly, very dignified, as if Mr Paradis was acting out a role, of a Cardinal perhaps, or even the Pope. *Nee hoor*, the chatty attendant added – no, they didn't say where they were going. Not one word. *Misschien*, she ventured, perhaps Mr Paradis had arranged a change of scenery for himself, possibly some sightseeing in Gouda or Edam, two very pretty towns not far away and for foreigners worth a visit. Oh, one last item. The orderlies informed clinic administration they would have him back by dinnertime. Oh yes, yes – *Natuurlijk!* – Mr Paradis would be informed that the embassy had called to enquire how he was doing. Most definitely!

~

Tourism for the invalid Paradis in one of the numerous scenic towns sprinkled about on the flats of Holland? Really? The administrator meant well when she speculated this, but had it wrong. The escorts in their starched, white uniforms did not take him for a day of gawking at cobble-stoned streets, cute bridges and toy-like squares in front of ancient, sumptuously gilded municipal buildings. The real destination was a kind of geographical opposite – the Akamas Peninsula, a place of nature on the northwest tip of Cyprus.

Around the same time the clinic administrator chattered on about the joy Mr Paradis would be experiencing being wheeled through narrow alleys and along sun-dappled canals, he was actually cruising along in a roomy business jet at 8000 meters. Though in one respect she had been right. The orderlies, Stavros and Aslan, now acting as cabin attendants, were treating him majestically, as if he really was an eminence of some kind. Paradis, for his part, his thick eyebrows dancing, addressed them in beguiling little growls, as if he wanted to be friends, yet knew he had to maintain distance. They served him breakfast delicacies and he lauded the compartment's spaciousness. When they fussed over his napkin to make sure it was in place, he extolled the quality of the deep leather seat. He asked where and how two such fine young men as Stavros and Aslan might have been trained. This brought on delirious laughter, though no answer. Paradis, nodding benevolently, then settled back to attend to the world outside his window.

He had watched Schiphol fall away and there was the loop out over the North Sea before the jet took on the familiar course to the southeast. For Paradis, nothing about this was different today except that he was travelling higher and faster than he had done in his own ill-fated turbo prop. The trip, therefore, would be three and a half hours one way, not six.

Ah, there are the Austrian Alps. How lovely their alternations – green-black valleys set off by inspiring white peaks. Soon they would be hugging Hungary's western border. Then a half hour of Serbian hilly backwardness before the brief glimpse at Bulgaria's southwest corner. He planned to watch it all. But over eastern Greece he would nap, Stavros being duly instructed to wake him at first sight of Anatolia's coast. He was unfailingly fascinated with the bird's eye view of that part of Turkey. The pervasive ancientness down there was spellbinding. He wouldn't want to miss the beauty of it for the world. Over Cyprus, the final descent to the Akrotiri airstrip would, as always, be enjoyable, not for the scenery so much as for the atmosphere upon landing. Paradis had concluded years before that nothing about flying was quite so satisfying as stepping into a military base at journey's end. The ease, the informality, the endless friendly saluting! One of Helmut's reliable choppers would be waiting close by. Which made him think forward to the final hop, from Akrotiri on the south coast to the north, to the Akamas Peninsula. At this, he winced.

"Do you have pain?" Stavros asked.

"Oh no. No, no. Not at all. I'm quite comfortable, thank you. I was beginning to think of Cyprus heat. A minor worry, that is all."

"Today it will not be too hot. Thirty-three, maybe thirty-four degrees celsius."

"Thank you. When we get there I will remove my sweater."

"And I will help you."

Paradis nodded. It was not the prospect of the helicopter ride that had put him off. It was the half-hour meeting scheduled with Helmut.

~

Not once, not ever, had Paradis felt at ease when he and Helmut talked in the hilltop enclave. The complex possessed rare physical beauty. No one could dispute that. The core was a villa built in the Roman style with a graceful atrium. Around the villa like a U were terraces adorned with rich, tropical vegetation. Staff quarters and technical buildings were located behind a wall of cypresses at the back. On the promontory itself in nearly every direction were panoramic views of the Mediterranean, which dazzled with its subtle colour variations of indigo, turquoise or azure. In a location like that, with any other patron, Paradis would have desired to visit long. But each session with Helmut made his gut feel tight. Pangs of apprehension hit; he was always thinking of a quick departure. The trouble was not entirely Helmut himself. Helmut could be chummy enough. He sometimes radiated a rough kind of goodwill, no doubt acquired as a big game hunter in South Africa. Helmut looked good too: blond hair now tending towards white, keen sapphire-blue eyes, a ready cowboy-like grin. Helmut could be comfortable to be with. So the problem wasn't Helmut so much as what Helmut stood for. When they first met face to face, within seconds Paradis had sensed something sinister in the air. He felt it coming at him, felt it coating him. A miasma. A miasma of what? Of … of … of some form of moral pollution. Immediately it made Paradis feel unclean.

~

A name was chiselled into the cornice above the villa entrance – *Bellonae Adytum* – and during that first time there Paradis halted before ascending the steps and entering. In his deep, rolling voice, the one he used to muster up his circus tent authority, he said, "my Latin is a touch rusty, Mr Steinmeyer. What does it mean?"

"Alistair, stop. Stop now. We're a team. Working hand in glove. I'm Helmut. If you don't mind."

"Helmut? Thank you, Helmut."

"The inscription means *Bellona's Retreat*."

"Bellona?"

"Roman goddess of war. This is her sanctum. We do not see her, but we sense her presence."

Alistair did.

That first time in Bellona's sanctuary, he felt her wooing him. For three hours she went at it, using Helmut as her oracle. He spoke for her in his South-African-musical accent; what she said through him was both spellbinding and chilling.

They were in a dual-level room with slabs of black, polished marble on the floors and walls. It must have been Bellona's personal space, because – in alcoves cut into the walls, on both sides of Helmut's desk and three steps down in the room's lower part, around sofas facing floor to ceiling windows – exquisitely miniaturized replicas of the latest lethal instruments of war were exhibited on pedestals.

"How beautiful," Alistair said softly. "Each one a work of art."

"Right. Masterfully sculpted. Rigorously accurate. See the details on the missiles and the tanks? This by the way is the F-35 Lightning Joint Strike Fighter, a deadly machine. And here is the F-22 Super Stealth Raptor. The cannon fires 480 rounds in five seconds, shredding whatever is in its sights. Under the wings, two Sidewinder heat-seeking missiles and a couple of one thousand pound satellite-guided bombs. Cruising speed, mach 1.7. Imagine something invisible approaching that fast. Only after this bird has vaporized its targets would anyone know she'd been coming. And there are the new glamour toys. Drones. Much in favour. Only enemy fighters die nowadays. Unstoppable power, Alistair. Humanly engineered beauty. Shall we go down and sit easy?"

"Righty-ho," Alistair said lightly, though now sensing Bellona's unmistakable breath in his ear.

Down in the sunken part of the room in a vast armchair Helmut smiled with business-like enthusiasm. "Right off the top, Alistair, I have to say that from the start we considered ourselves lucky to find you."

"Thank you most graciously. And I, when I was approached, was convinced I was ripe for these new horizons."

"Yeah. All good. From the beginning." Gazing out through the windows onto a placid Mediterranean, Helmut began rubbing the thumb of one hand against the fingertips of the other, as if to prepare himself for one or another dexterous act. "You didn't know then who I was. What I represent. But preparations are completed. It's time to fill you in. I run the Society, Alistair. That's what we call it. The Society makes sure the market for war equipment functions. I mean, no hiccups. Smooth transactions. Lots of sales. The Society has big interests. Huge. And needs you. Why?"

"I, well, perhaps I may be able to do what nobody else can."

"That's it. For years we had a blind spot. A bad one. We thought we had the angles covered. That we were everywhere. Not so. Information flow from governments was good. Accurate. All that. But not good enough. Not really good. The problem? The information wasn't complete. Case in point: that terrible international treaty banning landmines. Heard of it?"

"Yes, yes. No more landmines."

"Right. So you know it came from nowhere."

"Out of the blue, if I'm well informed."

"Just so. Hit the Society like a stealth bomber payload. NGOs pushed an agenda. I gotta admit this. We didn't focus. No one said NGOs were co-opting the bleeding-heart governments. As you say. Out of the blue. That's how the ban thing came to us."

"The spectacle was awful. Most painful."

"It was. We knew about NGO activism. Naturally. The fussing about global poverty. Super topic for them. Poverty is never going away. Same thing health. NGOs can busy themselves forever. No damage to our interests there. Then the shift. NGOs sticking their noses into the military-security front."

"A kind of metastasis, Helmut. As with cancer. Those were my thoughts at the time."

"Just like that. So a landmine ban is imminent. Puts the Society overnight into a pretty pickle. Crisis consultations. Goddamn stuff like that. We pulled out the stops. Yanked every string. Sat down with the governments we count on. Too late. Before the voice of sanity appears, the landmine ban treaty is signed. I have to say it. We were always good at timeliness. If we had a problem, we screwed a silencer on the barrel. Put the crosshairs on the problem. Squeezed the trigger. Total silence. Target gone. But that NGO stealth campaign. It flew right through us. We couldn't shoot. We couldn't bring it down."

"Pernicious, how it happened."

"Right. We had the post-mortem. Naturally. Conclusion? If NGOs get landmines banned, what's next? Grenades? Cluster bombs? Assault rifles? Tanks? That pretty raptor fighter over there? There would be no end to it. The lesson? Never again. The new priority? Countermeasures. Boots on the ground in the NGO camp."

"I do know the voices in the NGO camp. I do. Shrill. Very shrill. In tone, they are often most unbrotherly."

"Blinkered too. No common sense. No focus on the big picture. If NGOs go fuzzy again, we've got to know early. Which is, Alistair, where you to come in."

"Timely entrances are my speciality."

"I know. That's the reason we picked you. And thanks for the years you put in developing cover." Helmut uncrossed his legs before re-crossing them the other way. He ceased moving his thumb over his fingertips and cocked an index finger at Paradis instead. He held it that way for a while, as if pointing a gun. Then he smirked. "So you went back to school. Confide in me. How was it?"

"Best years I ever had, Helmut. I have always loved rehearsing and I never had it better than preparing for this role. I also liked the costumes. Six months in a cassock. A half year in a caftan. I confess, the saffron robe and shaved head period came to me most easily. As a Buddhist, I was scarcely acting."

Helmut beamed. The cocked gun disappeared and he began to play with one of the model inter-continental ballistic missiles that beautified the little coffee table between them. "I was goddamn proud of you. Taking in all that religion. Lots of good reports on how you took it. I thought, that Alistair, he does us proud. *Summa Cum Laude.* Alright. Fess up. How did they stack up? Is a Catholic seminary better or worse than an Episcopalian school?"

"I treated each institution as a lover, Helmut. We were very intimate. Each had its own subtleties, to which I responded tenderly.

Yes, I slept around a bit and enjoyed all. The best one? In the end, no contest. Roman Catholicism. No other creed comes close. She is the sulkiest, the most deeply brooding. Why love a woman if she doesn't grab you with her magic, if she has no aura of hocus pocus. The hocus pocus of the seminary in Quebec was easily the best."

Helmut chortled. "And the others?" His question had a ribald-story urgency. "That ashram in Sri Lanka. Islamic instruction at the Tunis madrassa. Were they freaky? Tell me."

"Rare experiences, Helmut. Ask me too much about them and my heart will start to flutter. Life in Katharagama was splendidly devotional. The acolytes held hands with the monks, sang songs, went down onto their knees to polish the temple floor. I loved my orange robe. I loved not having hair. And I loved their Buddha. Often I thought, why am I not him? Sitting in the lotus position. Lost in thought for decades. Afterwards, the world viewing you with reverence through all the millennia. Who wouldn't like that? You know, my body shape is not unlike his. As for the madrassa in Fez, that was a shade too rigorous, a touch too S&M for me. I didn't mind facing Mecca kneeling on a carpet, but it was a slog memorising the Koran from morning to night. Somehow, it didn't caress me, not as the mantra chanting did. There was no meditation either. Just those ever-nodding prayers. Silly. But ask me to do some Buddhism, right here this minute, and I'll go into deep meditation and slip off for two hours straight.

"Religion is in us somewhere, Helmut, and it's wonderful when we allow it to come out. From the imams, but also the episcopalians, I learned how religion should not be done. After two years my conclusion is that religious feelings are much improved if texts and prescriptions are thrown out. The rote stuff makes no sense. If you decide to get on with religion, start by looking for irrationality inside yourself."

"I support that," an excited Helmut cried. "I do. I was raised a Calvinist in Bloemfontein. Know what Calvinism says? You are predestined. You will spend your whole life sitting in the same old pew singing the same old hymns. The pastor glowers at you like the devil before he says you're doomed to hell. He says this is the product of reason, that it is reasonable. My childhood? Torture.

Fear-mongering only. I was scared out of my wits the whole time. I said to myself – Helmut, cure yourself. Where and when can't you be afraid? What's the answer? Got one, Alistair?"

"Uhm. I am not sure. Ideally, I suppose, no fear on one's deathbed."

"Pretty good answer. For me, I thought, when a goddamn lion or elephant or something like that is charging, hell bent, try being fearless. So I became a big game hunter. A heavy rifle. Good crosshairs. Steady aim. A little squeeze. Bang. What scares you drops dead two yards off. Wished I could have done that to Calvinism. I loved squeezing the trigger. I loved deciding when death should happen. Something living in the crosshairs, Alistair, is like your best mistress. That same hocus pocus quality. Then the squeeze. The snuffing out. Total death. Oh man." A shudder went through Helmut from deep inside all the way to his extremities. It was unclear for a second whether the intercontinental ballistic missile in his hand would take off, or crash. "So there's me and the animals that are alive then dead and we're all happy and the day comes when I'm giving tips on good shooting to a German. Executive manager of a bomb factory. I get him to stand his ground against a bull cape buffalo. The animal stumbles then drops. Not totally good. But not too bad either. Progress next day. A rhino goes down clean. He gets me to organize a big shooting tour. Guys from all over the world. Associates, he says. I ask of what. The Society, he answers. It took a while, but every Society Associate from everywhere came to South Africa. They shot. They killed. They signed a lot of deals amongst themselves. Since I shot better than all of them, they hired me."

"Thank you, Helmut, for not forcing the Calvinist experience on me during my training period."

Helmut laughed. The missile was put down and the index finger pointed at Paradis again. "We wanted you to come out of training functionally sane." He clapped his hands once. "Alright. All that theology. You got it done. Then you traveled as a world religious leader. You said hello to Desmond Tutu and the Bishop of Canterbury. All that. The grassroots work in the States with the goody-goody peace groups. First rate too. The credentials are there. Depth for your new role. The performance can begin. Agree? It's going to be a subtle one, Alistair. Subtler than the clown act. That act as … uh, your act…"

"As Wazzock."

"Wazzock. Right. Well. Wazzock impressed us. We were looking everywhere. Where was the raw material for the artfulness we needed? Who in broad daylight can be the bush that has bursting buds, but only blossoms undercover? Good luck. A Pentagon Associate vacationing in Tennessee took his kiddies to the travelling circus. He saw Wazzock. He knew he was seeing genius. Wazzock's refined sensitivities. The outpourings of pathos filling the tent. It blew his mind. He said that. He was pretty sure you were our man. Couple of weeks later he went back. With another Washington Associate. A second opinion. Twenty minutes at the circus and he was convinced too. Wazzock the confused holy man. Spiritual ramblings perfectly pitched. The character convinced. We thought, OK. A slight retooling only. Wazzock can emerge as the NGO peace messiah. After which the best revelations on NGO thinking turn into our intellectual property."

Paradis raised a finger.

Smiling warmly, Helmut said, "question, Alistair?"

"I have one, Helmut."

"Shoot, man. Shoot."

"I understand what's coming, generally. My lines are coming along. I have some good soliloquies on world peace. Also a few monologues on an underpinning spirituality and a couple of asides on core human values. The material is there. I look forward to stirring the masses. But your Society, and the Associates, that's not as clear to me. What are the aims? Where lies your promised land?"

Helmut chuckled. "Promised land. I like that. Here's the shorty. The Society promotes realism. The world must have wars. Aggression is basic. Part of evolution. It should flow. Don't deny it. Don't bottle it up. Confine aggression and the explosions get worse. The Society wants you as the window on peace, Alistair. Because that serves our conviction that all the nations on the planet should be armed to the teeth."

Paradis nodded, but was silent. A sigh escaped. "I have always wanted to participate in a grand scheme. Succouring the nations and their militias – what could be finer?" Helmut spread his hands wide in absolute agreement and Paradis gingerly continued. "And the Associates, who might they be?"

"Likeable men. Up front types. People you want to be friends with. Some are damn fine thinkers. You know, professors, professional philosophers. They are the Society's ideologues. Others are literary. They write. Books. Magazine articles. Letters to editors. Spread the word in the right way, is the motto. Most members are entrepreneurs. They make sure factories run. They are the wealth creators in the world. Soldiers are there too. Naturally. Same thing politicians. The soldiers know that preparedness for war brings peace. Politicians think if war must be, it should be crisp. The businessmen understand that war preparedness drives economic growth. The thinking members reason that conflict cannot be suppressed because it is an inherent part of life. The sum total? The Society is a microcosm. Of the forces that make humanity click."

"Righty-oh. Are you big?"

"What's big? Sixty-plus nationalities good enough? We've got our annual assemblies. Like any professional troop. We lease a cruise liner. A shiny big white one. Seven, eight decks. It fills up good. For a week, a couple of thousand like-minded brothers go to seminars, listen to debates, look at presentations on new weapons and armament concepts. Eye-popping stuff, Alistair. On the side? Military deals get reviewed and signed. In plenary? Fine-tuning of political directions. Decisions on the weapons embargoes to support. And the ones we don't want. Stuff like that. When done, the Associates go home. The Society's interests get put into the government hoppers. The mills grind. Not long then. What we want shows up as national security policies and priorities. The goddamn thing about all that? The world develops better on account of us."

"Splendid. Thank you. That background is important for me. Keeping the show rolling is your job, I take it, Helmut?"

"Yeah. Chief op guy. Listen brother, I'm promising you something right here, right now. Soon as you got a track record running the NGO flank, soon as that bears fruit, you'll have a cabin on the cruise ship."

"I would consider it a privilege."

"Sure. And I'd assign you to a study group. We got lots. Geopolitics, philosophy and religion, new scientific developments, commercial trends, economic forecasting – groups on everything. We think broad. We want to have early dibs on all the trends. I sit on economic issues. I've learned. The armaments business is over a trillion dollars a year. Isn't that a stat? We're talking millions of jobs. Take a dollar and cent view of wars. What pops up? The calculation that one war casualty generates a good income for five thousand hard-working souls. Think social good. What does that spell out? A lot of proud parents sending sons and daughters to school on account of just one crazy guy dead. A big plus on the political and economic ledgers of many nations. Small part of a bigger picture though. Armaments production drives research. Stimulates innovation. Everywhere, spin-offs. Medicine, aviation, new materials, lower costs, goddamn stuff like that. Said simply, we do good. Except we've got that one dark spot always on the horizon. The peace NGOs. They spoil it. They don't see the big picture. Conclusion?" The index finger was pointing once more. "Work. For you, Alistair. Lots of it. Big opportunities to make a mark. The reward won't be that bad. A sexy lifestyle. It's coming your way. Wazzock was good. But what's the point of brilliance in small towns? For you, capital cities from now on." Helmut made a popping sound with his lips as if the trigger had been squeezed, the gun had fired and Paradis's free will, without a stumble, had now expired.

"Wazzock was rather hand to mouth."

"Sure. That brings us to Bellona's generous side." Helmut leaned forwards. "Getting ready for the part. That was dedication. We're happy. Your skills, Alistair, are good. We think, a million a year isn't too much. Expenses on top. Naturally. And a plane to travel at short notice. For the NGO scene, you've got your imagination. For me, I sometimes need an emissary. Go here. Go there. Hobnob with the colonels and the generals. You'll help out there too. Hush-hush stuff. I'll make sure it won't cross over to the NGO role. Sound good?"

Paradis clasped his hands, brought them to his chin and closed his eyes. After a brief meditation, he answered in deep, bass reverberations. "If Bellona has faith in me, I am certain it will be vindicated."

"Well. That's good then. She has her way with us, Alistair. She's got hocus pocus too. Not like what stirred you in Quebec. She doesn't tease. She doesn't make you wait. Bellona is direct. You feel wanted on the spot. She wants you to work fast. If you do, afterwards, she does all she can to make you feel comfy. You know, warm. Listen, this is how it's going to work."

The million-plus for Paradis would come together through thousands of micro payments from all over the world, flowing through a peace website into a Vienna bank account. IT technical support was from Athens. A research network was ready to go. Historical statements on global peace, current utterances and new writings, all labelled *peace musings and confessions*, would feed into Athens from scattered places. A contribution counter on the website was being juiced with a hundred thousand fake contributions and subscriptions. Donation growth above that would be attributable to Paradis's work and trigger bonus payments.

Paradis listened, but made it seem this was mere nitpicking. He waved aside a more thorough exploration of the financial package. He had full confidence in Helmut's accountants. Let them manage the dollars and cents. "I have been thinking of my cover, Helmut," he said. "A good calling card does wonders. I believe it should say PEACE. In capital letters. I trust you will not mind. I will admire my card. Because it will hide my true new mistress. The best mistresses were always secret."

~

The jet had left the Alps behind, but Paradis, scanning the years since his first *Bellonae Adytum* visit, remained oblivious to the progress. He'd had radio and TV appearances, interviews with magazines, lunches with senior government officials, dinners with ministers, uncountable peace conferences, earnest discussions with grassroots groups. By turns, his act was schmaltzy-visionary and punchy-lobbyist. He knew right away that he was tapping into something big. The proof? The website subscription counter went berserk. Not two years went by before an additional digit had to be inserted – to accommodate the one-millionth contributor. Helmut's accountants took careful note and processed bigger and bigger bonus payments. Paradis saw a day coming when he would live opulently just off interest.

Sometimes he pinched himself. Was the change of fortune real? During the Wazzock decade, home had been a tiny trailer without ventilation. The smell then was of farts that lingered. Nowadays he rotated through jasmine-scented presidential suites. Whenever he slipped into yet another wall-to-wall jacuzzi to let the jets play with his loins, he contemplated his step up to limousines, gold faucets and princely food. No more shabby circus tents. No more performing before a hooting rabble. Who had Wazzock really been? Paradis asked. The answer. Wazzock was a high priest of wisdom casting pearls to swine. In contrast, the performances today played out in scintillating conference centers and on glitterati TV shows. Solemnly delivered lines challenged millions everywhere to dedicate themselves through thoughts and actions to the cause of global peace.

Routine reporting to Helmut took place once a month, the turbo prop taking him in and out. Accounts of NGO initiatives lasted maybe thirty minutes. Helmut on the sofa, his head thrown back, would smile contentedly at the ceiling. He may have been watching an enemy up there, a foe drawing up battle formations, while he below, empowered, saw their futility. He listened without interrupting and, when Paradis had finished, clapped his hands, just once, loudly, as a sign that he had made up his mind. His observation was always the same. "Couple of phone calls, Alistair, and the goody-doers will be on their arses again."

Sometimes Paradis received a postcard sent from Athens. The image on it didn't vary, always of a marble statue in the classical style of a woman armed, armoured and holding a sword high. The sword had the angle a warrior would use when getting ready to land the blow that separates the head from the torso. The message on the back of the card was alluringly sweet: *Wish you were here. Love, Emily.* Summoned in this way to the sanctum, Paradis traveled with the image of Bellona seared into his brain. He couldn't shake thoughts of the sword's angle, nor of her victim. It was like Helmut's pointing finger and the popping sound coming from his lips. Each time Paradis went, he held his belly, as if he could make make a pain there go away. At the sanctum, Helmut issued instructions in his breezy manner. At the end, Paradis, rubbing his neck, would say, "Righty-oh," and with a slow, grave nod depart, his role of envoy once more expanded. Ostensibly, as befits a peace prophet, he carried olive branches, though in fact he traveled to off-limit places where the only rules are military. The cliques of colonels were delighted with what he brought. When the parley ended, they palmed his cheeks, as if they loved him. As he climbed back into his plane, they stood in salute.

Only two days ago, Emily was at it again. And yesterday brought Stavros's bright voice into the phone to pursue the invitation. *It is my pleasure, Mr Paradis, to be in charge of your outing.* Stavros was a winning young man, as was Aslan, and the jet was comfortable, but Paradis wasn't enjoying his midriff cramps.

He slipped into a slumber without asking for a wake-up shake over Anatolia and did not come to until he felt his seat was being forced to upright. Through the window he observed familiar landmarks – the final approach to Akrotiri. "Slept right through the places where some of the bloodiest battles of all time were fought," he observed to his two caregivers, who now sat facing him.

"You bad man," grinned Stavros. "If no interest in that, why you visit Mr Steinmeyer's villa?"

After landing, Stavros and Aslan worked fast. The exit door was thrown open; the peace prophet in wheelchair was bumped down steps to the ground; a foot race began across the tarmac to a waiting Sikorsky; more huffing and puffing as the wheelchair was dragged up a ramp; a slam sealed the helicopter cabin. Total transfer time? Mere minutes. The helicopter engine whined, then screamed, and blades beat the air. The rise was smooth, the nose tilted down and the headlong rush towards the peninsula began. Some hours before, departing the clinic, Paradis had admired beds of sturdy tulips. Here, he looked down at ochre scrubland. It looked parched and, when he ran his tongue around the inside of his lips, he found his mouth was that way too. What would Bellona's insatiable, restless spirit have in store for him today? What would she exact? How big would be the slice of soul she would demand as sacrificial offering? *Soul*. Paradis sighed inwardly. *My soul?* His soul was gone. It had been signed over. And the return? Earnings so high that he had begun to notice the miracle of interest yielding still more interest. But all the same…

"A sip of water, Stavros," he said with closed eyes, "if I may."

On the Akamas Peninsula, on two golf carts – one with Paradis in it and Stavros driving, the other with the wheelchair, operated by Aslan – they sped along a path, which snaked from the landing pad to the front steps of the villa. Twelve sandstone steps confronted them. The quandary lasted less than a second. "To the side," Stavros ordered. "To the kitchen, then the lift." The lift's egress on the main floor was next to the dining salon and from there they swung around the atrium towards Helmut's door. Stavros knocked. Helmut's chirpy, lilting voice, sounding all the world to Paradis that Bellona herself was singing, rang out. "Come in."

Stavros opened the door, Aslan pushed the wheelchair forward and Paradis enlarged his chest. He wished to look like any other decorated veteran. Sonorously he said, "thank you, Stavros. Aslan, thank you too. I have seldom been so well handled. Ah, Helmut. You have my greetings. I can tell you, these boys are good. You know, nothing is more paralyzing than convalescing. Seeing the mountains and seas from your plane, then the beauty of the peninsula, and now breathing the sanctum's divine air, I am inclined to think you sent for me because you knew I needed some diversion."

Helmut laughed and spoke to the orderlies. "Twenty minutes." When the door clicked shut, Helmut, still grinning, studied Paradis in the wheelchair. "Am I well informed, Alistair? You are improving? Can you roll yourself to my desk? Or should I push?"

"Tireless as a robot, Helmut. No need to assist. Next week physio will have me doing sprints – behind a walker, but still."

"Bloody-awful thing, the accident. The pilot must have blinked."

Paradis worked the wheelchair, following Helmut who was moving to his desk, situated on the far side of the mezzanine portion of the room. "The weather, Helmut. In an instant it turned Dutch." The marble floor offered little resistance, but even so he worked hard to keep his lungs full and when he was next to Helmut's desk he exhaled, like someone who has reached the high point of a pass. "All I remember is a jolt," Paradis said between breaths, "a hard jolt, then being suspended upside down. A blow came next. It seemed to come from every direction." A laboured pause. "When I woke up next day I was staring at rows of TV screens with roving dots." A last deep breath. "I looked more closely and saw that a formation of medical devices was doing my living for me. I no longer had personal responsibility for my heartbeat, kidney function, lungs and bladder. I thought, I am free. I have been liberated."

"It freaked us out, Alistair. We thought our mother lode was disappearing."

Paradis manoeuvred the wheelchair into a casual angle so as to look out over the sunken part of the room, through the floor to ceiling windows, across the terrace framed by potted oleanders and out towards the sea which, in the midday light, lay lazuline. Helmut companionably turned his winged chair on wheels in that direction too. They sat like pals staring into the distance until Helmut began toying with a miniature replica of a sleek missile. He said, "I'm glad we didn't lose you. Neutering the NGOs. It's going good."

"They have become my choir, Helmut, if I may show a touch of pride. I wave a baton and they sing their hearts out."

"*Hallelujahs, Glorias* and *In Excelsis Deos*. Right? Them stirring tunes. I remember them. It still hurts. But your conducting job. It's good." Helmut bit his lip. "Got to get to the point, Alistair. A batch of Pakistani generals are coming in. As we speak. The choir stories. We swap them next time. OK? You're barely off intravenous. I know that. You're asking, why today's travel? I know that. This is the deal. There's a low rumble. A faint noise. Almost no decibels to it. All the same, it's been picked up. It could be nothing. Just a rock rolling down some mountain. But we must ask. Is it an early warning of a seismic shift? Something that will rock us like nothing else has. Not being sure. Being prudent. We ought to get close to the action."

Paradis had observed on earlier occasions that Helmut could become quite sunny when confronted by a challenge. This time, too, he began a low chuckle. He placed one leg crosswise over the other, lifted the little missile up from his desk into the air, gave it a nice trajectory to bring it back to earth and, just as the nose made contact with his desktop, said, "Boom." A grin broke out. "*Le Triomphant*, Alistair. A French model. Their latest submarine-launched, multiple warhead missile. It impresses the hell out of the Chinese. They've been here twice."

Paradis waited.

"The rumble I'm talking about. The noise deep down. We need certainty that no big time grinding is starting. We need your ear, Alistair. Nobody picks up the vibes of hell as you do."

"Thank you for that applause," Paradis said, not shifting in the wheelchair. He seemed to withdraw. His eyes emptied as if there was nothing left for him to look at. Not in front. Nor left, nor right. After a brief spell, however, he was back. With scarcely moving lips, he softly put forward a rhetorical question. "What is my situation?" A slow answer formed. "It is quite uniquely blah." He sent a glance at Helmut and with more robustness stated, "I am thinking longer term now. Longer-term thinking involves stabbing into the unknown. May I share one stab with you, Helmut?"

"Shoot, man. Shoot."

"What purpose can be served by my putting an ear to the ground if that very act prevents me from ever rising up again? They say I need at least another month of physio. I am an invalid for now. Do you know what I see when I look into the mirror? In the mirror I see blah."

It triggered no response. Helmut gave the missile another fanciful trajectory. Eventually he said, "Gosh, Alistair, I'm not asking you to put on a hard hat. You don't have to pickaxe your way through tough back country digging out terrorists. We need a piece of sleuthing. It can be done from your clinic bed. The sub-surface rumble comes from Holland. From The Hague. We think it's set off by the Canadian Embassy. Your passport is Canadian? I'd say that is convenient." Helmut let this sink in. A second later he warbled on. "You have no admirers in that place, Alistair? You can't call them? Your super-sized talent can't do that? You doubt you can get the embassy to come to you? Alistair. Come now. Why are you paid?"

~

153

When the Sikorsky lifted off, the next one was 50 meters off and hovering, queued up to use the pad. Stavros and Aslan were excited by the action, the VIP coordination, the helicopter cacophony. They waved enthusiastically at the incoming crowd, three men, South Asian, khaki uniforms, gold braids on low-slung caps. But they seemed out of humour, for like sullen predators they stared back.

In Akrotiri, the Challenger had a new crew in the cockpit. The wheelchair was heaved in with minimal jarring. The hatch was secured, belts were buckled, the jet cruised to the runway. Without a pause, acceleration was initiated. Aloft, the race against the sun began. Paradis consulted his watch. Schiphol at about a quarter past five, he reckoned. Entry procedures there for dignitaries were generally greased. Then the half hour ride to the clinic. ETA? Close to six. Ought he to dine in the common room, or privately in his suite? Perhaps he would not eat at all. Stavros and Aslan chirped away in Greek – or was it Turkish? – as an in-flight banquet was in preparation. They might feast on it. Not him. Paradis lacked appetite. He felt tired too. Tired of the hours in the sky and tired of his lot in life. Was there an alternative? Suppose, one inner voice said, suppose you go back. Become a second-tier clown again. Would you be happier? He heard a firm but negative reply from that part of the brain where pleasure reigns. A third voice came along to counsel him. You are a professional, Alistair. You are responsible for a show. It must go on. You can't stay backstage just because you're feeling blue. So, no, he had no alternatives. The show really did have to go on.

All the same, the thought of it was tiring and Paradis shuddered.

Stavros caught it. "A cramp?"

"Oh no. Thank you, Stavros. No, not at all. This is a fine chair and my limbs are loose. I'm very comfortable."

"I mean, a soul cramp." Stavros said with a slight sneer.

"Soul cramp? I see. A slight one possibly. I suppose. You know, I have been to *Bellonae Adytum* many times. Quick in, quick out. Always the same. Is there a lovelier seat on which to sit to contemplate the world? Rushing off makes me feel rather denied." A deep sigh welled up. "I worry that I'm missing out on tranquil contemplation."

"Bad thinking. Mr Steinmeyer's visitors never stay long. They come. They go. The next one is already waiting."

"I know, Stavros. I know. Mr Steinmeyer is a chief executive. It brings burdens. People like him cannot afford the many hours which true meditation requires. As for me, I play prophet, which is nice. But it does mean having to enjoy existence in a wilderness. Wild beasts roam in the wilderness and I confess I am growing too old to fight for my survival. A villa on a promontory with a broad view – it is a prospect to hanker for."

Stavros's nod was matter-of-fact. He had heard, but had no empathy. He asked, "you want lunch now?"

"No thank you. Perhaps later when I take my medicine. A small cracker then will suffice."

Over Anatolia, Paradis did not look down for an appreciative view of antiquity's great military acts. His eyes had shut, though he was seeing clearly. For him another shape from ancient times was making an appearance. It wasn't a landscape, nor a region. It was a creature, the one that once did its slithering in the tree of good and of evil. That happened to occur in a place which gave rise to his name. Seeing the snake at work, seeing the snake was him, he knew that his enslavement to perfidy had never been greater. When he had trained to serve Bellona, could he have foretold that one day his reporting would be needed on the thoughts of good people whom he had befriended? Could he have predicted that he would have a brush with death and would be spying next on the fine individuals who then nursed him?

The snake flicked its tongue, which caused Paradis to pick up echoes of Helmut's summery voice. Helmut was making four points. He counted them off on his fingers. It was to bring background and clarity to what Paradis would next have to do.

One: An associate in the Pentagon read a transcript about a table chat at a United Nations lunch in New York for a dozen or so prime ministers. Standard stuff. Images from surveillance cameras are always analyzed by trained lip readers. The transcript had some gaps, because if a prime minister bends over to spoon the soup his lip movements can't be seen. Also, lunch material like that is mostly pretty thin. It seldom has much in it to trigger the alerts built into computer screening procedures. The reason the transcript of this chat came to the Pentagon associate for his attention was that the screen was set to pick up references to topics such as soft power, people power, NGOs, democracy building, peace movement, peace building, R2P, etcetera. This transcript had a copious amount of red underlining.

Two: At the lunch, the Dutch prime minister threw interesting phrases at his table partner, the Canadian. *Protecting innocent civilians. Limiting the arms build-up. Promoting non-killing and peace building. Launching a new Dutch-Canadian initiative in this area. Taking the global community a giant leap forward.* It made the hairs on the Pentagon associate's neck stand on end. The Canadian prime minister said nothing. A bracket to the transcript said his body language showed boredom, although towards the end his thin lips did stiffly flutter. *Let's put the puck in the net.* The Dutch prime minister was observed to have responded with enthusiastic nodding.

Three: On this basis, the Pentagon associate was in touch with one of the Society's Associates in the CIA. The standard stakeout in The Hague was consequentially strengthened. Enhanced surveillance of the prime minister's office paid a quick dividend. Each Saturday morning, promptly at ten, the Canadian ambassador was caught on camera entering the building where the Dutch prime minister's foreign policy advisor worked.

Four was a question: Has something started that may undermine the Society's interests? Could there be a link between the wayward thinking of the Dutchman in New York and the sudden Saturday morning regularity of the Canadian ambassador in The Hague?

"See the challenge, Alistair?" Helmut had concluded. "Yours now. Wangle a situation in which you lift the good lady ambassador's hand to your lips. Say the right things. Focus on her fragrance. Say something nice about it. Whatever feels natural. But clarify what she is up to. Talking peace with a Dutchman? If that's what she's doing, no problem. It's easy to stop. It's just that, we don't want to bring in howitzers if not necessary. Get it? We want to be sure. Any insight on how to do that?"

Despite the guise of sleeping deeply, Paradis cringed. He had immediately proclaimed to Helmut that, although he had not met

Her Excellency, her husband was a close professional acquaintance. With a schoolboy's eagerness he also revealed having developed good connections to the embassy itself, to the consular section, for example.

Helmut had crooned. "Connections! Connections! You are indispensable, Alistair. Your sixth sense. It anticipates. You see far ahead. Uncanny. The Society loves you for it. Being in rehab, let's be frank, we didn't predict it, but mano, it's good cover."

Paradis had drawn himself up tall in the wheelchair then and had quipped, "call me *The Patient Spy*."

Helmut began laughing. He laughed until he wheezed, slapped Paradis on the back several times and rang the bell for Stavros.

The Adytum scene became too awful to stick to. Paradis opened his eyes. He pushed a button on his seat, bringing it back to upright. He saw that once again Anatolia had been left far behind. Turning to Stavros, he said, "that cracker now, please, if I may. And my afternoon pills." He worked them down, though he wondered why he bothered.

Chapter 11

Irving Heywood had fallen into a new habit. Nowadays, on Monday mornings, at precisely nine-thirty he rose from his desk to begin pacing. Three steps each way between the walls. A steady back and forth with seamless turnings – the psychotic rhythm of a caged wild animal. It was his way of waiting for Natalia's call.

The arrangement wasn't cast-iron fixed, but at the beginning of the week, mid-afternoon in The Hague, she usually reported in. They seldom talked long – her updates never went beyond a quarter of an hour – yet the prospect of it gave him a wonderful anticipatory rush and satisfied his craving for some solid peer-to-peer companionship.

In between his turnings he would hurl a thought towards the silent phone.

Ring, you cursed thing.

Another dozen circuits in the cubicle. More poisonous glances thrown at the inert device.

In the old days, the contraption used to peal non-stop, vibrant testimony to his influence. Each hour, at least one dozen sentient beings had required urgent access to his brain. And he satisfied them all. He had counselled and comforted, explained and decided, and if all that failed, he had cajoled, or just plain berated, since at the end of the day the only thing that counted was getting good results.

And now?

Natalia, come in. Elevate me. Take me up into the stratosphere, the place I used to roam.

He loved having her teasing voice resonate in his ear. *Hello Irving. All is well today? Juggling the world's affairs? Acting honestly? Answering boldly? Sprinkling your panache over all the issues on the go?*

He would grunt out an affirmative. A serrated tone of voice, he believed, had the merit of diverting compliments. But at home that evening, he'd level with Hannah. "Good day in the salt mine, Sweet. Busy as anything. Found time to take a call from Natalia. Remember? She and her husband came to the cottage last summer. One of our nicest dinners ever. She's doing well. A fine ambassador. One of the best. I'm proud as heck. Every day she vindicates my efforts to get her that promotion. Her pep! Unbelievable. Like mine when I was her age. It affects you even on the phone. Funny how she helps me understand the person I was when I was young."

Shuffling back and forth in his tiny space, Heywood often reflected on Natalia's resolve to get things done, on her purposefulness, her reasonableness and embrace of people, how everyone became her ally. He'd studied her file. He knew that on her postings the local intelligentsia flocked to her. Years ago in Moscow, before glasnost and perestroika, she had uniquely informative contact with local dissidents, though her real feat was avoiding *persona non grata* status under the Soviet regime and getting thrown out of the country. In Islamabad, she co-opted the military with sure-footed interventions. Imagine rank and file soldiers being ordered by the army high command to transport books. But they were. A bunch of platoons in heaving, rolling convoys, full of educational material for kids, inched their way up to Pakistan's far north where the Himalayas meet the Hindu Kush. Yes, in Natalia's presence, bombastic generals were like putty. Same thing in South Africa where she galvanized aid agencies. They adopted her idea for The

Year for Women. She got the apartheid Afrikaner government to accept it too and new cooperatives sprang up all over the country. They functioned smoothly and proved her point: in Africa the aid that delivers dependable results is that which goes to grassroots women. Natalia's file was crammed full of such stories. Wherever she went, the imprint she left was deep.

Natalia, what's happening? Are you stuck in a Dutch traffic jam?

At headquarters between the postings the pattern wasn't any different. At first she was desk officer for disaster relief operations and rewrote the manual on how to get supplies to stricken areas fast. After a promotion – Deputy-director, Human Rights – she took on the Chinese, Serbs, Iranians and Kenyans, annoying them to the point where they squealed, a sure sign of progress. Next step, Director, Global Democratization. What happened? She initiated the preparation of a guide – for journalists, lawyers, students, grassroots organizations and budding politicians still possessing a vestige of idealism. Also for judges who love freedom, but are afraid to come out of the closet. And for business people who understand that democracy and the rule of law are essential for long term profits. In short, for everyone everywhere under the thumb of authoritarian rule. In this guide, Natalia provided detailed, practical advice. On organizing non-violent civil resistance. On avoiding repressive state security machinery. On promoting solidarity and achieving legitimacy. For good measure, she threw in her own golden rules for success, such as listening, respecting and seeking ways to deepen understanding. The little guide became an underground best seller, appearing on the index of banned books in all the places where the concept of sovereignty remains a fig leaf for the exertion of totalitarian control. How, Heywood had argued, can you *not* make someone who has done all that an ambassador? He trembled with pride every time he reminded himself he was the one who plucked her out of the swollen ranks of Service over-achievers.

Natalia, my ward, please magnify my shrivelled soul by punching thirteen simple digits into your phone.

Admittedly, once the press release was out, once Natalia was formally ambassador and she and her husband came to the cottage for dinner, she did knock back quite a few martinis. Three before dinner no problem. But was there a problem? He raised it with Hannah afterwards.

"Come now, Irving," Hannah pooh-poohed. "You sometimes have three, four whiskeys on the porch on a hot afternoon." Hannah's tolerance for human foibles was legendary.

"Not the same, sweet," he had countered. "I have a bigger volume."

"You drank as much forty years ago in Nigeria when we met, and you were slimmer then."

"Sure, but I had a good reason. I lacked self-confidence at the time. You changed that."

"Well, maybe it's like that for her. Maybe she feels she is on stage when she is with others. Maybe she feels she has to perform. Maybe a drink or two helps get it going. Like you."

"Like me?"

Heywood thought about this and concluded it was true. Natalia was like him. In numerous ways. They both thrived on pressure, even if afterwards they occasionally took a couple of aperitifs. And their intellects were similarly dynamic, having the will to leap over obstacles. And now they were close collaborators. How truly wonderful was that? Furthermore, if through their partnership she delivered a new peace package in The Hague – a gift to the world – his reputation was bound to gain its final patina. Heywood had thought long about this, about his career ending in glory with one final, great achievement. If the peace package was decent, with him doing the headquarters anchoring, he would surely be called on to brief the PM. *That* was in the cards. And probably the PM would desire him to come along to The Hague. And there, at the peace meeting, he would sit behind, maybe even next to the PM who would want him to whisper salient advice. *That* would be noticed. Everyone would finally understand that as Co-Deputy Minister Irving Heywood had been working his butt off all these months on devilishly secret files.

Such were the unforeseen consequences of having made Natalia an ambassador and you just had to love them.

Natalia, I really need to know that the peace thing is on track.

Eventually the phone began its ringing and Heywood studied it. At the last moment, in dignified, slow ceremony, he brought it to his ear. "Irving Heywood here." He made his voice sound distant, as if his mind was elsewhere.

"Good morning, Irving." Natalia's voice was bright. "You sound preoccupied. Am I disturbing something?"

"Ah, Natalia. It's you. No, no. Just shooing three people out of my office this second. Hang on... OK. Now you have my undivided attention. Has the world gone through two millennia since we last spoke? It seems like it. So much happening here. Life on a conveyor belt. But let's you and I not feel rushed. By the way, the PM's people often ask me about your progress. Have I mentioned that before?"

~

Natalia's report was longer than usual and the news was good. Very good. Undeniable progress. When the phone was dead again, he replayed the conversation in his mind.

Right at the start, well, he kicked himself. A mistake to bring the PM's people into the conversation. Natalia immediately pressed him about their involvement, wanting to know if that crowd was doing some new thinking. Had they mentioned specific peace initiatives they wanted her to table? She had not had much help from anyone thus far. Heywood had to do some fast fudging. Smoothly, in grunted tones of authority, he answered: "What you've worked out until now has been thoroughly considered by everyone here with an interest. What you're doing is fine. You know as well as I do, Natalia, when that crowd says something is fine, it is an understatement. It means they're thrilled. No nitpicking from this end. They want you to forge ahead."

She seemed satisfied because when he next asked how the peace package was evolving, she gurgled out enthusiasm. The latest meeting with the Dutch foreign policy advisor was productive. Agreement that a Peace Summit would launch the initiative. Between fourteen and twenty selected prime ministers to be invited to attend. Canada's PM to give the opening statement. It was assumed he would talk about raising the famous Responsibility to Protect doctrine to a higher level of effectiveness, setting out a vision for how ordinary people all over the world would be guaranteed peace and security. Maybe a couple more speeches would follow, after which the prime ministers would individually sign a peace proclamation. *We declare that the greatest good to which humanity can aspire is non-killing co-existence.* After the signing, a communal press conference and, lastly, lunch or dinner with the Dutch Queen.

"Whoa, Natalia," Heywood hollered. "Hold on. Two things here. There's the substance in the proclamation and the protocol of the whole event. Let's keep them separate. Substance first. Go on."

"Well, you know I have the lead on substance. Heiko's thinking about the protocol."

"I do know that and I have to say I worry about his side of things, but we'll come to that."

"The latest on substance is this: we still don't have a really big new idea, something that's got instant zing, you know, star power, something the world can't help but notice. I'm mulling that over though. What new commitment to peace can we make that will be different from what we have? If you or the PM's people have a brainwave, please, let me know. Heiko has embraced the ideas I've tabled so far." Natalia reviewed what she had put into the draft peace proclamation, the preciousness of human life, important aspects of identity such as kinship, belief systems and collective memory, which form cultures and give life meaning, but also bring people into conflict and are used as reasons for killing. The political abuse of culture would be denounced. She came to the proclamation paragraph where prime ministers would commit themselves to reducing the size of the military, the resources freed up to be used to create legions of peace-builders.

"Peace-builders?" Heywood growled. "What's the difference between peace-builders and the blue-helmet crowd we have already?"

Natalia explained that *peacekeepers* move around in armoured personnel carriers and carry rifles, whereas *peace-builders* would be civilians, people trained to understand the causes of conflict, and why and how it deepens. They would be skilled in preventing and resolving hostilities using techniques of communicating, mediating and negotiating. They would speak local languages and understand the cultures they were working with. Peace-builders, she argued, win trust and bridge societies.

"Global social workers, right? Baseball caps instead of helmets. Feet wrapped in leather sandals."

"The prime ministers won't be quibbling about dress codes, Irving. The emphasis will be on relationship building and on long-term investments in cultures potentially in conflict or already so. Current and future hostilities shall be eliminated."

"Yeah, I get that. I'm with you. I guess it's true, now that I think about it. Patrolling barbed wire fences all day, that's sort of passé. For sure we'd get a supportive op-ed piece in the papers on the conceptual transition from *keeper* to *builder*. A plus for the PM. Let's say that's decided. Peacekeepers are out; peace-builders are the new sexy. What else?"

It was one thing, Natalia explained, to proclaim that legions of peace-builders would be as numerous as today's battalions of combatants, but for that to happen recruitment and training programs were necessary. Schools would have to be founded, maybe a new world university. Naturally, the standards set would be high. Peace-builders would have an intellectual preparation as tough and demanding as the physical one is for specialized commandos. Governments would have to reorganize themselves too. "Each attending prime minister would sign onto a commitment to create a national peace department. Ministers of peace would have a higher cabinet rank than ministers of defence. You have to send that kind of signal."

"Wait a sec," Heywood cautioned. "That's assuming a lot. I don't see a problem carving out peace departments. Taking a chunk out of the military and a pile of cash out of the aid folk – that's well-traveled terrain. The environment crowd is used to coughing up resources too. Ditto health. It wouldn't be that tough to put a decent bureaucracy together to get on with peace. And I agree, why shouldn't the peace minister be senior? One way or another, that's all do-able. But new schools? A new world university? My instinct says there wouldn't be much enthusiasm for that here. It's been a while since we opened the chequebook for an international commitment. That tendency is gone. The political culture has evolved, Natalia. We like to talk as much as we always did, but we no longer like to pay.

"Therefore, I ask this question. Will the Dutch commit themselves to paying for the schools if that is what's needed as a bribe to get the invited prime ministers to sign the proclamation?"

"Too early for that, Irving. All I can say is that when I put the idea of a global civilian peace service to Heiko, he was keen. Some countries already have a national peace service, so it is partially a question of joining up the existing efforts. To develop peace professionals, why not just turn war and defence colleges into peace colleges? They could link up as nodes in an international educational peace network with common entry and graduation standards. As you can see, lots of ways to go."

"Military colleges becoming peace colleges? Clever. Could have a good PR dimension. And it would save on uniforms, bayonets and ammunition. Yeah, I like it. Good forward thinking, Natalia. Am I right in thinking that all the substantive stuff would be in an operative part of the proclamation, or declaration?"

"That's right. After the preamble. The preamble would describe the causes of conflicts and the obstacles to peace. There will be a significant section on poverty, the single biggest conflict factor. In future, some of the trillions spent on war will go to women, children, health, education and strong programs to prevent young people from becoming interested in joining extremist organizations."

"I like that too," Heywood said gruffly. "The substance is in good hands. Congrats, Natalia. Innovative stuff. Crystal clear, too. Carry on, is all I can say. Now let's talk protocol. Can I assume that the prime ministers will sit at a summit round table, each one having an advisor behind or right next to him?"

"Something along those lines."

"It's the most sensible approach. As for lunch or dinner with the Queen, I imagine it's the same formula, prime ministers plus one advisor? Will it be in the royal palace?"

"I'm sure."

"Perfect."

"Heiko has spent some time on the pros and cons of countries to be invited."

"Yeah?" Suspicion crept into Heywood's voice. "Which ones is he thinking of?"

"He's looking at a reasonable global distribution. Democratic imbalances among regions pose some limits, but the peace club will be exclusive at the start anyway, making it more enticing for others to join later by signing on to the peace commitments. Founding members, he's thinking, should include Sweden, Norway and Malta from Europe. Malta is doing good work on training the new generations of diplomats. From the Americas, apart from Canada, probably Costa Rica and Chile. Africa we know is tough. Few credible democracies there. Botswana may be the best candidate. In the Pacific area, New Zealand rather than Australia. Some suspect Aussies harbour a latent xenophobia. Also Indonesia or the Philippines. The Maldives could be in. That would send an interesting signal to India. India would be excluded because it strives for global power status. Some countries such as Mongolia, Qatar, Jordan need more analysis. We'll have to see how Egypt develops."

"Ukraine."

"What about Ukraine?"

"Get them in."

"Why?"

"Aren't you from there?"

"My grandparents. On my father's side. So what?"

"From what I read, Ukraine has had a tough history, always administered from someplace else. Now they're running their own affairs. I would conclude Ukrainians are like you – forceful and creative, able to persevere, with a strong tendency to exist in harmony with neighbours. Ukraine could be perfect for the initiative. Plus, the Russians would be annoyed." The phone line stayed silent. Heywood pressed. "Agree?"

"Leave it with me, Irving. I'll test it with Heiko."

"Let's hope he doesn't take too much time mulling it over. If it were up to you and me, we'd have a peace package put together and the summit launched by now."

Talking with Natalia this way, Heywood felt contentment surging. Trading big ideas on the phone with others who had intellectual agility was what he did non stop during the glory days. It was coming back to him. "Have I ever told you I was in The Hague once?" he asked. "Back in the eighties. The PM at the time was keen on nuclear disarmament. There had been that, you know, NATO double-track decision to dot the German countryside with short-range nuclear missiles aimed at the Warsaw Pact. It caused some bother and the PM thought that with a little elbow grease he could get everyone to agree to reduce all kinds of missile deployments on both sides. It was a big time initiative. He planned to fly to all the capitals. The problem was, on his little plane, there was room for just one expert. Who would it be? The candidates were me or a windbag Brigadier General who wore a beret. The phone lines into the PM's office just about melted. It took a while to figure out what was needed. When cool heads prevailed, everyone realized that the Brigadier General had commanded a tank corps, whereas the PM required someone having the skill of framing subtle arguments. It was a squeeze for me getting into that little plane, but that's how I came to spend eight hours in The Hague. Good hours. I remember, the motorcade from the airport didn't stop once. When the current PM goes to our summit, I assume there will be that kind of good motorcade work again. Funny, isn't it? Twenty-five years go by and you find nothing is different. After The Hague we went to Moscow…"

"Irving, sorry, I've got an appointment in twenty minutes."

"Sure thing, Natalia. Off you go. Fly the flag. A noble thing to do. And let's not lose our vigilance. A lesson I learned the hard way is that people like Duhbrouyeen cannot fundamentally be trusted. We've got to second-guess him the whole way."

~

After the call, waiting for time to pass until the coffee break, Heywood turned to his computer and opened the Service Records browser. He clicked a few times and was soon looking at files from the early eighties on that disarmament initiative. The digital scans that appeared struck him as works of art. Nostalgia settled over him. His life, everything he once was, had been meticulously archived. His career, Irving thought, was sort of like a Pharaoh entombed. Imagine Tutankhamun still alive. Imagine him going on an archaeological dig. He discovers the early version of himself deep down in the ground and sees that what he once was has become gold-plated. "That," Heywood told himself as he clicked, "is how I feel."

Awe arose inside him. Awe for himself. It motivated him to click on, down through further layers, through memoranda he had written in the olden days and through the bygone battles. All of it lay there, accurately chronicled. Finally, he saw the things he valued more than almost everything – his ancient travel and expense claims. Goose bumps tightened his skin as he remembered confidently striding into five-star suites. With supreme authority he had barked orders into the phone – for caviar, champagne and whiskey chasers to be brought up. And why not, seeing as how the host country was paying for it.

Soon, The Hague again. A final VIP trip. Heywood felt excitement seizing his great gut. *Natalia, thank you. You cause the sun to shine and I am making hay again.*

Chapter 12

The air in Natalia's office felt burdened after the talk with Heywood, as if alongside his bombast a contamination had streamed in. She reflected on the conversation. Peculiar, how readily he had accepted all her suggestions. Setting up a global civilian peace service, governments slashing the size of war departments to create new peace departments – not exactly candidates for the flavour-of-the-month award. Nor was this all that smelled. Normal functionaries assume a bunker mentality when the status quo is threatened. Whiffs of change are treated like bombardments. They resist. They hide. They defend. But Heywood seemed immune. He put up no obstacles. What did that signal? That he viewed her proposals as minor? That they threatened nothing. He had not even brought out the pros and cons ledger. Was he treating them this casually because he had a larger strategy? Was something else, something big and ominous, going on? *Might get an op-ed or two in the papers.* What kind of justification was that for embracing proposals intended to force the world's political discourse up a few notches?

Listening to Heywood sometimes made you feel you were listening to a barker at a carnival talking into a megaphone. Today's *nays* and *yeas* were so flippant, so smooth and quick, that you couldn't help but conclude that he believed he was answerable only to himself. As if he had the PM himself sitting in his hip pocket. Could this be true? Had Heywood become positioned as close to power as he claimed? The PM was a wormy operator, a low-road traveller, not known for being interested in the well-being of generations to come. But suppose the man had experienced moral growth. Suppose that the New York lunch had changed him. Suppose the PM had been thinking, and concluded it was time he did some legacy building, that he should start doing some things today, which will benefit the generations of tomorrow. In this scenario, could it be that Heywood had convinced the PM that he possessed that most mysterious of diplomatic formulae, the one which leads – *Presto!* – to a respectable international reputation? Heywood, Chief Executive Diplomat to this PM? Natalia shuddered.

She reasoned further. If Heywood truly had become a kind of small-time Talleyrand or Kissinger, she should worry about the direction of the country's foreign policy, but not about her role in it. If Heywood had experienced an investiture of some kind and was now influential, then he had acquired the privilege for whipping off snappy judgements. He could on the spot say *yea* to a Peace Department and *nay* to a Peace College, if that pleased him. But if a fraud was on, if Heywood was playing a game – if that was the smell that had come wafting in – how would she, as an accomplice, fare on the inevitable reckoning day? *I was taking orders.* That excuse was long passé.

Natalia stared ahead, fingers drumming the desktop. Had she reverted to that time, months before, when the peace discussion began and doubt overcame her? A phone call to Ranford Tolman at the UN had settled that down. Ranford had confirmed that the two PMs talked at that lunch. In his kind, wise way, without prying, he'd encouraged her to carry on. Since then, she had contacted him several times to sound him out, or get advice on the substantive concepts she was working on. In confidence, he said that since in

New York no UN group, not even the Secretary General, seemed able to make progress on peace, it was important the flame continued burning elsewhere. Ranford provided steady support. He kept stiffening her resolve. Once, when he told her he would be in Ottawa for consultations, she asked if a few private minutes for him with Harry Berezowski were in the works. This was indeed planned, he answered.

"Would you mind doing a gentle probe for me?" she asked. "Would you mind asking Harry what he thinks about the peace work I'm doing on the side in The Hague? I would feel better having confirmation he is aware of it."

A week later, Tolman called back. "I met Harry. I asked. He said he knows you are doing high level, concept development work in the area of peace. That Irving updates him once a week. The updates are casually done, apparently. No paper side to it. But yes, he is in the loop. Irving is to show him the final product when it exists. So carry on, Natalia. Keep doing what you're good at." It settled her anxiety. For a while.

Today, again, Heywood really was too glib. Doubts about the Ottawa end were rekindled. Should she telephone Tolman again? Inquire once again about Heywood's standing with Harry? After thinking about it, Natalia concluded, that was pointless. Ranford would not know more today than what he knew a month ago. He might even be irked, having to repeat what he'd already said. Was there someone else who would know about the standing Heywood had with Berezowski. Who could confirm that it was as Heywood claimed, that they were each other's alter ego, conjoined twins? Natalia mentally flipped through her list of professional friends. Who might know? With whom could she chat off the record? She came to Michael. Of course. Yes. Michael O'Reilly.

Natalia's bond with Michael went back decades when they were both on a posting. Michael, Jane and their three pre-school aged children had arrived in Moscow for their first overseas assignment ten days before she and Donovan did. Michael was a part-time guitar player and soon enough was sitting back with Donovan, the self-appointed master on the instrument, to strum out some duets. Many happy Moscow hours were spent in the

O'Reilly household. Two married men crooned about thwarted loves and three kids laughed, screamed and went crazy.

Michael and Natalia moved up through the Service ranks at the same pace. His current fief was media and communications, which meant he sat on senior committees, met Harry Berezowski daily and had a wide view of policy trends. He would hear the gossip too. If Irving Heywood truly was roaming through that strange and rarefied landscape that surrounds political power, Michael would know.

Natalia dialled him twice in one hour and both times was shunted into voicemail, which she ignored. The third time, O'Reilly answered. He was in a cab going to a lunch. She asked if he had a couple of minutes.

"Natalia, this ride will take fifteen and each one is yours. How are you? We talk too seldom. Why is that? Don't answer. I know."

"You're busy?"

"Too busy even for a heart attack. Crazy work, Natalia. Every day the assembly line runs faster. It's lunacy. Six more months and I'm gone. I don't know where. Your spot will not be vacant, I assume. I hear you have a big garden. That sounds like room for occasional solitude. I hope you take the time for it. What's up?"

"Nothing special. It's spring here. The flowers are out. It's quite lovely. The mood is uplifting and I thought it was high time to connect up with you. Jane is fine? And the kids?"

"All good." Michel gave details on university achievements and the attendant tuition costs.

The newsy exchange went back and forth. Natalia learned that several of their generation really had been struck down by heart attacks.

"The good ones get hit," she observed, "while others keep barrelling along. I hear Heywood is still peppy. Not even his teeming flesh seems to stop him."

"True," Michael laughed, "when it comes to size, Mr Heywood is one of a kind."

"What's he up to?"

"He pinch-hits for Harry and does assorted things. When Harry took over last fall he ignored Heywood. That changed. Slowly.

Heywood comes to the coordination meetings again. He cracks us all up with his imperial ego. He likes to remark that the Service is lightweight now. Then he shakes his great gut and says he's the sole heavyweight left. We all laugh, naturally. What's with Heywood?"

"Part of my resolution to stay in touch more. Don't tell him this, but he was kind to me last summer. He and Hannah had Carlos and me over for a *bon voyage* dinner. I'm wondering now, if I call him, you know, show an interest in how he is, whether I should commiserate because he's been sidelined, or sound glad that he's still doing the sumo wrestling of old."

"Don't commiserate. Don't prod him on his current campaigns, either. That's my advice. Convince him to start drawing his pension." A renewed chuckle came to Natalia from the back seat of the distant cab.

"Maybe I'll ask him what it's like to be picking up Harry's overload. Is there a pattern to that, Michael? A focus on particular issues? Are he and Harry close?"

"There is a pattern. I can't be sure about the issues they share, but their body language is fine. Whenever those two are in the same room, Heywood teases Harry. He winks at him. Not exaggerated. Not too obvious. And Harry winks back. What's going on between those two? Is there a private joke on the go? The rest of us don't know. If you talk to Heywood, ask him about the winking, Natalia, and if what he tells you is wickedly funny, call me. Maybe Harry has done something naughty and Irving knows it. At the end of the meetings, though, as we file out, those two usually go into a corner. The way they talk then, it looks serious enough."

Michael's cab was arriving at the restaurant.

~

After they broke their connection, Natalia pulled the short talk apart. She discounted that senior-level winking. Something like it was always going on. Usually it was done more subtly than what Heywood managed. His wink to Berezowski merely said: *You and I both know you've got the job I should have had.* And Berezowski's happy eyelids signalled back that he denied it: *Not your job at all, Irving. You know as well as I do, it is the best that triumph.*

Michael's take on Heywood proved and disproved little. If anything, it corroborated what Ranford had reported. For the peace initiative, all could be sound in Ottawa. If the interest high up was genuine, as Heywood always claimed it was, she should consider herself blessed. But the situation could be the opposite too. Double-dealing could be going on. If so, should she continue?

Natalia reviewed her options. That last question, she decided, could be flipped. Did she have it in her *not* to carry on? Advancing the issues with de Bruyn had become meaningful. She believed more deeply all the time in the value of shaping a peace summit.

"Do I have enough conviction," Natalia thought, "to decide that I don't give a hoot whether Irving Heywood is a swindler or a saint? I hold a respected position. I am in the right place at the right time. Events have conspired to give me a chance to do good on a grand scale. An alignment like this is unlikely to come along again. I could decide to feed Heywood crumbs from now on, enough to keep him thinking that his game plan is progressing. For my part, I would let nothing stand in the way of pushing a new approach to global peace to the limits. If it has merit, it will acquire standing. Once a good idea has formed, it doesn't go away, not even if a summit meeting fails. It remains, somewhere it remains, simmering, waiting for the right moment to take on a new life. Take the International Criminal Court. If someone hadn't thought and pushed for it, would it be functioning today?"

With delicious recklessness, Natalia made a decision. The process with de Bruyn would continue. Heywood would be kept on a course that fed his ego, whereas she would set hers by rejecting bureaucratic boundaries. If that meant that one day she would be branded as a rogue ambassador, and censured, so be it. The cause was worth the risk.

With this as a fresh starting condition, Natalia sat in quiet exhilaration. She had taken control. "It is a *coup*," she thought. "A *coup de soi-même*. After all these years I have managed it."

Chapter 13

"Ambassador Plavniuk!" The greeting rolled across the residence patio towards Natalia like a sonic boom. "At last I meet the woman who graces Carlos." Alistair Paradis came hobbling forward, behind a walker. An attentive Carlos at his side held out a hand in case the old man faltered.

"Mr Paradis," she replied graciously. "Very glad to meet you. It's good to see you on your feet. You've had a terrible ordeal." Her first impression of Paradis was as Robbie had described him, only more so – taller, rounder, a larger head and wilder, longer white hair that dropped over his shirt collar at the back. He looked more like a fashion designer than a peace prophet.

"Your husband calls me Alistair," Paradis chided.

"And me, Natalia."

"He is a fine man. And you are right. Adversity struck me."

"Do sit down. My grandmother had a saying – adversity brings wisdom."

"And teaches us humility."

"And I shall run in to get refreshments," Carlos interjected. He saw these two would not be grappling with silence.

A warming, late spring breeze was rustling through the trees. In the flowerbeds, lupines and irises, the blooms still young, were ravishingly colourful. Amidst this serenity, Paradis thanked the ambassador vociferously for sending him a car, a driver and a husband to lend him an arm.

"We've been wanting to have you over for weeks," Natalia answered. She was wearing a dress that matched the lupines and the irises – streaks of dark blue and deep purple, with ruddy-rosy touches. A diamond pendant dangling from a gold chain around her neck scattered the rays of the sun. "Robbie has been keeping me informed on your progress. She said you were finally up to getting out."

Paradis sighed. "My guardian angel Robbie. She delivered me from a hospital in which death was pestilentially prevalent. Then she signed me into a rehabilitation center so glorious it really ought to change its name to mine. And precisely on the day when boredom was getting the better of me, she brought me brochures on fine apartments. Now I am pampered daily by a Filipino domestic, a virtuoso physiotherapist from Morocco and an oriental massage maestro. I have concluded that with Robbie in support a man could survive several airplane crashes in a lifetime."

"Robbie is convinced you are worth the effort. She admires your philosophy."

"My philosophy? It is all I have. May I ask how she describes it?"

"Let me think. That the finest aspects of life derive from our capacity for spirituality. Along those lines."

"Accurate enough. I like to think most people have it in them to arrive at that insight before their end. Robbie is special. She is young, yet radiates hard-won wisdom."

Natalia nodded and added her take on why Robbie was unique, which Paradis then augmented with more comments of his own. This character polishing continued for a while. When Carlos returned with a large tray, laden with cups and spoons and coffee, tea and pastries, they were animatedly comparing notes on the virtue of helping people in distress. "Good Samaritanism?" Carlos asked. "Is that what you're on to? Already? Before the cordials? I'm no good practicing it, but I know cultures that are. What brought you to that topic so fast?"

"Robbie," Natalia said.

"Robbie?" Carlos placed the tray onto the table. "I should have guessed. Has Alistair told you about her latest good turn? He is in an apartment now. In a wonderful building. It looks like a museum for modern art."

"You only saw the back of it when you came for me today, Carlos. There's a view on the other side. From my balcony, I look down on a landscape unchanged from the middle ages – farms and meadows full of fat cows. A dyke goes right the way around it all. One has the feeling it was designed that way just to give the people living there a feeling of snug enclosure."

"You have discovered the secret of polder life, Alistair."

"Is that good?"

"I would say so. Most of the time. But do watch the meadows closely. If you see a Spanish militia setting up camp, get away. Run as fast as your walker will let you. The Dutch get nervy when Spaniards show up in their polders. They've been known to slash their dykes to drive them out, and you don't want to be in a polder when North Sea waves roll in."

"Thank you, Carlos. As always, you give excellent advice."

"Carlos has a thing about Spaniards," Natalia explained. "Fortunately he's objective about everything else. He is knowledgeable about more than polder life, by the way. For example, he knew the meaning of the acronym on your calling card. It stumped me. Robbie too. All she was able to find that seemed to fit to PEACE was, if I remember right, Palestine-Europe Academic Cooperation on Education. Luckily, Carlos straightened us out."

Paradis chuckled. "Carlos would straighten the whole world out if it would listen to him. There may be an overlap of sorts between my PEACE and that Palestine-Europe one. Education. Every chance I get, I promote it. I mean real education, not indoctrination. A broad perspective, the onset of understanding – that undermines parochialism. We know that parochial minds conceive the most terrible things."

"I see it that way too," Natalia said with rising excitement. "Imagine if, for the last half-century, the world's foreign aid had invested in the goal of every child having twelve years of schooling."

"I *have* tried to imagine that," Paradis said, his large head vigorously moving up and down.

"I'm sure you have. Twelve years of schooling for every child, and developing countries would be much higher on the global development index."

"A few big rungs up that ladder, indeed," the old man agreed. He knocked the table top with a knuckle for emphasis. "And we would all be sitting higher on the global morality index too."

As Carlos set out cups and saucers and was distributing spoons, Natalia leaned forward. "I have a question." Paradis bowed slightly, the palms of his hands coming together with the fingertips up. A pose of respect. "Ever since Carlos informed me what your PEACE stands for, I've wanted to know more about the *People Everywhere* part of it."

"Coffee or tea?" Carlos interrupted. Paradis chose tea, as did Natalia. Carlos took coffee. "Which pastry?" he asked next. The tray had cream puffs, strawberry tarts and slices of chocolate cheesecake. Paradis pointed at a piece of cheesecake and Natalia lifted off a cream puff.

"What's your connection to the masses?" Natalia persisted. "What made you decide to link up with them? And, specifically, who are they?"

～

Paradis took a deep breath. "I was in the entertainment business once," he began. His great head quivered and his face looked pained, as if that part of his past shamed him. "I developed an act." His eyes closed, recalling it. "Like a priest, I wished to express pathos. The trouble was – only the burlesque stage would take me. It was perverse." Paradis fell back into the patio chair and sent Natalia a haggard look. "Most difficult was that the more pathos I injected into my act the louder the audience laughed. It caused me to think deeply about the human condition." He shuddered, as if once more he needed get the trauma of it behind him. Natalia and Carlos patiently sipped their tea and coffee.

"The human condition?" Natalia eventually prompted. "Please, don't hold back your thoughts on that. I'm interested."

"I wish to share them. I truly do. I admit, I could not really blame my audience for laughing. They were predisposed to do so since I was dressed up as a clown. But is a clown so different from a priest? Why is there no laughter when the priests dress up? Being a clown was my way of being a priest. Yet, the contrast between my feelings on the stage and the revelry in the crowd was dreadful and I concluded that the human condition consists mostly of stark contrasts."

"Life would be duller than an ant heap without them," Carlos said blandly.

Natalia lifted her teacup, saw it was empty and poured herself more. "Dressed up as a clown and shedding tears of poignancy while parading before raucous spectators – is that when you conceived PEACE?"

"Not so linearly. That insight sprang up along the way."

Paradis began to describe his thought journey. The narration had flair, as if the residence's patio was also a stage and his task was to hold the audience spellbound. He went back, far back, all the way to the beginning, to the origins of the universe, the big bang. From there he jumped to the dual nature of humanity coming to terms with that moment, science or religion. He rambled on, touching on a few great staging points of humanity's intellectual growth, such as the capacity for abstraction. Abstraction, Paradis claimed, is a prerequisite for the existence of beauty and morality, but also for evil.

Wherever could this be leading?

Natalia listened intently. She had arranged for Paradis to visit because she hoped to acquire something from him. She had a peace declaration to compose and wanted civil society's role purposefully woven in. But his answer to her direct question was convoluted and mostly mystical. Not too usable. For his part, he appeared confident that he was making sense. He kept count of his main points by taking hold of one finger after another, first on one hand, then switching to the other when fingers ran out. Each time a finger was grabbed, Natalia made a mental note, reducing what he was saying to what she thought he meant.

179

On the existence of the universe and humanity's role in it: *Generation by generation we add to our knowledge, from the very large to the very small, but not for thousands of years have we developed truly fresh insight into what it means. How is it that we can be so expansive, yet remain so limited?*

On biology: *The individual is beyond biology, but rooted in it. It is the reason why we constantly go back and forth between joy and suffering.*

On the mind: *If diligently directed, it renders riches unequalled in the material world. Is it not perplexing that gold, or diamonds, has permanence, whereas the mind is transient?*

On conflict: *The material world holds us as pawns in the ceaseless struggle between upheaval and tranquillity. This gives rise to our craving for security and peace. When conflict recedes and peace is achieved, the necessary preconditions for the mind's spiritual expansion are in place.*

When Paradis eventually stopped his face had hardened, as if his truths were stark but ultimate. Lifting his teacup, he emptied it in one gulp.

"More?" Natalia asked. Paradis pushed the cup forward.

"My thoughts reverberate in me," he said glumly. "Like thunderclaps in mountains. New ones crack while preceding ones still rumble. My apologies if your ears got boxed around a bit."

"But no." Natalia reached forward and placed her hand on his arm. The journey he described, she said, was winding. Its turns were fascinating and illuminating, and she thanked him for sharing them. To be sure she had it right, however, would he mind if she restated what she believed she heard him say?

"Please do. Improve on it. If we don't improve, we stagnate. Stagnation is the first stage of decline."

"Very true. Well, what I heard you say was that the universe appears, life begins and the mind emerges. So far so good?"

"That is delightful brevity."

"The mind assumes an overriding purpose for itself – the search for certainty. The certainty it arrives at very quickly is the most obvious of all, that to live is to suffer."

"That truly is, I believe, a supreme truth."

"Next, the mind discovers the antidote to suffering – spiritual expansion."

"Its salutariness is widely acknowledged."

"And, to engage in spiritual expansion we benefit from tranquillity and harmonious surroundings."

"You would be surprised how many people intuitively understand that."

A silence set in.

Carlos's irony broke it. "When struck dumb by magnificent wisdom only a good drink brings the voice back. I know what Natalia likes. What's your preference, Alistair? Will the doctors allow you to go beyond water with a sugar cube added?"

"Carlos, you are the most divine heretic." Paradis's broad smile sent cracks spreading into his jowls. "You say water with sugar. That sounds alright, though I will take it in the form of rum. Add nothing. Make it a double. We must not waste a single second of this delightful afternoon."

~

Paradis had his double rum, and then another. Natalia sipped on a martini and also took one more. For himself, Carlos poured white wine and did not scrimp on refills. In the garden in the afternoon under the large open sky, they fused into a cabal of three that enjoyed thinking that possessing life is like owning a good, engaging puzzle.

Throughout, Natalia continued to pump Paradis on PEACE, as if that, not rum or martinis, would make the afternoon delightful. Paradis had conquered his trauma, it seemed, because he now described more easily how, as the circus tent howling continued, he shed his alter ego as a clown. Meditation was next, a long period, though he was vague about where it took place. He came out transformed, having thought his way through the problem of contrasts and having developed a message – that, like the speed of light, humankind is an absolute. How so? Because nothing else has the capacity to conceive what is essential. Each of humanity's members has that special, precious capacity. Each has a spirit and each spirit must be nourished. This is a communal obligation achieved through peace, not war.

Paradis described how in the United States he took his message from town to town – receptions in ladies' auxiliary groups and at the Kiwanis clubs. He engaged with theology societies in annexes to religious buildings. He talked at shelters for abused women and held hands at AA meetings. Nor was he afraid, he claimed, of prison visits and academics. A network coalesced out of this wandering. A sect, a subculture, was linked up. News of the message spread. People everywhere adopted the simple tenet that the purposeful unfolding of the universe is one and the same as meaningful co-existence in a secure neighborhood. The network soon had a hundred thousand members. Two years later, it stood at a million. One million became ten. Next, twelve, or fifteen?

"One hundred million PEACE adherents in ten years' time is probable," Paradis claimed modestly.

As the alcohol in them slowly raised its conducting baton, the sense of community tightened. Natalia leaned forward. "You are the leader of ten million people prepared to intervene for what they believe in?" she asked. "That's a formidable collective. Are there more details?"

She wanted to know how the practicalities of it were managed. How these people everywhere were kept together? What promoted their sense of solidarity? Who maintained the websites? How were email lists kept up-to-date? Was social networking a tool? Were there chat rooms, blogs and other such techniques? Did mobile phones in large sophisticated cities and in poor small villages ring in unison if an important common message had to be delivered? And, if peace were threatened, if it became broken, could the millions who had declared themselves to be against conflict and evil be orchestrated to act as one? She went on to provide an overview of security challenges. Nuclear blackmail by North Korea, a despot in Zimbabwe actively destroying his country, a theocracy in Iran funding murder, a military dictatorship in Myanmar, state criminality in Darfur-Sudan so bad it was causing genocide – what could people everywhere against conflict and evil do about that? Could an injunction be delivered to the millions to begin a global demonstration against such brutalities? If so, who would push the *SEND* button?

Paradis's face had turned ruddier. *You have many questions*, his amused eyes signalled, *so many minor questions. With the roles we have, should we not be dwelling on the bigger picture?* In keeping with this, he answered with more blanket statements, such as raising oneself to a higher, a more important, a more mystical level.

Carlos had been listening quietly, not sharing views or offering opinions, but at the mention of Darfur-Sudan and holding up his glass to inspect the colour of the wine, he finally chipped in. He had been working on a monograph about that benighted place, he said, a contribution to an international investigation into the years of rampant civilian killings. "We read about it, but all the same it isn't easy for us to fully understand the horror of what's going on." He stroked his beard. "As we sit in this tranquil Dutch enclave we could try to imagine how it would be if brutal barbarians galloped in, right this minute.

"We hear them going from house to house. The air fills with pistol shots and rifle fire. As family members watch their kin get shot, they wail in terror knowing the next bullet is for them. With everyone soon dead or dying, houses are put to the torch. Now we hear them approaching us. We have no place to hide. All we can do is live a few last horrible, surreal minutes until we too slump forward, here, onto this patio table, with bullets in our heads. If you can imagine that, you will have an inkling of what's happening in Darfur."

The way Paradis was nodding, intensely and with foreboding, he really was imagining his life ending with a bullet. He said, "the unconstrained murder of defenseless people is a stain, a constant one, on the moral record of the nations of the world. If you are holding the pen explaining the Darfur genocide, Carlos, I am confident the UN will soon understand what has seemed inexplicable so far. We must know the causes if we are to work out solutions. What lies at the heart of it? Another politico-ethnic problem?"

"It is larger and deeper than that. It is an everything problem."

Natalia seldom heard her husband talk about his work, but when he did, it fascinated her. She also wanted to hear his take on Darfur. "What do you mean by that?" she asked. "What is 'an everything problem'?"

They sat so close their elbows touched. Carlos with his gift to render complexity simple, explained yet another of the many genocides he had studied.

~

For centuries in Darfur, a remote sultanate, people live placidly in rich African-Arab linguistic and tribal diversity. Farmers, herders, nomads. The land used is effectively communal. Tribal elders negotiate solutions to disputes.

Two hundred years ago or so the British arrive and bring with them concepts of public administration that involve hierarchies. The Darfur Sultanate is now part of a larger administered region, the Sudan. When the British leave in 1956, Sudan becomes a sovereign state, though lacking the skills, knowledge and ideas necessary to run itself. Sudan's experience is the same as that of other new sovereign states. Sovereignty means a strong man, or a small elite, who take over and then do as they please, answerable to no one. Which is to say there is power but no responsibility. Sudan is located in a predatory neighborhood. Libya is to Darfur's north-west, Chad directly to the west. A succession of post colonial shocks hit.

The 1970s and 80s bring one military coup after another. The government in Khartoum changes regularly, and weird administrative diktats stream into Darfur. In the south of Sudan, Africans struggle to free themselves from the influence of Arabs in the north, which triggers a rise in ethnic distrust. At about this time too, a nearly permanent drought sets in, so that land which used to be productive turns into desert, setting off still more rivalries. Farmers turn against herders; sedentary tribes dispute the presence of nomadic ones. With the ancient way of settling disputes gone, conflicts intensify, tribal loyalties sharpen and Africans and Arabs become enemies. Politics, economy, ecology, kinship, religion – a complex set of factors – contribute to an escalating, fierce competition for control of the land. The killing begins.

In Khartoum, the Muslim brotherhood has taken charge, and it picks sides in Darfur. Nomadic tribes, mostly Arab, continue to come in from Chad. Libya, not friends with Chad, begins a counter action and seeks influence as well. Weapons pour into the region. Rebel groups and militias, tribally determined, spring up. The government in Khartoum sees an opportunity to advance its ethnic agenda. Having no capacity to keep the peace in Darfur itself, it calls upon the nomadic Arabs to assist. They are given weapons, promised land ownership and allowed a free hand. These are the chilling Janjaweed, armed marauders who arrive on fast horses or camels, with the aim of killing off entire villages. State supported murder of sedentary Africans becomes pervasive. Once an African village is killed off, land ownership passes to the killers. It is genocide and the hatred it creates ensures that the peaceful, multi-ethnic coexistence of earlier centuries will not return.

In real time the international community watches all this unfold. The Security Council talks about Darfur, naturally, but is split on what to do about it, Nothing happens although, belatedly, the International Criminal Court decides to indict the president of Sudan.

For a while, after this neat piece of reduction by Carlos, they sat so silent it could have been a vigil – for every innocent villager who ever lived and was murdered because of a faraway political agenda.

Paradis recovered first. "You are a diplomat," he said, addressing Natalia. "Everything that could go wrong *did* in Darfur. Should diplomacy have become active early on?"

"Diplomacy?" Natalia's mind was on the way-forward plan she was devising with de Bruyn.

"Yes. The art of solving intractable problems."

"The art has limits."

"Meaning what, in Darfur's case?"

"Carlos said it. Sovereignty. The right not to be interfered with. Sudan has sovereignty. Khartoum did and will do as it pleases, including doing nothing for its people. As is the case with most of the juntas, theocratic power structures, oligarchies and dictators. Sovereignty stabilizes, but destabilizes too. Perhaps the world community will evolve and eventually adopt a more effective political stabilizer than sovereignty."

"We must expect that," Paradis responded enthusiastically. "It is the only way. We must agitate for it. It gladdens me, Natalia, that as ambassador you think this way. Myself, I am much encouraged by the Responsibility to Protect doctrine. *That* is political evolution. I have often wondered why the internationally community did not use it to save lives in Darfur."

"R2P!" Natalia laughed scornfully. "R2P *should* compel the UN to intervene. It *should* have done that in Darfur. The world's leaders signed onto R2P. But they excel only at assuming obligations that can be shirked. They adopted R2P, yes, then gave it no teeth. There are no specified *criteria* for when it should be used. So it doesn't get used."

"My apologies, Ambassador, I am misinformed. I understood the Security Council has the power to decide when to apply it."

"Good luck with that, Alistair. Five Security Council members can veto anything they like. We know the veto is an anachronism, but the famous five won't give it up. Even if a good majority of countries on the Security Council believed something had to be done to stop the Janjaweed killings, one Security Council member with a veto could prevent it. There is always one. China certainly would, because it believes the principle of non-interference is more important than state-supported killing. Russia usually thinks that way as well. Neither wants meddling with their own internal policies towards dissent, and they refuse precedents being set elsewhere. They apply their veto, the Security Council can't make a decision, the international community remains hung and genocide continues."

"I am having a powerful idea," Paradis exclaimed. "We must join forces." He stretched an open hand towards Natalia. "We will begin a process. Here in The Hague. We will attack obstacles to building peace. You have an ambassador's influence. I can contribute PEACE, millions of supporters. We can ask the Dutch government to join us. I know senior individuals here. I believe they will bite. We can do this, Natalia."

Natalia began to answer, for her body shifted forward, but an invisible hand came out, took hold and pulled her back. She met Paradis's intense gaze for some time, then took his hand and squeezed it. "I will reflect on that. I like spontaneity. I am for enthusiasm. Your millions of supporters fascinate me. But ..."

"But?"

"What you propose would be a great departure, not to be lightly undertaken."

~

Natalia strolled across the residence grounds, this way and that, in no special direction. Paradis and Carlos had said affectionate goodbyes, then flopped into her car – two burly men with enough drink in them to be at their convivial best. Dirk in his stately manner meticulously shut the doors and drove off, Paradis returning to an exquisite suite and Carlos going to the airport for a flight to Chile. She remained behind. Time to collect her thoughts.

Natalia walked slowly from shrub to blooming shrub, touching the blossoms. This tactile act, the fingering of a flower, was like putting that same finger on what the afternoon had brought. Paradis had been entertaining. It wasn't difficult to imagine him on a stage, keeping the audience on the edge of their seats as he transformed mystical concepts into high entertainment. And she made some progress understanding where PEACE came from. But absent entirely was a sense of how it practically functioned. Paradis had shied away from that. Was PEACE a stand-alone organization or was it more of a coalition, a grouping of peace NGOs? PEACE seemed fairly incomplete, Paradis saying nothing to fill in the gaps. Was that because, as its leader, he didn't understand the working details tended to by underlings?

Tea with Paradis had been lively and funny. Yet something about it was odd. His bombast had been a touch too heavy, in the same way Irving Heywood could overwhelm you with fine words strung together into an irresistible wave that overpowers you. The town-to-town wanderings story, the peace messages for ladies' groups and prison populations – it sounded borrowed and overly souped up. The saga of himself was biblical: suffering, deprivation, catharsis and meditation, self-cleansing, mystical insights, preparing a gospel, then circumambulating. But in a subtle way he had interrogated her too. A deep interest was expressed. A barrage of questions were posed about her work and ideas. As if he had come to find things out. Well, she questioned him and got nothing, which was how it was the other way around. In that respect, the tea had been a draw.

The oddest moment was at the end. After Carlos's explanation of the Darfur-Sudan disaster and the discussion of national sovereignty as an obstacle, the veto problem and the Security Council's dysfunctioning, the stillbirth of R2P – after their dialogue on the obstacles to peace – Paradis proposed cooperation on solutions. What lay behind that? Why would he suggest they do the very thing she was already doing? An odd coincidence. For a fraction of a second she debated bringing him in. He had access to, and possessed, influence. The optics of civil society being linked to the peace summit could bring advantages. But she caught herself. Something about PEACE was not transparent, although she was unsure of what that meant and what to do about it.

Natalia repeated the circuit through the garden. Again, she looked at the the powerful colours of the lupines, irises, azaleas and rhododendrons. But this time she wasn't seeing them. She was too deep in thought. In her mind, she was defining the path for a world moving beyond sovereignty. The only things missing were a few acts of supreme statesmanship.

Chapter 14

"Did Alistair awe you?"

Robbie, comfortably sunk back in an easy chair in Natalia's office, was swirling tonic water around in a glass. "Shockingly good isn't it, how he's bouncing back? He isn't young, but he isn't mouldy. What did you talk about?" Eager eyes pressed Natalia for details.

Some hours before, Robbie had taken a call from the ambassador in her car. "You had him over at the residence?" she'd exclaimed at the news.

Natalia's reply from the car's back seat was of the cloak and dagger variety. "Carlos was doing the chaperoning, Robbie." In a near whisper she added, "He was with us the whole time. I felt safe." Robbie gushed a *ho-ho-ho* at that.

Robbie's Monday afternoon had been slow. The office walls were pressing in and the backlog of consular reports was ripe for an enlivening. Natalia's conspiratorial theatrics on the phone dispersed the humdrum. It also brought her own new secret to the fore. She had an urge to share it with Natalia right then, but Natalia cut the conversation short. "I'll be back around five-thirty, by which time I'll need a drink. It's been weeks since we last had a good confab, Robbie. Got time for it?"

"For sure."

Great Provider, reveal to me why I deserve to have this woman as my boss.

~

After hours, the embassy was as still as a body that has exhaled its final breath. But when Robbie entered Natalia's office the mood was instantly vital.

Right away, Natalia began to describe her day. Only meetings: one with the chair of the board of a large international conglomerate, another with someone who had a similar position with a well-connected arts funding trust, and so on and so forth and, basically, who cared about all that? What mattered was the ambassador's panache, the way she told the stories. She had seen lewdness in male hands holding teapots; she had been at the unveiling of an awful gothic-like piece of artwork that was supposed to make a bare wall look appealing; she had endured a grown man snivelling about high corporate taxes and another who must have had a good lunch because twice he burped. She had even studied one who for one full hour had froth at the corners of his mouth. Natalia slung an open vodka bottle through the air as she painted the pictures of her days' happenings and a shot or two escaped. "Baptizing the carpet!" she murmured.

An imperfect martini was made, Robbie's tonic glass stood fizzing, and they settled in. "Did you like him?" Robbie prompted. "Did Alistair draw you into his space? Did he light up the immaterial regions?"

"Oh, he did. In fact, he described a place I don't know much about, the one from which all guardian angels hail. I have heard of its existence, but who gets there to experience it? He claims he has. He said, Robbie, that that is where he found you. He is a very grateful man."

Robbie blushed. "Stop talking that way. You'll make me mute as a mouse. I just do my job."

"Good show all the same." Natalia raised her glass, extended it in Robbie's direction and finished the toast with a sip.

"What did you really talk about?"

"Work. We all have work in common. It got a proper airing. Did you know, by the way, that Alistair used to be on stage? Vaudeville I think. Something in that vein."

"I know he wanted to act Shakespeare when he was starting out."

"Well, it seems he became a stand up comic, or a clown, though he treated it like the priesthood. Then he went through a further conversion and is full of metaphysics now. Humankind's spiritual evolution – he has it pretty well worked out. As you know. He gave me some new peace ideas to think through. That's how yesterday was for me. So tell me, what happens when you do your Sunday afternoon socializing. Did you have a good day too?"

Robbie reddened. "I was in the dunes."

"The dunes? The place that wherever you look you see nothing but sand? Were you alone?"

"Maarten took me. He showed me places where he used to play when he was growing up."

"Maarten? The detective? Well that's lovely. Plus you explored his childhood. Not necessarily a trivial pursuit. I hope he showed an interest in yours too. The Dutch can learn from Newfoundland. I mean, it would shake up their sense of order."

"He's very considerate."

"How far did you get?"

"You mean, into his childhood?"

"No. Into the dunes. Did you walk north or south from Scheveningen?"

"We bicycled. We went to a place that seemed remote. Almost nobody around. We had a picnic."

"You bicycled?"

"Yes, I bought a bike a while ago."

"Suddenly you're like Carlos. His bike frees him, he claims. He ambles around carefree on a saddle, while I have to ride in a posh backseat of a car with no end of worries. It doesn't seem fair. And you picnicked too? Do you know what eating does to people? It stimulates their appetites. Can I ask where yours took you?"

"I don't know, Natalia. To a dead end maybe. There's a ringing in my ears and it doesn't sound like common sense."

~

Buying a bike is a practical thing to do, but for Robbie it assumed symbolism. On one level, with a shrug, she had signed a transaction slip for a gadget consisting of steel tubes and chrome bars, all of it resting on two large wheels. But the act had an undercurrent that came from the heart. Buying the bike was the latest in a string of consequences all derived from that first primal hour spent in the café with Maarten.

She couldn't help reliving it. Although not much happened at the time, as days passed the little there had been was further distilled in her thoughts until it came down to some simple behaviours – eyes met, subtle gestures registered, a few spoken words were remembered. This became reduced still more until finally there was only the essence of two psyches meshing. This lived on. Thought conversations with Maarten rose out of it. She was not aware of topics, only that a conversation was taking place and he was in on it.

Chief Hearkener, just so that you know, if you listen in, I don't mind.

Beyond the silent conversations lay a question. Should she let him know, despite the last strained minutes at the tram stop when he played police officer, that she enjoyed drinking tea with him? Should she find a way to show that the café hour lingered? But would he welcome that? She wasn't sure. There was the risk that he wouldn't appreciate an overture from her. Robbie's inner debate was ceaseless.

A week passed. On impulse, her heart beating loud, she jabbed the buttons on the phone.

The call must have caught him off guard, for he stammered a hello. He recovered fast. "Nice," he said. "Yes, nice. Very nice that you are on the phone."

Robbie made it sound casual. "You don't mind me interrupting?" She judged that she had her voice reasonably under control.

"No," he laughed. "No, no. I don't mind."

It was not, she thought, too policeman-like a laugh.

She said if he came to The Hague again, if, say, he attended another meeting on global crime, they could meet again in that same café. Or, if the global criminal problem had been solved, they could do it somewhere else. "Maybe there's a café in Nootdorp?" she said with a questioning inflection. "I think Nootdorp is about halfway from here to Zoetermeer." Maarten answered that her call could not have been timed better, since the task force on trends in global malfeasance was scheduled to meet again the next day. They could meet tomorrow.

~

The same place. Tea and coffee again. Except this time the atmosphere was familiar. At the end, Maarten offered to show Robbie Delft. Delft was only twenty minutes by tram from The Hague. In three years, Robbie said, she visited Delft only once and she was sure she had not seen it properly. They agreed on Saturday.

In Delft, she stepped off the tram into a steady drizzle, but why let that be bothersome? They walked through medieval alleys. When they crossed a street, since many were bisected by water, they also crossed a canal. They entered old buildings, even standing on the stairwell where William the Silent, Holland's founding father, the one who got the Spaniards on the run by using the North Sea as an ally, was assassinated. They peeked into a renowned porcelain factory with wonderful white-blue crockery. And they sauntered around in the great church on the central square, which has the crypt where over the centuries the members of the House of Orange have been laid to rest in neatly lined-up sarcophagi. Maarten revealed he had acquired the civic duty of sitting on the board of directors of the cathedral's gift shop. They climbed the tower and, up top, stepped onto a balcony where a cold wet wind attacked. Beneath them lay a sea of wet, gleaming red-tiled roofs. Maarten got Robbie to look down along his extended arm and pointing finger. See it? His roof. It covered a narrow row house on one of the canals. "It was built in 1568. It has been in the family for hundreds of years. Would you like to see it?"

It was tiny. Two small rooms downstairs and two upstairs accessed by a steep stairway. At the back, a bathroom was squeezed in. Downstairs there was a small kitchen with a door leading to an outdoor space not big enough to be called a patio. "I have to adjust my thinking," Robbie said when he was finished showing her his house. "I imagined you would live in something modern, a loft maybe, open and mostly empty. What do I see instead? Racks of silver tea spoons on the walls and sheets of lace covering the furniture." Maarten explained he had not yet taken the time to change the atmosphere the place had when his grandmother lived there.

A bike stood in the hallway. With a surge of mischief, Robbie rang the bell loudly. "Oops. Didn't want to let the neighbours know there's a visitor." Maarten asked if she had a bike. No, she did not. She liked the tram and for the rest of the time relied on her feet. This baffled him. No bike? How could she be living in Holland for three years without a bike? Had she ever had one? Are bikes not common in Newfoundland? Robbie explained that Newfoundland was fairly large, seldom flat, had gales that made the ones from the North Sea seem like teapot storms, plus, in the winter, there was freezing rain by the buckets, or snowfalls measured in meters.

"Sorry, Robbie. Sorry. Yes, I can see the problems of Newfoundland, but you are in Holland now." He listed some good reasons for bicycle ownership. "If you buy one," he argued, "I could take you to very nice places around here. And I know a store close by that sells good used bikes not very dear."

"This minute?"

"Sure. Or next Saturday."

"I have to think about it. Maybe next Saturday."

That week, as Robbie considered matters, the symbolism emerged. Buying a bike would be buying into an idea. Suppose she and Maarten enjoyed going on outings. What would the consequences be? According to one line of thought, certain self-imposed limits would disappear. In that scenario, her existence, simple until now, would go topsy-turvy. Common sense forced her to shake her head at it.

But another aspect was worth pondering too. She had observed the scenes of Hollanders on their bikes, fluently sailing along on broad smooth paths. Could she and Maarten be active like that, chattering happily as they went, hair pushed back by the wind, roaming past waterways, crossing drawbridges old as history, stopping for a picnic? The images were powerfully alluring.

Delight in the short term? Upheaval in the long? Or both? In the end Robbie decided nothing except to go with the flow. A bike was bought at a shop near the Delft railway station. Its design wasn't too sexy, more of a middle-class device built for comfort. The shopkeeper made a good sales pitch, predicting it would be dependable – *betrouwbaar* – and light to pedal.

Because of the symbolism, Robbie was wary of touching the bike, which Maarten interpreted in his straightforward way. Therefore he marched her and the bike to a quiet lane away from the canals and with a watchful eye had her go back and forth a few times. She was told to practice braking and to shift the gears. No mishaps. Robbie was declared ready for the countryside.

The bike was stored in the narrow hallway next to his, which by itself was a good reason to call each other during the weeks, so as to plan its use. Maarten had many ingenious ideas for going places, all fine with Robbie, and regularly on Saturdays she found herself taking an early tram to his place, where a picnic lunch was packed into carrier bags.

The first time out they made their way to the railway station and jumped on the 10:08 train from Delft, south through Rosendaal and into Zeeland, the bicycles along in the hold. The destination? The Scheldt River delta – a special location for biking. High dykes, deep polders, windy country lanes and manicured farms. For their second excursion the departure was on a Sunday, at 11:22, this train taking them from Delft through Rotterdam to Gouda. The same bikes-on-bikes-off procedure. The following Saturday, the train chugged east to rolling hills on the German border. Another time they went north, past the Zuiderzee, to Friesland's choppy lakes.

And so it was that on the same Sunday when Alistair Paradis drank rum in the company of the ambassador and her husband, Robbie and Maarten were enjoying a playful breeze coming onshore from the North Sea. After a short train ride to Haarlem, they had made their way deep into North Holland's dunes. A substantial picnic was in the bags slung from Maarten's back carrier.

~

The path winds around and up over relentless mounds of sand. The vegetation is sparse, a few tough shrubs and clumps of swaying grasses. After about an hour they stop at a row of metal racks to which bicycles can be chained. From there a narrow boardwalk leads into the dunes towards the sea. Maarten has the bags slung over a shoulder and Robbie carries a blanket. It is a long, curvy walk that rises and falls, the surf's dull clamour becoming steadily louder. A final crest, then an ample beach comes into view. In straight lines it stretches away in both directions and disappears into a maritime haze. The sea is calm, Robbie's practiced eye observing that the tide is low and rising.

This being a remoter part of Holland's coast, not much is happening: a horse and rider plod along the water's edge, a few people stroll on the wet, firm sand, a family flies a kite, some dogs run free and chase the gulls. When the boardwalk ends, Maarten turns right. It's slow going on the dry, loose sand and after a few minutes along a wire fence, which is a kind of boundary between the beach and the dunes, he decides they have come far enough. Shoes come off, the blanket is spread, a feast is unwrapped. Maarten sits cross-legged; Robbie has both feet to one side. Bread rolls, cheeses, a jar of pickled herring, raw veggies and fruit. The talk is of growing up near the sea. Robbie describes the hours of sending flat pebbles skipping over the water in a becalmed cove. For his part, Maarten constructed sandcastles. The design was standard; they all had a wide moat. "As the tide came in, the moat filled and the castle sank away. Shall we build one later?"

"Sure."

"I'm glad we met, Robbie. It's been so much fun." He reaches over and strokes her arm. "Who would have thought when you first came to my office that we would go to the beach together?"

"All because of that plane crash," Robbie answers whimsically. "Do you believe everything has a purpose, that there is direction?"

Maarten thinks. "I believe much happens by chance."

196

"Do you? I used to think that too, but now more and more I believe there is a force of some kind that has intentions for us."

Maarten nods. "That's fine. I guess people who believe that have an easier time dealing with certain things."

A dreamy pause occurs, which Robbie breaks. "Are you still working on that crash?"

Maarten hesitates. "We weren't going to talk about that. Not outside office hours."

"Sorry. Just curious. I shouldn't have asked."

"The crash is history. I don't know what the insurance settlement was. Mr Paradis, on the other hand, still has a tag."

"A tag? What's that?"

"It means some monitoring is done. Many people have a tag. The one for Mr Paradis allows us to know that he has been moved from the clinic and now lives in an apartment near Leyden."

"I know that too," Robbie answers, smirking lightly.

"And I know you know that. You located the apartment for him."

"Pretty good tag."

"I didn't ask for the information, Robbie. It happened to cross my desk."

"Sure." Robbie, lulled by the warming sun and the sound of the surf, wants to continue the lazy conversation and distantly asks, "is it interesting for you to know that an old man has rented comfortable accommodation for himself?"

Maarten's expression transforms. He squints in the direction of the sea. "We can talk about more agreeable things than Mr Paradis. But since you ask, you may as well know that he has had a fax machine installed in his flat."

Robbie takes this as an attempt to poke fun at official information and starts to snigger. "A fax machine? That's thorough police work. Did they say he also has a microwave and a flat screen TV?"

"It is a secure fax machine." Maarten's voice has taken on an indignant edge. "Which suggests he wants to hide his communications."

Robbie stiffens. "And what does that mean?" Her tone is changing too, to the one she uses when an embassy program head at a management committee meeting goes out of his way to cross-examine her work. "Alistair runs a large organization," she continues. "Why would he not want confidential communications?"

"It could be linked to something else. Some weeks ago, when he was still recovering in the clinic, he went on a trip. Only for that day. The clinic people understood it was to see the nice towns near the Zuiderzee. A van with two men in white uniforms came for him, but did they go sightseeing? No, they did not. They drove to Schiphol. From there a private jet took him to Cyprus, landing at the same military airfield from which he took off last February on the day his plane crashed. We do not know why he went or whom he met. The military administrators of the airport will not share their information with us. All we have is civilian air traffic control data. One and a half hours after landing the same jet took off and returned him. He was back at the clinic in time for dinner. A very nice outing, but what does it mean?"

She considers the question and replies testily, "Why not ask him? I could do it for you."

"It would not be wise."

"And what do you suspect it means?"

Maarten sighs. He spreads his hands and gestures at the delicacies arranged on the plates. "We're here to enjoy ourselves, Robbie. I want to build a sandcastle with you, not have annoying discussions about my work. It's only a low profile watching brief we have going. I'm sorry I surprised you with it. I should have kept it to myself."

"Wait a second." A cold efficiency has crept into Robbie's voice. "Let me say that I'm not surprised Alistair traveled somewhere. There could be all kinds of explanations. That airport on Cyprus, maybe it's also partly civilian. Maybe he attended a meeting of the board of his organization somewhere nearby. Maybe the board members of PEACE come from all the corners of the world and the Mediterranean is centrally located. Maybe what we really have here is just another instance of a security suspicion which doesn't want to consider innocent explanations."

"Robbie, please. Let us not spoil the day. What can be more awful than having an argument over security work? It is too theoretical. Let us drop it. Let us enjoy the picnic." He takes her hand and squeezes it.

Robbie, stunned how the day has turned, not liking the new feel of it, inhales deeply. As she watches Maarten's hand massaging hers, she gives in. "Sorry," she sighs. "First I pry, then I overreact. It's because I helped Alistair when he was vulnerable. When I got to know him, I developed a respect for him. He has a rich personal philosophy."

"I see."

"Plus he's an activist for a very good cause. He tries to change the things that are wrong with the world. Everybody else just *talks* about stuff like that."

Maarten turns his attention to the plate with herring, taking a piece, savouring it. He makes an *hmmm* sound which says the fish is truly yummy. Smiling engagingly, he repeats Robbie's words: "The things wrong with the world." He shifts his pose, from sitting cross-legged to lying on his side, head propped up on an elbow. "That's a very good picnic topic. I like to talk about such things."

~

On the tram taking her home from Delft, her bike stored once again in Maarten's hallway, Robbie sat stiff. How could it have happened, she asked herself. How could a lovely summer day, beginning very simply, have taken several sudden turns to end up in a terrible tangle? One minute there was a lovely picnic mood. In the next, the atmosphere turned frigid. Suppose Paradis's name hadn't come up. Suppose that next tangent, their exploration of what's wrong with the world, had not happened either. Suppose instead they had gone down to the water, carefree and playful, to build Maarten his castle. Would her illusions have shattered?

She thought back to Maarten stretching out before her full length. He looked innocent and contented. He yawned before delving into the topic she had put into play. He said that, in his opinion, humanity's main problem was competition. She nodded agreement and said it was a problem you could see everywhere, every day. Maarten, on his back, stared into the sky and lazily elaborated on what he meant. No species can compete with humanity, he explained, meaning humanity competes only with itself. The competition has become a giant race, which is going ever faster and getting more chaotic all the time. He believed humanity would soon trip over itself, that a big stumble was coming. Many, very many, would get badly hurt. This was not preventable, he said. For two reasons. He lifted his index finger. One, humanity has no idea why the race is necessary, it being pointless that everybody wants more and more of all the things they don't really need. And two, his middle finger said, the race has few rules and no referee. A crazy race without rules always ends up in chaos.

Up to a point, Robbie found this interesting. She could agree there was something like a race, but she saw it as having two contestants – the good and the bad side of humanity. Nor did she think there would be a stumble, not by the good side anyway. It was destined to remain upright and win. How could it not? The good side always showed it had better staying power, although one tricky problem was that each time the good side wins, the bad side, in some new disguise, pops up once more, meaning the competition had to start all over again. The overriding reason for the good side having stamina, for always winning, was its motivation, its spirituality. The good side drew its strength from its capacity to stand in awe at the complex functioning of the universe, coupled with the conviction that meaningful design guides life.

Maarten mulled this over. Some of that is true, he said. Good and evil are in a struggle, but he doubted that the struggle was the central feature of that crazy race. The main characteristic of the race, the reason it was so crazy, was that billions of people in it had no say, no say in slowing it down, changing the direction, or drawing up rules to maximize order and minimize chaos. No say. None at all. When people have no say, eventually there is trouble. Therefore humanity was in for a bad stumble.

Robbie was surprised. How could Maarten put her view – of the struggle between good and evil and the spiritual force behind what is good – so lightly to the side. For her part, she didn't accept at all that people have no say. People do have a say, she argued. Everyone can decide to live in accordance with high moral values. Those who do elevate themselves. When people put their consciences to work, they give themselves a say. Living according to one's conscience is a contribution to the unfolding of the grand design.

Maarten remained unconvinced. In his opinion, in the practical world, the conscience of any average individual had at best a modest impact.

Robbie winced at that. What is the practical world? she asked. It was almost nothing. A mere blip. In the real scheme of things, the immaterial guiding force in the universe was in charge. It was far bigger than humanity's silly internal competitions.

Maarten could not accept that. The practical world is all we have, he said. Think about any global ill. Take poverty. Suppose an ordinary person thinks this through and puts his conscience into overdrive. What will he discover? That he can make a little financial contribution, but that is about all. He has no say in how that problem is managed. It was the same with all the global ills. Most of them were hardly managed at all. More than that, the little management of global ills that did occur was done by steering committees operating in the shadows. These committees consisted of anonymously appointed officials. "Want a simple example of what I mean? The people of the world cannot even vote for the head of the UN – is that not an absolute absurdity?"

The sun was shining, but Robbie was beginning to feel chilled, which weakened her voice. That example, she said, was so excessively practical that it clouded what was truly important. She again tried to explain that in every person something more fundamental than simple practicality was at work. People can discover deeply meaningful experiences within themselves, and she was sure that if everyone searched for them, the ills of the world wouldn't need active management. The ills would cease to exist.

This was how it went, back and forth, the overlap between them shrinking the whole time.

Maarten smiled a lot – he was enjoying the debate – although the sentiments he expressed were grim. Robbie, on the other hand, felt driven to explain that her thoughts were uplifting and wonderful, though she knew they sounded trite when she put them into words. How do you describe a magnificent insight – that an infinite reservoir of spirituality, including the souls of humans, coexists with the physical universe – to someone mired in thoughts about practicalities? She tried to describe her inner joy, yet was feeling steadily gloomier. The debate, which Maarten was savouring, hit her, in contrast, as a fundamental clash of values, and that pained her.

The topic ran its course. A long silence ensued. Maarten finally made a reference to the great global, meaningless mess of things, and pleasantly asked Robbie where she thought she and he fit in?

She wasn't ready to answer.

Maarten took the initiative once more. He repeated what he said when they first sat down on the picnic blanket, although more earnestly. He said that being with her made him happy. "I have been wondering," he added – he began to massage his forehead as if a new thought had to be worked through – "I have been wondering why you and I are not yet lovers?"

A shock went through Robbie.

"What I mean is that it would be natural since we get along so well."

More seconds passed. Tears formed in Robbie's eyes. Immediately she rubbed them away and Maarten leaned forward to take her hand.

On the tram to Scheveningen, Robbie sank deep into that moment. She asked herself, was his interest in intimacy surprising? Well … just then … actually … yes … it was. It did not fit at all into the situation. They had differed over their elemental views on the purpose of existence. They had not come anywhere close to working through some kind of accommodation. Without a meeting of minds, how can the meeting of bodies deliver meaning? Apart from that, although he was suggesting love, he made it sound terribly clinical. When you ask someone to be your lover, shouldn't you make sure it doesn't come across as a reading from a logic book? But all the same, though Maarten's tone and timing weren't the best, the subject wasn't unexpected. It had been there from the beginning. It had merely been impossible to know how it would crystallize. You could even say, Robbie admitted to herself, that she had given her answer weeks ago – because, well, she had bought the bike. And she did agree to park it in his hallway. With this day's awful turns, could it be that the time had already come to discard it?

Consummate Observer of the foibles of humanity, where in the ranks of sadly failed seductions does this one fit?

No, Maarten's overture to become lovers hadn't caught Robbie unprepared. When he took her hand, he may have thought her tears were flowing at the prospect of future happiness. In truth, struck hard by the gap between their separate outlooks, Robbie was overwhelmed by an image of how the afternoon could have developed. In her alternate version, they spread the blanket in a much more private spot. Not a word was exchanged. No pointless references to Paradis. No blathering on about the world's existential problems. Instead, slowly, they simply fell into making love.

And what happened in reality? First, she got the policeman in him going. Then she promoted both debate and philosophizing. She had lined up a neat row of disasters. With what results? One, she learned he still had an unspecified suspicion of Alistair lingering, which bugged her to no end. And second, worse, she found that his core he wasn't like hers. He wasn't spiritual. He was a rationalist and a materialist, someone who picks the universe apart, someone who can't stand back to be infused by its grand purpose. Her tears hadn't flowed because she was overwhelmed by thoughts of happiness to come, but by the sudden, brutal corruption of a once lovely dream.

On the beach, she had pulled herself together. She released herself from his hand squeeze and mumbled she was sorry, but she had to think things over. Maarten amiably asked why. She latched onto an obstacle she had not yet dared to think about too deeply. Because, she answered, because their lives were on different tracks. Maarten in his uncomplicated way had no problem answering that. He reasoned, since the world is beset by so much misery and awfulness, is it not better to seize contentment when it presents itself and after that just let the future happen?

When Robbie recalled this part of the picnic, she smiled wryly. The picnic, she saw, had been like the tides. For her optimism had risen, but ebbed and given way to pessimism. For Maarten it went the other way. He set off as a malcontent about the dismal state of planetary management, but rose and emerged from the discussion radiating happiness. Rarefied happiness. No other word could describe better how he had looked when he said they should jointly fashion their contentment. Its great meaning didn't strike Robbie until later when she was alone on the tram. That suggestion wasn't rational, materialistic or pessimistic. It was the opposite. Maarten demonstrated faith. Acting on faith, he was prepared to make a great leap forward.

In the end, no sandcastle was built. Even after her tears dried, she didn't feel up to engaging in childlike joy. Soon they rolled up the picnic blanket, walked the boardwalk and were back on their bikes. The way they pedalled away – no laughing, no chattering – misfortune could have been driving them on. On the train to Delft they scarcely talked. After she parked the bike and was opening his front door to depart, Maarten asked Robbie if something was upsetting her. "I'll try to call next week," she replied.

~

Robbie, sitting back and looking like a poor lost urchin, sighed and saw that Natalia was emerging from a pose of concentrated listening. A sudden verve, or ruthlessness, must have welled up in Natalia, because she bounced to her feet, came straight at Robbie, energetically yanked the empty tonic glass from her hand and, with determined steps, took it to the side table in her office where the bottles stood. She grabbed the gin, poured a hefty measure, added a squirt of lemon juice and a portion of fizzing tonic and returned to hand Robbie the refilled glass. She settled back in her own chair. Nothing in all this looked anything like what should happen in diplomatic offices. It was more of a form of midwifery that had been put into play.

"Drink that, Robbie. Pour it down," Natalia ordered. "No buts. It's medicine to stop the ringing in your ears. Come. Bring the glass up and tilt it backward." Robbie did. "Good girl. Once more ... And once again ... Good. What do you think of it?"

"It's not as if I've never had a drink before."

"In that case it's no big deal. Alright, we have some confusing terrain to wade through. Mind if I summarize what I heard?"

Robbie lifted the glass to her lips again and waited.

"You've been bicycling on your weekends with a nice man. You obviously like each other, because you picnicked on a blanket in the dunes. In that situation you have an inappropriate discussion about the ills of the world. You draw weird conclusions from it, whereas he proposes that you two make love. You think that takes you to a dead end, at which point you conclude it's best to seek shelter in common sense. Sound about right?"

"Why do you say I drew weird conclusions?"

"Don't stop sipping."

"It was confusing for me, Natalia. Ever felt you were way up the creek and only had one oar?"

"That's how I live, actually. Two oars are dangerous. Two oars are a temptation to try to row upstream. You're in your prime, Robbie. Relax, go with the flow, steer only a little and enjoy. There isn't much more to say."

"There are complications."

"Meaning?" Natalia asked crisply.

"For one, Maarten's roots are here."

"That sure is thinking ahead. You don't like the idea of sinking roots?"

"I've become used to not having any."

"Why think about it? If you sink roots, you sink roots. If you don't, you don't. Both are good. For the time being, relax."

Robbie continued to work on her glass and was beginning to understand the claim that tonic tastes better if altered with gin. She was also understanding that on Sunday afternoon she'd gotten herself wound up pretty tight. Was she *not* at a dead end? Was there a gate, which could be opened onto some other place? Ought she to be more relaxed, as Natalia was advising. How strong was the streak of hyper-practicality and rationalism in Maarten, since there was an incredible strong faith in him too?

"If I were you, Robbie, I would go see him and I would take along a bottle to show I meant business. How on earth did you get around to talking gloom anyway? The ills of the world? During a romantic Sunday picnic? For heaven's sake!"

"It wasn't planned. We stumbled onto it. I said I admire people like Alistair who are committed to doing good, who act out the good that's inside them. Maarten's view was different. He believes the world is in a mess because people don't have a say in what affects them."

"And that caused a flap!" Natalia continued to be astounded. "Did Maarten elaborate? When he said people don't have a say, what did he mean?"

"He said that as long as the big issues facing humanity are addressed by shadowy committees consisting of appointed officials they won't get solved. People don't respect decisions that affect them being made behind closed doors, without them at least having a say in who makes the decisions. He used the example of the Secretary General of the United Nations. It is ludicrous, he said, that the person in that job isn't popularly elected. He is convinced that the way the world is run these days no longer makes sense, given how humanity is developing."

Robbie observed Natalia lifting her martini, but she stopped with the glass halfway to her lips, where it froze into position. Her eyes went lifeless too. "You OK?" Robbie asked.

Natalia shuddered and came back. "Sorry, Robbie. A brainwave. A shiver went up my spine." She put her drink aside. "That policeman friend of yours, have you thought he's too smart to be a detective? A global voting process for the UN Secretary General? That has some very interesting implications. Your Maarten, I am asking, is he brilliant in the same way you are?"

Chapter 15

Natalia, alone in the residence, was restless. The last martini with Robbie in her office was hours ago and, on any other evening, she would have convinced herself by now that one drink can never be enough to defang a hectic day. Not only that, but Carlos, the dependable absorber of stress, was in Chile for the week, the separating time zones making phone chats inconvenient. So no calming words from him, and no chance of it for days, not until his return on Saturday. The situation really did call for a couple more martinis. Yet, this evening, the urge scarcely figured. There was an occasional seductive whisper – that a proper evening unwinding promotes health, that she really ought to give in to the temptation to pour herself a soothing double – but Natalia's stance was resolute, and she stayed away from the room with the liquor cabinet. She wanted a clear head. She had to wrestle down a new idea.

Robbie started it in the office when she bravely sipped her gin and tonic. She'd been dismissive when she described Maarten's opinion that ordinary people have no say in how the world is managed, but that didn't sidetrack Natalia. On the spot, a whole bunch of rapidly developing images had swooshed through her brain. Of muzzled multitudes, of people in their billions standing by, abjectly gagged, of a very large plurality prevented from saying a single word about what was on their mind. She remarked to Robbie that Maarten could be right. Why shouldn't ordinary people vote for the head of the UN? Wouldn't the office carry more legitimacy and be more powerful too?

Robbie shrugged. Casting a ballot for someone that far removed from reality didn't seem such a big deal to her.

This took Natalia into a higher gear. She admitted she had not read up on the cultural, sociological, or even psychological origins of voting, but it was fairly obvious that somewhere in the past the notion emerged that every view for or against something should be counted. Maybe the ancient Athenians were responsible. Maybe it was some prehistoric tribe that lived in what is Switzerland today. No matter. For humanity, voting was a breakthrough, a practice with a high likelihood of creating long-term order. The use of the ballot box was still evolving and wouldn't it be reasonable, therefore, to take it a step further, such as democratically deciding who would be the next Secretary General of the UN, or President of the World Bank, or others of that ilk?

Robbie remained skeptical. It sounded fairly dewy-eyed to her.

Natalia was undeterred. "It's an interesting idea, Robbie. Ideas have to be put out. If ideas aren't put out, there's no chance for them to grow. It wasn't all that long ago that freely elected parliaments were hard to find. Today a few dozen decent ones exist. The notion that people should have the right to vote according to their conscience has been coming along. Who says we've arrived at the end of that road?" Natalia began to speculate on the practicalities of organizing a free vote on a global scale and Robbie, true friend that she was, listened patiently.

On the way home in the car Natalia tapped the armrest, such thoughts not leaving her. Her excitement over the notion of global voting was actually growing. Could it be made part of the peace package? Was this the big idea, the zing thing, the concept with star power, the summit commitment making the world take notice? She continued to mull it over as she ate dinner. Her head remained high up in the clouds and she was scarcely aware that the residence staff had bid her good night. But she did manage to focus on a message from Carlos, recorded hours earlier as the Chilean day was starting. He said he was fine, though he missed her. Well, she missed him too. Thinking out loud with Carlos always injected order into scrambled up questions, something she badly needed now. With thoughts of all kinds jumping about, Natalia went to sit in the drawing room for a while. Not finding calm, and because not moving was unbearable, she began wandering from room to room.

~

Reasoning while pacing works for some, and Natalia was one. The physical rhythm caused the formation of something like a psychic membrane. It closed around her, placing her inside a pure thought bubble.

Her route through the house was circuitous and repetitive. She would grab a finger sometimes, as a way of underscoring this or that new insight. When the ground floor rounds delivered nothing further, she ascended the stairs, slowly, physically disengaged, as if sleepwalking. In her study she picked up a pen and jotted words down on paper, but immediately considered them foolish. Many sheets were discarded. More scribbling caused more shredding. Much was thrown away, though she did think that some of what was left could have value.

Later, in bed and out of the bubble, she came back to herself, only to discover she could not sleep. Did she get too worked up? Or was it because she hadn't taken a nightcap? She could go downstairs. She could still have one. Natalia decided to tough it out. Fitful hours followed, a confusion between a waking imagination going strong and seemingly real, remembered dreams. A wasted night, like the ones she used to have before she discovered the curative power of martinis. Haunting her during the nights back then was Papa. He was always dropping by as a bad dream, or a troubling memory. A scene would unfold, a simple scene, a distillation of what he said to her over many years. This night too that clip started to run.

He has finished his shift and is doing his drinking. The wife is not home. She has escaped to do her rounds as neighborhood beautician, which means he can't confront her. Insensitive to the fact that Natalia is doing homework, placing a chair opposite her at the kitchen table he mutters: *Vile bastards. They're out to keep me down, Natalia. Today they made fun of our last name again. I tell 'em – Please, I'm Plavniuk, not Spastiuk. They laughed, the morons. Don't let 'em do that to you, Natalia. Never. Don't let 'em treat you second class. You go high, way above that type. That's what I want. Promise me you'll rise so high that you'll be able to kick all the morons that cross your path in the nuts anytime you like.* Natalia didn't respond. Not back then and not now. But tonight she did wake up. She sat up in bed, took her head in her hands and shook it. Why wasn't Carlos there to tease her out of anger and crack a joke about the pointlessness of self-pity?

The next morning was like living behind a dark veil. In the office, Natalia instructed Marge to take her name off the guest list for a dinner that evening. Other appointments were cancelled too. A worsening headache, she claimed. Marge solicitously brought in a pot of tea and her personal pillbox. Natalia removed two tablets, hiding them away in a desk drawer. Home early, she declined having a martini, wolfed down some food and went upstairs. This time she fired up the computer. The few sheets of jotted notes that had survived the previous evening were laid out on the desk before the monitor. Hesitantly, she began to type – a few keystrokes, a long pause, more intermittent tapping. It continued until midnight, when Natalia wondered whether rest that night would once more be sporadic.

It was. Restorative sleep refused to come. But Papa did.

He is in bad humour. Again. And into his drink. He is explaining to her how he stood up against them that day. *Listen, Natalia. Like me, you were born with a few strikes against you. So don't make my mistakes. Don't settle for a job run by the bastards. You can spot the bastards. They call themselves managers. Taking a job where there are managers is like striking out. That's me. They've been out from the start to keep me from getting to first base. Don't let that happen to you. Hit a home run, Natalia. Win a prize. Any kind will do. You're smart enough to figure out how. When you do, know what's gonna happen? I'm gonna stick it under them bastards' noses. It'll show 'em who the Plavniuks really are.*

The next day, Wednesday, Natalia's program was too full to ignore. A run-around kind of day, continuing late into the evening. But Thursday was different. Thursday after dinner, itching to make progress, she was back at the computer. The document in it received another thorough going over, was printed and taken for a residence walk, Natalia clenching a pencil between her jaws. She read the paper repeatedly and lowered it onto a table or buffet, where sections were crossed out or new words inserted. Arguments were honed and the flow sharpened up. Back at the computer, the cycle of revising began all over again. That night when she went to bed, fifteen pages were in decent shape, she thought. Friday evening was a repeat. More filing away at the text, paragraphs emerging that were crisper still. Natalia mumbled to herself – and incidentally to Papa – that if this kind of progress continued the document might well win a prize. That night she slept well.

Saturday she was up early and felt fresh. She printed out the latest draft, reviewing it as she drank her morning coffee. A few last blemishes remained. Having pencilled in the changes, she went up to the computer for last adjustments before the final version was printed. Back downstairs in the drawing room she placed the two versions side by side on a coffee table to make a close comparison, an ultimate check. It was finished. She would go with this. Back upstairs, she made a duplicate of the final version, each copy being put into an envelope. Time left to dress for the appointment with Heiko. She chose a pleated, calf-length skirt in dark purple and a jet black, short-sleeved top in fine cashmere. Over this a white silk jacket. Her necklace was delicately worked, in silver, her favourite ruby pendant hanging down from it.

Carefully dressed, festive yet business-like, she was ready to go plant a new, oak-sized, peace idea.

~

Dirk dropped Natalia off in the Binnenhof, the square defined by medieval buildings. Clutching the two envelopes, she entered the building that had become familiar. The guards knew her too. *Good day, Your Excellency. One moment please.* Telephone buttons were punched. *Meneer de Bruyn. Zij is hier … Ja, goed. Ik breng haar.* The hand piece went down. *Your Excellency, may I escort you?*

The corridors of government were lifeless; the unused doors down both sides standing like numbered gravestones. In this catacomb, the guard's shoe creaked with each step, the stillness excruciatingly amplifying it. Creak, pause, creak, pause. He whispered an apology. Up the stairs and around the corner, where one door – the usual door, like a wormhole to the universe where government business never sleeps – stood invitingly open.

De Bruyn came out. "Ambassador. Good morning. You look very bright today, but when do you not?" To the guard he said, "*dank U wel,*" to dismiss him.

"And you look relaxed today, Heiko," Natalia countered as they passed through the anteroom into his office. "How many crises for you this week? Or don't you keep count? According to the papers there were at least seven. Was the true number double that?"

"We had the usual quota," he admitted pleasantly. "Please, sit down. Coffee? A propos crises, can I tell you what happens to me? If the morning is without one and nothing explodes in the afternoon, I begin to doubt my own importance. Odd, how one feels one is defined by the crises. I don't mind them. I am fortunate that my prime minister insists on knowing their root causes. It makes shaping the solutions more rewarding." He poured coffee with aristocratic formality and pushed a plate of cookies forward. "Do help yourself to cream, please. Let me add that, despite the week and all that adrenalin, what excited me most was our project. A successful summit with a meaningful outcome could mean fewer future crises."

"Good progress on the substance, Heiko."

"I'm sure. Your proposals have found favour here." De Bruyn jabbed his thumb to the wall behind him. "As for us, we have the protocol planning effectively completed. The list of countries to be invited has been capped at fourteen. You know which ones. We propose that the invitations to the heads of state and government will be from both our prime ministers. Will that be acceptable?"

212

"I will check."

De Bruyn nodded. "An answer in a week perhaps? We should be checking some details off now." He initiated a methodical review of the summit program. The foreign ministers of the invited countries would convene for a working dinner the evening before, to give the outcome a final polish. "My prime minister intends to chair the discussion. If yours wishes, they could do it as a duo. Foreign ministers sometimes get picky. One or another may have to be subjected to some prime-ministerial strong arming." De Bruyn found this prospect amusing for he made an arm-wrestle movement, with an imaginary wrist buckling under his pressure. "My prime minister will inform the foreign ministers that presentational improvements to the declaration will be acceptable, but he will not yield on substance. No haggling, no watering down, no replacing hard commitments with bland generalities. He will not allow the pace of progress to be set by the slowest. The next day, at the summit, leaders will participate in a televised session with our queen, in the International Peace Palace. She will give a major address. Your prime minister will speak about ways to take the Right to Protect doctrine towards more predictable methods of implementation. One or another of the presidents and prime ministers may add short statements.

"That over with, they next assemble in our ancient Hall of Knights, across the square from here, the place where the Queen otherwise opens the Dutch parliament. We chose the Hall because, over the centuries, Dutch engagement in policies of peace were publicly expressed there. Its atmosphere inspires. In the presence of the foreign ministers, the leaders, one by one, will sign the declaration, then it's off to celebrate over lunch. The program is rather compressed, which has the advantage, we think, of reducing time for waffling and haggling. Each participant will have to decide quickly whether or not his country accepts the distinction of being a founding participant of our major reorientation towards policies of peace. How does that sound? Once your side is comfortable with the program, we would explore dates."

De Bruyn's protocol intentions were not new. In the previous weeks Natalia had heard them aired in dribs and drabs and had relayed them on. Heywood's habitual response was a condescending snort. With disdain, he would enquire if that was all. "What about the press?" he asked once. "Do the Dutch plan a communication strategy? There's nothing on that. You and I, Natalia, have made the transition to this new century. We would have websites ready for launch by now. You would be enjoying the green light for your own blog to start on summit day. We know how to get the message out. The Dutch had their last peace conferences a century ago. I wonder, are they searching their files for the communications strategies used back then? Do they want our summit to be a replay? A period piece? Will they be issuing pin striped tails to the men and forcing the women upstairs to observe from the gallery? Ask Duhbrouyeen about that next time."

Heywood's hubris was sometimes difficult to take. All the same, communication aspects were not trivial. "How do you plan to deal with the media, Heiko?" Natalia asked.

He stirred. First came a leaning forwards in his wing-back which was followed by a sideways turn. "My expert had a field day." He lifted a thick binder off a side table. "All done. Live TV feeds to the national networks of the countries attending. An electronic press release in multiple languages to be sent out as the summit's substantive session is ending. The mailing list thus far consists of over two hundred thousand journalists worldwide. A dedicated server will ensure fast access to a peace documentation center and database. Some customized portals too, for researchers, students and children. If you are interested in details, please borrow it." He thrust the binder towards Natalia who took one look at all that paper and, with a motion of her hand, declined. De Bruyn shrugged and put it back on the side table. "So much for protocol and process. Another go-around on substance? Good progress, you say? Your side's policy minds have sealed a package?"

My side? Natalia thought. *Policy minds?* She lifted the coffee cup with two fingers, delicately bringing it to her lips before returning it to the saucer. This was her moment. She took the two envelopes and passed one over.

De Bruyn received it like an unexpected gift. "Documentation," he murmured. Half-rimmed glasses appeared from a silver case.

"Thin documentation," he added, positioning the spectacles on his nose.

"Brevity is powerful."

De Bruyn laughed. "That can be true. I am also a fan of concision." He fingered the envelope flap and slipped the contents out.

Natalia removed her copy too. De Bruyn began reading and she synchronized her speed with his, flipping the page when he did. Now and then a low noise escaped him, an undercurrent, a short *hmm* or *ahh*. "That's right," he sometimes said, or, "Indeed yes. We had agreed on that." Two-thirds through, he stopped. "This is good, Natalia. A persuasively organized hierarchy of commitments, progressing up from a dependable foundation. I like it. It makes sense to begin by setting out our universal values and humanity's basic aspirations – possessing security and living in peace.

"The next description, the ascent of civil society, follows logically – ordinary people who demonstrate by their acts that they live in accordance with the universal values. They wish to contribute to human security, but too often governments frustrate them. So much creative energy wasted. Governments ignore civil society at their peril. The related issue, of NGOs gaining ever more influence and responsibility, is cogently put. We must make the commitment to tap into the huge productive forces that reside beyond governments.

"And I do like the next step up the hierarchy – promoting the role of peace builders. A global service is long overdue. Establishing elite academies to develop them will be an investment bringing high returns. Your succinct description of the qualities of this new breed of professionals – individuals adept at pursuing their negotiating and mediating skills in other cultures   convinces the reader.

"Higher up again, the Summit commitment to adjust government structures. Governments who pledge themselves to the primacy of peace ought not to place departments geared to fighting at the expenditure apex. The time has come to create Peace Departments funded in proportion to the military.

"There we have it – expanding the role of civil society, creating civilian peace services, establishing peace departments – a fine commitment triad. A global wake-up call."

Natalia scanned her copy as de Bruyn worked his way through his and ignored the accolades. The substance was not solely hers. She and Heiko had been hammering away at these ideas for weeks. Her contribution was largely in the presentation. He was coming to the final section now, the last few pages. She held her breath.

"I see there's more." His forehead wrinkled. "Have we not covered the waterfront?" He read on.

Natalia glanced in his direction to pick up signs. How was he taking it? The short grunts of approval had stopped. No more tightening of playful lines around his eyes. All she saw was a concentrated plodding forwards. He was weighing the words. At measured moments, he stared into space, squinting, taking his time. The quiet in de Bruyn's office was absolute, save for the fluttering sound of pages being flipped forwards, then back, then forwards again. When done, he shook his head. "I am somewhat surprised. Can you really be proposing this?"

Natalia was ready. She responded in a monotone. "We must include it, Heiko. It's the final, logical step. Peace without democracy is not peace. Only a coerced stillness. Coerced stillness, we know, is inherently unstable." De Bruyn's silence was intense. Natalia pressed. "Think of this tabula rasa. If you look past the clutter of daily crises, a compelling picture forms. Progress towards peace requires the establishment of a world body with legitimacy, a legitimacy that only comes with democratic credentials. It will inject purpose and stability into the other commitments we're planning. If we are serious about peace, we must begin to wean ourselves off sovereignty."

De Bruyn looked up towards the ceiling. "Sovereignty? We talked of it at the start. Yes, sovereign states squabble like children. It is an entrenched political style. But replacing the bickering with an elected assembly? Our European Parliament isn't exactly a success story. I don't know, Natalia. I admit I sometimes think this way. In the abstract, an effective parliament constituted by likeminded nations, making decisions on global challenges, may be a good thing. It may even come eventually. But I have never dared to hope that it would be seriously discussed in my lifetime."

"Political evolution, Heiko. It's taking us there. The choice is simple. Do we continue with today's way of making decisions, closed room deals fashioned by appointed officials? Or, since we know that democratic values will migrate anyhow to a level beyond the nation state, do we force the pace of change?"

De Bruyn was wavering. Was he listening to his instincts, or making complex political calculations? "Is this going too far and too fast?" he finally asked.

Natalia knew this was the pivotal point. She would have no second chance. Her voice remained devoid of inflection. "Today's global governance inspires no one. Actually, it's a mess. If someone were to stage it, what piece of theater would you be looking at? You would see the puffed-up heads of state front and center. Behind them are their foreign ministers, aching to have VIP treatment. Off to the side, the finance ministers strut about as always, though really they don't move. All around swarm international officials, quota-appointed, who pull strings. That forces the heads of state to do a jerky little dance, which they hope will impress the audience. The audience, by the way, consists of a few hundred thousand excited journalists and seven billion bored people."

De Bruyn was laughing. "You are good at parody."

"It is a failing."

"Parody, I suppose, sometimes helps get us closer to what is real."

"Real? We have been inside those closed off, international chambers, Heiko. We have helped throw lofty words together and wring out the communiqués. Only occasionally does a political leader come along who actually wants to effect what has been undertaken. Even the steering councils that consist of representatives from democratically elected governments aren't democratic. Executive authority rules there too. You see the issue. As you said, today's governance is a recipe for ensuring progress at the pace of the slowest.

"I will rant for one more minute. What was the starting point for the peace summit? The R2P doctrine, the world community's responsibility to protect people tyrannized by their own state. A fine enough doctrine. Too bad it's flawed. Take the Darfur genocide as one example. Darfur was a prime candidate for the doctrine. But nothing happened. Why? Because a UN Security Council decision was required. The Security Council seldom takes principled decisions because too many members are there to posture. They worry about this or that national company losing a contract. They fear that what's done to others could apply to them. Set no precedents! The Security Council's biggest flaw is the five permanent members having a veto. Those five happen to be the world's largest arms exporters. They have industries that depend on military threats and armed conflict. Are we sure that peace is a priority for the veto-enriched five? The Security Council served its purpose after the Second World War. It allowed the victorious powers to neutralize each other. But it's an anachronism now, incapable of developing into something better. It will never be a representative council. The five will never give up their veto. That is the peace summit's opportunity. It can create a new model. At first it will be small, but it will grow. Peace-building, pursued with democratic legitimacy, will eventually force the Security Council to implode."

De Bruyn waved Natalia's document like a fan. He seemed to be recalling a past debate. "A year or so ago, at a seminar arranged by our foreign policy think tank, we talked about this very topic. The Security Council's dysfunction is indeed a concern. But is your model the answer, Natalia? A World Peace Assembly, democratically elected, with certain defined supranational powers? The ring is nice, but too glib for now?"

Natalia patiently continued. "Imagine the Peace Assembly, Heiko. The individuals elected to it wouldn't be your standard, hack politicians. They would be exemplary individuals, leaders in our societies from all the spheres that matter. The arts, academia, the media, the judiciary, business and finance, the professional ranks, labour, civil society. A World Peace Assembly will symbolize what the Security Council cannot – decision-making in accordance with humanity's core values. The Assembly would represent global compassion. It would be a place to pursue moral truth. No superpower rivalries allowed there. No posturing autocracies rotating through. The only council on a global scale today that comes close to having that kind of standing consists of the leaders of the religious faiths. Their work inspires individuals, but it doesn't drive solutions to problems. Furthermore …"

De Bruyn raised a hand. "Supposing in the abstract that we agreed a representative assembly for peace is needed, the details would be daunting. We have to remain realistic."

"There are details, of course, that will need sorting out. But they are not insurmountable. Less so, I would say, than what you went through with you new constitution for Europe." Natalia pulled a few further pages from her envelope.

He watched with slight alarm. "What's that?"

"The details."

"On those few sheets?"

"Concision, Heiko. Are you interested in a sampling?"

De Bruyn sighed.

"I put the details into categories. An important one is the apportionment of Assembly seats and how the seats are filled, because for people that is democracy in action."

"Have you included the Assembly's role and powers as a category? It's hardly less significant."

"Some details there too. We could also explore whether in a structure of peace governance the World Peace Assembly is merely a lower house. Peace building may be important enough to have an upper house as well. Wisdom, experience, symbiotic relationships between peace and other global issues would be brought to bear there. Plus, there is the issue of expansion. Other countries will wish to join."

"You have answers to all that?"

"Not answers. Ideas. Possible answers."

Natalia began listing them. As she did, an ardency crept into her voice, a fluidity of expression, a timbre rising and falling. Her career, the years spent seeing the world's political disfigurements up close, the trudging off to international meetings in pursuit of the high-minded aim of promoting democracy, the hours given over to absorbing Carlos's insights into cultures, which ones flourish and which ones flounder and the reasons for that, all the time spent probing ideas, her own and of others – all this came together in her lyrical petition.

The details of a World Peace Assembly, as with any constitution, were basically unglamorous, but Natalia's eyes flashed as she described processes for ensuring that only the best would be chosen for the task of drafting global peace laws. With hands that danced, she outlined the path to parliamentary oversight for a global peace judiciary, the International Criminal Court included. Parliamentary oversight too for civilian peace building services and their conflict prevention purpose. Human rights work would fall into the Assembly's purview too. A few wrestling bouts with the UN could be expected, but the UN would not win. The reason? Human rights are synonymous with freedom and transparency in politics. By virtue of its make-up, the UN would never have this. Witness, too, the dismal spectacle of regimes with brutal records presiding over the UN's human rights interests. As for the upper house – a World Peace Senate – it could be constituted by individuals *ex officio*, Natalia argued, by Nobel Peace Prize laureates, for example, and by the President of the World Bank and the Secretary General of the UN. Each member country would nominate one supreme court judge and one retired head of state. Who could argue that a Senate like that, constituted by the great and wise, vetting, amending and improving laws framed by a high calibre representative Assembly, would not give peace decisions the highest standards of legitimacy?

De Bruyn sat as motionless as a wax figure and when he spoke he was subdued. "A not uninteresting model for global peace government, but I fear it will be more complicated than you make it sound. Countries are tightly enmeshed by treaties. Putting a parliament with supranational power over that, even if the focus is narrow, will be very complicated. What are the implications for NATO? Or for the NPT? A range of circles need to be squared. But let us suppose we take it further. Let us suppose we ignore our security establishments and UN experts and the sudden massive cardiac arrests they will all have if this comes to pass. How do we get ordinary people to understand it? Which leads me to a final question, which I will formally put to you as ambassador. Can I inform my prime minister that your prime minister wants this?"

Gazes locked. Natalia said slowly, "That is delicate. It could be put this way. If your prime minister were interested in moving from a triad of commitment to a quartet, he would not be alone. I'm sure you understand."

Heiko nodded. "I see. Well, why not? Concepts that go beyond established thinking should sometimes be floated and prime ministers should not lack the courage to consider them. It appears your prime minister is not afraid of governance innovation and therefore, Ambassador, this is what I will do. As you request, I will present this quartet approach to my prime minister. The implications are clear enough. If he is inclined to go along, I will inform you that we will play. If there is a disinclination, if he thinks that at this time more will be lost than gained, I will tell you it will be the trio only. It goes without saying that we would then expect you to agree to let this last part lie."

The discussion with de Bruyn had taken forty-two minutes. In the back seat of the car returning her to Wassenaar, Natalia felt humbled more than elated. She had put all she was, her judgement and experience, into the summit document. Never before had she developed ideas on that scale and she was convinced it was her finest, freest piece of work. It might not live. Perhaps the ideas stood no chance. What mattered most now, however, was that they no longer existed only in her head. After forty-two weighty minutes they had assumed a little bit of life in that a serious prime minister was scheduled to consider them.

Chapter 16

Carlos felt dull after a long journey back from Santiago. Turning the key to the residence door, he silently lamented. "Why do I endure the airline torture? I am not a masochist. Why not cut the travel by half? Better still, go nowhere from now on unless it's on a bicycle."

Deep down, however, he knew such resolutions stood no chance. A good night's rest, another flattering request to be the featured guest, and off he would be traversing the continents and oceans again. Despite some tut-tutting to the contrary now and then, he had an ego. He enjoyed being the star academic. He liked the audiences fawning over his exotic knowledge. Nor did he mind the fat consulting fees. Cheques arriving in the mail were further vindication that he was a valuable commodity, though he mostly ignored the money. When bank drafts and other such pieces of paper had piled up, he took them to the bank and forgot about them.

In the vestibule he let the suitcase clatter to the floor and banged the front door shut. It brought on no whoops of joy, no sound of quick feet coming down the stairs. Disappointment pricked him. Then he realized. Saturday morning. Natalia would be at the weekly foreign office briefing. And so he dragged his luggage up the stairs, extracted toiletries, showered and brushed his teeth to get rid of the smell and taste of travelling and, in fresh clothes, went to the kitchen to brew tea.

Usually, if Natalia was absent, Carlos didn't notice the stillness in the house. When his intellect was in high gear it generated all the sound he needed. But it was barely turning over now and the quiet began squeezing him. Were Natalia home, her weekend brio, her verbal chromatics, would be jolting his humour. With much irony he would be admitting that his week had been mud-flat dull and dreary. For three days, hotly contested academic opinions were thrown around in a stuffy Santiago seminar room. Painful theories were promulgated on what should be most valued: cultures remaining true to ancient customs – of which a few, with practices such as female circumcision, may seem barbaric by today's standards – though continuing to have a primordial authenticity; or cultures that are open and progressive, willing to embrace new ways, but thereby losing their ancient, defining edges? *It was like a farmyard dust-up between geese and chickens, Natalia. Don't laugh. There was quacking and cackling. Three days of seminar noise to which I contributed nothing. I tried, but failed, to doze through it.* When she came home and asked, that's how he would summarize the week.

Carlos took his tea into the drawing room and flopped into a chair. Picture books on West Coast native art and Canada's magnificent northern parks lay scattered on the coffee table before him. Would the most recent edition of their weekly news magazine be there too? Yes it was, the front cover portraying a burning oilrig. And beside it? What was that disorderly pile of paper? It looked much handled and was covered with notations in Natalia's joyous, swirling script.

Piqued, Carlos put his mug to the side. Because the pages had a rumpled look, were in a messy stack and didn't look professional, or perhaps because jet-lag had him in its grip, he did not hear an inner bell chiming out a warning. Not for one second did he think he was about to violate a codicil to the unwritten covenant that sustained his marriage – that he and Natalia would always and fully respect each other's professional privacy.

~

NON-PAPER.

The big black letters, as in a screaming headline, stood centered at the top. No further markings on that first page, nothing that said the document was confidential, secret, or should be read only by certain, security-indoctrinated eyes. He was used to noticing such designations from a distance. One or another alluring term implying national secrecy was usually stamped in an imposing font on the heavy binders emerging from Natalia's double-lock briefcase. She would open them, be immersed for hours, then lock them back in. Compared to that, **NON-PAPER** looked playground-innocent.

What is a non-paper, anyway? What is a non-magazine? Or a non-book? Something that exists, yet doesn't? The word *non* sometimes crept into Natalia's vocabulary. Returning from a diplomatic jamboree she might say, *That truly was a non-event.* Or, if they were on a holiday, again marred because Ottawa had found her, even at a tiny, out of the way hotel, she would sigh and say, *another non-vacation.*

Non stood for the opposite of what should have been. Let's think opposites therefore, thought Carlos. What's the opposite of a solid academic paper? A spoof? Continuing this line of reasoning, Carlos wondered if this document, this non-paper, might also be a mockery. Were the pages autobiographical? Had Natalia been writing about her own existence, setting it down as a parody? She had a gift for that.

Carlos smirked and took the sheets.

Right away he saw it wasn't personal at all. No caricaturing of self. Not one personal pronoun to be found. He began reading the document.

And once he started he couldn't stop. The prose was succinct, shorn of Natalia's love for embellishment and the content was immediately captivating. Leaning forward over the coffee table he stroked his beard with one hand and flipped the pages with the other. His brain shook off the problem of too many traversed time zones. His dullness morphed into ferment. Before him lay a description of a vastly better world. And it seemed close. Actually, according to this paper it was no more than one short shout away. A summit of political leaders from fourteen principled countries to be meeting soon in The Hague? Commitments to force humanity's mania for violence into remission? A huge leap towards credible global peace governance? Undertakings to bequeath future generations with representative institutions possessing credibility?

A non-paper? Or an audacious declaration? It was as high-minded as … as … Carlos thought. What magnificent political paradigm shifts had mankind produced? When did humanity step up to become a species with a higher level of political morality? There was the Magna Carta, a pretty fine document. Also the American Declaration of Independence. He sucked in his breath. What led Natalia to draw up a blue print for the planetary management of peace on that kind of archetypal scale? Why did she develop a conviction that international discourse had to be lifted above the current, self-interested, effrontery-driven one typical of the UN?

He thought back. In recent months she had at times been distant. Or preoccupied. Often she sat in a reading chair, not moving, her eyelids drooping down, her gaze inward. Sometimes she questioned him, asking for his opinion or for explanations. How did belief systems built up around a culture of military rigidity and aggression work? What made the ones based on comity and cooperation tick? How, she wanted to know, do cultures arise that are driven by vengeance? What allows others not to take that route? Why do social groups – and nations – turn myths into truths and truths into myths? What inclines humanity to see the atrocities it perpetrates on itself as acts of righteousness? She was often intense. *What's your view, Carlos? You're the world's foremost expert on identity and culture. Why do we distrust people who are different? Is that learned? Is it genetic? Does distrust impart a higher survival advantage than concord? If so, are there ways to address it?*

In various ways his thinking, creatively distilled, was in this non-paper. He also recognized Alistair Paradis. Last Sunday with a rum-lubricated tongue he had grandiosely described the unstoppable force a million people become when they organize themselves to act as one. But mostly Carlos saw Natalia in the document – her values, her capacity to jump hurdles, her decades of encounters with the causes of world-scale failures. Peace ministries as counterweights to the war departments? Why not! Money allocated to civilian peace building in proportion to military budgets? Why not! Peace professionals engaging proactively in areas of tension? Why not! And, most intriguingly, this newness would be wisely steered. The governance system she proposed was the most innovative, he was sure, of all the ones that have come along since the Peace of Westphalia was signed by the warring Europeans five hundred years ago.

Carlos's tea went cold. He read each page, then read them all twice more. He eventually decided that the title was wrong. This was not a non-paper. It was not a spoof. Nor a caricature or mockery. This paper showed his wife at her intellectual best. This paper explained why, on Malta's ramparts, he had instantly fallen in love with her. What he felt then, he was overcome by now.

The stillness was broken by the opening and closing of the front door. Hurriedly he hid the dishevelled pages under the pile of picture books, stood up and placed his tea on a different table. Natalia came rushing up for an embrace. "Carlos," she cried, "my gorilla in life!"

The next morning Carlos rose feeling like a lion. Natalia's mood upon his return had been iridescent and, naturally, that affected him. For the remainder of Saturday, they had clung to each other to make up for days lost. A tender hour in the bedroom, a neighborhood walk afterwards, a nap for him, then chatty drinks together, an excellent restaurant dinner, after which more tenderness before a long, deep sleep. Could life get better?

In the kitchen after the restful night, waiting for the espresso machine to fill a demi-tasse, he planned the week. Tomorrow he would visit Alistair. That old grizzly bear would enjoy another diversion. He would ask him when he would show himself on the international peace circuit again. In Santiago, Paradis's metaphors and stirring cadences had been sorely missed.

A phone call after breakfast set it up. "My dear Carlos," Paradis replied volubly, "you are the augur of truths that future generations will eventually discover. Do come, please, yes do. Some quacking going on in Santiago, you say? And clucking? Was there cuckoldry too? By the way, please tell Natalia that no rum was ever more enjoyable than last week's."

Next morning Carlos nearly cancelled it. Storm and rain arrived overnight. He didn't feel up to hours of being lashed by bad weather while cycling forty kilometers to Alistair's condo and delayed his departure. When the fierceness outside appeared to be tapering off, he pulled on an oilskin coat, donned a rain hat and set off. Cycling's rhythm brought on the usual euphoria. To the left beyond the dunes, the North Sea was roaring. The high tide whipped on by the wind would be two meters higher than he was. But down here, in the pit, so to speak, the ditches were straight and draining, the trees pruned in winter were greening up and all that lived was well-orchestrated and protected.

North to Katwijk and on to Noordwijk, then east past Lisse in the direction of Aalsmeer. A variety of routes would get him there and Carlos took paths randomly, though in the right general direction. Eventually, breathing hard, he parked the bike inside the complex where Paradis enjoyed his opulence. The architecture of the buildings in park-like surroundings was north-European urbane: units with glass walls, setbacks for privacy, hanging gardens and spacious balconies ringed by flowers. Beauty, calm and innocence. At the door he pressed a button.

Almost simultaneously, from a speaker, Paradis's voice jumped at him. "Watched you coming up in that Aussie coat, Carlos. A poor disguise. Come up. There's brandy and a mountain of Dutch cookies."

In the apartment Paradis hobbled about on stiff legs in a side to side swagger. He barely had balance. All the same, Carlos complimented him on his mobility. "You're moving like a stag now, Alistair."

"Watch me leap," Paradis replied. With care he stepped from the hardwood floor onto an oriental carpet and shuffled towards an immense chair. Sinking into it, he explained, "Every part of this chair is adjustable, the footrest, the back. I like the massage feature best. Our party is in the kitchen, Carlos. My domestic did the shopping and put it there. I would get it, but that would take hours. Would you mind?"

Over coffee, cookies and then cognac, they gossiped like two palsy soldiers off-duty. Carlos took Paradis though the debate minutiae of Santiago. Paradis shook with laughter. "I miss it," he said. "The delegates, the accents, their spectral backgrounds. I used to think, they speak the same language, but the atmosphere is more like at the Tower of Babel. Noble individuals forced into insularity because they don't understand each other. Watching the spectacle – that capacity for getting nowhere – always fascinated me. High time I got back to it."

Carlos nodded. "We're always planning to stir up ideas and develop deeper understanding, but it seems we mostly stir up muck. Should more be expected? With thirty experts in one room, each one convinced he knows enough to lecture the others for five days running, a coming together gets difficult. Let's be thankful there are higher decision-making levels."

"Higher levels? Come now," Paradis pooh-poohed. "With muckraking, the higher you go, the thicker the stuff gets. At the top, the muck is so dense you can no longer rake it. What you get up there is absolute paralysis. You smirk, Carlos. You see it otherwise?" With an expansive swing, Paradis brought his cognac glass to his lips and emptied it. "It is not yet noon," he added. "Let's squeeze another in before then." Carlos poured more cognac for them both and Paradis sighed with pleasure. "Such bliss when two comrades have a chance to talk. Back to decisions made at higher levels. You claim we should be thankful for them. What do you know that I don't?"

~

The question took Carlos back to the seminars, to the esteem that came his way for having unique knowledge. Speaking openly brought respect and sometimes applause, which in a special way was seductive. After all, he had that little challenge with his ego – the gratification derived from being central. This now welled up in him.

"Something has been on my mind, Alistair. Something exciting," he said in a complicit tone. "I was thinking about it the whole way up. When I returned from Santiago on Saturday, I happened to read about a political development at the highest levels. It has been stirring me since. Historical instances exist when politics was refined, when political nimbleness brought results, when there was no paralyzing muck. Why shouldn't it happen again? Not only that, but imagine trench dwellers like you and I contributing to it."

Paradis, deep in his chair, had the appearance of a serene and tolerant Buddha. "But Carlos, I have been prophesying that," he answered smugly. "Remember the Luanda workshop on eradicating racism? I said our voices would eventually be heard. Then, at the conference in Ulaanbaatar when we explored the fundamental right to commingle culturally, I stated that the political level would one day realize we were providing them with a recipe for a world crackling with creative social energy. And at the colourful religions festival in Menaus, you recall, I argued that ritual dance is not appreciated nearly enough for its extraordinary unifying power. I added that the next UN summit was bound to recognize this, that the world's leaders would surely be proclaiming a World Day of Dancing for Peace. If I recall correctly, you agreed with me. I also remember you saying with your usual smirk that every head of state should set a personal example by doing a tepid little tap dance on a New York sidewalk in front of the UN. So all of us, we, the muck stirrers and trench dwellers, have been showing the way.

"This refined, new political development you mention – is what we were forecasting beginning to happen? You must tell me, Carlos. We have been friends too long for you to hold back."

Paradis's curiosity was eager, like a child having the urge to rip ribbon and wrapping paper off a present. His interest, Carlos had experienced, often flipped into enthusiasm. If a nugget of information or insight was shared with him, it generated instant praise. *That's cutting edge, Carlos. A unique and true perception. Absolutely so.* Questions would follow, intense but sympathetic, which made you want to share still more. And today Carlos had more to share. Much more. But not yet, he thought. Munching on cookies, sipping cognac, conversing without effort, the opportunity to tease – it was too enjoyable. It should continue a little longer. So Carlos held back. Instead, he invited Paradis to reply to a question. "In your opinion, Alistair, what in the last few centuries is the best example of great political refinement?"

Paradis frowned. "Gorbachev ending the Cold War?" he ventured.

"Endings don't count." Carlos gave a hint. "Think of a beginning. A magnificent beginning." Paradis refused to guess a second time and Carlos answered for him. "Has there been a political advancement more far-reaching than the American Declaration of Independence?"

"If endings don't count, why should revolutions?"

Carlos took another cookie. "What has been on my mind, what I was mulling over as I cycled up this morning, is that in nearly two and a half centuries nothing has come along to match that Declaration. In that time no new constitution has been written that matches the one the Americans composed. Thirteen colonies got together. In population terms and relative to the empires then existing that was small beer, fairly minor nation building really. The political class in Spain or Portugal were probably amused by it. But what did that constitution beget? A nation with an overwhelming global presence. The founding fathers of America could not have foreseen what their Union would look like two hundred years later. In their small sphere, driven by idealism, they devised a balanced political framework allowing decisiveness when necessary. Of course, America is now losing its enlightened impulse. It says it wants to lead, but really it intends to dictate. Nevertheless, in 1769, the thirteen colonies engineered a fine moment, a highpoint of politics."

As Carlos set out his latest piece of historical simplification, Paradis lifted a hand several times and wrinkled his lips to try getting a word in, but now he scowled as if annoyed. "I am always too slow to get your meaning, Carlos. The Americans did give themselves a fine start and, yes, they are losing their greatness, but what is your point? Are they returning to that earlier state, to the inspiration they had at the beginning? Do you know of them planning something that is politically new and possibly elegant?"

"Something like America's birth may be happening again. Imagine this statement. I conjured it up on my way here. *We hold this truth to be self-evident, that all humanity is created equal and is endowed with the unalienable right to live in peace. That to secure this right, humanity will initiate new governance. That this governance shall derive its power through the consent of those it governs.* The wording could be improved, but you get the idea. Imagine further that this expression will be the first paragraph of a peace constitution for the whole planet."

Paradis sat static. His face, always expressive, and his head, normally restless, were stock-still. His scowl had melted away too, replaced by narrow eyes, which studied Carlos with suspicion. A minute passed. At last he moved a hand. It edged down to a switch on the chair's side. With a flick the massage function became activated and to the tune of its low hum his body began quivering. "I prophesied that," he said casually. "*Our voices will be heard.* I said that two years ago, March 17, in Luanda. You smirk again, Carlos. It is incessant. Are you playing with me? Who is the 'we' in that line you quoted? Is your wife working on something? Is that how you know about things happening at higher levels? I have not seen reports in the papers and my clipping service doesn't miss a thing." He looked at a clock. "We are past noon now which means we ought to feel quite free to have another cognac."

"A small, final one for me. Bicycle paths are safe, but not always straight." Carlos poured himself a drop and half-filled Paradis's glass. "This must stay between us, Alistair. The strictest confidence. Agreed?"

"You are not here, Carlos. Nor have you been. I have been alone all-day and dozing. In a dream I ate cookies and drank cognac."

Carlos shifted forwards. "I've seen a remarkable document. You have a right to know about it since it's partly based on what you and Natalia talked about. She is the author. I am sure of that. It has her special style. I don't know its status. She has been visiting the Dutch Government on Saturdays, but I cannot tell if there is a connection. It deals with a peace summit. Fourteen countries to attend. Not one of them a great power. That's what made me think of 1769 when thirteen minor colonies came together."

"A Peace Summit? How enticing. Where?"

"In The Hague. At the Peace Palace."

"I prophesied that!" Paradis cried triumphantly.

"You did?"

"At the colourful religions festival in Menaus. August 7 last year. I said a peace summit was coming."

"You said there should be a World Day of Dancing for Peace."

"To be launched by a peace summit. Don't quibble, Carlos. Just now you said something that fascinates me. Did I hear correctly? *Governance arising through the consent of the governed.* Is that the purpose of the Summit?"

"Partly."

"That is truly grand. Think of all the breath we have expended on that objective. Prospects for it always seemed beyond the horizon. But we did not give up. We did not stop chasing our dream. May a day be nearing when humanity will steer itself according to enlightened principles?" Paradis made no attempt to suppress his excitement.

It spilled over, for Carlos began nodding energetically as well. "I'll predict something," he said. "If what is in Natalia's paper comes to pass, you will be part of the new governance, Alistair. You will be in at the top level."

"Oh my! Truly Carlos? I think I may swoon. How would that be? What are the intentions?"

"I don't know the document's status. It may be in transition. But as of last Saturday, this is what it says." Carlos's eyes had fixed in a direction down and away from Paradis on a spot near the cookie tray. He was unable to restrain himself and recited from memory. The non-paper's introduction and the doctrine of the responsibility to protect and the action items were accurately described. His voice dropped when he arrived at the provisions for global peace governance – an elected Peace Assembly and a Peace Senate constituted by humanity's wise elders. Carlos described the constitutional mechanics, how member states would transfer certain of their national rights and privileges to the new governing structure. With a hint of triumph he announced a day was coming when the Security Council, anachronistic and dysfunctional, would be muscled to the side.

Carlos finished and looked up. The massage function was continuing to stir Paradis. Tears were trickling down through the stubble on the old man's cheeks. Carlos handed him a paper napkin. "My apologies," Paradis said, dabbing his eyes. "Crying like a baby. You took me to see the promised land. What I witnessed overwhelmed me. The audaciousness of it. The magnificence. Will it happen, Carlos? What are the odds? What do you think?"

Carlos spread his hands. "Think once more of America's founding fathers. What allowed them to lift democracy to a new level? The people. The people were sick of Britain's colonial ways. A revolution in thought and deed became viable. Natalia's peace governance may start small and may take some time, but when people see the moral force, they will be won over. As I said, should one day the wisest members of humanity take their seats in a Peace Senate, you will be among them. Much in Natalia's paper hinges on the people whom you lead."

"It is too much, Carlos. It is too much. Such utter happiness. It makes me weep."

~

In the hallway Carlos slipped into his oilskin and asked, "ever traveled with the wind, Alistair? Going somewhere at twice the speed with half the effort – it is sublime, I tell you."

"Seldom, Carlos. Always fierce head winds for me. Nothing but struggle. But with Natalia pushing peace, perhaps the sails will billow." He seemed to lose his balance and struggled to maintain it, taking Carlos by the shoulders. "A lovely visit. Come back soon." Carlos patted Paradis muscularly on the upper arms and was gone.

Tottering back to his chair and nestling down, though not to drift off into a restoring nap, Paradis's first thought was, what now? First recapitulate, he decided, then act. Such extraordinary luck! Years had gone into gaining Carlos's trust. Not easy years. Not necessarily. Carlos had his smug side – that smirk of hubris, the overplayed modesty, the diplomatic password which he acquired through marriage, did not deserve, yet liked to show off all the same. He'd spent years shooting arrows in the dark and today, unexpectedly, one hit the bull's eye. Yes, signs had been accumulating that a breakthrough was coming, that Carlos was softening. He came to the clinic to visit. Last week that favourable opportunity, spending the afternoon cheek to jowl with his wife, drinking happily and sounding her out. That had been a strikingly civilized time. An investment, since by itself it brought little. But today! Today an over-sized supertanker of good fortune had eased into port. A bounty beyond his wildest dreams was there. Helmut would be thrilled.

Bellonae Adytum. Paradis began to visualize Helmut in the black-marble sunken room, toying with the weapons in miniature. The image stiffened him. Shoulder-slapping, sharp-shooting, death-loving Helmut. Savannah schmoozer, issuer of bone-chilling orders and godfather of doom. Helmut demanded more than any mortal man seeking some late-life comfort could deliver. No matter how much news he provided over the years, it was never enough. Helmut demanded more detail. With ice in his voice, he insisted on precision. Often the facts Helmut required did not exist and Paradis would have to set about inventing some kind of scourge to rationality arising from the NGO netherworld. In the vibrating chair, Paradis reflected for a long time on how to report to Helmut so as to maximize his thrill. The story would be smooth, highly polished. Like a billiard ball. One soft spot, one imperfection, and Helmut's probing claws would sink in and snap it apart. With the chair working hard to bring suppleness his back, Paradis reviewed the picture Carlos drew. Many contours in it; plenty of crosshatches and shadings; lovely depth. A masterwork. Yet too much as well. How could all that be transformed into something hard, into a kind of verbal billiard ball? Thank goodness Carlos departed feeling high. But then, people usually are when they come out of the confessional. The ancient Wazzock act, some moaning, a show of tears, it never failed to soften people up and cause them to feel good about themselves.

Paradis switched the massage function off. Martha's cooking shift began in two hours and he ought to file the report before then. He hauled himself up using the cane. A hobble brought him to the spare room. A key, which he always kept close, turned the lock. Behind the door in the mostly empty space stood a small table, a hard chair, a shredder and, on a stand, a device with so many buttons that Paradis always worried he would be electrocuted if he touched it.

He lowered himself onto the chair, pulled a pad over and began to copy that which lingered of Carlos's picture down, with some reworking to make it flawless. The ballpoint sat heavily in his hand. Pressing down on pens was his habit, his style. It took some time. On governance, he recalled, there were many details. Elections, allocations of seats – nuances aplenty – but, no longer sure of all the fine points, he omitted them. Who could forget the broad strokes of an elected World Peace Assembly, though, and a Peace Senate? Paradis pushed the pen. It was not long until the hard chair caused the muscles in his buttocks, hips and back to cramp up. He winced when he pushed himself back onto his feet. One final act remained.

Two wobbly steps delivered him to the device with all the buttons. He stared down and gathered the resolve to operate it. He had done it only once, after installation, to test it. He had then taped the idiot's guide to its operation to the wall behind, and now he meticulously consulted the necessary steps. Place the report face down in the slot. Lift the receiver and push that button. Wait for three rings. Listen to a recorded voice that says, *Speak*. "Message," Paradis answered loudly, reading from the wall. A wait for his voice print to be checked. The quiet broke. *Proceed*. More jabbing at buttons. A beep. The wall chart instructed that a special key be turned. That done, another silence, another beep. A small red light glowed. A message lit up a screen. *Secure link*. The next step, according to the idiot's guide, was to put the receiver down, then press the Start button. The sheet began moving. He watched it disappear and re-emerge from a slot lower down. Once it was fully out, the machine beeped yet again, a signal that the security key should be reversed. A final beep, with the red light cutting out. *Bellonae Adytum* was in possession of its latest pound of flesh.

The pain in his back was worsening. He left the room, locked the door, and with a yelp or two stumbled to his chair. A fresh round of massage began. By the time Martha arrived he was his old cheerful self. She went into the kitchen and sang her Filipino songs.

Amidst this domestic bliss the fax machine could be heard ringing. It startled her, for she came out of the kitchen.

"Sir?"

"I'll handle it, Martha. My staff in Geneva. Be so kind. Pull me onto my feet." Steadying him by the elbow, she led him to the locked door. He ordered her back to the kitchen. Inside the room the same process was repeated. Buttons and beeping, the strange key, red lights, this time to receive. A sheet emerged from the machine. He turned it over.

Too vague. Almost useless. A new Assembly? A Senate? How? Where? When?

Paradis turned the fax off, locked the door as he went out and shuffled to the dining table. Martha had prepared a curry and he chewed on it in gloom. "You no like?" she asked.

"It's delicious, Martha. My apologies. Someone on my staff in Geneva has become ill. It is on my mind."

"For that, very sorry. Why you no bring here? Doctors pretty good."

"Excellent suggestion. Thank you. We may do that."

"You tell me. I help."

Help. He could use some. Helmut's demands were undoing the chair's good work. He was tensing up again. Why? What was that problem's source? Paradis knew. His memory wasn't what it used to be. He could not recollect all the details Carlos had so fluently spilled out. He remembered there were prescriptions for action. Numbers too. The information had entered his brain, paused, done a U-turn, and fled out. Paradis sighed. He waited for something, anything at all, to come back. Martha cleaned up and left with a cheerful *God bless. You sleep pretty good tonight. OK?*

Once more, he laboured to the forbidden room. Again he pulled the writing pad towards him. What had Carlos said? What thoughts had cascaded through him as he bicycled up? Of course, yes. The peace initiative was comparable to America's struggle for freedom. A government came into existence that was representative and moral. Some of it was coming back. Carlos had rephrased the Declaration of Independence. Also there was a formula for elections. But how, precisely, all that was to function, Paradis could not remember. Was it that important? Wasn't one governance formula as good as another? If Natalia, or Carlos, could resort to inventions, as they must have, why not match them? Paradis took the pen again and began to move it weightily. Helmut's lust for specifics had to be satisfied somehow. The alternative was to share in the fate of that rhino caught in the crosshairs and get dropped cleanly at two yards.

~

Following a Peace Declaration by the Summit of fourteen countries, a convention of these states will determine governance for peace action by modelling it on the American Constitution, which is considered to be the most sublime such charter in the world. It was written by founders who were motivated by high moral values.

The time is considered ripe for a similar action.

The US House of Representatives is the model for a World Peace Assembly. The US Senate is the model for a Peace Senate.

CONSTITUTING THE PEACE ASSEMBLY:
- *each member state shall be allocated a seat for every ten million inhabitants*
- *no member state shall have fewer than two seats or more than twenty*
- *candidates to the Peace Assembly from each member state shall be nominated to stand for election by a national peace conference, designed to make sure they are of the highest calibre*
- *for each available Assembly seat, three candidates shall be nominated into a pool*
- *in the election each voter shall mark one vote for no more than three candidates*
- *the candidates will be ranked according to votes received, the top ones filling the allocated seats*
- *terms for elected peace representative will be six years*

- *through a phasing in period at the start, eventually one-half of Assembly seats would come up for re-election every three years*

THE PEACE ASSEMBLY'S ROLE AND POWERS:
- *pass laws which build global peace*
- *ensure member states implement the laws*
- *determine the actions of peace builders and peace academies*
- *allocate funds acquired through guaranteed drawing rights on member state tax revenues (revenues to be in proportion to military outlays)*
- *provide parliamentary oversight to important peace-related organizations such as the International Criminal Court*

~

Paradis wrote with his imagination in overdrive. The page filled up. Then another. He did eventually recall how the Peace Senators – humanity's wise elders – would be determined and wrote that out too, adding some personal embellishments. His excitement mounted as the work progressed. The pain of sitting was forgotten. He was beginning to feel that he was himself a founding father writing down a constitution. The glow it caused allowed him to come up with ever more abstract thoughts. How could this or that constitutional provision work? He thought, then wrote it down. When the follow-up report was finished he felt pride, the pride of creation and knowing it was good. This material was the best he had ever conjured up. Better than the Wazzock acts. Better even than his speeches as a PEACE prophet. It was detailed too. It would overwhelm Helmut's love of quibbling.

Rereading his paper before sending it on, Paradis began chuckling when he saw he had come up with his own non-paper. It surely matched Natalia's and in parts was possibly better. He placed it in the fax machine, initiated secure activation and saw it go through. After shutdown, he took it and the day's other pages and shredded them.

A final thought. A smug one. Should Natalia's peace come to be, he would arrange to have a new card. *Alistair Paradis, Senator for Peace.* Of course, he would also have to find a way then to jilt his current, demanding mistress.

Chapter 17

Heywood consulted his watch when the phone began ringing. 9:45 am. An early disturbance for a Monday morning. The name and number appearing on the screen were not familiar, and he let it ring a few more times before lifting the receiver. "Heywood," he announced gruffly.

"Mr Heywood." The voice was that of a bright young woman. "Glad I caught you. I'm Jenny Chou, Mr Mckilroy's Executive Assistant. He has to see you. Right away. How long will it take you to get here?"

Heywood's mind spun into action. Urgency from the prime minister's office? What was happening? The peace summit? Experience had taught Heywood that when surrounded by unknowns, sounding cocksure provides the advantage. He growled, "what about?"

"No time for that." The voice was sweet, eager, a touch angelic. "He's with the prime minister this moment and wants you here when that's over. In about fifteen minutes?"

"Should I bring something? Documents? A briefing book? My desk is stacked to the ceiling. One on every current crisis going."

"My understanding is, on this issue, it's best there's no paper."

"Fine. OK if we make it twenty minutes? I'm not who I used to be. I need a detour in the men's."

"Five minutes for that?" Jenny giggled. "How about just one?"

"I promise to get there when I can."

Going unprepared into encounters with the higher levels was contrary to Heywood's standards. He ought to at least get the latest from Natalia. But Jenny, despite the sweet voice, had been forged from steel. She scarcely bended on the fifteen minutes. In the cab, Heywood did some speculating. Mckilroy was coming out of a meeting with the PM. That suggested the Dutch PM had called. Probably for some final fine-tuning of the Summit, along the lines he and Natalia had worked out. Co-hosting and co-chairing, the main conference speech, sitting at the queen's right hand for lunch, that sort of thing. Maybe the two PMs had agreed on dates, meaning the PM would require a wagon master, a dependable workhorse, familiar with the background and the substance, able to shape the complexities into a nice tight package and write two or three short sentences for statement to the media. "It is happening," Heywood thought, staring fiercely through the cab window. "And they thought they could get on without me."

~

In Mckilroy's suite of offices Heywood never did catch a glimpse of sweet-tongued Jenny Chou. The receptionist, in between smacking loudly on a piece of gum, said, "Yeah, gotcha on this list here." She pointed at a small boardroom off the open space. "Wait there." He looked at the room. A table and four chairs, not one of them a leather swivel. Ascending eyebrows questioned the receptionist. Was this spartan space a mockery? Her reply was a commanding finger snapped towards the door. A minute later she came up and loudly banged it shut.

Without the bureaucratic comfort of a thick briefing book containing more answers than are ever needed, waiting in tight confines, Heywood felt uneasy. He had expected sunny Jenny to be waiting for him, to whisk him through security like any standard VIP. He had imagined her happily babbling in the elevator about how impressive it was he got there so quick. What happened instead? A surly guard had demanded his ID. He'd snarled back that he was a high-ranking official in the government, that in his own building the guards knew him, were kind, and often enquired about his health. It hadn't helped. In retrospect, he was probably lucky to get past them without a strip-search. The escort in uniform who brought him up had viewed him with similar aggression. And the reception up here wasn't exactly of the let's-uncork-a-bottle-of-champagne variety either. "Gotta get myself a cell phone," Heywood reflected. "I could call Hannah in situations like this. She'd keep my spirits up. Plus it looks good yakking into the phone, as if you're busy all the time." His watch now said 10:15. Was Mckilroy still with the PM? What could those two be wasting so much time on?

Just before 11am Desmond Mckilroy swept in and slammed the door. Heywood had been practicing a greeting. In an amiable, musical voice he had planned to say, *Hello Desmond. It's been a while. How are things?* But Mckilroy scored first. "Never experienced this kind of monumental screw-up before," he snapped, dangling a portable tape player before Heywood's nose.

Heywood studied the tiny machine, then looked up into Mckilroy's raw eyes. "I got here as fast as I could," he answered peaceably.

"Last winter I clearly said to you that we were too busy for the Dutch. Our ambassador there was supposed to hop to it."

"You did say that. Absolutely. The ambassador has been doing a great job on your behalf."

"Then how come this?" Mckilroy brandished the tape player again. "The voice you'll hear is that of Colonel Y. William Goht, military attaché at the US Embassy. He called me at home at six this morning as I was sitting down for breakfast and demanded an appointment at nine. I don't like being dictated to and tried to fob him off. Let colonels deal with colonels. He flat-out told me that my receiving him was in my interest, not his. He said, does the Canadian Government want to go down in flames? That didn't sound nice, so I agreed to an appointment." Mckilroy placed the player on the table and pushed a button.

~

Goht   Well, Mr Mckilroy. Mighty kind of you to have me at short notice. Before we start I oughta let you know my colleague in The Hague, Brigadier General Rory Bessy, Air Force, is seeing the right hand man of the Dutch prime minister this very minute. Same topic. Close coordination. You with me?

Mckilroy   It makes your visit only slightly more interesting.

Goht   Not just interesting. Fascinating. This is the background. We got this neat unit in Pentagon communications called Media Early Warning and Liaison. MEWL. OK, not the best acronym. Anyways, MEWL does good stuff. Never mind how, but they prevent problems, I can tell you. Political hassles, embarrassments, misunderstandings – MEWL gets stuff like that to sink below the radar.

            So now MEWL picks up an item, a story that's been penned. Day after tomorrow it's supposed to appear in the *New York Times* page three, fourth column I think. All nicely written up, ready for printing. The item in question is about your government and that of the Dutch. The US government is friendly, as you know, altruistic, and I'm here to share the item with you, in case you want to avoid yourselves some embarrassment. The item says your two governments are planning a peace initiative. New goody-goodies for mankind. Changes in the structures of governments, which would see outfits like the Pentagon in other countries play second fiddle to some kind of new department for fluff with money for the fluff work to

243

be heisted from defense budgets. Brigades of long-haired types are supposed to invade the world, to offer wise thoughts to local insurgents who, overnight, are supposed to become respectable, God-fearing middle class types like you and I. And, get this, there's gonna be a peace constitution for the whole world. It seems a lot of preparatory work took place in The Hague, secretly, and according to the article things are ready to roll. So now, Mr Mckilroy, I'd like to ask you – is any of that true?

By the way, my friends call me Billy. Billy Goht. A silly joke I know. Played on me by my parents. You smile. That's a good sign. It qualifies you for Liz and me having you over for a meal real soon. Can I call you by your first name too? Des OK?

Mckilroy	Desmond, please.

Goht	That's OK. Desmond and Billy we are. Look, Desmond, you and I, we both know this can't be true.

Mckilroy	It isn't. It's absolute rubbish.

Goht	Sure. I predicted that. Last night I said to Washington, "MEWL is out of tune". Problem is though, this *New York Times* piece is detailed. Makes it seem plausible. It's also been noticed that for months your ambassador in The Hague, elegant lady, touch on the round side, has been visiting the prime minister's office there every Saturday. We couldn't get a spot for taking a sound reading off a window where she was, so we don't know what was said, but you oughta have an inkling of that. So now, please tell me, were they busy planning the creation of a World Peace Assembly to be modelled on the US House of Representatives? You have to agree, that would be pretty damn grotesque.

Mckilroy	The article is bogus whatever the contents. For years my prime minister, this Government, has shunned an international profile. You know that. It's on the record. My prime minister would never waste time seeking votes through an international initiative, let alone a peace agenda.
Goht	Well, I do know that Desmond and I said so to Washington. I think they bought it. So obviously we both want this news item to go away. You, because there's nothing to it, and Washington, because it doesn't want to be asked questions about why our allies snub us. The world knows that the US has a standing right to be part of all things peace. America fought for peace in the Korean war. It fought for peace in Vietnam. It was the reason why we freed Kuwait. The US was a steady ally of regimes in Latin America fighting the leftists. We invaded Grenada and went into Somalia. We fought for peace in Iraq and now in Afghanistan. Peace, peace, peace. All the time and everywhere. Our credentials are impeccable. It would actually be a slap in the face for us not to be asked to take a seat at a peace table. Not just that. When our constitution gets hijacked to serve as a model for something global – the word in my briefing note is "usurped" – we consider that a blasphemy. The world needs nothing other than the supreme effectiveness of the American Constitution deployed by Americans to look after others. That ensures justice, peace and liberty for all. Do you see it that way too, Desmond?
Mckilroy	Since the news article is not based on fact, the question is hypothetical.
Goht	Right. OK. So how do we get rid of that bad article? As a friendly neighbour, I've got a suggestion. Here

is a name and a number. The US Government has
no official knowledge of any of this and therefore
we believe it best if you dialled that number
yourself, and formally, on behalf of your government,
inform the individual answering the phone that
you categorically deny all Canadian knowledge and
involvement in the events described in the article.
Sound doable? For quality assurance, what you say
will be recorded.

Mckilroy   *[After a long silence]*: I'll call you.

Goht   Before lunch if you don't mind, Des. Those big
papers, you know, bureaucracies unto themselves.
Some of their inside pages take shape early. It gets
tough for stuff to come out.

~

Mckilroy silenced the tape player with a contemptuous jab. He
took a deep breath and said, "A preliminary comment, please."

Heywood sensed slaughter. He also knew that a magnificent
last stand would at least bring honour. Drawing on forty years of
acquired aggression he answered with icy scorn. "Preliminary?"

Mckilroy exploded. "Goddamn it, yes! Something preliminary
such as, *Golly, I guess my little game is up*. What in hell have you and
your ambassador been doing?"

"We have been serving the public good, as is our duty."

"Mr Heywood, you have two minutes to explain. You bloody
diplomats refuse to understand my use of language so I will resort to
yours. Please do allow me the courtesy of expressing, with my loftiest
esteem and with every assurance of my highest consideration, that
since Colonel Billy Goht met me this morning I seized the honour
of consulting the prime minister. The prime minister listened to the
tape and availed himself of that opportunity to become more pissed
off than I have ever seen him. The prime minister's initial reaction
was that the Dutch were doing something stupid. He asked why
the fuck were they dragging us and others in? The Yanks, he said, are

always getting wind of shit. They were probably using this Dutch crap to test our loyalty. So screw the Dutch, the prime minister concluded, and call the American bluff. Let the journalists dig away, there being nothing to find. I did remind the prime minister that he sat next to his Dutch counterpart at lunch in New York last autumn and that their conversation topic, apparently, was about taking advanced measures to implement the R2P doctrine. The prime minister didn't recall that. All he remembers is explaining the game of hockey, which has the objective of putting a puck in a net. I then informed the PM that back then the Dutch PM's foreign policy advisor tried to call me several times to follow up on the lunch conversation and that I had left it to you and the ambassador to turn him off."

Heywood's posture became erect and his eyes blazed as much as Mckilroy's. "That is rubbish too. You said, *Manage the issue.* You used the word *success*, or perhaps *successfully*. You said you wanted us to run the show so that the PM would get the credit. The instruction could not have been clearer. You wanted a sound foreign policy initiative prepared. It was to be done deftly and privately, to be ready for future use. I understand that motivation. One never knows when an international initiative will suddenly turn into a domestic godsend. Every prime minister has come to understand that, and we all expect that someday this one will too."

Mckilroy looked up towards the ceiling, seemingly half-crazed, and groaned. "I am not hearing right. Truly I am not. Holy heavenly saints and dear Jesus on the cross, how brainless can anyone be?"

"The instruction you issued was important and I wrote it down verbatim," Heywood added.

"Can't you read tea leaves? Aren't you paid to know political priorities? This government cares about penal institutions, oil and gas and subsidized hockey lessons for kids. There is no international interest. You heard me say that to the billy goat. There are no votes in it. So why in hell would you assume we want some teensy-weensy peace thing cluttering up the policy closet?"

Because Mckilroy was losing his composure, Heywood had a sense he was gaining ground and pressed on. "Your order was explicit. I followed up with all my energy. We have prepared a gem of an initiative. If I may ask, have you counted the number of people in this country who want more justice and peace in the world? If this initiative is rolled out with a touch of clever empathy, the editorialists will come around for you. And by the way, all that stuff about a World Peace Assembly being modelled on the US Constitution is absolute rubbish, as you pointed out to the billy goat. Nothing like that was discussed with the Dutch. Three discrete initiatives have been worked out, only one of which brings costs, for training, with the Dutch agreeing they will open their wallet. That is a firm understanding. Fiscally, for us, it's neutral, as we want it to be for international initiatives. And don't forget, that for the lunch the PM will sit next to the Dutch Queen. On her right side. There are votes in that."

Mckilroy planted both his hands on the conference room table. "No more wasting time." He spat the words out. "It is this simple. The prime minister gave his orders. If the Dutch got carried away because he sat next to their guy at lunch and if since then there has been some slight contact with them on peace, the *New York Times* number must be dialled. So here is the slip the billy goat gave me. You call that number and you deny. If there are follow-up questions, slur Dutch diplomacy. Who cares? Next, you inform the billy goat it was done. After that you instruct Madame Ambassador to goddamn well get onto the same page as you and me and stay there from now on. Got it?" Mckilroy lifted a finger, snapped it at Heywood, swooped the tape player off the table and rose. At the door he said, "I will not be presenting my compliments to you again. In a few days you will find that the assurances of my highest consideration for you will have been expressed to someone else. For now, I have the honour to request that you get the hell out of my sight."

~

Heywood did not ask the receptionist if Jenny was around to say hello. In the elevator he looked at the uniformed escort with the same disdain she sent him. When he returned his temporary pass to building security he slapped it down onto the counter without saying a word. Outside, he waddled down the sidewalk to the spot where a cab could be found.

Heywood was thinking. Mckilroy's silly game of spoofing diplomatic language showed he was small-minded, and made you feel sorry for him. Perhaps it wasn't Mckilroy's fault he was that way. It could be that to be successful in his job he had to be sort of a replica of his boss. That happens. The replication theory could also explain why Mckilroy came across as one-dimensional, the type of man that swings as aimlessly as a punch-drunk fighter. What prevented him from doing political work with elegance? You had to wish that one day, after his PM's office stint, Mckilroy would become normal again.

For now, though, the billy goat needed an answer.

Where did ultimate responsibility for the fiasco lie? With the Dutch, obviously. The initiative was their idea. They forced the pace. And clearly they had leaked it. Why? What was their rationale for arranging a *New York Times* announcement in such a way that it would cause the Yanks like Pavlov's dogs to yip and yap and yelp, thereby ensuring the initiative would end up in flames? Was the Dutch PM suckering us from the start? Was the whole "joint effort" a planned sting? This was not outside the realm of the imagination. The Dutch could have wanted access to the best ideas obtainable and turned to Canada. Once they had them, they manipulated the Yanks into killing the effort. Then everybody downs tools and walks away and, after a decent wait, the Dutch would arrange an opportunity to do some recycling. The peace package comes back to life, gets put on the table again, this time as theirs alone, meaning the Dutch are the ones going into the history books. That could have been their game plan. If so, how could it be answered? What counter strategy could be put into play so that he, Heywood, would emerge with his reputation enhanced? Not only that, he should do something to shield Natalia. She ought to be left unaffected. That policy brain of hers was too precious for the likes of Mckilroy, or the billy goat, to chuck into a trash bin.

Back in his office, Heywood drew up a list of numbers and began dialling.

Chapter 18

That same Monday, early in the evening Holland time, Robbie was at her desk clearing off a backlog of consular reports. But no complaints. The summer solstice was a mere ten days off and, despite the late hour, rays from a resilient sun continued to illuminate her office. Peering at the computer screen, she felt the light gathering around her head, as if a halo was forming, as if she was blessed. So different from the previous week, when hurricane-strength storms raged and rain was never-ending. Everyone had been gloomy. In each eye you saw a silent question taking shape – was the summer already over for the year? Had the loveliness of the spring used up all the outdoor freedom for the year, so that there was none left for the months still to come? Even Robbie had to admit the gales had been howling pretty good. Weather bulletins announced that North Sea waves propelled to shore at high tide were mauling the dykes (though they held), which was freakish for this time of year. A seeming miracle then. The weather turned, the winds died, the sea calmed, the skies cleared, the sun warmed, nature's nurturing side came out again and people went back to anticipating the bounties of the coming summer.

Robbie, humming to herself as emails got fired off, wasn't feeling blessed only on account of the light. Her existence was newly scintillating too. Very scintillating. Suddenly, shockingly so. Coincidental with the outdoor tumult, she had been experiencing some personal heavy weather. Two weeks of it. Two weeks of chomping on broccoli shoots and carrots during contemplative lunches. Night upon night of light dinners that were deeply pensive. She had much to figure out. As she gnawed on raw veggies, her future gnawed at her. At its center stood one issue, Maarten. That is, Maarten and her.

After the picnic in the dunes – Robbie was never so disoriented – Natalia's counsel made her predicament worse. *If I were you, Robbie, I'd go see him. I'd take a bottle along to show I meant business.* Stark advice. Robbie could picture Natalia meaning business in that way when she was younger. She probably followed her own advice all the time. Back then, maybe she never went anywhere without cradling a bottle of vodka in her arm. Natalia could carry that off. It wasn't difficult imagining a young Natalia steering her way into a liaison and happily sailing away the next morning. But that wasn't Robbie's way. Which posed a question: if she went to Maarten, say with a bottle, what would happen next? Not during the following hour – no problem there – but long term? Could they be a fit?

Overseer of All Time, no need to shock me with a preview of fifty years to come, but I'd appreciate a peek at where I might be at twelve months from now.

Robbie, having wrestled for more than a week with alternative versions of the future, had then on the Thursday bumped into Natalia in the embassy foyer. Natalia was rushing in from an afternoon of calls. She had looked majestic: a radiantly white, open-collared, lace-enhanced white blouse, a dark blue satin pantsuit, lush hair with every strand in place and, naturally, a ton of jewels. All the same, fatigue showed in her eyes. "Robbie, apologies," she had said soberly. "Crazy schedule. The whole week. I hoped we would have an hour to confab, but there wasn't one. All is well?"

"Good enough."

Natalia studied Robbie. "How resonating. Tried disconnecting your mood from the weather?"

"I'm fine."

"I'm sure. You're strong. The strong conquer. I would love to know how that conquest of yours is going. Sorry we can't natter about it for a while yet. I'm off tomorrow for the ambassadors' conference in Helsinki and right now there's still a dreadful pile of impatient papers on my desk screaming for me to rush upstairs."

"I know."

"End of next week. Soon as I'm back. We'll catch up then. Some good things have happened. With you too? I mean the conquest. You're on track with your detective?"

"Still thinking, Natalia."

"Still thinking? Gosh. Sometimes you have to stop thinking and start knowing. Get to know him, Robbie. Totally."

"I heard you, Natalia. I should get a bottle."

Natalia had laughed. "It works. You won't regret it. Go with the tide, Robbie. See you in a week. I'll be dying to hear what's happened."

Natalia had gone upstairs to spend hours reading and signing, and Robbie had then stepped out into the storm. The whole way to the tram stop she had to lean forward, although she scarcely heeded the force. For ten days she had been reasoning. Ten days with no advance. Then Natalia comes along. *Get to know him. Totally.* It sounded so simple. Long before she arrived at the tram's rain shelter a feeling of reckless abandon set in, replacing her indecision. Near her flat she detoured past the local shops to buy a single item and the minute she was home she made the call.

"Ah, Robbie. Yes. How are you? It is very nice to hear your voice."

"Are you in this evening?"

"Yes. Actually, yes. I plan to be home."

She arrived with a bag. In the hallway, she extracted a bottle.

"Champagne? Nice. Very nice. Shall I open it? Are we celebrating?"

They clinked glasses in the front room, drank and talked until they could no longer stand it. Surrendering to an unseen hand, they felt it taking them upstairs.

~

Now, bathed in sunlight in her office, after a weekend of ascending and descending the stairs in Maarten's house – more often than she could ever have predicted – Robbie felt luminescence and scintillation inside and out. Her thoughts strayed from work. If Natalia were in the embassy, they would probably be talking in her office this minute. Not that there was much to say, but Natalia had claimed the right to know everything. Natalia would listen and not say much, except maybe that her counsel had once again proved sound. It would have to wait until Friday when she would be back from Helsinki. Robbie planned to whisper a quick update into her ear at the staff party. *Not only that, Natalia. Guess what's in my glass right now. You got it. Tonic water with gin. Is this progress?*

Robbie's phone rang. This late? Another juvenile delinquent at the airport unable to fly home because he's lost his passport and is at his wits' end? A suspicious Robbie lifted the receiver. "Hello?"

"Robbie."

"Natalia! Hi. I was thinking of you this very minute. I've got good news."

"Your detective? Doesn't surprise me. You had a certain look last Thursday."

As Robbie listened she also tensed. Natalia was not sounding herself. No energy in the voice. It came across hollow. "We had a lovely weekend," Robbie said cautiously. "Everything OK? You're not in a fog or anything, are you?"

"It's over, Robbie. The peace summit is done for."

Since the day she began consular work, Robbie had been exposed to the sentiments that come with loss, mishap, and doom and gloom, which taught her a style for dealing with it. Calmly, professionally, she would dig for information. And she did this now. She asked Natalia questions. Then more. And still more. There is therapy in the method, which calmed an overwrought Natalia. An insistent Robbie dragged the story out.

~

At the end of the first day at the ambassadors' conference, Natalia was back in her hotel room. A late afternoon Blackberry message from Marge urged her to call in. Sitting on the bed, Natalia entered the number.

Marge was cheerful. "Hello Ambassador. Two calls here for you. Mr De Bruyn and Mr Heywood. Mr De Bruyn was first, by about half an hour. Both said the same thing. They want you to get back to them right away. Big deal, right? I felt like saying everything around here is acute and critical. Here are their numbers in case you haven't got them with you."

Natalia considered which one to go for first. Something must have happened, but was it good or bad? More likely bad. Good news usually arrives in an orderly fashion. For which of the two should she be best prepared? For Heiko, obviously. Therefore, call Heywood first.

Heywood's phone scarcely rang, he was on it that fast, though his first words were not particularly frantic. If anything, he seemed delighted, as if he had just learnt she had won a prestigious prize and wanted to be the first to convey congratulations. "I'm told you're in Helsinki, Natalia. How goes the hobnobbing with all my many protégés?"

"What's going on, Irving?"

"Good news. Excellent news, really. Won't keep you in suspense. In a nutshell, we're freeing up some of your professional time. The peace summit will be on ice for a while."

The phone line went silent. Heywood had not said much, but as in all poor spin doctoring, there was a disconnect between the words and the tone. "On ice?" a suspicious Natalia asked.

"I'm fresh back from my Monday morning meeting with Des. We have a standard slot to review stuff, you know, compare notes at the beginning of the week, review the issues likely to require high-level steering. Well, given what's been happening, the landscape for everything changing early this morning, we agreed it was best to stand back from the peace file for a while."

Natalia thought about the last days' headlines. Had she missed something? Did something rear up when she wasn't looking? What peace landscape changed? Had North Korea declared nuclear war? Was Iran caught out planning to build a plutonium reprocessing plant?

"You still there?" Heywood asked.

"I don't get it. The initiative is just about ready. We want to set dates. What's changed?"

"It's been leaked. Relax. Not through us. On our side there was Des, you and me – only us three talking. Nothing was by email or put on paper. We were careful about that. The leak has to be Dutch."

"How? Where?"

"Not clear yet. A story has been in preparation for Wednesday's *New York Times*. Des got a tip from the American military attaché. Damn decent of the Yanks to share their intelligence. We agreed with them to talk the story out of existence. No problem on that front. I'll call myself to deny everything. What we need to figure out, though, is why the Dutch did it. We have to assume they had a purpose. I'm guessing that as part of their scheme they will be assuming that we will disavow having an involvement. That gives the leak the smell of an end run. The assumption here is – now that they've got solid policy concepts out of us – that they're having a go at muscling us out of the peace game."

"Does the story quote sources?"

"Don't know. I haven't seen it."

"This is bizarre, Irving. Heiko de Bruyn has asked me to contact him urgently. Maybe he has heard about the leak too. Suppose he assumes we're responsible."

"He also tried to get through to me, but I'm not talking to that guy. If he claims we are at fault, he's resorting to the oldest trick going – accuse others of what you've done, to cover your tracks. I hope he doesn't go that route. I truly do, because we've got the smoking gun."

"Meaning?"

"The *New York Times* article apparently refers to all the good things you and I have been talking about, you know, people, money, government structures changing – the doable stuff we've put on the table. But the article goes further. It says a world peace parliament is planned. That's news to me. And listen to this, Natalia, that parliament would be modelled on the US Congress, you know, an assembly like the House of Representatives, a senate like the American Senate. A peace charter seems to have been drafted, setting this out. It's supposed to have a lot of lofty rhetoric in it, a kind of rewrite, apparently, of the American Declaration of Independence, plus chunks drawn from the US Constitution. That's clever stuff if you ask me, but it doesn't come from us. So if Duhbrouyeen says it wasn't his side that leaked, you ask him where this copycatting of American greatness comes from."

Natalia tried to think so fast she couldn't think at all. "You're going to deny the story?"

"Yeah, in a couple of minutes. The reason why you and I should feel good about that is that the denial won't be for all time. I've got something in mind. We'll recoup what was taken from us. What you have to do is smoke Duhbrouyeen out. Listen to him, but don't say too much. We need a fix on what he is planning. If my hunch is correct – if they want us out now that they have our policy ideas, intending to refloat them as their own at some other time in some other way – then we've got to act fast to outflank them. They're using the *New York Times*. What they don't know is that I have a good acquaintance who gets stuff published in the *Times of London*. I'm going to get something planted there. We want this scheming to boomerang on them, hit 'em where it hurts."

"I can't see that, Irving. De Bruyn wasn't out to do an end run. What has happened is awful, but we can't let it make us paranoid."

"And your explanation for them leaking would be what?"

"A mistake. A piece of paper in a recycle container. A memory stick left on a train."

"Not real world scenarios, Natalia. In our line of work everyone thinks three, four moves ahead. And it's dog-eat-dog. The Dutch were at it centuries before us. When it comes to the art of double-dealing, they have a head start. We can't trust them for a second. So once you've got Duhbrouyeen set up, when we get some home truths out of him, call me and we'll coordinate. Until then."

With the phone inert in hand, Natalia sensed her field of vision narrowing. *Holy God*, she whispered, falling back on the bed. *Can this be happening?* The summit dead. Irving Heywood half-mad and galloping off like Don Quixote. A wave of nausea rolled over her. It passed and her thinking cleared. Heiko de Bruyn could not be behind it. They were equally committed, to everything, including advancing some form of peace governance. Mystifying her was the article's reference to the American Declaration of Independence and the American Constitution. Where did that come from? Robbie? Robbie knew about the initiative and contributed in various ways. But Robbie didn't know she had written her non-paper. The leak's source did have to be Dutch. Unless? A third party? Natalia thought. A bug in de Bruyn's office?

In lament, on the edge of the bed, Natalia took the phone and placed the second call.

De Bruyn's assistant sounded relieved. *Daar bent U*, she said quietly. It is you. She put Natalia through. All calm and orderly so far. Synonymous with the connecting click, de Bruyn was in her ear. No more calm and order now. A verbal assault began. Natalia had expected a degree of commiseration. She had anticipated a world-weary de Bruyn to use words saying that once again a good piece of work somehow got loused up. Instead, she listened to accusations of duplicity and piercing allegations that amateurs in Ottawa managed to bungle things. The hectoring was bad; Natalia struggled to change it.

"Heiko, slow down, take a deep breath. I have Ottawa's version of what happened. What's yours?"

De Bruyn's anger cooled. By degrees, a patrician detachment returned. Brigadier General Rory Bessy, Air Force, once wounded in covert action, had limped into his office at 3pm to discuss tactics for dealing with a pending *New York Times* story. His manner was folksy. The story couldn't be true, right? So no problem denying it, right? De Bruyn, in generous diplomatic terms, told the Brigadier General to go to hell. The Brigadier General replied he was picking up some kind of a negative vibe which, he allowed himself to conclude, was meant to apply to the pending story, not to him, and therefore he expressed his appreciation for full Dutch cooperation.

Fulfilling his instructions, he next kindly requested the foreign policy advisor to call a certain person at a certain number within three hours so as to deny that the story had a basis. He handed de Bruyn his instructions. *Keep that sheet. I got no use for it. You can read as well as me what'll happen if you don't call. I have to say it, I love living in Holland. Nice meeting you Mr Brine.*

"I tried to talk to Mr Desmond Mckilroy in Ottawa," de Bruyn said darkly. "They said he was in a meeting with his prime minister. He didn't return my call. Nor did Mr Irving Heywood. I had no choice. I had to break the news to my prime minister. He didn't take it well. He had been giving the initiative close attention and was eager to proceed. Only last week we met to discuss your side's proposal to include peace governance. His opinion was favourable. Despite the obstacles – Security Council opposition, the NATO dimension – he became committed to it. He recognized that accountable governance provides a sound moral platform, that today's structures are counter-productive, that we must reach far."

"We were that close?"

"A productive dynamic was shaping up. With this American counter, my prime minister decided we have no choice but to abort. If the story appears, the fallout would be unmanageable. The American administration will strong-arm the invited countries, cajoling them, threatening if necessary. With that, no country would accept the invitation. The initiative is over and he instructed me to take the denial route. What angered him most was the disconnect, that your inspired policy thinking was coupled with the stupidity of leaking it."

"Not us, Heiko," Natalia said quickly. "In Ottawa only Mckilroy and Heywood were in on this. Very senior. People at that level don't leak."

"What are you saying? That it was us? That is unimaginably preposterous."

"How many people knew on your side?"

"The prime minister, myself, and three senior officials in the foreign office. Experienced men. Absolutely dependable."

"One of them may have left the paper where others could read it."

"Not possible. I brought copies of it into our meeting. We reviewed the contents, prepared advice for the Prime Minister, highlighted where political decisions were needed. Then I collected the copies and took them with me again. They are here, locked in my cabinet. It was your side, Natalia. Absolutely."

"We don't think so. I haven't seen the text of the article the military attachés passed along. I don't know the name of the journalist who wrote it. Apparently it contains a reference to the American Constitution as a model for governance. That wasn't in the non-paper. That was added. Who and where? We conclude it occurred in The Hague after I passed the non-paper to you. Maybe some listening was going on during your meeting. A third party must have embellished the text. It's worth investigating."

"There's nothing to investigate. Why should I investigate myself? Are you going to investigate yourself?"

~

"It was awful, Robbie. His anger came to the boil again. It became unpleasant."

"What happened is a sin, Natalia. I'm so sorry for you. I know you put everything into it. No one could have pushed it farther. I think you'll have another chance some day. I know you will. What happens now?"

"Nothing. The summit is over. There could be more fallout. Nasty truths may come to light. I took some liberties. I believed in what I did, but I was well aware it had a flip side. The chances of me remaining ambassador are not good. Carlos's future will be different too. He should be home by now. I'll talk to him next."

"News like that passed on the phone? Don't you want to do it face to face? You could leave Helsinki."

"I'll soldier on here for the week, Robbie. Make it seem the world is unfolding as it should. If I leave early without a reason, the rumour mill will start. It's not fair to Carlos to let him wait until Friday. I'll call him now. Once I've gone over the situation with Carlos the problem may begin to shrink. Misfortune and fortune are neighbours. I hope better days lie ahead."

"Come to the staff party Friday if you can. We'll share the martini shaker."

"Martinis? Robbie! If you've started sinning that way, I would forgive you."

Chapter 19

Tuesday morning and Carlos was on the move, cycling in radiant sunshine, though his temper wasn't at all like the weather. A fury was driving him. He scarcely saw the flat fields where hay lay drying and the pastures filled with masticating cows. Normally, rustic serenity gave him a high. He would revel in creative thoughts, one leading to the next, then on to another, an endless chain of happy inner notes. A self-indulgent whisper would come on too, saying life was worth living. But anger? On his bike? In a polder? In good weather? Never. Today was an anomaly. No creative insights about his own mental state were registering. Not even simple ones. There was only an all-encompassing wrath, and it was blinding him.

Carlos was a deep thinker but seldom a quick thinker, and the night before it took a while for a realization to set in. The full impact of Natalia's news took about an hour to register. Of course, right away, her call from Helsinki worried him. Natalia was mostly up and seldom down. If her dark side did come out, he usually remarked she should focus not on herself but on a bigger, happier picture. This often helped. When in a flat voice she informed him that she had bad news, that her position in The Hague was likely to end soon, he therefore answered, it is how you live, not where you live that is important. He also dismissed this news as the dumbest he had heard for quite a while. "You're their best performer, Natalia. Why would they dismiss you? Does a dance group amputate the legs off its prima ballerina? What gives you such ideas?"

A story came out about two governments working in secret, a security lapse not yet explained, a scramble to go into public denial and her certainty that this would lead to the usual sacrificial rite. "I went beyond my brief, Carlos. I developed some new concepts. I badly wanted them aired. I thought, if the Dutch buy in, I could present them back home as having full Dutch government support. It was too clever by half. The price will have to be paid. I suspect I'll be recalled. I'm sorry, because Holland was turning out to be so agreeable for you too."

He soothed her again. "It's not as if we've never moved before. Why worry?"

"The tragedy is that it could have worked. The Dutch PM seemed to like my ideas. Some things are strange, though. Military attachés from the US took charge. That suggests the Pentagon issued instructions. But why the Pentagon? Peace initiatives are State Department turf. I can't fathom it. Also peculiar is that the *New York Times* story claimed that the concept for peace governance was a kind of recasting on a global scale of America's way of being democratic. It is a neat idea, but we didn't think of that. We never talked about using the American Constitution as a model. Where that comes from is a mystery."

Carlos guessed it was the journalist. "You know journalists. They fall back on speculation and insinuation to fill their column inches. Do you have to stay in Helsinki, Natalia? Can't you come home, take some time off, develop distance?"

"I'm alright. I'll plod on. I'll be back Friday afternoon. I'll act as if nothing has happened. I'm planning to go to the embassy Friday and show up at the staff party. If you're going, I'll see you there."

～

Natalia's revelations simmered on the fringes of Carlos's consciousness as the evening ticked away. As if he had an inner timer, however, after an hour, something chimed. Suddenly he understood. The reference to America's democracy – a mystery to Natalia – was not a mystery. That lens on the peace initiative had come into existence a week before when he'd happily battled a head wind to visit Alistair. What path, he wondered, could have led from his mind to the *New York Times*? Carlos's blood froze. Paradis? Paradis had sworn not to breathe a word. But suppose he did. Was he, Carlos – a happy-go-lucky man, an internationally feted ethnographer, the consort of a gifted ambassador – a blabbermouth? Was he an unwitting double agent inside a thriving marriage? Had his ego and the impulse to impress Paradis with insider knowledge inflicted terrible damage on his wife? Carlos groaned as, blow by blow, the cold spike of guilt was hammered into his soul.

Struggling to maintain calm and think clearly, he hurried to the kitchen to make tea. Trembling with shame, as he poured the hot water into the pot, he resolved that as soon as Natalia was back he would take both her hands in his, sink to his knees, reveal all and beg her to pardon him.

To reveal all, however, he needed more, much more. The link between him and Paradis was clear. But what about the jump from Paradis to the article? Had a rumour mill been at work? Had Paradis blabbed to someone else in the way he had blabbed to Paradis? Paradis loved to gossip. It could have happened inadvertently. Sipping tea, Carlos constructed a chronology. He had been with Paradis a week ago today. Not much time, really, for a rumour mill to crank up so high that US military attachés were instructed to kill the initiative. If Paradis had dropped hints to friends in the NGO world, wouldn't months have to pass for the rumour to gather momentum? A journalist serious enough to write copy for the *New York Times* would have taken more time still to research the story.

The rumour mill could not explain this. The story had traveled too fast and too directly. That suggested Paradis had fed an information service of some kind, an efficient one with instant media access. No inadvertency there. Which left the Pentagon. How had they learned about the story before it was published? Or was the Pentagon part of the jump? Either way, something existed on Paradis's other side.

Sitting on a kitchen stool, watching his tea get cold, Carlos's fury built.

~

Throughout the night his thoughts had churned. Who was Paradis really? A silver-tongued spiritualist? Front man for a grassroots movement with faultless ideals? A vaudeville actor still playing out roles? A snoop marching to the beat of an unknown, but perverse, drum? Or, in one or another psychologically twisted way, all of this? When dawn arrived, Carlos's head was in such a mess that he methodically beat his brow.

Pedalling along to confront Paradis, he rehearsed his lines. Skirting Katwijk he went through some opening remarks; near Nordwijk he began phrasing questions he would ask; making the east turn at Lisse he was composing a powerful rebuke, and by the time he closed in on Aalsmeer the threat he would deliver had been finely tuned.

At the condo complex, bike neatly stowed away in accordance with local custom, Carlos pressed the apartment button. His mouth was grimly set; the height to which he drew himself was that of an inquisitor. He waited. Once more, he hit the bell. More seconds ticked by, and more seconds still, until the speaker crackled, though no voice came on. "Alistair," Carlos commanded.

"Uh, wait." There was a sound of something banging into the wall, an out-of-control walker perhaps, and a clattering, maybe of a cane, crashing to the floor. "Oh. Damn. Who is it? Wait. Ah. Yes. Who's there?"

"It's me. Carlos."

"Carlos! Oh. Well. How lovely. A sudden, gentle sweetness fills my day. Wait. Ah, here is the button. Yes. Do come up." The door catch buzzed and Carlos entered. One floor up Paradis stood in his doorway wobbling on two canes. "Carlos, Carlos, on the day when no one sweeps my floor you decide to come. Oh, this *is* lovely. A reason for a drink before noon. But I see you are not smiling. I … well, do come in. If there is sorrow, we must ensure it is short-lived." He shuffled in, went to his chair, made an about turn, fell backwards into it and heaved a cane in the direction of the glass cupboard. "Cognac? My heart fluttered last week when you visited, so great was the pleasure."

"No cognac, Alistair. No pleasure. No niceties. Not today. I'm here because I'm worried about slime."

"Slime? Good heavens. Well, do sit down. I'm sure we will come to the cognac in a while. Slime? Isn't that a form of cell life which predates the beginning of rational human beings?"

"Yes, that's slime. What have you been up to since my last visit?"

"I have been continuing my recovery. You must notice it goes well."

"Recovering? Or earning your keep? But which keep? Shall I tell you what I know, or will you disclose what you've done since I was here? It doesn't matter who goes first. I think the end location will be the same."

Paradis's features softened as if he was a mushy grandfather. Charity began shining in his eyes. "Carlos, Carlos," he murmured. "When have we entertained views that were in contradiction? Not once. Never. Not that I remember. Think of the occasions when I marvelled at your work. Which of your insights has not brought me stimulation? When did your humour not strengthen me? Do you recall – in Port au Prince I believe – that you drew for me your image of God, today's God, the rather biggish one. You said he had two tattoos, one on each cheek. The first portrayed a lovely crescent and the second was of an exquisite cross. How we laughed at that. And did we not agree – was it in Dubai or Singapore? – that the other God, the one before the latest one, the wrathful one, the one who didn't like the competition, demanded death for other gods. Baal was one, I think. Did we not both see that that slightly earlier God had a patch over his right eye because he had so much warfare in him? In truth, Carlos, has there been a single topic on which you and I have not seen eye to eye? Of course we will arrive at your single location. We always do."

"To get beyond the crap," sneered Carlos, "I'll say my piece." Like a seasoned prosecutor he set forth his facts.

Throughout, Paradis remained gentle, with his adoring gaze on Carlos unwavering. He closed his eyes for a while and seemed to indulge in happy memories, for he smiled and nodded vigorously. Then he leaned back and threw the switch activating the chair's massage function, which made his body quiver. He waited and listened and was patient. When Carlos finished, his reply was instant. "All of that is wrong. I am very sorry, but my nature is not barbaric. It cannot bring forth deceit, nor cause disgrace. Suddenly there is discord between us, Carlos. I don't want it and I insist we end it."

~

In the showdown, Carlos had planned, he would confront Paradis with facts, then move to a moral high ground. Once there, he was sure, Paradis would confess. But it wasn't working out that way. Gracious and avuncular, Paradis insisted he had not done what he was accused of. He took his cane, raised the point up and stabbed the air to drive this home.

Finally, Carlos asked a simple question. What was Paradis's explanation for Natalia's peace proposals becoming public, within days of them talking about them here, in this condo?

The response was ornate and long. Governments, Paradis sermonized, enjoy presenting themselves as gilded arks. Like the ancient one. They enjoy creating an appearance that national covenants are sacred. But on the inside, governments are the opposite. No precious things exist there. No sanctity, no morality. Inside governments, all one finds is an etching substance. It corrodes morality. It causes gaping holes. Inside governments, the sacred national covenants – such as truth, honesty, probity, rights, responsibilities and obligations – are violated. Eventually, knowledge of this oozes out and the media, naturally, feast on it. That is how the *New York Times* must have got into the picture. "It was the Dutch, Carlos. The Dutch. Look to them for an explanation. They present themselves as holy. As holier than holy. They love their morality, their ark, their covenants. But they are not perfect. One of their holders of high office has transgressed. I feel it."

Carlos drew on what Natalia said the previous evening. Not the Dutch, he answered sternly. Not possible. The proof? The *New York*

Times article contained a reference to the American Declaration of Independence. That was not in Natalia's paper. That allusion was his. He thought of it one week ago cycling up through the storm. The only person he shared it with was Paradis. It was in this condo that the leak had originated.

Although Paradis had nothing in his mouth, he began to chew like a ruminating cow. "I will explain," he said, his jowls in energetic motion. "It is simple. You brought me wonderful news that day. I wrote it down because my memory is not good and I wished to savour it some more the next day."

Carlos nodded at this progress and said, "the article also contained material that didn't come from me. It seems detailed prescriptions were developed on how a Peace Assembly would be elected, apparently including a formula for the number of seats to be allocated to each member country. Where did that come from? Were you working with someone?"

"Oh no. I wrote that down also. My joy overwhelmed me. I thought, the tidings from Carlos are nearly perfect. What he has brought is flawless, save for one or two small nicks. I thought of the great sacred texts of the ancients, the wonderful Sutras, the Vedas, the Pyramid Texts, the Pentateuch, the Dead Sea Scrolls, the Bible and the Koran, and I saw that Natalia in her paper was getting close to reaching such heights. I began to think that Natalia, through her writing, a thousand years from now, would enter the pantheon of humanity's great prophets. I desired to be part of that. To be, you know, her first disciple. I have been much cut off these last months, Carlos. I miss the flux of great ideas. I miss the drama of conference debate. Your visit caused my thoughts to stir again. I thought, I could add to what Natalia has achieved. I knew it could be no more than an addition of a few minor, prosaic details. Even so, as the origins of the new peace creed become searched out, future scholars may come to my slight elaborations too. It sounds immodest, I know, but St Augustine, an imperfect man, once managed to add value, so why not me?"

"You gave that text to someone."

"No."

"Yet others acquired it. How can that be? You passed it along."

"I didn't … Wait … I understand now. I see what happened. It was Martha. My domestic. No, she is not Martha. She is Delilah. Clearly."

"Martha?"

"Yes, her. What a fool I have been, Carlos. Martha must be employed by others. That explains other strange occurrences. You know, some exist who envy me. They wish to know the secret of my strength. And they sent Martha to find out. Martha is always cheerful. When she arrives she serenades me with bright good mornings. In the kitchen organizing breakfast she sings too. She maintains her happy hymning as she dusts and sweeps the floor. It is not natural. But the real proof, Carlos, is her camera. I have been photographed. Yes, it is true. She claims she is proud to be my domestic and wants her family in the Philippines to share in her pride. She has photographed the apartment as well, everything in it, even the fresh-cut tulips she brings along over there on the table. She has gone onto the balcony to photograph there too. My God, Carlos, how did I not see this? The Dutch are plaguing me with Martha's charms. They are the Philistines in this."

"You think Martha saw your text?"

"She photographed it. The text was there on that table. I trusted her. I spent the morning reading it and thinking blissful thoughts, but did not take it with me after lunch when I lay down to rest. It is completely obvious. The Dutch fear me, I mean, my control over ordinary people. They are out to smear my reputation. It is a subtle framing job. They abused Natalia's work to get at me."

"How long was your text?"

"My script is dense."

"May I see what Martha photographed?"

"My text? You can't. It is gone. I shredded it."

Carlos looked around. "I see no shredder."

"There isn't one. I shredded it by hand when I noticed its position on the table was not as before. I was sure it was dangerous to keep and I tore it into tiny bits. The wind was strong last week and that evening I took the scraps onto the balcony and heaved them high. The wind dispersed them."

Paradis was speaking more and more like someone whose brain had cracked, and Carlos began humouring him with constant nods, occasionally muttering a *yes-yes*. No prospect for arriving at the truth existed here. Was there another way?

Paradis fell silent and shut off the chair. In the stillness he brought his palms together as if next he planned to say *Namaste*. "Natalia's peace will live," he whispered and began to weep quietly.

Carlos answered that he understood the ordeal Paradis must be experiencing. He was going through one too. But neither of their ordeals came close to what Natalia was having to endure. "We have both erred, Alistair. Let's face it. We cannot undo our mistakes, but our way forward can be honourable. I suggest that, together, we explain to her how we fouled-up."

Paradis nodded. "We must. We shall."

"Can you come to the embassy on Friday? She will be back from Helsinki. Be there at four-thirty. And let us also make a vow this minute that we will not share a drink again until we have been forgiven."

"Redemption, Carlos. We will seek it. Friday at four-thirty it is."

For the remainder of the week, as best he could, Carlos focused on a new monograph, but the damage he had created weighed on him. He saw no way to make it good. In the drawing room he checked if Natalia's paper remained where he had placed it. It would prove he stumbled on her secret diplomacy. And if Paradis appeared on Friday, perhaps she could extract from him what lay on his other side. *If* he appeared. Part of Carlos doubted it. Martha as Delilah and shreds of paper cast to the wind – Paradis was far-gone if he believed all that. If he were still rational he would know Carlos had not believed one word. In which case he would not show. "If he does not come on Friday," Carlos concluded, "it will prove there is another drummer. And in that case I will ensure PEACE is thoroughly investigated and then disbanded."

Friday came. Carlos felt ready. He counted the hours. He rehearsed what he would say to Natalia if Paradis showed up. He went through another narrative in case he didn't. Just before four, he got onto his bike. Gathering speed on the residence driveway, he used the bell to salute the rhododendrons. A forceful ring. Another. Emerging onto the street he made the turn to the right.

Behind him, fifty meters away, two repairmen in overalls and caps ceased tampering with the bus shelter and hopped into a van.

Chapter 20

Most days now when she finished work, Robbie didn't take the tram home to Scheveningen. She jumped onto one going in the opposite direction instead, end station Delft. She carried a small bag containing a change of clothing for the next day and the things you need for an overnight stay.

The journeys were not unlike travelling into an exotic, imaginary land. An enchantment, a unique sense of completeness would fill her. Rocking with the tram's side to side motion, she tried to pull the feeling apart, but didn't succeed. The sole conclusion she drew, the same one each day, was that when the tram entered Delft her heart beat faster.

Beyond the enchantment lay an anxiety, however. Over Natalia. The Helsinki phone call caused Robbie to search her memory. Had she let a remark slip to someone about the ambassador's project? A stray comment to Gus perhaps? An incautious statement to one of the local girls? Robbie thought and thought and was sure she hadn't. Which left the worrying. Was Natalia coping with her setback? Was some kind of toxic fallout still awaiting her? Robbie decided to keep Friday evening free. When Natalia was back she might want to talk things through. No Delft that night, for the first time in a week.

Friday afternoon she popped by the ambassador's office to say hi to Marge. "All's good, Marge? Things are quiet?"

"Yes, all is good, but no, it is not quiet. The diplomatic invitations to the ambassador just keep rising. Ten or fifteen new ones every day. Deciding between the worthy and the trivial, which ones should go to Gus, which ones to Marcel, which ones into the garbage, and so on and so forth, takes hours. And yesterday there were too many phone calls from Ottawa. People insisting on talking urgently to the ambassador. She told me to park them. Think that's easy? It's been nightmarishly busy, if you want to know."

"The ambassador's return is on schedule?"

"It seems so. It's two o'clock now. She'll be leaving Helsinki in thirty minutes. Dirk will go to Schiphol in an hour and bring her back to the embassy. For some reason, the ambassador wants to go to the staff party. Are you going?"

"I sure am."

One look at Natalia would be enough for Robbie to read her mood. Eyes sparkling with mischief versus eyelids that droop. The program managers, naturally, would jump at her the minute she stepped in, wanting to know what was concluded at the ambassadors' conference. In three minutes or under the ambassador would summarize everything worth knowing. What happened next would be telling. Natalia would either disengage with a drink and stand by herself for a bit at the back of the room, lost in thought, or she would fire the party up by delivering a perfect mimic of this or that colleague at the conference. If the latter, Robbie would relax. If the former, she would approach Natalia resolutely. Her opening line had been practiced. *Want to halve your troubles, Natalia?*

At four-thirty, Robbie cleaned her desk, locked the cabinets and turned the computer off. She called Maarten's number in Delft and left a message saying she would see him tomorrow, then headed over to the Friday social. With the weather continuing brilliant, the party would be outside, in the embassy atrium.

Clusters were already forming. Only Gus stood alone. No one was interested in listening to his methodical long-windedness in a social setting. The local girls formed a circle around Robbie. Small talk. Lots of it. Mostly about the coming weekend, which was looking very promising. Marge came in. She had relaxed and seemed prepared to cope with Gus, for she went up to him. Twenty minutes passed. Robbie was about to refill her glass and sidle up to Marge to ask if the ambassador's flight arrived on time, when a stately looking Natalia entered. Around her neck hung a double string of garnets. The dress was loose, silk with a sheen, the light amber shadings changing with every movement. A narrow belt brought the waist in. A grand presence as always. But what about the eyes? Robbie could not make them out, not right away, because Natalia was half-turned, talking to several staff members at once. While conversing, she scanned the atrium, picked out Robbie and sent out a glance. It was only glance, yet was much more. For Robbie it arrived as a burst of severity and it rocked her. Natalia, continuing to talk, ended the scan. There was no second look at Robbie.

Robbie concluded that matters had not improved since Monday, but so many were clinging to the ambassador's every word that Robbie couldn't bring herself to break in. Amidst the clangour of the Friday social, Robbie inched to the side to stand alone.

More minutes went by and another searing glance from Natalia pierced Robbie. A signal of distress, Robbie was sure of it. She became resolved. She moved quickly into the circle around Natalia, saying, "Ambassador, may I have a moment of your time? I have a consular emergency you should know about." Natalia excused herself. In an atrium corner they stuck their head together. "Are you alright?" Robbie whispered urgently.

Natalia didn't answer, not right away, but locked her eyes on Robbie's. Then she said, "bad news. It's over. The axe came down last night. Harry Berezowski called. I will be replaced."

"What? I don't understand that. I don't understand at all. You said on Monday that the leak wouldn't get into the media. It seemed under control."

"The problem was bigger, Robbie. I went too far. I should have been a skeptic, but I began living a dream. All along I suspected I should be more concerned about whether I was far out on a limb. I checked, but not enough. The dream grew. Dreams give wings to fools, Robbie. Harry Berezowski said as much."

~

Natalia. Hello. Harry here. Caught you in Helsinki, right? Conference is going well? Sorry I couldn't come. Competing priorities. You know how it is.

I won't beat around the bush. I've got tough news. You're coming out. Right away.

What happened? Desmond Mckilroy contacted me late yesterday. He said our management of the relationship with the Dutch has been abysmal, that the PM, and he, had zero confidence in Irving Heywood and you. I asked how that was and had to listen to a weird tale about an unauthorized peace plan, with the Dutch. I knew you were working on something academic there, but a full-blown bilateral initiative? The Americans got wind of it and are mad as hell. You know what, Natalia. That caught me with my pants down.

What exactly do I know? Not much. Only that you and Irving acted contrary to Mckilroy's orders. Irving was here about an hour ago. I asked him where Mckilroy was coming from. Irving wasn't exactly coherent. From the story about you and academia he moved on, describing a complex Dutch gambit to suck peace ideas out of us, which started at a PM's lunch in New York. Really? Irving seemed unbalanced, actually. I sent him home. His building pass has been cancelled.

But you surprise me, Natalia. You're known for your judgement and élan. What am I to do with you?

You want me to listen to your version of events? I will. Tell me what happened at your end. Who were your partners in this?

~

274

"Berezowski did listen. Without interrupting. At the end he asked why I took Heywood's word for everything. Why didn't I call him to check? I explained that in a roundabout way I did check, with several people who put me at ease to some extent that he and Heywood were on the same page. My mistake was not contacting Berezowski directly. And an overwhelming enthusiasm for the file got the better of me too. None of that will change anything. He confirmed to Desmond Mckilroy that I will be recalled. I did get Berezowski to agree he wouldn't announce my leaving for eight weeks. The condition is that I resign. I start looking for new work on Monday."

"That is so unfair, Natalia. You must be terribly upset."

"I'm still adjusting my thinking. I'm expecting Carlos to be here any minute. At least he knows this outcome was likely. I'm sorry I'm causing disruption for him too. Feel like dropping in on us sometime this weekend?" Robbie nodded. "I should get back to the staff for a few more minutes."

A queasy feeling took hold of Robbie watching a valiant Natalia easing herself back into the party's laughter-filled center. A disaster, Robbie thought. Natalia was downplaying it, but she had to be hurting bad. Robbie couldn't comprehend it. What unwritten rules turn success into failure? How can you be sure that in doing your best you won't be judged to have done the worst and pay the penalty? Could anything be more wrong than Natalia's excellence as ambassador causing her to get the boot? Robbie shook her head at her loss.

Great Comforter, we need you now, we really do.

Another quarter of an hour went by. Robbie noticed Gus was having quality time with the ambassador and that Georgette was butting in on it. The local girls, on the other hand, were wandering off to get on with the weekend. She observed the embassy guard coming into the atrium, going up to the ambassador's cluster, speaking briefly with the ambassador, then Natalia following him out. Gus and Georgette were left stranded together, a future viticulturist confronting a keen duck hunter. It was funny how those two, having no overlap, looked past each other. Georgette finally peeled off with a rough, *You enjoy yourself, you hear,* and

Gus was on his own again. The party was dissolving fast, yet Robbie hung on as if an instinct was at work, one that said she should not leave Natalia alone.

The guard came back, this time marching up to Robbie. His countenance was military hard. The ambassador wished her to come to her office, was all he said. Robbie followed him out the atrium and went up.

~

What had Robbie's encounters with death been? She was a baby when the sea took her father and an infant when her mother succumbed to a disease. Growing up on the little island off the island, death had been present enough. But death was always fairly distant – mothers of second cousins or uncles of friends. Not one of the departures had given her a feeling of painful loss. Next, death became part of her work. Expats and travellers who expire abroad require a fair amount of administration, meaning that for Robbie death was a review of filled-out forms which she stamped to make official. All in all, she had seen enough death, but none of it was close. Death never having been a near reality left Robbie unprepared when she arrived in Natalia's office.

Natalia sat slumped in one of the low chairs. Her eyes were ghastly, as if she had turned primitive, or wild. "Carlos is gone," she said hoarsely. Horrified by the starkness of her own voice, she clasped her hands over her mouth. From behind them, she added, "he's dead. The police just told me."

Robbie stood mute. No shriek of pain escaped. There was no racing up to take Natalia in her arms. No pouring out of comfort. Only silence while her mind raced. Considerations of all kinds jumped into all directions. Remaining immobile, falling back on her training, she formulated questions and posed them. Factual questions. Where, when, how? What did the police say exactly? Natalia, not answering, began swaying backwards and forwards. Her eyes went strange, more haggard, as shock was taking over. She was going into breakdown.

Robbie, on reflex, perhaps having seen something similar during childhood, marched to the wall cabinet, took out the vodka bottle and a glass, poured three fingers, came back to fall on her knees before Natalia and ordered her to drink. Fight shock with shock. Natalia gulped, then gulped again. It seemed to revive her, for her eyes lost their distant stare. They focused on Robbie, who saw fear was invading them. She took Natalia's head and drew her close. Natalia whimpered and, as Robbie wrapped her arms around her, began to sob. Robbie couldn't help it. She was crying too.

They rocked back and forth and then let go, their faces soaked.

"Another vodka?"

"Yes."

Robbie poured three more fingers and a small one for herself, grabbed a stack of napkins, returned and placed herself at Natalia's feet. Natalia wiped her face and blew her nose. Robbie dabbed her eyes.

"Tell me what happened."

"An accident. Carlos was on his bicycle. A vehicle hit him."

"Where?"

"On his way here."

"What else did the police say?"

"A hit and run. On an intersection. They believe the vehicle made a right turn without checking the bike path. Near where you live. You know how it is all trees and shrubs there. It can be difficult to see cyclists coming.

"I feel I've been ripped open, Robbie. I'm so sorry for Carlos. He lived sublimely. I accessed another universe through him. If anyone deserved life, it was him. I can't think. I can't grasp it. Let's not stay here."

Robbie ran to get the bag she brought in that morning and took Natalia down the stairs, holding her close. In the foyer the guard stood like a pillar, watching them come, then sprang to life and rushed to open doors. Outside, Dirk, ashen-faced, was attending the car.

They scarcely spoke during the ride to the residence. Natalia took a small mirror from her purse and looked into it. A small tissue package came next. She wiped her face with care, removing some make-up smears. The activity helped. In the residence, they went to a small sitting room, which they had used before when they shared and halved troubles. Robbie was sure Natalia should talk – about the accident, about Carlos, and perhaps about what might happen next – and asked, "can I get you something? If you tell me what goes into shaking up martinis, I'll make some."

Natalia shook her head. "A coffee, maybe. Later. I'm at the end, Robbie. Nothing is left. With Carlos, I could survive anything. But now? The peace summit is gone. I'm gone. Carlos is gone. Three blows. In one week. I'm not sure I can take it. I'm strong, but not that strong." She began to cry again.

Chapter 21

The following week, Robbie went to the residence to console Natalia each day after work. Mostly she listened, for Natalia had a need to talk – to tell discursive tales of life's strange, sad twists – and to explore the feeling of loss, how she was dealing with it. As days went by, the administrative imperatives of death confronted Natalia too. They arrived as if sucked along in a slipstream and seemed queerly disconnected from what was real. All the same, quickly enough, they dominated.

This being Robbie's area of expertise, Natalia let her do the running. Robbie explained the impact of laws and regulations and how the many practicalities should be managed. For example, the autopsy result was available fairly quickly and was unambiguous: multiple organs crushed and massive internal haemorrhaging. But since Carlos had not died of natural causes, the body could not be released, not until the police investigation was complete. Natalia remained on sedatives and did not want to meet with the police about the accident's details, fearing they would be too raw. She didn't want graphic images etched permanently into her memory. Therefore, as Natalia's proxy, Robbie was empowered and found out that clues, such as foreign paint remnants on the bicycle, were going through forensic analysis. The investigating officer was certain that the make, type and year of the vehicle that struck Carlos would soon be known. For the time being, however, the body had to remain in the morgue.

Police niceties were only the start. An obituary had to be prepared for publication and death announcement cards would have to be mailed out to Carlos's friends and acquaintances. Beyond that, the issuance of a death certificate proved troublesome, since obscure aspects of Carlos's quasi-diplomatic status had to be unravelled. Bureaucratically worse was the question of inheritance. Carlos left more than Natalia could have imagined. As a global ethnographic expert he had hauled in top fees, yet spent very little over the years. His will named Natalia the sole beneficiary. This was all well and good, except he wrote it in longhand Spanish, necessitating a certified translation. That was a small obstacle compared to the legal questions arising from precise Dutch law concerning the witnessing of his signature on the will. The witness, as a minutely scribbled endnote explained, was the chief of a nomadic tribe called the Penan, which inhabits certain forests on Borneo. The arboreal eminence had placed his thumbprint in a blue-green pigment on the will. When punctilious Dutch officials saw this, they threw up their hands in horror and ran for the few hills on offer in Holland. None of it fazed Robbie, however. Tirelessly she sent in affirmations, drew up *aides memoires*, and signed personal affidavits. Even the official diplomatic seal was hauled out of the consular vault. "It is my job," she assured the ambassador. "On a wing and a prayer we'll get through."

The subtlest decisions concerned Carlos's physical remains, their disposal, and honouring his memory. Natalia and Robbie got to this after a short, tasteful event at the embassy, which allowed the staff to express their compassion and sorrow. They had individually signed a card which they presented to the ambassador along with a large bouquet of dark red roses. Natalia, the initial shock of the accident behind her and now sleeping somewhat better, thanked them warmly in a voice that was firm once more.

Afterwards, in the residence, Robbie sat slouched forward on a kitchen stool. She was watching Natalia clip the rose stem ends off before arranging the stalks in a vase. "Let us imagine this …" Natalia said introspectively, "let us imagine he knew he was about to die, what would he have said? What would he have wanted to be done with him?"

"To be buried at home?"

"Buried in Spain? Not too likely. We exchanged our vows there, but that was because of me. I wanted exotic surroundings. He probably felt awkward about it. Even if he could lie in state in the Alhambra, I think he would decline. No, he and Spain got a divorce. The problem is, for Carlos everywhere was home. He had no single place. What does that tell us?"

"A burial at sea?"

"Hmm. Better than in Spain certainly, but …"

"But?"

"Well, he didn't mind the sea, but he preferred land."

"Not in one place and not in the ocean," Robbie mused. "That narrows it down."

Natalia nodded. "It does." She soon made a decision. Cremation. Cremation followed by ashes scattered to the wind. But which wind? Where should it be blowing? Robbie, still enamoured by the chief's thumbprint on the will, suggested Borneo. Natalia agreed it was an option. The place meant much to Carlos. On the other hand, if Borneo was suitable so were the Amazonian highlands. The Mongolian steppes should not be ruled out either. Nor should one or another sacred Hindu lake in the high Himalayas be overlooked. Even the front steps of the Mormon Tabernacle in Salt Lake City could qualify. In all these places Carlos had reflected on the flamboyancy of people's identities, and been delighted by the quaint structures of local beliefs.

For a while Robbie and Natalia remained silent, thinking the options over. "You know," Natalia broke in, "these places won't work. One of the reasons I loved Carlos was for his sense of irony. Scattering his ashes will be his last event, physically. We can't make it serious. It has to be done in a place where, were he there, he would roar with laughter. Where he would wave an arm to the

sky and yell up to himself, *Carlos, you crazy Spaniard, you did it!
You trumped the culture you were forced to inherit; you bested your
upbringing!*"

"Bless your cotton socks, Natalia. I like that way of going about
it. I do. But where do you think his urn being turned upside down
would let him see himself as a posthumous comic hero?"

Natalia went back to attending to the roses. "I know the place,"
she said finally. She pulled a few rose stalks out of the vase, adjusted
the spaces between and meticulously stuck them back in. "It has
just come to me. Carlos's best parts were secret to everyone but
himself. That's why he liked going about on his bike. It allowed him
to be unobserved. That's where he enjoyed himself clandestinely.
He went into the polders all the time not caring how strong the
wind was blowing. Once he told me he went close to Leyden
and stopped on a dyke, dressed himself up as a sixteenth century
farmer and spent the afternoon sitting on the grass smoking an
old clay pipe. He began to imagine he was witnessing the Spanish
army besieging Leyden. He could see seawater pouring into the
polder after the Dutch breached the dykes, sending the Spaniards
scrambling. He would chuckle for an hour straight if he knew his
ashes would be scattered there. He would see it as his remains
anointing a piece of history when Spain's Catholicism failed."

"Was Carlos anti-Catholic? I never thought he was against
religion."

"Religions fascinated him. 'Gods are the most colourful of
humanity's mental inventions', he said. He studied them all. He
was sure religion had an evolutionary dimension. As the species
developed awareness, it began to search for purpose. Most people
find survival easier if they agree on something they can all believe
in."

"Essentiality," Robbie said. "It explains everything."

"And why not? Why not believe that the essence of being
human – having lofty thoughts and living morally – makes us one.
Carlos would not have trivialized that sentiment. He appreciated
the power of ritual too and liked participating in it. We must give
that some thought as well, Robbie. We should stage a suitable rite.
After that, the anointment in the polder can take place." The rose

vase was done. "Would you mind taking this into the drawing room? I'll be right behind you with some drinks. Juice? I have a new one. Very exotic. Just for you."

Robbie walked the magnificent rose arrangement from the kitchen to the drawing room and placed it on a low table. Absent-mindedly she moved about, looking at the paintings, the furniture, the immaculate carpets, the pristine upholstery, the silver trinkets on the coffee tables, the cabinets standing along the sides like statues. A brittle, designer-contrived perfection. Robbie had been in this room many times, including once when it was full of cocktail-guzzling guests producing a din that grew so loud they all had to scream to be heard. She sent a silent observation up that day while hiding in one of the room's corners.

Most Excellent of Excellencies, I hope this way of living isn't in your plans for me.

Robbie took a seat next to an end table, picked up a book from a pile, flipped through photographs of national parks, put it down and grabbed the next one. She worked her way down. Lifting the last book, she saw some loose sheets of paper, typed and scribbled on, a dozen or more pages altogether. She glanced through them, as she had the books. She had never seen these pages, but she recognized them – Natalia's peace initiative, the document that the Dutch government was unable to keep under wraps. How sad that lapse had been for Natalia. How it had shocked her. How awful that a few days later her position as ambassador was taken away. Robbie studied the pencilled markings, then compared them to what was typed. She had to agree, each pencilled-in change improved the original. A pretty decent paper. But it was history now, even if the episode continued to bring pain to Natalia. Robbie put the document down and, in a gesture that said it was best to keep ideas of peace governance buried, replaced the book pile on top.

"Peach-maracuya. Sound good?" Natalia stepped in with a tray. "I tasted it. I think you'll like it. Hope it didn't spoil my palate for what I'm drinking though. Mind those olives, Robbie. They aren't pitted. Macadamia nuts OK, or would you prefer crackers?" She put the tray down, handed Robbie a glass, lifted her martini off and settled in her favourite chair with a sigh of cosy intimacy. "Where were we?"

"A ritual for Carlos."

"Yes. I've been thinking. Probably the only church he ever entered where he did more than study the layout of altars and pillars, where he actually felt something, was the cathedral in Delft. We went there first thing when we arrived last August. He raced in, and went back again and again. It was connected to the Leyden event, you know, the polder full of water, William the Silent defeating Spain. Eventually William was assassinated in Delft and buried in the cathedral. Carlos felt an affinity to him – his tolerance, the drawing of a line in the sand against tyranny – and liked to pay him homage. One day Carlos said, 'Where William is, I wish to be.' He might have meant that metaphorically, but for what we're planning, that is telling. That settles it, don't you think? If we can swing it, the place for his final rite should be the Delft cathedral."

"God strike me dead," Robbie exclaimed. "I know that church. I've climbed the tower. It's Maarten's church. There's a gift shop on the ground floor. He sits on the board of directors."

"He does?" Natalia's free foot began swinging. "Are we thinking the same thing? Would Maarten help? Could Carlos's ceremony be there? It would be very fitting, a perfect complement to us pronouncing our vows in the Alhambra. I'm just thinking out loud, Robbie, but suppose Alistair Paradis delivered the eulogy. Imagine that great voice of his reverberating up to the ceiling and back down to William the Silent in the crypt below. If Carlos were to have known that William would be listening to the kind of individual he was, to his outlook on life and his accomplishments, his rejoicing would have been out of this world."

Robbie and Maarten went to see the pastor, who was reluctant at first. Were they not aware that church rituals are only for the baptized? Maarten soothed the man, talking about traditional Dutch tolerance and liberalism. Not yet won over, the pastor speculated that the deceased, being Spanish, could have lived a life full of grave delusions and doctrinal errors. For example, he had probably been a Catholic. Definitely not, said Robbie, jumping in so fast she nearly cut him off. The deceased, she explained vigorously, when still very young had rejected the Pope. Totally. The pastor grudgingly admitted this was a point in favour. His opinion turned further still when he learned the deceased had not only idolized William the Silent, but also spent his life advancing values identical to those the Prince had lived by. A moment came when the talk switched seamlessly to practical issues, such as timing for a service. The cathedral was much in demand. As was the pastor. He would not be able to preside over a ritual, especially a custom designed one, until Saturday three weeks hence. It would have to be held after the cathedral had closed to visitors. It was incumbent on him to be frank on one further point. His fee for Saturday services was always double, plus of course a levy for doing it in English. Robbie nodded all that was fine. Being a no-nonsense cleric, he next grabbed a notepad and quickly scribbled out a liturgical outline.

~

"That man is pretty big on himself," Robbie observed when they were outside. She scanned the scrawled-out liturgy, which looked like a medical prescription. "Anything in your fridge for dinner?"

Until they sat together with the pastor, Robbie and Maarten had not seen each other for over a week, not since the accident. With Natalia now more robust, most of the bureaucratic clutter straightened out and a cathedral ceremony for Carlos on track, Robbie looked forward to being with her man, chatting with him about the last ten days.

"Sorry, Robbie. Sorry. It's Tuesday. Tuesday, you know, I eat with my mother. She cooks. If I don't come she will be disappointed."

Robbie's expression dropped like a stone. "I ..." was all she got out before her voice faltered.

"Join us," Maarten said quickly. "Why not? I have told my mother about you. She is not opposed to meeting you." Robbie, with a single, emphatic headshake, conveyed that the niceties of dinner with the mother would be too sad a substitute for the evening and night she had envisaged. As the extent of these shattered expectations sank in, she shook her head once more and hurried off in the direction of the tram stop. With a few long strides, Maarten caught up. "Why not eat with us? It will not take long."

"Not ready for it." Robbie quickened her pace. "Not now. Maybe in a few weeks when the funeral things are over with."

He became resigned. "I'll accompany you back to Scheveningen. My mother lives there too."

Neither managed small talk. In the tram, they sat side by side like a silent old couple that has learned the hard way that a steady sullenness isn't nearly as bad as outright acrimony.

When Robbie closed her apartment door, she absorbed the tranquillity of her sanctuary. She ate some fruit and drank some herbal tea, then lit aromatic candles before sinking to the floor to sit cross-legged. A dead weight had seized her midriff and her thoughts were sour. She seldom felt such spiritual suffocation and it puzzled her. What had happened? For a start, Maarten had not been himself. That was obvious right away. When she got to Delft for the meeting with the pastor he was waiting at the tram stop, but showed no joy, no echo at all of the elation she was radiating. Was his reserve a form of empathy, she wondered, a way of recognizing that she had spent much time dealing with sorrow? Then, after the scene outside the cathedral when she had stomped off, he was still more subdued. Did I sink too far into myself? Robbie pondered. Was I caught up too much in expectations? Did self-centeredness take over? What prevented me from being generous? Why did I make it seem like his mother is my competitor? Suppose I had a mother. Suppose she and I could plan to eat together once a week? How precious would that be? Wouldn't I do everything to fit it in? Robbie's head dropped in wretchedness. To begin to make amends she dialled his number and dictated a first, brief explanation, saying she would call first thing next day.

Arbitrator Full of Glory, feel free to be there when we work this through.

Next morning Maarten beat her to it. Robbie's phone was ringing when she got to the office. "Hi," she said warmly. "Get my message?"

"Thank you, Robbie. Yes."

She perceived no warmth. "Everything fine? I was pig ignorant yesterday. Sorry."

"You were not, Robbie. I am sorry. I was not sensitive."

"This evening is good?"

"Yes. I want to see you badly. But I must meet with you before. In my office, or in another place if it is more convenient. I must talk … officially."

"Officially? What's happened?"

"I will tell you when we meet."

"I can't … I don't want that. I don't want to see you in any office."

"Shall I come to The Hague then? This afternoon? The coffee shop?"

"No. I'll go to Delft. I'll meet you at the cathedral entrance after work. I want to turn the clock back. To yesterday. Start over. I want to walk with you. In step. Holding onto your arm. I don't want to feel sour. Not ever again."

"We will walk, Robbie. Yes, it is a good thought."

Robbie departed the embassy with foreboding. An official talk? She tried to ban the thought, but it clung to her like an unclean patina. Probably something had occurred, major for him, but minor for her. The police often blew issues up to the point where, like balloons that can't take one more molecule, they burst with a bang. On the other hand, maybe it wouldn't be minor. Maybe something awful was happening. She yearned for the hours with Maarten to be uncomplicated and happy. As sourness seeped in again, she tried her best to dispel it.

~

At the cathedral, Maarten stood waiting next to the entrance. They embraced. She took his arm. He asked if she would like to walk somewhere in particular. "You know Delft," she replied, leaving the choice to him. From the cathedral they crossed the market square. Crowds of people were out and about; cafés and restaurants buzzed with business. From there it was down a narrow lane, across on old stone bridge to the far side of a canal, much like the one his house stood on. "Did your mother cook you a good meal?" Robbie asked. He replied it was very good. Roast chicken with mashed potatoes, cooked green beans and a delicious sauce. She squeezed his arm. "I'm glad." On the canal's far side they turned right and proceeded along it under a thick tree canopy. "What did you and you mother talk about?" Robbie learned that the topics were his mother's plants, her friends and the medicines she takes. "Are the topics always the same?" Maarten smiled and said that sometimes there was also the weather. "I suppose," Robbie mused, "I would talk about those topics with my mother and it would be fine." From the canal, an opening on the left went into a picturesque alley. He led her into it. Down the alley, they passed a cemetery before arriving at another pretty canal and another scenic bridge. And more tree cover. Soon then, on the left again, came a narrow opening through a wall, behind which was a passage leading into an open area. A sign there listed the visiting hours of a museum; the museum itself was a compact, old villa. Maarten explained it was famous. "William the Silent was assassinated there. It was the seat of government when Holland fought Spain. Spain put up a ransom. Twenty-five thousand crowns. A French Catholic shot him through the heart."

Robbie tugged playfully at Maarten's arm. "How terrible. Is that what you wanted to tell me officially?"

He took Robbie into a small garden, densely planted, next to the museum with a modern statue of the Prince in it. They sat down on a wooden bench. The sounds were of nearby birds singing. "I am very sorry for what I have to say, Robbie. It is not easy for me. It has been on my mind for days. I know we promised each other not to talk about Alistair Paradis again, but I have to do it."

Robbie let go of his arm and stiffened. "We promised and we shouldn't. I've been trying to reach him, actually. The ambassador wants him to deliver the eulogy at Carlos's funeral."

Maarten ignored this. "When I promised I would not mention his name again, I believed the investigation into his travels and contacts would take a direction that would not have anything to do with you. For several months it was so. But it is no longer so. I was informed you are acting for Ambassador Plavniuk on all matters relating to her husband's accident. Therefore I must ask you officially for advice on how I should proceed."

"You don't need to," Robbie says coldly. "I'm already dealing with the police on the accident. They have identified the type of vehicle that hit Carlos. It was a white Renault van. They are now doing a search of the owners of that model. I would actually prefer it that you didn't mix in."

"They will unfortunately not be successful with their search for the vehicle. The situation is this. I am able to access the information of the traffic police, but the traffic police are not able to access my information. They will soon come to you to say they have reached a dead end."

"I hate it when you talk that way, Maarten. It's really difficult for me. It destroys something."

"For me, too, it destroys. I also hate it. I hate it very much. But please, I must talk to you for ten minutes officially. If you really don't want me to do it, then I will not, but in that case someone else will call you tomorrow for the same talk. Ten minutes and it will be over and I hope to God, after that, I will never have to talk to you officially again."

Robbie, feeling an intense cramping of her stomach, struggled not to wince. The rational part of her mind was telling her this would be more awful than she feared. Another side made her want to run. She fought back with a kind of last stand at getting all this to stop. Summoning up all the disdain possible, she said, "Carlos's accident and Alistair Paradis? Are you suggesting there's a link? What on earth have you DINPOL types dreamt up this time?"

"You say you have tried to contact Paradis?"

"Yes."

"Did you have luck getting through?"

"I only tried once. Last Friday."

"He did not pick up his phone?"

"No."

"You do not know why he did not. I do. He did not answer because, one hour after the ambassador's husband was hit, he moved out of his flat. He took his clothes and some equipment. The van that took him away was a Renault. The colour was white."

Robbie took a deep breath and sat upright and still. She turned towards Maarten and her eyes, fixed on him, began to fill with tears, which in little streams dribbled down her cheeks. She begged, "don't do this to me, Maarten. Please."

"I am sorry, Robbie. This has been in me for nearly a week. It is eating me. I am truly sorry. I wish I did not know it. I wish Carlos's accident had been a simple hit and run, with the driver found and put in jail. It would still be a story of terrible injustice, but at least it would be simple."

"Are you just being suspicious of Alistair again? Are you without evidence putting the worst interpretation of circumstances again? If you are, if all you have is innuendo, I don't know what I will do. For sure I will be sick. How can I respect you if I can't respect your work?" She shuddered and heaved, and for a few seconds sobbed heavily.

Maarten took out a handkerchief and placed it in her hand. "Hear me out, Robbie. Let me explain."

~

Inspector Maarten Valk's reconstruction of events was based on three separate investigations. The traffic police were looking into the accident. As part of the international group, Valk had maintained a monitoring function on Paradis. The third, internal to the Dutch government, was a probe initiated by Heiko de Bruyn into a possible lapse of security leading to the *New York Times* story. The third line of enquiry brought the other two police actions into its ambit.

De Bruyn's probe took several directions, and one was a database search. Information was pursued according to various names and word-strings. *Natalia Plavniuk, Canadian Ambassador, Canada, diplomats, Canadian officials, peace initiative, peace organizations, journalists, New York Times.* A few disconnected items of information showed up, one being the hit and run accident that killed Ambassador Plavniuk's husband at the end of the same week that the US military attachés made their demarches. Another item was the acronym PEACE, which showed up in relation to a plane crash in February. PEACE being Inspector Valk's dossier, he received printouts of several miscellaneous facts that de Bruyn's probe had so far uncovered.

The information appeared disconnected, but all the same, when Inspector Valk first saw it he immediately paused to struggle with a point of professional ethics. Since he and Robbie were now

290

lovers, was it appropriate for him to continue with this dossier? His superior brushed the concern aside. What link could there be between a possible government leak, a traffic accident and the convalescing leader of a peace NGO? At DINPOL, Inspector Valk continued to be the point man.

He proceeded with thoroughness. He requested a copy of the accident's forensic report. Separately, he looked at communication data for Paradis's flat and noticed right away that the secure fax machine in it, generally not much used, ran hot during the days prior to the threatened *New York Times* story. Also, numerous scrambled fax messages arrived and left Paradis's flat on the day before the accident. Yet another check was made with European civilian traffic control for arrivals and departures at Akrotiri airport. There was an interview, too, with the janitor of the complex in which Paradis lived, which uncovered relevant facts. Paradis's domestic turned out to be helpful. Finally, a forensic search done in the flat itself produced fingerprints, smudges, leftover hairs, the lot. Among the things that came back was a pad of writing paper with nothing on it except indentations on the first page or two, caused by heavy, laboured writing. This went off for electronic analysis.

Within a week, Inspector Valk knew this: a diplomatic car had come for Paradis on a Sunday several weeks before the accident. The janitor also saw him delivered back by the same car, accompanied by a man with much facial hair, rather like Karl Marx. The bearded man was fifteen or twenty years younger than Paradis. The two appeared to be friendly.

A confidential interrogation of the driver of the Canadian Ambassador confirmed that Paradis had been a guest at the residence that day, for several hours and, yes, the ambassador's husband went along to pick him up and drop him off.

About ten days later, a Monday, the Karl Marx type was back at the condo complex, the janitor reported, this time arriving by bicycle in strikingly awful weather. Paradis's domestic confirmed the presence of a guest in the flat that day. She had provided cookies for the occasion. Fingerprints in the apartment matched those of the ambassador's dead husband. On that day the secure fax sprang to life, several messages going out to an untraceable destination.

Eight days after that, a Tuesday, Karl Marx was in the complex again, his stay this time was fairly brief. Afterwards, more secure faxing. Within one hour of the last incoming fax, a private jet departed Akrotiri for Brussels, where two men – of Mediterranean complexion – disembarked. Their European identity cards were swiped. Both were apparently Spanish, though Inspector Valk's closer check of the magnetic data showed that both cards were high quality forgeries. Twenty minutes after the Brussels arrival, a white Renault van was rented. By whom? Not known. The driver's license was Spanish, but also fake. The credit card used was linked to a numbered account at an offshore bank. Therefore untraceable. One hour after the van left Brussels airport, the private jet, no passengers on board, returned to Cyprus.

A gap in the details until Friday mid-afternoon. The hit and run occurred about twenty minutes past four. Approximately one and a half hours later, just before six, Alistair Paradis hobbling along between canes, plus two men of small stature with dark hair, one carrying a big box, another a small suitcase, were observed coming out of the apartment complex. They were in a hurry and were urging Paradis to go faster. The stuff was dumped into a white van, Paradis got muscled into the rear seat and they drove off.

Concerning the writing pad, a computer examination of the indentations on the first few pages allowed most of what was written on it to be recreated. The text written on the pad closely matched the purported *New York Times* story.

Inspector Valk presented his findings to his superior. Next day, both were summoned to The Hague to a meeting in the prime minister's office; a meeting, Maarten told Robbie, he would never forget. When it was over, he carried away a wrenching instruction. For several days he deliberated over what to do next.

~

"Almost incredible." Heiko de Bruyn is shaking his head. "What a set of events. I expressed my view to the ambassador that her side was responsible. I was sure the leak was in Ottawa. But in her own household? Who would have thought it? We knew it could not have been us. Fine work, Inspector."

Five men in suits and ties are assembled around a large round table. The room they occupy has two doors, one to a corridor, the other opening to de Bruyn's office. To de Bruyn's right, tense and on the edge of his chair, is an official from the foreign ministry identified as having advised de Bruyn on the peace summit; to the left is the head of internal security in the prime minister's office. Opposite them is Maarten Valk, who has just delivered the briefing, and his superior who has been silent.

A debate begins.

The foreign office advisor's favourite word is *calamity*. He blinks furiously behind horn-rimmed glasses. So close to a brilliant success, he claims, then uses the word *calamity*. *Yes, it is a calamity. A true calamity*. Loose talk sank the initiative. No doubt it took place in the most dangerous of locations, in the bedroom, with two heads comfortably resting on soft pillows. However it happened, wherever the loose talk occurred, the ambassador should not stay in her position. If she did, it would be an affront to Dutch principles of accountability. Ottawa had to be told to recall her. He would be pleased to organize it. To show he means what he says, he rips his glasses off his nose and uses his tie to give the lenses a vigorous polish.

The head of security pitches in. He points at an important fact. The ambassador's husband, having delivered secret information, was obviously killed for it. Gangsterism at play. In Holland! Care had to be taken to avoid the development of a negative reputation. Individuals, including foreigners, working on new foreign policy should not get the feeling they could be knocked off for it, not in Holland.

The foreign office advisor – who, in Maarten's opinion, is living proof that the people who work in that department truly are la-la-land types – asks rhetorically how this explosive problem can be contained. He speculates on a variety of subtle diplomatic ways to communicate to Canada that Holland no longer has confidence in them.

After more such back and forth, Maarten risks a personal observation. "Some key evidence is missing," he points out. His aim is to get some logic into the room. "We cannot prove that the van rented in Brussels was the one that hit the ambassador's husband. The van could be anywhere in Europe. I doubt we will ever find it. Nor can we prove that the ambassador's husband had access to the text of the ambassador's non-paper. Personally, I doubt it was pillow talk and there is a logical possibility that he was not the leak's source. Furthermore, without knowing to whom Paradis sent his fax, or what has been going on in Cyprus, we are far from demonstrating a clear link between the diplomatic initiative here and the threat of public disclosure through the *New York Times* story.

"Let us not lose sight of the fact that the story apparently contained a number of details that we were able to attribute to Mr Paradis through his notepad, but which were not in the non-paper that Mr De Bruyn and Ambassador Plavniuk worked on. There are gaps. The Canadians would likely counterclaim that a link, between what the military attachés said and the ambassador and her husband may have done, has not been conclusively proven. They might well counter-speculate that all this happened because a spy network of some kind was active in Holland and that we were unable to infiltrate it."

Reactions to that bounce back and forth, ping-pong-like, across the meeting table.

De Bruyn has heard enough. "Ambassador Plavniuk is a controlled individual," he says. "I agree with Inspector Valk. I cannot imagine her discussing the non-paper with her husband. On the other hand, circumstances make it look fairly certain that her husband, innocently or not, played a role. The individual we would like to get our hands on is Alistair Paradis, but we believe we will not find him, or the van. Which brings us to the Cyprus military airport. How much effort are we prepared to put in? The airport is well located for playing a role in America's counter-terrorism efforts. I strongly doubt, even if we pursued it at the highest levels in the US Administration, that we would get any help there with the missing information.

"Therefore, I think we should do this. We throw the mess at the Canadians. Mr Paradis is their national. Canada has close links to US intelligence. Let them pursue the whole, sorry embarrassment and try, with their own investigation, to find out who Paradis is and what goes on in Cyprus. I propose the following: Inspector Valk will give the same briefing he has given us to the Canadian Embassy, ideally to Ambassador Plavniuk directly. It will be painful for her to hear the facts and she may choose not to believe what they imply. Nevertheless, she will have to make a decision on what happens next, whether an attempt should be made to find out whom Mr Paradis works for, and why, possibly, they killed her husband. Are we agreed?"

~

When Maarten finished, Robbie's head had sunk down into her hands. Her defiance, her every conviction that in this world good outweighs evil had been broken. The groan she gave was of a soul having splintered. "He inspired me," she whimpered. "He owned truths. He showed me who I am, how I fit, what my role is, why my life is meaningful. He made me feel more complete. I trusted him, Maarten. I can't bear all that collapsing. Alistair is a murderer?"

He tried to console her, but it came out as police objectivity. "Not necessarily a murderer, Robbie. Not strictly speaking. He was in his flat when the van hit Carlos."

"But he was responsible. When Carlos brought him details of Natalia's work, Alistair could have chosen to do nothing. He didn't need to send it on. He could have kept a lid on it. He must have realized he was compromising Carlos."

Maarten wished to soothe her, but again his words did little except bring more factual precision. "We are not certain Carlos took that information to Paradis. We have no way of being sure that Carlos had access to the ambassador's work. If not, he could not have passed anything on."

Maarten was in a peculiar position. His sleuthing had convinced high government officials, although it had gaping holes. He fully expected Robbie, with her skepticism, to come at him strong because of those holes, and he was bracing himself for derisive observations about circumstantial evidence acquiring meaning solely through assumptions. But strangely, he wasn't having to defend his scenario. She was buying in. Peculiarly, therefore, he was in a position opposite to where he thought he would be. He was highlighting all the uncertainties. He nailed his final point again. "There is no proof Carlos knew anything."

"But there is," Robbie replied abjectly. "He did know. I know he knew about Natalia's non-paper." She used his handkerchief for a good blow and with a blouse sleeve dried her eyes. "I've just now realized it. I saw a copy of it in the residence. In the drawing room. Hidden under a pile of books. Carlos must have stumbled onto it."

Maarten pondered this. A slip-up. An innocent lapse. An important element for his scenario. "I see," he said. "I see."

Robbie began talking. In a strange monotone she reviewed what must have happened: Carlos living for peace and believing Paradis did too; Carlos, proud of Natalia's competence, seeing it on display in the non-paper; Carlos visiting his friend; Carlos wanting to share the news that something they both worked for was to be launched onto the world; Carlos cycling off, effectively towards his death.

"And so Alistair is a murderer," Robbie said with a frightening finality. She stared into the garden without emotion. "In a way, Carlos betrayed Natalia, and Alistair built on it. Suppose I had taken your suspicions seriously. Suppose I had told Natalia about them. Everything would have been different. Because I didn't, I'm also responsible for Carlos's murder." Her expression had grown ash grey.

"Robbie!" Marten took her shoulders and shook them. "Stop this. Don't talk that way. If you go back through all the circumstances that led to Carlos being run over you will never stop. The fog last February is responsible. I am responsible. Your ambassador is responsible. If we had all acted differently over many weeks, of course the future would not have been the same. I could have given a louder warning. The ambassador could have been more careful with her document. But this way of thinking does nothing except heap up regret. It makes no sense, so stop it."

"I am convinced I am more responsible than you. More than anyone." Robbie stood up. "I think we should walk again."

"Yes. We need time for this to settle."

Beyond the wall, back along the canal, they were surrounded by late day noise. A cyclist sparred with a car; he rang his bell and balled a fist. Further along, a determined figure in an electric wheelchair raced by like a sovereign. Walking mothers kept watch on their children on pushbikes. Robbie took Maarten's arm. He interpreted it as an emotional jam having been broken. "One last issue," he said cautiously. "I was instructed to inform your embassy, the ambassador herself if appropriate, about my findings. How should I do that, Robbie? What is your advice?"

Five steps later she quietly answered, "You have done what you were told to do. You have now informed the embassy. Leave the ambassador to me."

Chapter 22

Perhaps it was because she was speaking to a policeman, or because she was speaking to a man, or because she was speaking to her own man. Or perhaps it was because she decided instantly that a gut wrenching, stone-cold constabulary briefing on a harsh reality was the last thing Natalia needed. Whatever the reason, when Robbie took on this new burden she sounded very certain of herself. She exuded a calm superiority, the same superiority she bestowed on every other protector of the public peace when she became determined that henceforth the management of this or that poor sod's troubles should be hers.

"Are you sure?" Maarten weakly asked. "I admit I haven't been looking forward to briefing the ambassador, but I was instructed to make sure it happened."

"I'll deal with it," she repeated, borrowing a whiplash tone from one of her aunts, the one who liked to claim that men, generally, were tits-on-a-bull useless.

Robbie's firmness was calming, and Maarten became chattier.

She didn't dampen his mood, not that evening, not that night, nor during the days that followed. Yet it was a mask, for her inner state was one of chaos. She had been violated and betrayed. She had been stupid and so carried blame. No matter how hard she tried, she couldn't turn such feelings off.

Alistair Paradis had provided her with a deeper understanding of her own existence, but since the PEACE man turned out to be a conman, what did that say about his metaphysics? Was it deceitful too? Should she stop believing in essentiality? Should she cease to have faith that her small niche in the universe had value? But she also asked herself about the flip side. If new insight heightens consciousness and allows you to transcend, is the source important? Can something good not arise out of evil?

Thoughts like these, often half-formed and mostly jumbled up, roiled about inside. Each day she felt a weight grow bigger.

Untangling the assault on her emotions was one thing, but she also had that other problem to attend to. Assuring Maarten that she would brief Natalia was easy; doing it was something else. Sometimes she imagined the conversation.

I have something to say Natalia and I want you to sit down, next to me, here, at the coffee table. Please, take the pile of picture books that's before you and move it. Pick one book up and put it down beside the pile. Then the next one. Yes, like that. Please, don't stop. Ah, no books left. And what's that? Yes, I know. It's your peace paper.

That paper, Natalia, was carried by Carlos – in his head – to our friend the prophet from PEACE. But unfortunately, Alistair was not who we believed. He was a fraud. When he represented people everywhere against conflict and evil, he neither spoke for them, nor from the heart. We don't know for whom he really spoke, but it was not for PEACE. He learned about your paper from Carlos and passed the contents on. No one knows to whom, but it stopped your peace summit in its tracks. Carlos found this out. It was the reason for his "accident".

You were careless, Natalia. It killed the initiative. It killed your career. And it killed your husband too.

Robbie groaned with pain when she heard herself saying this.

And questions bombarded her: What moment should I choose? In the office? In the residence? Should I invite her for a walk along the Scheveningen boulevard? How will she react? How utterly total will her breakdown be? Will she die inwardly on the spot and remain dead that way for the remainder of her days? Can I do it to her at all? Should I do it to her? What if I don't? Would that be right? Is it right for me to know why Carlos died, yet withhold that knowledge from my best ever friend, his wife? She beseeched me to be honest. Your honesty will be my balm, she said. Does that still apply? And what about my promise to be frank, to rub her nerves if need be, to rub them raw? If I don't do what I promise, doesn't that make me a fraud too?

Robbie, in torment, weighed and pondered and became more indecisive all the time. Occasionally Maarten asked if the ambassador had received the briefing. After all, he had that obligation to report back to the prime minister's foreign policy advisor. "Not yet," was Robbie's reply. "The time isn't ripe." The foreign policy advisor, as far as she was concerned, could go fly a kite.

When Robbie felt her dilemma could not get more intense, the embassy's morning mail produced a letter. It was mailed from Geneva, not showing a sender. Robbie closed her office door and pushed the *make busy* button on the phone.

~

My dear Robbie,

How does one move a mountain? I have one in my heart and it obstructs. I wish to hammer it away, chip by chip, so that when it is gone I can reach out to you again, but too little time for it remains. Forgive me, therefore, for coming to you in this roundabout way.

This is my confession.

I fear few would understand it, but I know you will. Your empathy is special.

I know now that my life did not go right. I made decisions that I rue. For a very long time I refused to look into my soul because I was too busy manipulating it. I confess this to no one but you. Why? Because you are the only one I know who is my perfect opposite.

If only, when I started out, I had tried harder to be the opposite of what I was becoming. Had I made an effort I might have turned out more like you. I would be charitable. I would be generous, honourable and magnanimous. I would be genuine. You prove, Robbie, that in this world it is not impossible to live according to such qualities.

I am a beneficiary of your decency and kindness and how can I repay you? How can a life imprisoned by avarice repay anything? This is one of many questions to which I do not have an answer.

Another question. As I grew up why did I turn to pretending, when what I really wanted was an existence which, for the entire world to see, would be high-minded? Acting can earn a living, but acting is not living. Through you, I came to understand that.

Those I acted for have now discarded me. I also acted for myself, wherefore, I have concluded, I must discard myself. I will do it soon. Before that, intensely, I wish to express shame. I am ashamed I got caught up. I am ashamed I did not get out. I am ashamed and sad that I caused harm. My crimes are terrible. Unpardonable. Therefore, please, now, if you wish, punish me with the worst retribution I can imagine. Expel me from your memory.

In the time left to me, I will weep. I will weep thinking how life would have been had I done more than only acted. Suppose I had met you when I was young. Suppose I had taken your hand. Suppose that had enabled me to take nourishment from what you essentially are.

I weep, Robbie. I weep.

And now expel me.

Alistair Paradis.

~

Robbie's immediate reactions were all inadequate, each one too shallow. She reread the letter, and then again. She cried a bit. What was this letter? A confession? An apology? A suicide note? All three? Or something else entirely – just one more deception? What was she supposed to feel? How much longer could she bear being played with?

But suppose it was true that Alistair sat somewhere weeping. Suppose the tears were not called up, not just another act. Suppose they were real. If he was recognizing that his human existence had been wasted, should she not be sympathetic? If he was understanding the extent of the misery he caused, should she expel him for that? And imagine, too, that in full contrition he had already killed himself. Where would that take him? Back into essentiality's vast pool of spirituality? His cleansed spirit would be commingling there with others, becoming part of the many new spiritual configurations lining up as dots of light, coming into the energy universe and illuminating it for a spell. His newly found contrition – a good – would be morally strengthening for future people. Having failed to fight evil in his own energy-universe existence, he could be contributing to the fight against it through others' lives. Robbie took some solace from this way of thinking.

She showed the letter to Maarten.

"Very cruel," he declared the instant he finished reading it. "He blames you, or someone like you, for not being present long ago, to prevent him from becoming corrupt. Do you know how many claim that they kill others or themselves because, long ago, life did not treat them well? That is too easy and cheap. Anyway, it proves he contributed to the plot."

"You don't think it's a suicide note?"

"I think he's saying, *Please believe that I will soon be dead, so why don't you call off the hunt.*"

"But his remorse could be real, so deep that he can no longer live with himself."

"His type, Robbie, lies and betrays. Such people will do anything to acquire an advantage. Unfortunately, such people are very numerous." Protectively he added, "I will keep looking for him and you should stop thinking about him. All I can say is, when you brief the ambassador, if she is doubtful, show her that letter."

~

Robbie didn't. The funeral day was approaching and although Natalia, immersing herself in the arrangements, was obviously strengthening, Robbie dreaded what the conversation would do to her. It seemed she spent each hour convincing herself the time was not yet right. So she was mostly silent, and continued to support Natalia by listening.

There was much to listen to. Natalia was back to being manager. Mostly she focused on Carlos's funeral rite. She wanted it structured in such a way that Carlos, were he present, would consider it quixotic. The obstacle, Natalia told Robbie, was the pastor. The prescription for a liturgy that he had hastily scribbled down did not impress Natalia very much. Renegotiating it was proving troublesome.

Carlos, in his casket, lid closed, was to be present in the church. No problem with that, said the pastor. He protested, however, when Natalia insisted that the casket should not face the mourners in the pews as per normal practice. Rather, she wished him angled in an opposite direction, towards the monument of William of Orange. When the pastor dug in his heels Natalia asked him: When we are in the House of God, with whom are we face to face? God, the pastor grudgingly admitted. And where is God when he is in His House? The pastor, as if to say the question was silly, spread his hands. Exactly, Natalia replied. He is everywhere. So the direction faced by anyone, including the deceased, does not matter. Therefore, the casket can be angled any way at all. Furthermore, why shouldn't Carlos face the most telling of all the monuments to Dutch history? That was the spot where he spent hours reflecting on the power that arises through tolerance. The pastor squirmed in his chair.

The pastor next learned the cathedral organ would stay silent. Natalia had located a professional trio in Amsterdam. She had met with them and signed a contract for certain musical arrangements to be part of the service, arrangements based on Saint-Saëns's *Danse Macabre*, Schubert's *Wanderer Fantasy* and Manuel de Falla's *Nights in the Gardens of Spain*. The pastor flared up at this, especially at the *Danse Macabre* and *Nights in the Gardens of Spain*. It took some effort, but Natalia calmed him. He then caved in to yet another interesting idea she had. As the rite was starting, she wanted the clock bell in the cathedral tower to ring.

But no dissension from the pastor – no climb-down required – on the concept for floral arrangements. He nodded when he heard that an importer had confirmed that fresh flowers would be flown in from every continent in the word, except Antarctica of course.

That left one final detail unsettled – the eulogy. Natalia didn't say it out loud, but she definitely didn't want a pastor, certainly not this pastor, to be entrusted with a description of a life that celebrated the fact that human existence is random.

She conferred with Robbie.

"He's gone," Robbie categorically replied when Natalia asked about Paradis. "He's moved out of his apartment. I don't know where to look for him."

"He'll surface, I'm sure. But it may be too late by then. A pity. Alistair would have been good. Well, I'm in touch with a French anthropology professor who knew Carlos. He plans to be at the funeral. I'll explore the eulogy with him."

The funeral Saturday came. Robbie and Maarten walked the few minutes from his house to the square. In the early evening, promptly at seven, the cathedral bell's tolling began. It tolled and tolled, on and on, like a stuck record. After about three dozen reverberations, casual strollers on the square lost count. And still it continued, not stopping until precisely fifty-three peals had rung out, one for each year of Carlos's life.

In the cathedral, tourists had cleared out and the mourners filed in – embassy staff, some dip corps types, a small elite from different walks of Dutch life. Mostly they had a link to the widow, not the deceased. Heiko de Bruyn stood out because he came dressed formally in tails. Robbie, in contrast, wore a plain, loose black frock and Maarten looked gangly in a dark suit, a touch too small now, acquired years before for his father's funeral.

The church doors closed. The stillness was broken by the trio, which began with *Nights in the Gardens of Spain*. As notes, portraying mysterious goings-on during Spanish nights, formed and rose up to the ceiling and spilt out towards the walls and back down, the ambassador made her entrance from the transept, as if she walked through *her* night in a Spanish garden. She wore a large black hat and a veil. Her dress had a high collar shielding the neck. On the front, prominent buttons went down to the waist, which was pulled in tight, and from there the satiny material descended to just below the knees. Black gloves, a small black purse. She walked regally to the front pew and sat down, alone. The music finished. The pastor entered. In a flowing gown with large drooping sleeves, he briskly approached the pulpit steps. He began with a prayer, spoken with a strong Dutch accent. With eyes shut tight, he tilted his head nicely up towards the cathedral roof. Next, in the vast echoing cathedral interior he expounded God's infinite greatness and mercy. He read a passage from a modern English translation of the Bible. More music from the trio – the *Wanderer Fantasy* – after which the French anthropologist came to the front. He was a methodical man, for he listed every worldly location he knew of where Carlos once did field work. Speeding up, he described the academic papers he and Carlos co-authored. Now he turned ardent, his enthusiasm rapidly growing and feeding on itself. Unable to control himself, he began quoting from memory, mostly in French, lengthy scholarly passages describing all manner of unusual customs he and Carlos had unravelled. Natalia didn't move a muscle. She didn't seem to mind that William the Silent below might not be getting the best impression. She might even have convinced herself that the freakier the proceedings, the more aligned they were with Carlos's quirky side. How he would have loved his rite unfolding in this way in Holland's most important church. The professor finally expended his store of memories. The trio, relieved he had finished, played the *Danse Macabre* with special intensity. A short sermon from the pulpit then, gutturally delivered, on the topic of *God's Master Plan*.

Three rows back from Natalia, Robbie felt sadness deepening. She listened to the pastor's words about God's obscure intentions and she thought back to six months before, to the fog and the plane crash. Much had come together, but still more had broken up. Circumstance had driven circumstance. As a result, she had gained a man, while Natalia lost one. Still hanging over it all was that sword – the truth of Carlos's demise. It threatened terribly. She still had no idea what to do.

A final prayer, then the pastor descended the pulpit as if in flight. He consoled the widow with a single, much overdone handshake before hurrying off. The mourners rose. Some cleared their throats. The noises were amplified by the surrounding stone and, bouncing back, sounded yet more hollow. The ambassador led them in single file to the cathedral doors. Outside, she marched them to a restaurant on the far side of the square, where a post-service reception awaited them in the upstairs party room. And in that place, in no time at all, the mood became chatty and convivial.

Natalia, having shaken every hand, briefly came up to Robbie. The party would last an hour or so. Could Robbie stay on afterwards?

Of course.

Robbie had become separated from Maarten, but she spied him on the far side listening closely to the tall man dressed in tails. She began to make her way towards them through the crowd. When she got there, he had been efficiently squeezed aside by a group of ambassadors eager to introduce themselves to the foreign policy advisor, whom they knew but seldom saw.

"Robbie!" Maarten exclaimed as she was taking his arm. "You didn't say you briefed your ambassador on everything having to do with the accident. Meneer de Bruyn just thanked me for that happening."

"What?"

"Yes. He said the ambassador came to him yesterday for a meeting. He asked her if Ottawa was acting on all the information made available, and she said yes. Meneer de Bruyn was very satisfied with that."

"The ambassador had a meeting with Mr de Bruyn?"

"She did. And now he is happy. Therefore I am happy. Therefore I think we should leave. I don't like receptions. We will go home and change and I will take you out for dinner."

"Maarten ... wait ... I have to think ... sorry, I can't go for dinner. Not yet. The ambassador asked me to stay on. I don't think it will take long. Did Mr de Bruyn say anything else?"

"Only that everything was working out. The ambassador is staying on to continue her peace building work. He is expecting great things from her. It is alright if you stay with her, Robbie. I will go home and wait."

~

Away from the reception noise, in a corner where there was a screen hiding a door to a service area, Robbie used her dark frock as camouflage. Making small talk was the last thing she wanted. Her mind had gone empty; no thoughts there, at least none she could put into words. Mostly she had an urge – to get at Natalia, to find things out. Ottawa acting on information? The ambassador to continue her peace building work? Had some powerful clock been turned back to one or another past circumstance, following which everything somehow got flipped around? Was Natalia suddenly on a new track, taking her into the future? Had her career come back from the dead? Was the peace imperative alive again? And, what did all this imply for her personal, awful burden of knowledge?

The ambassador finally freed herself from the last guest and Robbie sprang at her. "I was watching you, Natalia," she gushed. "You were so graceful and confident. I am full of admiration."

"It was for Carlos, Robbie. I wish the memory of him to be like a large, gracefully arranged bouquet of colourful flowers that will never wilt. Thanks for staying on. I have news, not troubles, to share. Shall we lose ourselves amongst the diners downstairs? So nice at last to meet Maarten. He has a clear, straight look in his eyes. I like that. And his height is right for you."

In the restaurant, they settled at a table in a bay. Both waved the menu away. For Robbie, dinner would come later. As for Natalia, she explained, "I'm eating less now. I'm turning a page. A weight reduction program, Robbie. Ten pounds is the target. The first three are in the bag. Want a drink?"

"What are you drinking?"

"Tea."

"Tea?"

"Yes. As of two weeks ago. Part of the page-turning. No more booze. I confronted my martini habit. It had been growing, and the time had come to take a holiday from it. The more so since I'll be doing much pure and constructive thinking from now on. Perhaps I will learn to do it with the same peace and contentment my grandmother had. I can't tell you how restful the nights are becoming. But first, what did you think of the service?"

"I was moved by it. There was sadness, naturally, but I was glad Carlos had his moment in the cathedral."

"I was pleased enough with how it went. The pastor was … well, we knew what to expect. Part of the price for having that location. But Monsieur de Brégançon was unfortunate. He assured me he knew what was needed, except I didn't know he was the type that talks well only when it's to himself. Too bad Alistair never surfaced. Any news on him?"

"He is …" Robbie looked down.

"He is what?"

Robbie took a deep breath. "I mean, his whereabouts are still not known. You said you had news, Natalia."

"Yes. Very interesting news. Something good has come out of last month's terrible events. I'm starting out fresh. Yes, I am. It's a tragedy that Carlos won't be part of it. I miss him terribly. But I think the future may be better than I dared to think some weeks ago. Earlier this week I met the director of the foreign policy think tank here in The Hague. I gave a talk there some months ago and got to know him. This time I went to explain that I was resigning as ambassador and was looking for an unpaid fellowship with an academic institution, to develop a program of peace-building studies. I wanted to know if I could join his group. He was not enthusiastic. Not right away. He asked about my credentials. Being an ambassador doesn't qualify you for much, I suppose. I asked, if I were to provide a reference from a highly respected source, would that make a difference? Possibly, he said. I managed to get an appointment with Heiko. That was yesterday."

"I understand now," Robbie interjected.

"You do? How do you mean that?"

"I mean, you said you would be looking around for something else to do."

"Yes. Well, I met Heiko. Sometimes the first minutes with him can be strange. He often makes remarks that seem disconnected to the topic at hand. When I entered his office yesterday, I thought he might apologize for his staff leaking the peace initiative, but he didn't. Nor did he ask about Carlos's funeral. The first thing he said was that he had been expecting me to come and see him. Typical of him to say that. He likes you to think that he knows more about you than you do yourself. I informed him I had resigned my post. 'It has come to that,' he said. 'Resigned?' I didn't want to give him all the details – you know, the Irving Heywood-Desmond Mckilroy disaster – and I only said that certain miscues on the peace initiative had come to light and were being followed up. Because I was extensively involved, I felt it best to step aside. He mumbled something to the effect that this was no doubt wise. Then he said he was sorry Carlos was killed. I thanked him for his sympathy and advised him that the embassy – I meant you, Robbie – had received all the relevant information from Dutch authorities. I thanked him for their thoroughness and openness. 'Well then,' he said, 'let us hope the investigation will get to the bottom of it.' I replied that as far as I knew, no stone would be left unturned. He said he was happy to hear that and added, 'You are a brave woman, Natalia. Your setbacks were serious. I admire you for facing them.'

"I asked him if he was he planning to be at the funeral. He hummed and hawed. Eventually he confirmed he would come. I then asked if he would help me with one thing. 'If possible, it would please me,' he said. I explained I had become used to living in Holland, that I liked it here. Since there was no obvious place for me to move to, why should I not stay? I explained I had decided to continue to push the peace agenda outside government, because I had concluded that way I could make a greater contribution. I said I wanted to become a fellow at the foreign policy think tank. Could he put in a word for me? He thought a moment. 'Put in a word for you?' He began to laugh. 'Impossible, Natalia. I won't put in a word for you.' He stood up and took my hand in both of his. He said, 'That think tank gets its budget from me. As of this moment, consider yourself a member.' Then he said, 'Wait.' He picked up the phone and called the director. They spoke in Dutch. The conversation was over in a minute. So you see, Robbie, I'll be going to international peace meetings. I'll be giving speeches. I'll be cajoling governments. I'll be free to push a big agenda. I think I am entering the most productive part of my life. I'm looking for a small house or apartment to move to. Maybe in Scheveningen. And I hope you'll show me all the places you've been to on your bicycle, because I'm getting one."

"That truly is shockingly good, totally wonderful," Robbie exclaimed. "Heiko de Bruyn really said he was happy that everything having to do with Carlos and his accident was going well?"

"I think it's history for him."

"That is good. I can't tell you how good. We're looking forward now, right?"

"We are looking forward, Robbie."

"Maarten and I are too. It would be so nice if you came with us when we go on picnics. You would love it."

"Oh, I don't want that. I don't want to be an old aunt tagging along. You and Maarten need to spend time together, just the two of you."

"We're beyond that. It was that way for the first week, not any more. We're socializing with his friends all the time. It's different I tell you. They're all married and having baby after baby. In between the mothers nursing and the diapers getting changed we do have good times, but mostly its laughing about babies sitting and crawling and standing and taking first steps. So it would be good for us to socialize with you. With you we would go to a higher level. You and Maarten would enjoy discussing the big challenges facing the world."

"His friends are busy having babies?"

"Pretty well of all of them."

"I worry about that, Robbie. I worry about you spending too much time with people whose main form of recreation is procreation."

Robbie laughed. "I'm so relieved you met de Bruyn and that all that is settled."

"I've got another bit of news," Natalia said with mock darkness. "Irving Heywood. He called some days ago and waxed lyrical about the joys of being at home. He has never had more time, he claimed, to conceive important new initiatives. He asked me to collaborate with him on a series of articles for the *Times of London*. About what, I asked. He said, about political leaders these days having no vision, no energy, no sense of responsibility for taking the world to a higher level of peace and security. And he wants me to co-author a book with him, a joint memoir to be called, *The Peace Left Behind*. I don't know, Robbie. Collaborating with Heywood? I think not. I said goodbye to him. Actually, I had to say it three times. He didn't want me to hang up. I think he'll be doing the reminiscing on his own."

"So you'll be moving," Robbie confirmed brightly. "I'll come around next week to help. I'll begin by packing your books into boxes."

~

Robbie did. She began with the books in the drawing room, the big ones there. One by one, they were lifted off the coffee table and disappeared into a cardboard box. Natalia's paper was still there, in the same spot she last saw it. Robbie resolutely took it and folded it twice into a quarter size, although the second fold was thick and nearly didn't work. The ungainly bundle disappeared into her purse.

The next day, in the office, Robbie opened her purse. Natalia's non-paper came out and she undid the folds. Then she unlocked her safe and retrieved Alistair's confession too. Her next act was to throw the shredder switch to on. The machine's appetite was voracious. In seconds, to the crisp sound of rotary knives cutting, all the sheets, one after another, disappeared.

Sources

It is not necessary for a novel to set out the very many sources which an author draws on before or during its writing. *Natalia's Peace* took nearly four years to write and especially in the first years I read many books and academic monographs, numerous documents available on the internet, as well as magazine and newspaper articles. Of the treasure trove of information, historical and current, on the broad topic of "peace", which anyone can easily access, I would like to mention a few which were especially helpful.

The proposal for a Canadian Department of Peace made by CPDI: http://www.departmentofpeace.ca/. This proposal was the basis for Bill C-447 which received First Reading in the House of Commons on September 30, 2009. Part of this proposal was the creation of a Civilian Peace Service in Canada.

Glenn Paige's book, *Nonkilling Global Political Science*, first published in 2002, second edition published by Xlibris Corporation in 2007.

A Diplomat's Handbook for Democracy and Development: http://www.diplomatshandbook.org/. In chapter eleven of *Natalia's Peace* I attribute the preparation of this important, fascinating and far-reaching guide to Natalia. Actually, this work was done by my one-time colleague, former Canadian Ambassador to Russia, the EU and the UK, Jeremy Kinsman.

Concerning the passage in the novel on the Darfur genocide, after reading several detailed books on the historical underpinnings of the human disaster, in the end I mostly used the clearly written and readable 2005, Report of the International Commission of Inquiry on Darfur to the United Nations Secretary-General: http://www.un.org/News/dh/sudan/com_inq_darfur.pdf

I found much interesting and useful information on the web site of the International Relations Directorate of the EU. One example was the checklist on the root causes of conflict: http://www.ceipaz.org/images/contenido/European%20Commission%20Check-list%20for%20Root%20Causes%20of%20Conflict_ENG.pdf
This material was especially helpful when writing chapter eight.

Throughout writing the novel I drew inspiration from the *Charter for a World Without Violence* drawn up by the winners of the Nobel Peace Prize at their Eighth World Summit: http://www.nobelforpeace-summits.org/charter-for-a-world-without-violence-2/